By MORGAN JAMES

Purls of Wisdom

DREAMSPUN DESIRES
Love Conventions

With Ashlyn Kane
Hair of the Dog
Hard Feelings
Return to Sender
String Theory

HOCKEY EVER AFTER
Winging It
The Winging It Holiday Special
Scoring Position
Unrivaled
Crushed Ice

Published by DREAMSPINNER PRESS
www.dreamspinnerpress.com

CRUSHED ICE

ASHLYN KANE
MORGAN JAMES

REAMSPINNER PRESS

Published by
DREAMSPINNER PRESS

8219 Woodville Hwy #1245
Woodville, FL 32362 USA
www.dreamspinnerpress.com

Crushed Ice
© 2024 Ashlyn Kane and Morgan James

Cover Art
© 2024 L.C. Chase
http://www.lcchase.com
Cover content is for illustrative purposes only and any person depicted
on the cover is a model.

Mass Market Paperback ISBN: 978-1-64108-696-7
Trade Paperback ISBN: 978-1-64108-695-0
Digital ISBN: 978-1-64108-694-3
Mass Market Paperback published February 2024
v. 1.0

Printed in the United States of America
∞
This paper meets the requirements of
ANSI/NISO Z39.48-1992 (Permanence of Paper).

This one's for the village: Sibel, Curry, Amanda, Laura, Jeb, and Aurora. With special thanks to the always-helpful Liz for her editing expertise.

WARM-UPS

THE LYFT pulled into the driveway of Russ's Miami house in the middle of a September downpour. It was only two in the afternoon, but the sky was black and rain sheeted against the windshield. Occasional lightning illuminated the palm trees.

"Nothing like the Florida welcome-home," his driver, Stef, commented.

Back in Winnipeg they had a saying: *We don't have earthquakes, we don't have hurricanes, we don't have alligators.* Russ's parents and sisters repeated it to themselves when they were cleaning snow off their windshields six months a year. He liked teasing them with it over video calls from his sunny poolside.

At least this was just a thunderstorm, and Russ's covered front door would keep him from drowning while he unlocked it. "You can drop me off here."

"Sure thing." She put the car in Park. "You want me to get your other bag?"

Russ's hat would keep his hair dry and he had plenty of clean, dry clothes inside. He had no idea how far Stef would have to drive damp. "It's okay, I got it."

"Guess hockey players are kind of weather-proof, huh?" She smiled. "Go Caimans."

Russ smiled back. "Thanks. You got something you want me to sign before I get out?"

Stef beamed at him, and he fished out the Sharpie he always kept in his carry-on. When he looked at her again, she was presenting a team-branded alligator bobblehead. "Perfect." He scrawled *Hey Stef, thanks for the ride!* on the base, signed his name, and ventured out into the wet.

His cleaning and grocery service had been in, so when he finally got the key in the lock and went inside, it didn't smell musty. He waited until the car's headlights disappeared, then stripped out of his wet clothes and put them right into the washing machine. He hadn't brought any clothes home with him—he kept a set at his lake house outside Winnipeg—so his bag was just toiletries and a six-month supply of Coffee Crisp. He left his suitcase at the foot of the stairs.

A quick towel dry later and Russ was waiting for a late lunch to heat up in his microwave while he leafed through the stack of mail on his kitchen table. Credit card statements, flyers, endorsement contracts—who sent those via regular mail instead of courier? Oh, never mind, they were just copies forwarded by his agent for his records. He set them in the folder next to the fridge where he kept anything that he needed to file. A postcard from Paris from his sister, Andi, who was touring Europe with her best friend, another from Milan.

He stuck them on the front of the fridge.

By the time the microwave dinged, he was down to the last item—an embossed black, white, and silver envelope that could only be one thing.

Russ ignored the microwave and fingered the edges of the envelope. The return address confirmed his suspicion.

He slit it open.

In block print on a loose sheet of blank paper, someone had scrawled *Get in, loser! We're getting married!*

Russ snorted as he set that page aside and flipped to the actual card behind it. *Save the date! Max & Grady tie the knot July 10 in Moncton, New Brunswick.*

The card was postmarked from Canada. This time last year, he'd have bet money that Grady Armstrong would've called Max his Public Enemy Number One. They'd only gotten engaged a few weeks ago, and now they had Save the Date cards out.

Russ assumed Grady had his shit together. This level of preplanning seemed beyond Max. Then again, summer only had so many weekends to accommodate NHL players getting married. They probably wanted to stake their claim on a date.

Russ added it to his Google calendar, put the invitation on the fridge with the postcards, and retrieved his lunch. But when he set his plate on the counter, the cover page fluttered to the floor.

The back held Grady's spidery handwriting, accompanied by Max's all-caps sparkly gel-pen print.

Hey, Russ, I know you like to mark your calendar. Hope you can make it.—G

Russ snorted. "Mark your calendar." Right. That was one of the kinder ways someone had called him obsessive about his planning. It didn't hurt coming from Grady, who had his own Type A quirks. Besides, Russ had suffered through two seasons on the Firebirds with the guy. A little light teasing couldn't touch that bond.

Max's addition read, *I dare you to bring a +1. Otherwise you'll get stuck at the singles table. Just saying.*

The singles table at Max Lockhart's wedding could mean anything from "I'll seat you next to my horny gay cousin" to "I'm throwing you to a group of widowed biddies." Max probably didn't even know yet.

Unfortunately that only made the threat more effective.

For most people, ten months was plenty of time to find a date to a wedding. For Russ the main issue was finding someone he actually wanted to spend time with when most of the days between now and then were filled with hockey.

He wasn't picky or anything.

He rubbed his hands over his face, pushed the paper away, and reached for his plate. The time of off-season eating was over.

He was chewing determinedly through the second half of his chicken-and-pasta dish when his phone started to vibrate and edged toward the side of the counter.

Right. He'd forgotten to text his mom when he landed.

He answered on speaker. "I'm not dead," he promised.

"It's not like you to forget about me, baby," she chided him. He could hear the worry in her voice. "Did something happen?"

I didn't forget about you. I just got sucked into a spiral thinking about the future.

Russ had always been a planner. It ran in the family. He'd always known he wanted to be a professional hockey player, and he'd worked hard to make it happen—not easy when his parents had different plans for him. Being a Black athlete in a predominantly white sport didn't help. It had taken five years to convince his mom and dad he was serious about his plan and another to prove he could make it and thrive.

His mom still wanted him to get a degree when he was done, but at least she had two other kids to fulfill those dreams for her. He hadn't yet figured out how to make her understand he wasn't going to play for Winnipeg if he could help it—only partly because she'd spend the rest of his life trying to matchmake him with every eligible bachelor in Manitoba.

Russ loved his parents very much, but his mom was nosier than a hungry elephant. If he told her he needed a date to a gay wedding, she'd fill his calendar with Zoom interviews featuring Winnipeg's Most Wholesome Honey Trap. "No, Ma, unless you count the rain. I wanted to get my wet stuff off, and then I was hungry, so I made lunch."

"Well, we can't have that. I'm glad you're home safe, though. Usual call next week?"

They had a standing Facetime date on Sundays when Russ didn't have games. "Wouldn't miss it."

"All right. I'll let you get back to your lunch. I love you, honey."

"Love you too, Ma."

They hung up, and Russ flipped through his apps to clear the notification of her text as well as the generic *Welcome back to the United States* message from his cell phone carrier.

There was a third notification, this one from the Caimans' leadership team group chat.

Russ unlocked the phone to a string of messages from Mo, the team captain and, today, a convenient distraction. The first one was a selfie of Mo on a jet ski, backward snapback in place, the dock of his beachfront property visible behind him. *Preseason party at mine y/y?*

No one would ever guess he had graduated from Harvard.

On the other hand, Russ's defense partner had real himbo cred. Jonesy wasn't technically a captain or an alternate, but he'd been with the team forever and he was basically Russ's left hand… or at least his left defense partner. They didn't have a second alternate yet; their last one had left during free agency. But Russ didn't think Jonesy wanted the job, what with the brand-new baby at home. *Yes bro!!! let's talk theme and drinks. Russ, you got catering?*

Obviously Russ was going to take catering, since he didn't want to be eating crappy pizza at nine o'clock at night, which was what would happen if he let Mo and Jonesy sort it out. *Pick a date first*, he suggested.

OK dad! Jonesy replied, with zero irony or acknowledgment of the fact that he was the only father among them. *What u thinking Mo?*

Russ let the two of them hash it out while he finished his lunch, keeping half an eye on his phone to make sure they didn't plan anything absurd.

Finally they settled on a date and food, and Russ considered his job done. Now he could work out and shower to combat the lingering stiffness of having been stuffed into a plane seat for six hours, and then he'd research catering options while he made dinner.

But before he could make a move toward his home gym, Mo texted again, in their private chat this time. *So don't get mad but Shelly has this friend—*

"No," Russ said out loud. He hated being matchmade. Why did no one think he could find his own partners?

Probably, said a quiet, annoying voice in the back of his head, because he never found his own partners.

—and she wants to invite him to the party to meet you.

Russ sighed. He loved Shelly. She was smart and funny and happily put up with Mo and Jonesy at the same time, something only other hockey players had been able to manage before. Many a previous girlfriend had broken up with one of them because they couldn't deal with the codependence. *Tell her thanks but no thanks.*

At this point Russ was mostly in the closet because if he were out his parents could keep tabs on his dating life via the internet. He'd always been pretty sure no one on the team cared that he was gay, but any doubt had died over the summer, because the team group chat basically exploded when the Caimans signed Dante Baltierra. No one cared he was bi; they cared that he had two Cup rings and a deadly shot.

Mo sent a thumbs-up emoji to show he got the message, but then he added, *I reserve the right to sing Are You Lonesome Tonight whenever you look like you need to get laid.*

God, he was the worst. *I am begging you to get a normal hobby.*

You're gonna die alone in a swamp mourned only by one of your rookies, Mo replied.

Helpful. *Which one?*

This time he got a thinky-face emoji. *Guess we'll find out in 2 days. I gtg, Shelly just got out of the pool and she looks HOT. See you at camp bro!!*

Russ sighed, pulled up his Spotify workout playlist, and shoved his feelings about Mo's ominous prediction deep into a box in the back of his head.

LIAM PUT the rental car in Park but left the engine running. The Miami sun was punishing, and the second the air-conditioner kicked off, he'd start to sweat.

If he was lucky, he'd be doing enough sweating in the next few months. For now, he picked up his cell phone from the cupholder and took a selfie. The picture showed the logo on his snapback and the hockey gear that hadn't fit in the compact's trunk, crammed into the back seat.

Then he opened the family group chat.

He had a handful of unread messages—Bernadette sent a link to an article about the project she was working on for her aerospace company and Bastian had uploaded a video of his daughter's baptism. His parents and second-oldest sister, Marie-Jean, had replied enthusiastically with emojis and words of support. His mom had added a picture of Liam's favorite barn cat.

Liam used the heart reaction button and then sent them the selfie. *Souhaite-moi bonne chance*, he wrote. *Wish me luck.*

He turned off his phone before he turned off the car.

At eighteen, Liam had left home on a hockey scholarship to study at Boston College. He hadn't had a goal beyond getting out of his hometown, and hockey was the best way to do it. He couldn't figure out who he was in a town that would always see him as the little brother of someone more accomplished. Marie-Jean was a doctor, Bernadette sent things into space, and his brother married his high school sweetheart and was poised to take over the family business that kept their town in tourist dollars.

In high school Liam had been too small for the draft, especially as a defenseman. He hadn't had the skills yet either. But college hockey, with its faster pace and less focus on checking, fit perfectly, and Liam was good at improvising. What had started out as an escape for escape's sake led to an NHL scout inviting him to rookie camp the summer after graduation.

Now he had a professional tryout.

If this worked out, he would owe his former coach, like, a really nice steak dinner. Actually he might owe him a really nice dinner even if it *didn't* work out, but it would be harder to afford. Liam didn't have any student debt, but he'd only worked in the summers, so he didn't have a lot of savings either.

So… no pressure or anything.

He shouldered his gear bag and made his way into the arena.

He'd been here a few days ago to meet the coach, so he knew where he was going. Mo, the team captain, had texted him to introduce himself as well, so Liam wasn't completely out of his depth.

Just, you know, mostly. But he was good at faking it, so he took a deep breath and pushed open the locker room door.

It hit something firm and bounced back. Someone said, "Fuck. Ow."

So much for faking it. "Calisse de tabarnak," Liam said. He hadn't even gotten on the ice yet and he'd already injured one of his teammates. "Sorry."

The door opened. Mo stood on the other side, smirking, so clearly he wasn't the one Liam had hit. "Hey, Liam. Making an entrance?"

"Not on purpose," Liam said sheepishly.

Mo laughed and clapped the shoulder of the man standing beside him, who turned around—this must be the one Liam had hit with the door.

Oh God, Liam hadn't known you could wea-ponize handsome like that. The man had sparkling black-brown eyes, coiled black hair, and cheekbones for days. Just looking at him knocked the wind out of Liam for a moment.

And then he recognized Russell Lyons, the Caimans' alternate captain and the de facto leader of their defensive corps—a corps Liam very much wanted to join and would not be able to if Russell Lyons hated him. And Liam had just bruised his backside.

"I am so sorry," he repeated. But he was already here, and the damage was already done, so…. "You need an icepack for your ass?"

Lyons twisted his mouth in a wry smile—how was he so much more handsome in person—and his voice sounded amused when he said, "No, I'm all right. My ass has had worse." At least he had a sense of humor. He stuck out his hand. "Russ Lyons."

Liam switched the hand he was holding his hockey bag with so he could shake. Russ's hand was big and warm. "Yeah. I know."

Mo snorted. "This is the part where you intro-duce yourself, kid."

Wow, Liam was making *such* a good impres-sion. "Sorry. Again. Liam Belanger."

"All right, all right." Mo nudged him forward. "We're the dumbfucks standing in the middle of the doorway, eh? Get in and get dressed. You can ex-change life stories later."

My life story is not that interesting anyway. Mo was right—this wasn't the time for chitchat. This was time to prove he could be the guy they needed on the ice. If he couldn't do that, there was no point impressing them off of it.

He found his stall and dropped his bag on the floor. The locker room felt weirdly divided, with the development-camp group on one side and the team veterans on the other. The development guys had a harsh, brash, frenetic energy. They knew they were competing with each other, but a lot of them would be teammates in the AHL season, so they had to keep their competitive edges in check.

Then there was the vet side. Most of them knew each other too, though a few guys like winger Dante Baltierra—Baller—were new to the Caimans. That side of the room gave off a relaxed, jubilant vibe; they were *already* a team.

Liam didn't fit in anywhere yet. He hadn't been invited to development camp, and he didn't have a contract or know anyone on the team. Even the eighteen-year-olds who'd just been drafted had more experience than he did. At least they'd had dev camp. Liam knew Mo and a guy he'd hit in the ass.

But if Liam and his strong French-Canadian accent could make friends in Massachusetts, he could do it here, in a much more international locker room. Baltierra was even queer, so he wouldn't be the odd guy out.

Ha.

"It helps if you actually put your gear on," came a voice from his left—the veteran side.

Across the room, a guy he recognized as Riley Jones—Russ's usual defense partner—snickered. "He does this every year. You'll get used to it."

Liam glanced at Russ, who'd made the suggestion, and then back at Jonesy. "This?"

"Yeah." Jonesy pulled on his Under Armour shirt. "He has a thing for adopting rookies. Looks like you're it."

Russ tossed a stick of deodorant across the room. "Part of the leadership role, asshole. Which you'd know if you ever took responsibility for anything in your life." Then he turned to face Liam, smiling with those kind dark eyes. Not the worst guy to share a locker room with, for sure.

Liam had three older siblings. He could recognize the vibe when it was being projected at him. "Wow, I'm learning so much already," he said innocently. But he unzipped his shorts.

When their immediate neighbors stopped laughing and their attention went elsewhere, Russ nudged Liam's elbow. "Seriously, you'll be fine. You wouldn't have gotten a PTO if you didn't deserve it."

Did Russ think he was nervous? Okay, he was, but in an anticipatory way. He shucked his shorts. "Yeah, man, I know. I zoned out trying to figure out how Jonesy gets his hair like that."

Russ laughed. "It's a mystery for sure."

Despite his late start, Liam was one of the first on the ice. Maybe he hadn't played professionally, but he'd played an outdoor game at the Big House in Ann Arbor in front of a hundred thousand fans. That was more than any NHL arena could hold.

It had been colder too, not that Liam had felt it in the moment.

He did a few slow warm-up laps, keeping to himself, then picked up a puck and put on some speed to get his blood pumping. At the end of his first quick lap, he drew back for a slap shot and nailed the crossbar with a *ping*.

Liam smiled with satisfaction and collected the puck from the net. He might be a defenseman, but that didn't mean he didn't like to score.

A moment later, the ice was suddenly crowded with players. Then a whistle blew and everyone circled round the coach.

"Welcome to the first day of training camp! Hope you brought your pacemakers. Green and white jerseys, you're starting out on this end of the ice. You'll be working special teams drills first. Purple and red, other end of the ice, you're with me."

Liam and most of the newly drafted guys had purple or red jerseys today, so he guessed Coach wanted to put them through their paces and see who stood out.

Liam would make sure he did.

RUSS DROPPED into the lounge chair by Mo's pool and closed his eyes as his skin soaked up the last of the day's sunlight. His muscles thrummed pleasantly with exertion the way they did after a good skate. Lifting weights and off-season training weren't the same. It might be only the first day of camp, but this was what his body felt like when it had done what it was made to do.

Jonesy dropped a bottle of Corona on Russ's bare stomach. "Heads-up."

Despite the shock of the cold, Russ caught it before it could roll off and shatter on the concrete. "Dick."

Unrepentant, Jonesy straddled the lounger next to his. "So. Thoughts?"

Russ cracked the beer open. "Good group. Lots of energy. Mo's gonna need some luck with Baller."

"There should be a rule about slowing down after thirty." Jonesy was cruising for a smackdown.

Mo emerged from the house with taco dip and plates. "Are we dissecting the team already? Wait for me."

"Can't wait for your Harvard insight," Jonesy deadpanned, already sitting up and reaching for the food.

Mo set the plates on the table and grabbed one for himself. "We're going to be awesome. There, I said it." He paused. "Offensively, anyway." He cast a look at Russ as if daring him to take the bait.

Russ didn't back down from dares. "You're awesomely offensive." He bit into a chip. The Caimans didn't have any defensive openings on the main roster, just that seventh D slot that usually got filled with someone who'd rotate in to cover for injuries or give someone a rest day. "Defense prospects look young." Experience mattered more than speed when you were trying to keep someone else from scoring as opposed to doing it yourself.

"*Too* young?" Jonesy asked. "Or are you just feeling old?"

Russ flipped him off, but he wasn't wrong exactly. He kept his body in great condition, and he still felt good on the ice, but he was thirty-two. He'd slow down sooner rather than later. Maybe not enough that other people would notice, but Russ would. Even the most rigorous diet-and-exercise regime couldn't keep him from the natural effects of aging.

He'd mostly come to terms with the fact that he probably wouldn't be a Caiman again next year, but he wasn't keen on changing teams again. He hated the upheaval. Unfortunately the Caimans had too many big contracts coming up to keep him on next year at what he was worth.

Even Russ's innate need to plan for every eventuality shied away from thinking about what was in store for him after *that*.

"Probably the second one. Belanger might be good if he can get his checking game up to par."

Jonesy snorted out chip crumbs. "Yeah, we already know he's your favorite."

Russ said seriously, "It's because he made fun of your hair."

Mo laughed when Jonesy made a face. "Did he? Ballsy move, chirping someone on day one of training camp. Now he's my favorite too."

Russ kicked at him. "Get your own rookie."

"He's not your rookie yet."

"He probably will be, though," Jonesy said. "I mean, it's kind of perfect. He's a left D, you're a right D. He's Canadian, you're Canadian—"

"Like 90 percent of the league is Canadian."

"It's like 60 percent now, Harvard," Russ corrected with an eye roll.

Mo flipped him off.

Jonesy continued, undaunted, "You're into dick, he's into dick—"

Russ paused halfway through a bite of taco dip. Mo, who didn't have his mouth full, found words first. "Wait, seriously?"

"Uh, yeah?" Jonesy looked at Russ. "What, you didn't know either?"

Russ finished chewing and swallowed. "No."

"Man, how do you ever get laid? Your gaydar *sucks*."

Maybe because it hadn't gotten any practice in the first twenty-five years of his life. Yeah, so Russ was a late bloomer. It happened. "Shut up."

"Anyway," Jonesy went on, "he's going to be our call-up guy. Pretty sure. Which means Russ is going to make him his rookie. So you're gonna have to pick someone else, Mo. Hughes, maybe?"

"I wanted the college boy," Mo sulked. "I wanted to make fun of him for his shitty university."

"Too bad. Finders keepers." Russ had mentored a lot of rookies over the years, but he'd never had one who was queer. Maybe he could drag Liam with him to brunch one week.

No living with his rookie this year, though. Someone would *definitely* joke about Liam being his pool boy.

He tuned back into the conversation as Mo was giving Jonesy the third degree. "How'd you know he was gay, anyway?"

Jonesy kicked his feet up on his lounger. "I did research, Harvard. Never heard of Google? I got like, three newspaper articles about it. There was one in the Athletic, even."

Russ didn't realize the Athletic covered college hockey. "Can we focus?" he broke in. "I thought we were here to talk about hockey, not gossip."

"Most of hockey talk *is* gossip." Mo wiped a smear of taco dip from the table with his finger and wiped it on a napkin. Why didn't he just clean it up with the napkin in the first place? Did they not teach common sense in college? "But fine. Who's going home? Place your bets."

They spent the next ten minutes debating. Two of the promising prospects—a forward and a defenseman—would likely go back to their juniors team in a day or two. Most of last year's AHL forwards would get sent to the minors, though one of them would probably get called up when the Caimans had injuries.

Connor Hughes, an eighteen-year-old forward, had lit it up in juniors last year and would probably go right to the big leagues.

And as far as Russ was concerned, that would fill out the roster.

"Guess we'll see in a couple days," Jonesy said, raising his beer bottle.

Mo and Russ touched theirs against it. "Cheers to that."

THE FIRST two days of training camp left Liam wrung out with exhaustion. But on the third morning, when he checked the posting list outside the locker room, he saw he'd been squadded with some of the Caimans' best players—including Mo and Russ.

Fuck yes.

The team had assigned Ivan Havriushenko as their goaltender. Havvy was six foot eight in bare feet and the only other player on the squad who wasn't a regular on the roster.

The locker room was louder today, as if everyone was starting to get comfortable with each other. Liam bumped fists with Hughesy on the way to his regular stall. Next to it, Russ was already mostly dressed, only his jersey and helmet missing.

"Morning, rookie." His gaze flicked over the dark circles under Liam's eyes. "I hope you brought your A game."

"Why?" Liam chirped back as he dropped onto the bench next to him. "Am I going to need it?"

Russ snorted. "You should be nice to me, you know."

Liam flung his shirt into the stall and shimmied out of his shorts. "Yeah?" He grinned. "What's in it for me?"

Russ grinned back. "I won't fine you for sassing your betters."

Oh, it figured. Of course Russ was the fine master in this locker room. That meant it was his job to impose financial penalties for various infractions. Sometimes those infractions were superstitious things like stepping on the locker-room logo—not a worry here since the Caimans' logo was on the ceiling. Sometimes they were things like being late for team dinner. Liam had even heard a story about one guy who got married and then got fined a thousand bucks every time he said "my wife" instead of her name, because it got so obnoxious.

Liam wondered how much Russ would charge him for sass. He should probably work it into his budget.

Tough to make a budget before he had a job, though.

"You wouldn't fine a poor college student." Liam did his best wounded Bambi impression.

"But I *would* fine a guy with a pro hockey contract," Russ said sunnily. He pulled on his practice jersey and grabbed his helmet. "So look out."

How much could the fine for sass possibly be? Liam would survive. With a little luck, he'd be eating most of his meals with the team anyway. Great way to save money and time and avoid doing dishes.

Of course, he needed to make the team first.

Time to prove he deserved to be here.

It wasn't easy. The Caimans had six regular defensemen already, including Russ and Jonesy. Their bottom-six pair were playing on one squad, the middle pair on another, and Russ and Jonesy had split up—Russ to play with Liam, and Jonesy with a big Swedish guy named Carl.

Liam hadn't gone up against a lot of players of Carl's caliber in college, never mind guys like Jonesy, with years of elite NHL experience.

Not to mention they all had thirty or forty pounds on Liam, and college hockey was fast, not physical. Liam spent 30 percent of every scrimmage getting absolutely bodied and another 10 percent trying to reinflate his lungs afterward.

"Heads-up," Russ shouted as Liam skated backward, watching the forward he was covering. He didn't have the puck, but Liam could *feel* it coming sometimes. He knew the center was going to pass. All he needed to do—

The center passed. Liam closed on his man and flicked his wrists just enough to slide the puck off his stick and onto Liam's.

Perfect takeaway.

Liam didn't waste time holding on to the puck—Mo was open. Liam snapped the pass off—

Carl creamed him into the boards.

Liam tried to keep his feet, but his spine had stopped talking to his legs. He went down like a lead balloon.

He did manage to get his head up in time to see Jonesy put the puck in the net, though.

A second later Russ sprayed to a stop in front of him and offered him a hand. "I said heads-up!"

Liam took it, and Russ pulled him to his feet with no appreciable effort. Hot. Too bad Liam's body was too busy rebooting to appreciate it. "You should have said 'Look out for the Swedish freight train' maybe."

Russ clapped a hand on his helmet. "That's what heads-up means." He paused. "You good?"

Liam flexed his toes. He wasn't hurt, just winded and surprised… and embarrassed. He needed to be able to stay upright for those hits. "I'm good."

Russ took him at his word, which was maybe more faith than Liam deserved. "Good, 'cause we're going again."

By the end of the day, Liam was sure the team would send him home. He'd made a few good moves, but nothing that stood out, and he hadn't played his best. Meanwhile Carl had played two seasons of professional hockey in Sweden and one in the AHL, even a few games in the NHL. He had size as an advantage too. The Caimans only needed one more defenseman. It seemed pretty cut-and-dried to Liam.

But he didn't have to start packing yet. There was plenty of training camp left, and hopefully he'd get to play a preseason game or two where he could really make his mark.

Liam hit the showers and pointedly put off making any decisions about his future.

He'd never been much of a planner. He'd done his best in the moment and taken all the opportunities that came his way, but that meant he didn't know what he'd do if this *didn't* pan out. He could go home and work at the sugar shack, but the whole point of getting out of his hometown had been *getting out of his hometown*.

His English was good enough that he could do some kind of government work if he moved to Ottawa, maybe—work in an office all day and slowly lose his mind behind a desk while he stared at beige walls. But it would be enough to keep him living indoors.

Or he could try his luck getting a teaching degree. He liked kids. He could teach them French, or French literature.

Teachers worked fucking hard, though, and parents…. God. *Parents.*

Didn't matter. Today, Liam was still a hockey player.

One who smelled like a locker room. He reached for the soap. Shower now. Plan later. Maybe.

Pregame

RUSS WAS torn about the defense prospects.

On the one hand, Carl clearly had the advantage of experience. He was big and strong and followed the Caimans' system no problem. That made him the obvious favorite for the job.

On the other hand, there was Liam—less experienced, half as wide, but smart and fast, and he had a creativity that Carl lacked.

A good percentage of the time, that creativity got him into trouble because he didn't have the experience to know when to use it. But if he could *get* that experience? He'd be a lot of trouble for the other team. And if he could learn to take a hit without falling over, he could be heir apparent of the Caimans' defense.

Given the choice, Russ would sacrifice a few early season losses to have Liam on the team instead of Carl. Unfortunately, it wasn't up to Russ.

Liam's play wasn't perfect. In their fourth scrimmage, he badly misread the ice, which resulted in a wide-open shooting lane and a perfect screen for

Havvy. Baller sniped the puck top shelf and hit the back of the net.

"Fuck." Liam huffed in frustration and circled around the back of the net like he was skating off his mistake.

When he returned, Russ gently shoulder-checked him. "Hey. It's okay. He's done it to everyone." Baller was one of the most sought-after free agents this past summer for a reason.

"I know, I know." To his credit, Liam managed a small smile. "I thought I had him. Won't make that mistake again."

Russ couldn't help it—he laughed. "Yeah, you will."

"Hey." Liam bristled. "I can learn from my mistakes."

"Oh, no doubt." Russ looped his arm around the kid's shoulder and nudged him back toward the action. "And you will. But then one day you'll be tired or hurt or hungover, or you'll just have an off day." Russ believed in practice and preparation as much as anyone—probably more than most people—but you couldn't prepare for a cold or a toothache.

Liam gave him a look of horror.

"You had bad games in college, right?" Russ said. Surely to God this kid hadn't just made his first-ever hockey mistake. For one thing, he'd made several others today, and he definitely knew about them because he'd paid attention when Coach was talking.

Liam deflated. "No, I have, but…." He shrugged. Russ let the motion dislodge his arm. "In college I wasn't hoping to get paid to play hockey."

How? Didn't every Canadian kid who played dream of one day going pro?

But that wasn't important here. Liam needed a pep talk. If Russ wanted to keep him, he'd have to snap him out of this. What kind of pep talk, though? Liam didn't strike him as particularly serious. He was usually smiling and joking. So should Russ try to talk to smiling Liam, or the solemn one?

Maybe both. Russ tapped his stick against Liam's. "And if you're lucky, all your professional mistakes are going to be broadcast on television and dissected."

Liam groaned, but it turned into a laugh and a rueful smile. "Also every time someone bigger than me dumps me on my ass."

Russ gave him a shove back toward the action. "Let's go. Shake it off, reset, make a different mistake this time."

Liam snorted. "I can see why Mo delegates the pep talks."

True to his assertion, Liam didn't make the same mistake twice. He did make a couple of other ones, but he handled them well, and when Russ left his man undefended, leading to a scoring chance Havvy only barely got a piece of, Liam caught his eye and nodded. Russ figured he got it. Russ didn't like fucking up either, but not dwelling on mistakes was as important to a good game as not making them.

The last time they ran through the set play, Yeti really *did* dump Liam on his ass—so conspicuously that it had to have been intentional, as opposed to the way they were meant to run the drill. Baller and Jonesy hooted with laughter as Liam's gloves and stick went yard-saling over the ice.

Typical way to welcome a new defenseman. Russ snowed to a stop next to his temporary partner. "How you doing down there?"

Liam muttered a handful of French-Canadian expletives. He reached up with a bare hand and Russ hauled him to a sitting position. "I feel like I got hit by a truck."

"Yeti'll do that to you. You good?"

Liam shook his head. "I'm good." He got to his feet. "Jesus. How much does he weigh?"

"Significantly more when he's moving that fast." Russ clapped Liam's shoulder as they skated off to let the next groups practice. They were done for now, so he had time to give Liam a little more feedback. "That's something you'll have to get used to."

"What?" Liam pulled himself up on the half boards.

"Checking." When Liam looked at him, Russ elaborated, "You flinch."

Liam's mouth dropped open. "I do not!"

"Twenty bucks says the video review shows otherwise." Russ had seen it before with guys who came up through the college system, which focused on speed over hits, since they wanted their players to keep their brains unscrambled long enough to graduate. "It's fine. You're not the first. You're going to have to work on it, though."

"Not a lot of guys in college are Yeti-sized." Liam's mouth twisted into a wry smile, but he seemed genuinely upset, like the root of the problem bothered him.

Russ snorted. "Not a lot of guys in the NHL are either. Or outside of it." Yeti was six foot nine and built like a linebacker. "Are you trying to bulk up for the season?"

"Was that a hint?" Liam grabbed his water bottle from the bench and waggled it. The joker was still there, but Russ was pretty sure he meant the question. "Think I should fill one of these with Ensure or something?"

God. "That's one way to make sure no one ever steals your drink."

"Seriously, though." Liam put the bottle down. There was a smudge of blue at the corner of his mouth. "Do you think I'm too skinny?"

Russ must've given him a look that broadcast his thoughts, because Liam rolled his eyes and amended, still more than half serious, "For *hockey.* I'm not asking you to compliment my figure. I know I'm hot."

"I think you're a kid." At that age Russ could've eaten his body weight in M&M's and barely gained a pound. "Putting on weight at your age when you burn calories like we do isn't easy. But you could work with the trainers on some exercises that'll help you stay upright when someone his size hits you. Or when you hit them."

Liam made a sad noise. "I always used to think those videos were funny. You know, tiny forward tries to check an absolute monster like Mikhail Kipriyanov, then ends up on his ass."

"You're going to be one of those videos," Russ assured him. Maybe he shouldn't inflate the kid's hopes, but if he did his time in the AHL, he'd make it. It wouldn't take long.

Liam straightened his shoulders like that was a great compliment. "I'm going to be one of those videos." He shook his head and more of his usual humor returned. "I'm not even tiny. Just tiny compared to him." He looked sideways at Russ and his voice dropped and took on a suggestive tone. "And you. You're big. What do you eat?"

Russ glanced over and found Liam watching him with trouble written all over his face.

Surely he couldn't be serious. He didn't even know Russ was gay.

Which meant he was being a little shit. Russ shouldn't encourage him, but he couldn't let him get away with thinking he had the last word either. "Anything within range."

This kid's sass was going to cost him so much money if he officially joined the team. He hopped off the boards again and leaned close enough to put himself directly into Russ's space. "Sounds like you have a pretty healthy appetite."

Good grief. Russ had to laugh, because there was no *way* Liam was trying to pick him up with a game that bad. "Do these lines really work for you?"

Undaunted, Liam grinned and cocked his hip so his ass stuck out. "Don't usually need 'em."

Between Liam's body, the slight dimple in his cheek, and the unruly curls, Russ could see why, but he wasn't going to pump his tires. "Well, kid, welcome to the Big Show. Get used to putting in another level of effort."

Then he skated off to the next drill before Liam could decide he should start putting in that effort now.

THE LAST day of training camp practice before the preseason was officially the most tired Liam had been in his life. He felt bad about the way he kept nodding off during the seminars, where someone had decided to cram in all the compulsory classroom-education bits that didn't fit during the week. Liam might be impulsive, but he wasn't going to invest all his money in cryptocurrency, lend it to his parents, or start collecting vintage cars. He had enough common sense to know he was probably on video all the time when he was in public. He didn't even take dick pics that showed his face—though, based on the haggard expression on the long-suffering woman giving this talk, he might be in the minority on that one.

He *definitely* didn't need to worry about collecting his used condom after a one-night stand in case his partner tried to use the sperm inside it to baby-trap him.

"What the fuck," he hissed to Dante Baltierra, who happened to be seated beside him. "Do people do this shit? I don't believe it. Like… this feels misogynistic."

"Don't look at me," Baller replied under his breath. "Gabe and I can't even get pregnant the old-fashioned way."

Liam filed the whole thing under *weird straight-people problems* and closed his eyes to get a few minutes' rest.

Despite the exhaustion, Liam hadn't slept well all week. He should probably cut back on the energy drinks, but they were all that kept him awake during the day. He didn't like this anxiety, if that's what it was.

Before he filed out of the arena for what might be the last time—the Caimans had a habit of cutting a few players before the preseason started—Russ clapped him on the shoulder. "Hey."

Liam jumped half out of his skin. He was on edge. Russ's general… Russness didn't help. He was handsome and confident and competent and nice to Liam even though Liam was a nobody and kind of a fuckup. And all that would've been enough, but then he went and…. Liam didn't know. He certainly didn't seem to mind Liam's flirting, which was good since that made up about half his personality. He definitely hadn't gotten the awkward "thanks, but I'm not interested" straight-guy turn-down he expected.

Which didn't mean anything. Russ could just be, like, actually chill. But if he *was* into the idea of getting naked with Liam in a more private setting, Liam wanted to be clear he'd be all over that.

"Um," he said after a moment. Damn. He couldn't think of a plausibly deniable come-on. "Hey."

"Good camp." Russ squeezed gently, and his thumb brushed the base of Liam's neck.

Liam's dick, which was the only part of him not totally wrung out with exhaustion, woke up and licked its lips. "Thanks." He wished he'd had more time to implement Russ's suggestions and insight into his game.

Russ smiled. "See you around, I hope."

"Me too."

Russ gave a two-fingered wave and disappeared into the Florida heat.

Caimans Cut Training Camp Roster to 57
By Rocky Sanderson

The Miami Caimans have reduced their training camp roster to 57 players.

Forwards Jordan Ryan and Rocky Clifford have been released to their juniors teams. Center Grayson Wood will report to the Lexington Thoroughbreds, the Caimans' AHL affiliate. In addition, defenseman Byron Spitz and goaltender Mathieu Rocheleau have been released from training camp.

That leaves forwards Connor Hughes, who put up 87 points with the Windsor Spitfires last year, second-round pick KC Courvoisier, University of Michigan center Hunter Fisher, and veteran Raff McCleod, who is on a professional tryout.

Goaltenders Ivan Havriushenko and Jagger Nyman, as well as defensemen Liam Belanger, Mattias Schaefer, Michael Petterson, Carl Bjorklund, and Tomas Koskinen, remain with the team for now.

The Caimans are expected to announce the final twenty-three-man roster prior to the final game of the preseason.

THE CAIMANS' annual pre-preseason party arrived, and Russ headed over to Mo's early. It wasn't that he didn't trust Mo and Jonesy to set up, just... okay, it was. Russ had Older Sibling Disease. And he didn't know Baller well enough yet to gauge what he might bring to the table.

Besides, he knew they'd planned some kind of initiation ritual without him, and he wanted to make sure it wouldn't traumatize anyone before he let it proceed.

Which, come to think of it, was probably also a symptom of Older Sibling Disease.

It turned out he'd worried for nothing, because his teammates had come up with the mildest, dumbest ritual possible. The worst thing they'd done was ask the rookies to show up half an hour early to set up. When the doorbell rang at two thirty and Mo answered it, Hughes looked at them all, groaned, and said, "Oh no, so this is a hazing thing."

Well, Hughes already had one thing on Jonesy. He could recognize the obvious.

"Rookies!" Mo crowed. "You're half an hour early. It's so *nice* of you to volunteer to help us set everything up."

Liam rolled his eyes. "You could have just asked. You didn't have to trick us."

"Pfft." Mo dismissed that with a wave of his hand. "Where'd be the fun in that? Come in, come in, there's work to do."

Hughesy grimaced at Liam. "Next time we'll be fashionably late."

Way smarter than Jonesy.

Baller clapped. "Funny you should mention fashion." And then he presented them each with a custom white tank top. "We got you presents."

"More of a uniform," Mo put in.

Russ suffered silently. The leadership team needed to present a united front, even if that front looked dumb as fuck.

But at least it didn't look as dumb as three pasty white-boy rookies wearing custom tank tops with their party duties written on the back.

Unlike his own clothes, the POOL BOY shirt fit Hughes properly. Someone should tell him it was okay not to need a size Large. Havvy's BEER BOY top was straddling the line between "I accidentally put this in the dryer" and "stripper about to go on."

This left Liam with the shirt that read WATER BUOY.

Liam tried to look over his own shoulder at the writing on his back. His nipples showed through the oversize armholes. "Is that a spelling mistake?"

"No, man, you're on lifeguard duty." Mo clapped him on the shoulder. "Russ'll explain. Right, Russ?"

Russ figured this was related to the jet ski and life jacket rental. "I will explain," Russ repeated dutifully.

Liam grinned as he put his hat back on. "Lifeguard duty? Do I get a Speedo?"

"Only if you brought your own," Russ said dryly while Baller cackled. "Come on, I'll show you around."

Russ still hoped Liam would crack the Caimans' roster, but he wasn't holding his breath. A lot was riding on what happened in the preseason. If Liam did well, he should at least get an offer to play in Lexington for the Caimans' AHL affiliate, where he'd have plenty of ice time. Russ stopped short of hoping he'd get to play with Liam sometime this season, because that would mean someone was injured, but if it happened, at least the cloud would have a silver lining.

"Bathrooms there and there," he said as he led the kid through the house. "Beer in those coolers, premade mix drinks in the bar fridge." He glanced over his shoulder. "You're twenty-one, right?" Russ couldn't tell by looks anymore. Anyone under twenty-five looked like a baby unless they could grow decent facial hair.

Russ would've bet his Cup ring Liam couldn't even grow a beard if you covered his face in chia seeds.

"Twenty-two," Liam corrected in the tone of a very recent college graduate.

"Pool house is there, there's another two bathrooms in there." Totally necessary for the number of people who'd be at this party. Russ's place didn't have enough toilets to handle a full team gathering.

"This is kind of wild," Liam said as they went out the back gate toward the dock with the life jackets and jet skis.

Russ gave him a sideways look. "What, you never dreamed of playing pro hockey in Florida?"

Liam pushed his sunglasses up his nose. "I pretty much only got as far as 'I need to get out of my hometown.'"

That was interesting, but before Russ could ask a follow-up, Liam turned it around on him. "What about you? Did you dream about playing for Winnipeg?"

"Thought about it." His mom would cry tears of joy, but Russ would rather pull his toenails out with pliers than play for their coach, a stodgy old-fashioned type who gave Russ bad vibes. But he wasn't going to say that to a rookie he just met. "You have to admit, though, the weather here doesn't suck. I don't miss shoveling snow."

Liam wrinkled his nose. "I like snow."

Of course he did. "Ever been snowmobiling?"

"Like every day in the winter until I moved out?" Liam laughed and dipped his toes in the surf. "My parents have a sugar shack—you know, to make maple syrup? It's a big tourist thing in the winter. So, yeah. We snowmobile a lot."

That was the most French-Canadian white-boy thing Russ had ever heard—especially with the accent. They stepped onto the dock. "Different protective gear for these things."

"You're not going to make me clean them with a toothbrush or something, are you?"

Russ laughed. "No. Shit, that's creative. Don't say that around Mo and Jonesy. You'll give 'em ideas."

"So, what, then?"

Russ flipped open the top on the deck box and revealed Mo's collection of life jackets, all sizes, from Yeti to baby. "Ta-da." He reached into it and retrieved a bright red whistle on a cord. Mo knew how to lean into a theme. "C'mere."

Obediently, Liam came over and ducked his head. Russ didn't realize he was making a mistake settling the cord around Liam's neck until his fingertips brushed the edge of Liam's shirt.

Then Liam tilted his head up just a bit—a gesture that would've been an invitation if his sunglasses hadn't ruined it.

He still didn't even know Russ was gay, so Russ wasn't going to take the flirtation seriously. Even if he did have the momentary urge to lean in and kiss him.

Obviously he'd been out in the sun too long.

Russ pulled his hands back and resisted the urge to wipe his palms on his shorts. "Safety first," he said. "Welcome to Baywatch. You're now officially in charge of making sure anyone under eighteen who gets on a skidoo has a life jacket rated for their weight."

Liam ran his thumb over the mouthpiece of the whistle. Russ wrenched his eyes away. That seemed… unnecessarily suggestive. "You're not gonna teach me how to give mouth-to-mouth?"

God save him. Russ was starting to worry about the kind of invitation Liam would offer once he knew Russ was into guys. "Shelly's in charge of the actual lifesaving. Mo's girlfriend," he added when Liam didn't seem to clue in. "She's got a lifeguard certification. You're responsible until they get in the water, she's responsible once they're in." He pointed at the closest skidoo. "That one's Shelly's. Make sure no one takes it out in case someone gets into trouble."

"Yes, *sir*," Liam said with a flutter of his eyelashes. But then he frowned a little, his eyebrows drawn together in a wrinkle. "Okay, but is Mo really making his girlfriend work his party? I mean it's one thing for the new guys to get the shitty jobs, but…."

What a softie. If he did make it to the NHL, the whole team would eat him alive. Russ would have to take him under his wing.

"Shelly insisted," Russ corrected. She was very focused on safety. "And you're not here all day. Probably not even two hours. Once the food gets here, people start drinking, and then it's time to lock up the jet skis."

"Sweet." He looked down at his shirt, then back up again, lips pursed just so. "And then I can lose the uniform?"

"You can do whatever you want when you're off the clock." Though maybe Russ shouldn't give him free rein. Before Liam could take advantage, he moved on and pointed next to the deck box. "The cooler here has water and Gatorade for you and

Shelly so you don't get dehydrated. Stay sober until you're off-duty. Got it?"

"Ouais." And then there was a long, low growling sound that echoed like a burp in the Grand Canyon. Liam's cheeks went pink. Well, pink*er*. "So, um, what about lunch?"

It was almost three. "You didn't eat before you came?"

He scratched at the back of his neck and gave Russ a sheepish hungry-orphan look. "Uh, I maybe need to get groceries. I ate, like, an egg and some leftover pizza and a protein shake for breakfast."

"*Possible* you need to get groceries."

Liam spread his arms and put on an innocent expression. "I got distracted picking my outfit?"

"Jesus." Russ made a mental note to text Liam's captain on the Thoroughbreds and suggest he find the kid a babysitter—if he made the team. He put his hand on Liam's shoulder and turned him back toward the house. "All right. Let's refuel you first, and then we'll talk refueling the jet skis."

Russ had said *let's*, but he ended up making Liam a stack of sandwiches while Liam sat at Mo's breakfast bar, out of the way. Russ blamed that on instinct and the fact that Liam didn't know where anything was.

But it felt awkward to stand there and do it silently—it called too much attention to the out-of-place intimacy of the act. Russ figured he might as well satisfy his curiosity, so he reached back to their conversation from earlier. "So. You took the long way getting here. What's your story?"

Liam picked a baby carrot off the veggie tray and popped it in his mouth. "You don't believe me if I tell you."

Liam had spoken slowly at camp, like he was watching every word to make sure he didn't make mistakes. It was good to see him relaxing a little. Russ held up the mustard. When Liam nodded, he said, "Try me."

Liam tapped a piece of cauliflower against his lower lip. "I have two older sisters and an older brother. Like, a lot older. My youngest sister is ten years older than me. I'm an oops baby."

That explained a few things. Russ finished the sandwiches, cut them in half, and slid the plate in front of Liam. "Opposite scenario. I'm the oldest by eight years." He washed his hands for a second time and then leaned against the counter. "So, youngest of four. And?"

Liam snorted. "*And* my siblings are all over-achievers. The oldest one is a rocket scientist. Her fingerprints are on things that are actually in space. My brother did an MBA, got married at twenty-four, basically took over the family business, and has two kids. And my other sister did a tour with Médecins Sans Frontières and now she runs her own family practice in our hometown." He picked up a sandwich and took an enormous bite.

Russ whistled under his breath. That was a lot to live up to. "Remind me not to go to a family reunion at your place."

Liam nodded as he chewed. Then he said, "And we are from a *small* town. Everyone know my parents. All my teachers had my siblings first. Everyone always said, 'Oh, are you going to be like Bernadette, are you going to be like Bastian?'" He made a face. "I didn't even get to be the first one to be gay since Bernadette's a lesbian."

Russ stifled a laugh. He didn't want to come across as callous. Plenty of queer folks would've killed to know how their parents would react to having gay kids before they came out.

Which reminded him he had to have that conversation with Liam. Preferably in a way that didn't lead to Liam hitting on him and meaning it.

First things first. "I can see how that would be hard."

Liam wiped a smear of mayo from the corner of his mouth and licked it off his thumb. "Like, imagine graduating high school—the biggest thing you've done in your life so far—the same day one of your siblings is launching something into space."

"That's rude. She couldn't have waited a couple weeks to send up the rocket?"

Liam burst into laughter. "Oh, wow, you don't know anything about space launches, do you?"

"Almost nothing," Russ promised cheerfully. Liam had a good laugh, especially when he was surprised.

"That might be my favorite thing about you."

Yeah... Russ *really* had to tell him before one of his teammates witnessed this and made assumptions.

But before he could, he heard footsteps coming downstairs. With Baller, Mo, Jonesy, and the other rookies outside, that had to be Shelly. "I'm flattered," he said instead, bone dry. Then he pointed out, "You still haven't answered the question, though. Why hockey?"

Liam picked up his water glass. "I have three smart, civic-minded, accomplished older siblings, *but*—important—none of them are good at sports."

It was Russ's turn to laugh. "That's not really what I expected."

Liam shrugged. "My parents either. Mom wanted me to be a priest."

Now *that* would've been trouble. Russ wasn't Catholic, but he was pretty sure priests were supposed to discourage sin.

He didn't say that out loud, though, because he was right, that had been Shelly coming down the stairs. He stood up as soon as she saw him, because he knew what would happen next. He had four seconds to brace himself before a five-ten brunet in red swim shorts launched herself into his arms. "Russell! I can't believe you haven't come to visit before now."

Russ swung her around in a circle—not too fast; he didn't want to smack her legs on the kitchen cabinets—and then lowered her to the ground. "I did too. You were up to your eyeballs in fish jizz."

Shelly slapped his chest when he set her down again. "Gross. Thanks for that." She turned her attention to Liam and assessed him head to toe. Well, head to chest, which was what she could see from their side of the breakfast bar. "Is this your new rookie?"

Liam swallowed his last bite of the first sandwich. "Right now I'm just the temp." He wiped his hand on a napkin and offered it to shake. "Liam Belanger, at your service."

While Shelly was shaking his hand, Russ said, "Liam's in charge of life jackets today."

Shelly grinned. "Very important part of not drowning. Nice to meet you."

"You too." Liam tilted his head, eyes dancing as he flitted his gaze between Russ and Shelly. "Should I ask about the fish jizz?"

"Kind of an oversimplification. I'm doing a PhD in marine biology, focusing on the effects of climate change on marine reproductive habits."

"Fish jizz," Russ repeated teasingly.

Shelly shoved his arm. "Stop. Don't you have a party to cohost? Get out of here."

"I will. I had to feed the kid first. Didn't want him passing out during his duties."

"Don't forget interrogate me about why I don't become a priest," Liam interjected.

"Oh, yeah, you kinda missed the mark on that one." Shelly paused, and Russ just knew she was going to fall right into the trap. "Why didn't you?"

Liam shrugged with feigned nonchalance. "Too hot, too horny… too gay."

"Oh my God," Shelly said to Russ. "I love him. Are you sure we can't keep him?"

"Go love him outside," Russ suggested. He was lucky she hadn't said something more pointed. She absolutely would've if she thought Russ had come out to him. "I'll clean up the dishes and you can teach him how the jet skis work."

Liam sighed, long-suffering. "He's tired of me already."

"Well, come on, then. Let him be tired of dishes while we take the first spin on the water."

IT DIDN'T take long for Liam to fall deep in platonic love with Shelly, who was hilarious and full of weird facts about animal sex.

They chatted for an hour or so between helping the Caimans' kids into life jackets and supervising to ensure nobody fell off the dock or got on one of the machines after too many drinks. For the most part, the mood was jubilant, except for a few minutes when Baller got on a jet ski while his husband and toddler watched from the dock, and the kid screamed louder than the engine as he roared into the waves.

"I saw this coming," commented Gabe Martin, one of Liam's childhood idols, as he held the wailing girl against his chest. "She's in a daddy's girl phase."

Liam still wasn't sure he wasn't dreaming.

Okay, he was pretty sure. He'd had this dream, but he was like eight years younger at the time, and there were a lot less clothes and no toddler.

"She be pretty cute if she isn't screaming," he offered.

After about thirty seconds, Baller pulled the jet ski back up to the dock and scrambled to take the kid from Gabe. She quieted immediately.

"Sorry, sorry," Baller said sheepishly as Reyna hiccupped into his neck. "I let my enthusiasm run away with me. I'll go sometime when she's not around to witness it."

"She's fine," Gabe said. "She'll forget all about it in two minutes when she sees the kiddie pool."

As if to prove the point, Reyna looked up from under her oversize sun hat. "Pool?"

"Absolutely. Let's go do that." Baller lifted her above his head and blew a raspberry on her tummy. She shrieked again, but with laughter this time. "I guess jet skis can wait until you're older."

"Or never," Gabe said. "Never would also be fine."

They walked back up to the backyard together, shoulder to shoulder, just as Russ came back down from the house. He stopped and exchanged pleasantries with them—something Liam couldn't hear over the breeze and the waves—and then came out to the dock.

The afternoon light was particularly kind to him, highlighting the dark bronze curves of his shoulders and shadowing his cheekbones. He looked like some kind of modern sun god, with the sunglasses and the languid way he moved. "Think we're ready to close it down. Everyone's getting a bit too deep to drive." He raised his own drink, as though Liam was going to look at that when he could look at Russ instead. Then he met Liam's eyes and added, "Besides, the food'll be here soon."

Would it be too much to suggest Liam had a different kind of meal in mind? He'd been a very good boy to avoid peeping at Russ's dick in the locker room. And now training camp was moving into the preseason, and he was running out of time to misbehave.

"Sounds good," Shelly said before he could decide. "We'll get things squared away here and be up in a few."

Russ raised his eyebrows—and the drink—and then turned and left. The rear view was pretty great too.

When he was out of earshot, Shelly cleared her throat. "You know, the male argonaut octopus grows its penis on its head."

That finally snapped Liam out of his trance. "I'm sorry?"

"The argonaut octopus. Literal dickhead." She flicked him between the eyes and then turned to start piling the life jackets into the deck box. Liam bent to help her. "It's an evolutionary thing. The argonaut octopus is sexually dimorphic—the female is so much bigger than the male that she'd just eat him if he tried to mate with her. So he grows a penis tentacle in a pouch on his face, and when the moment is right...." She placed her fist against the middle of her forehead and then opened it with wiggling fingers. "He shoots his dick off and inseminates the female." She paused meaningfully. "And then he dies."

Where was this going? Liam handed her the last of the life jackets. "Wait, he dies anyway?"

She closed the box and locked it with the jet ski keys inside. "Yeah. Like, if you're gonna die either way, you might as well go out with a bang, right?"

"You would think." Then again, maybe octopuses weren't wired for sexual pleasure. In any case, Liam had the feeling he'd missed a point that Shelly thought was obvious. "Uh, not that I don't like to learn new things, but… is there a moral to this story?"

Shelly hooked her arm through his as they started up toward the house. "I'm just saying." She gestured in front of them, to where Russ was just taking a seat on one of the lounge chairs by the pool. "Shoot your shot. It won't kill you."

Liam caught the edge of a flipflop on one of the stairs, but Shelly hauled him upright before he could faceplant. "Oh my God."

"Maybe wait until you can walk and look at his ass at the same time without falling, though."

…. Yeah, that could take a while.

Liam grabbed a Gatorade and polished it off. Then he joined the line to get a plate of food.

After that, the afternoon wore on in a pleasant blur of good company and plentiful alcohol. Liam played two games of pool volleyball and kicked Havvy's ass at lawn bowling, then found himself staring blankly out at the water and listening to the waves.

He really liked this team. He was going to miss these guys—and this view—if he didn't make the cut.

He was debating whether he should have a nap when Jonesy appeared at his elbow. "Hey, bro, you look like you need an A/C break."

That sounded like a good idea. "It's very hot here," Liam said as he followed Jonesy inside.

"Yeah, man, Florida's like that. Here." Jonesy handed him another Gatorade and pushed him down on the couch. "Sit here and cool off for a few minutes, okay?"

By the time he'd downed half the drink, Liam realized how badly he'd needed to get out of the sun. First he felt light-headed and dizzy, then almost nauseated. His skin felt tight too—he definitely had a sunburn despite the half pound of sunscreen he'd slathered on before leaving his Airbnb. He hadn't had enough alcohol to earn this kind of suffering.

Clearly he needed to reevaluate how much he could drink if he was going to be out in the heat.

Mo's couch was comfortable, and Liam must have dozed off for a half hour or so, because when he opened his eyes again, the backyard was bathed in shadow and the setting sun had painted the room he was in a brilliant orange. He finished the Gatorade, felt better, and stood up to go back outside.

He had just put his bottle in the plastic bin designated for empties when the patio door slid open.

Russ quickly glanced behind him into the yard, then did a double take when he turned around again and almost ran into Liam. "Jesus, kid. You should wear a bell."

Liam's heat-and-booze-addled mind considered this. "Wear it where?"

Russ gave him a wry look. "Never mind. Come with me, I need your help finding something."

Bemused, and maybe still a little more drunk than he wanted to admit, Liam followed him down the hallway. "What are we looking for?"

"Karaoke machine," Russ answered absently. He poked his head into a room that seemed to be a den, then must have decided it was a likely place to look and stepped inside fully. "Hurry up."

Hurry up and do what? Liam followed him. "Why are we looking for it, exactly? And what's the rush?" Was there some kind of karaoke emergency?

Russ opened the closet, which turned out to be full of electronics. "Mo's been into the absinthe. If we don't find it before he does, he'll use it."

Surely worse things than karaoke happened at NHL parties. Liam had definitely heard stories about lost dentures and chipped teeth, and that could only be the tip of the iceberg. "So?"

Finally Russ turned away from the closet. "So one guy monopolizing the karaoke machine to serenade us with Rat Pack standards all night is a party-killer."

"Oh. Well, why don't you say so?" Liam paused. "What's a karaoke machine look like?"

Russ answered with a noise of triumph. "Found it."

But before they could make off with the loot, Liam heard the sound of the patio door opening again. Mo's voice echoed through the house. "I've just got to go grab something."

Russ and Liam met eyes in a panic. There was no way they could hide *that* thing—it was huge!—at least not before Mo found them.

Then Liam had a jolt of inspiration. "Just get the power cord," he hissed.

Russ's eyes widened, and he reached into the closet just as footsteps started in their direction.

"Where do we go?"

Russ grabbed his wrist. "This way."

Mo's house must've had some weird-ass open concept floor plan, because they circled back around to the kitchen a different way than they'd come. But before they could escape outside, the door slid open *again* and Shelly came in.

"She gonna rat us out?" Liam whispered.

Instead of answering, Russ yanked Liam backward and into a… closet?

"This is such a cliché," Liam muttered into the darkness, putting his arms out to steady himself as the world spun.

A second later Russ flicked on a light and revealed that they were actually standing in a walk-in pantry, which made a lot more sense, because who had a closet in their kitchen?

Then he turned around and realized it was a *small* walk-in pantry, and Russ was really close to him and still very handsome, and Liam was drunker than he thought. And also kind of horny, now that he could smell Russ's bodywash and the salt of his sweat and feel the body heat radiating off him.

The timing on that last revelation could have been better.

Shelly's words echoed in his head. *Shoot your shot. It won't kill you.*

Liam licked his lips, his gaze glued to Russ's. Russ looked half mischievous, half startled; a little-boy smirk hid at the corner of his generous lips, but his eyes had gone serious, and they pulled Liam in with all kinds of promises Russ probably didn't intend to make.

In an effort to put a little more distance between Russ and his dick, Liam took a teeny, tiny, insignificant step backward.

"Wait," Russ hissed, darting forward. "Don't—"

Liam's shoulder bumped against something firm. The door latched shut behind him.

"Fuck," Russ groaned.

Liam's heart sank. He turned around.

The pantry door didn't have a knob on the inside.

"Oh," he said. "Calisse."

Silence reigned for a few interminable moments. Outside the pantry, Liam could just hear Shelly and Mo discussing where the power cord to the karaoke machine might be. *Are you sure you put it away last time? Maybe it's still in the rec room.* Then their voices faded into the distance.

Another heartbeat passed.

Liam couldn't help it. He giggled. "Oh my God. I cannot believe this is happening to me."

When he looked back over his shoulder, Russ was laughing too, quietly, with a hand over his eyes. "Fuck, what's wrong with me? We could've just thrown him in the pool when he started singing 'My Way.' That's what we did last year."

Figuring he might as well make himself comfortable, Liam put his back to the door and slid down. He had just enough room to stretch his legs out. "Why he keeps getting to host?" Alcohol and sun made English harder.

Russ sat too. It took a moment of awkward shuffling to find room for all their legs, and now Liam was distracted by the way Russ's shorts rode up his absurdly muscular thighs. Russ's warm calf brushed the outside of Liam's leg… which drew Liam's attention to his own left leg, which was between Russ's.

Could Liam, like, arrange to fall over with his face in Russ's lap and make it seem like an accident, he wondered. That would be a good way to gauge if he was interested, right?

"Jonesy hates it—plus his wife just had a baby, that's why he left early—and I don't live on the water."

Shit, what were they talking about? Oh, right—why Mo kept hosting. Liam cocked his head. "Why not?"

Russ gave him a wry look. "I don't trust the ocean not to sneak into my bedroom when I'm sleeping."

Ugh, it should be illegal to be handsome, good at sports, *and* funny. "Ha! Okay, that's fair." Liam had never ridden out a tropical hurricane, though he'd been in Massachusetts for plenty of nasty nor'easters. "But like, maybe you don't know, but at least in Quebec you can have a party without an ocean."

"It's a division of labor thing. Mo cleans and hosts. Jonesy wrangles the details. I deal with the catering." He paused. "I don't know what Baller does yet. We'll figure it out."

"A well-oiled leadership team." Oh God, why that choice of words? Now he was thinking about it. For the first time, he wished he knew less English. He'd get into less trouble.

Russ really did look like someone had oiled him, damn it.

He did not look like someone who was particularly perturbed by Liam noticing. "You really can't help yourself, can you?"

"It's a reflex," Liam sighed. "We can get you a squirt bottle, maybe." Then he paused. He didn't need a squirt bottle. He was perfectly capable of knocking it off if his attention was unwanted. "Or you just tell me to stop. I don't actually want to make you uncomfortable."

For some reason *that* was what made Russ grimace, like the idea of telling Liam to stop was worse than being hit on. "Look, I don't care. I think it's funny. But if you're going to keep it up, you should know some of the guys are going to assume you're serious."

Liam blinked. "Seriously trying to get into your pants?" He absolutely would if he thought it was an option.

Russ pulled his right leg back toward himself, bent at the knee. Liam tried not to stare at his crotch. "I'm gay. The team knows, so at some point they might figure you're…."

Doing exactly what he desperately wanted to do? Liam thought hysterically.

Like, he didn't really want his teammates thinking he was… soliciting favors? Going for extra credit? Trying to earn a spot in the big leagues on his back or his knees?

It just so happened that he wanted both a spot on the team and a spot on Russ's dick. He *didn't* want to worry about a causal relationship between the two.

Ugh. He was going to have to dial back the flirting. And like, probably not suck Russ's dick. God damn it. Liam hated being an adult. "Right, yes. Good point. Thanks for telling me."

It figured. He'd just found out Russ was actually into guys and now he couldn't even try to get up on that.

Which, actually. "So, wait, did you think that coming out to me is going to get us out of the closet?"

Russ groaned, but there was a laugh buried under it. "This is a pantry."

"Sorry for my English," Liam said innocently.

This time Russ laughed out loud. "God, you're trouble."

"You're the one who think it was a good idea to hide in a room with no doorknob." He paused. "Are we actually trying to escape, by the way? Because I leave my phone in the living room, but if you have yours, maybe we just call for help. 'Hello, 911, two gays stuck in a closet. Send RuPaul.'"

Liam had not accounted for the way Russ digging in his pocket for his phone would pull the material even tighter around his crotch and thighs. "I'll text Shelly."

"We can tell her we get stuck playing Seven Minutes in Heaven." He paused. "Uh, assuming she know you're gay."

"Yeah, she knows. Most of the guys' partners know, but not all of them."

Russ seemed pretty comfortable with himself, but maybe Liam was biased. After all, it was easier to come out to someone you knew was queer. "How come?" Sure, it was a personal question, but if you couldn't ask personal questions when you were locked in a pantry together because you were committing karaoke sabotage, when could you?

Russ shrugged as he tapped out a message. "It's...." He sighed, sent the message, and rested his arm over his knee. "I don't know. It started as a rule that only the guys' wives could know, in case someone breaks up, but marriages end too. I mostly just don't want someone to blab to the press before I come out on my own terms. It's a glass closet, but the view is pretty good most of the time." He quirked his lips. "Unlike this one."

As if Liam could resist an opening like that. He licked his lips. "Hey. The view look pretty good from here."

Russ rolled his eyes—ouch—so Liam moved on. "If you're worried about being outed, you could just come out. Get it over with. Then you can do it how you want."

"They teach you all this logic at college?" Russ asked dryly.

As if. Liam grinned. "Nah. I majored in French lit and beer pong."

"Good. You can be on my team later if Shelly ever lets us out of here." Russ leaned his head back against the shelf. He'd lost his hat at some point and now the short springy curls on the top of his head were squished against the cereal box on the shelf behind him. "Did you like college?"

Were they playing Twenty Questions now? At least it would distract Liam from the other things they could do with their privacy. "It was okay. I made good friends, played good hockey, learned some shit. All I care about was leaving home."

Russ smiled. "I guess it's working out okay so far. And you're doing something your siblings will never do."

Of course Russ got the point he was trying to make. "It was this or write a book," Liam said earnestly. "This seem easier."

Russ laughed again, scrunching up his face until his eyes crinkled. "Good to have a backup plan, though."

Liam made himself look away. Clearly it had been too long since a handsome man paid this kind of attention to him. "What about you? Did you always want to be a hockey player?"

Russ shrugged. "Pretty much. The best quality time I got with my parents as a kid was on the way to or from the rink."

Liam understood that. Apparently they had lots in common. Like the fact that they were both sitting on a hard tile floor in a kitchen closet. "Fuck, where is Shelly? My ass going numb."

Russ reached for his phone again. "Maybe I should call her instead of texting."

Before he could, Liam felt the vibrations of footsteps. "Russ?"

Liam scrambled away from the door, which unfortunately meant he nearly ended up in Russ's lap—*actually* by accident this time. He was just getting to his knees when the door swung open. Shelly stood in the doorway, drink in hand. She stared at them for a moment, obviously on the verge of cracking up, and then asked, "Do I even want to know?"

Russ held up the karaoke cord. "We didn't have time to hide the whole thing. And then Liam accidentally locked us in."

Shelly laughed. "Oh, well. My heroes." She leaned over to offer Liam a hand up, and he took it.

She pulled him to his feet. "Though I'm just saying, it never hurts him to get thrown in the pool."

Liam turned around and made the same gesture to Russ. He did not have as easy a time hauling him up as Shelly had with him, and he made a mental note to spend more time in the gym.

Russ didn't give him a hard time about it, though. "Thanks, Trouble."

"Don't mention it."

Pregame Report: Caimans At Firebirds
By Rocky Sanderson

The Miami Caimans play their first preseason game tonight in Philadelphia. With 43 players on the training camp roster, they'll be looking to get a good feel for their younger players, which means most of the veterans are sitting this one out. Expect to see alternate captain Russ Lyons paired with Boston College alum Liam Belanger on the top defensive pairing. Forward Connor Hughes will also play. Ivan Havriuschenko will start in net.

RUSS HAD played for the Caimans for most of his career, and like any NHL team, the Caimans had a system when it came to road trips.

But the system for a preseason away game was basically chaos, because most of the regular team members wouldn't travel to many preseason games, which meant the plane was full of AHL and juniors players who didn't know the system.

Russ usually sat with Jonesy or Mo, but they weren't coming—they'd get a few extra days to lie around on their couches before the Caimans came back to play their preseason home games.

This meant two things. One, Russ was the de facto captain. Two, he felt like a babysitter. He was ten years older than the majority of the guys on the plane, and the excitement made them loud. For a lot of them, this would be their first time on NHL ice, even if it didn't count for anything. Some of them would never make the Big Show. Most of them would be waiting a few more years for their shot.

"I swear to God I was never that young," Baller commented as he dropped into the seat next to Russ. "You don't mind, do you?"

It wasn't like Russ had been saving the seat, and sitting next to someone who had some chill would keep him from grinding his teeth during the flight to Philly. "It's all yours."

"Thanks."

"So… ready to earn that letter on the jersey?"

Baller gestured at the chaos around them. "Who else were they going to have help you? One of these infants? They'd wet themselves."

"Probably true."

"So who's your bet for overachiever of the night?"

"Hughes, definitely." Eighteen, bright-eyed, fiercely determined to prove he was big on the inside, even if he was only five ten in skates.

Baller hummed happily. "Perfect. He's my liney for the trip. He can do all the hard work." Then, having lulled Russ into a false sense of security, he continued with, "Speaking of lineys, your rookie is being weird."

Unfortunately, Russ couldn't disagree. They'd had a whole weekend off after training camp, then another rest day before regular practices started. The weighing and measuring and fitness testing were done, and now they could buckle down and play. It had taken Russ a minute to put his finger on what was different about Liam, but then he realized Liam had stopped flirting with him.

But he hadn't stopped batting his eyelashes at the rest of the team. The other day Mo gave him shit for zoning out while they ran shooting drills. Liam shrugged innocently and claimed he was hypnotized by Mo's stickhandling.

Russ had no right to feel grumpy about it. Liam could flirt with whoever he wanted. Besides, Russ had no more intention of acting on the flirtation than any of the straight guys Liam made silly passes at.

But he still felt like he'd lost something—like an inside joke that didn't land anymore.

Agreeing with Baller would lead to uncomfortable follow-up questions, so Russ stalled. "Weird how?"

"Weird like ever since the two of you disappeared at Mo's party, he's totally stopped inviting you to bend him over the nearest convenient surface." Baller didn't blink. Russ knew he had a reputation for being direct, but damn. "Something happen between you and Trouble?"

Russ should've known that nickname would catch on. "Nothing happened. Unless you count getting stuck in Mo's pantry while we were hiding the power cord to his karaoke machine."

"Oh, so *you're* the buzzkills. I was looking forward to showing off."

"The captain doesn't share the mic when he's drinking absinthe," Russ said dryly. "Sorry."

"Hmm. Okay, I accept your intervention." Sadly, this didn't put him off the subject. "So nothing happened while you were locked in close quarters together? He just magically came out of that situation having decided he could live without your dick in his mouth?"

All the air rushed out of Russ's lungs. He'd been trying *not* to think about it, and now he had a vivid mental image and it wasn't even his fault. "He didn't know I was gay before. So I told him, and he came to the conclusion on his own that people would think he meant it if he kept it up."

"Hmm."

He kept saying that. "What?" Russ snapped, harsher than he meant to.

But Baller had apparently decided to shut up. "Nah, nothing. Don't worry about it. You know rookies—they're flighty. Always changing their minds."

Russ was pretty sure he was being a smartass, but he accepted the peace offering.

Russ generally wrote preseason away games off as scheduled losses—the teams they'd play against would ice more of their regular lineup at home. But the Firebirds' regular lineup had one of the worst records in the league, so maybe four Caimans and a ragtag group of rookies and minor players could give them a run for their money.

As long as he and Baller could keep the rookies focused, they had a shot.

Team dinner at the hotel skirted disaster. Hughes looked like he might throw up at any moment. Havvy knocked over a water pitcher—not a great sign for a goaltender, who had to be aware of body positioning at all times.

And Trouble kept checking his phone under the table after every bite of steak.

Maybe he could start with figuring out what was going on with Liam now. This quiet brooding didn't suit him.

Russ nudged Liam's ankle under the table.

Liam snapped his head up, cheeks flushed.

No point beating around the bush. "What's going on?"

Liam went redder and set his phone facedown next to his plate. "I'm trying to decide if I should ask if Bernadette wants to come to the game in Houston, since she lives there anyway, but maybe it's late notice."

The family issue explained the lack of confidence. It probably wasn't any easier being the younger sibling of a group of accomplished adults than it was being the semicloseted older brother.

Still, the answer was easy. "Ask her," Russ said.

Liam looked up. "What if she says no? What if she says yes and I don't play?"

"What if she says yes and you get to show off for your sister?" Russ tilted his head. "If you get cut that night, you could just hang out with her. Give her the VIP access tour." It was just a preseason game, but most people would still think that was a big deal.

"You're right, I know, just…." He shook his head. "I'm bad at talking to my family. That's pathetic."

Thanks for reminding me I have the same problem. "Practice," Russ suggested, though he chafed at his own hypocrisy. "No time like the present. And then get your head in the game, yeah?"

Liam straightened and the pink faded from his face. He gave a cheeky grin. "Yes, *sir*." He batted his lashes afterward too.

Russ groaned. "Trouble." He shook his head. He had a feeling it was a word he'd be repeating.

But he was glad to have the flirtatious Liam back, even if it did make him feel like a dirty old man.

LIAM DRESSED for his first NHL game with butterflies in his stomach and gasoline in his veins.

Sure, it was still the preseason, and he didn't have a contract. This might be as close as he ever got to professional hockey. But it counted to Liam.

At Russ's advice, he sent the family chat a short video clip from the bench during warm-ups, so they could be a part of the action, and he invited

Bernadette to the preseason game in Houston. She might not show, but at least Liam could set his expectations, and next time he wouldn't have to think about whether he should offer.

Pregame in the locker room, Coach went over the game plan—focus on speed, maintaining puck possession, and capitalizing on chances. Liam was an offensive defenseman, so that suited him.

Before the puck dropped, Russ bumped Liam's shoulder. "Hey. You'll be fine."

Some of the butterflies settled. "Again with the pep talk," Liam teased. "How long did it take you to come up with that speech?" And why did the terrible attempts to make him feel better keep working?

Russ poked him with the butt end of his stick. "Fuck you. I was improvising."

Liam laughed. Improvising—yeah, right, he thought fondly. He probably went through three drafts. "I can do this."

"That's what I said."

Liam wanted to ask for advice—he doubted Russ would tell him anything he hadn't heard, but hearing it again would help anyway, either because Russ had a way of soothing Liam's nerves or because the familiar advice would remind him that he knew what he was doing. But before he could, they were skating out onto the Firebirds' ice for the national anthem.

Not *Liam's* national anthem, but that was familiar too. He let the melody wash over him and kept his eyes on the rafters as he shifted from foot to foot.

Once the game started, he'd be fine. He wouldn't have time to think.

The puck dropped, and it turned out he was right.

The Firebirds had experience on their side. They kept Liam and Russ busy pinching off shooting lanes and shutting down breakaways. The first time Liam took a full-force check, the breath went out of him and his teeth clenched in his mouthguard, but he kept control of the puck and got it out to Hughesy. He did his job.

At first intermission, the score was tied at zero, Liam was drenched in sweat, and his nerves had burned off.

"Defense, great job out there," Coach said. "Way to control the puck. Remember you can count on Havvy too."

"I don't like be cold," Havvy piped up. "I can do my job, yes?"

Cold meant he wasn't facing enough shots. Some goalies couldn't get in the zone if they didn't have much to do.

"Sorry," Liam said automatically. He *knew* that. He could've let some of the lower-risk shots go through. Knowing what the goalie expected was part of being a good defenseman. This was basic stuff.

Russ's hand landed on his shoulder. Through his pads, Liam couldn't feel the squeeze, but the weight—and knowing Russ thought Liam was worth making an investment in—helped.

Meanwhile, Coach was going in on the forwards, who apparently hadn't taken enough shots.

The second period opened with Liam taking a penalty ninety seconds in for coming on too early. He sat in the box with his stomach clenching, kicking himself for getting a bench minor in his first game while the Firebirds capitalized on the power play. *Fuck.* How did he expect to get a contract if he couldn't even count to five?

He must've been wearing his feelings all over his face, or maybe Russ was psychic, because he bumped their shoulders together again when they were setting up for the next faceoff. "Lots of hockey left."

Even Havvy seemed in good spirits. "I said I wanted to do my job. You let me do my job. Is my fault I don't stop."

Liam might get an earful from the coach later, but he could worry about that *later*. Right now, like Russ said, he had plenty of hockey left to play.

Hughesy won the faceoff against a veteran Firebird, and he snapped the puck back to Liam. Liam took in his opponents' position and tried to feel out which way they'd break and who might misread him. The Firebirds' centerman gave himself away when Liam feinted left, so he passed right without looking, directly onto Baller's tape.

Baller carried the puck cleanly into the zone, with Hughesy running interference and creating a screen. Russ and Liam hung back to keep the puck in the zone if the Firebirds tried to clear it.

Instead, the goalie got just a piece of Baller's shot—but he missed the rebound Hughesy batted in backhand.

Baller whooped. "Attaboy!" Then he half smothered Hughesy in a hug. Liam skated in too, until he collided with them hard enough to knock them half off balance. Russ smashed in on his other side.

"Good trial run, Hughesy." Liam patted him on the bucket.

"Nice secondary," Russ pointed out.

Liam jerked his head up, caught in a flush. Right—he'd gotten a point too. He beamed.

The Caimans scored again late in the second, Baller off a wild stretch pass from Yeti.

This time when they came off for intermission, Liam was panting with exertion. His legs ached, his face hurt from grinning, his jaw was sore from clenching around his mouthguard, and his stomach was tight with anticipation rather than dread.

Coach patted him on the back on his way into the locker room. "Good hustle, Trouble."

Liam was glad he thought so, but he worried he didn't have anything left in the tank for the third.

Unfortunately, Liam turned out to be right about that. Coach cut his minutes in the last period. Liam was plainly exhausted. But Coach didn't switch the pairings, so Russ stayed on the bench with him, which soothed the sting, even if it didn't ease Liam's worries about his performance.

The Firebirds tied it up with five minutes to go, and Liam's heart sank. He knew the game didn't mean anything, but he wanted to win. Somehow he felt like if they won, he'd have a better chance of getting called up in the regular season. He wanted to be *part* of winning, but he couldn't help much with his limited ice time.

Both teams pulled the goaltender for the final two minutes. Apparently no one wanted to start the preseason in OT.

Liam and Russ went on for a shift of six-on-six. The Firebirds got possession of the puck at the Caimans' blue line. The left winger had a clear shot at the net, but Liam had him just within reach. He managed a quick stick-check that turned the puck over, and now they were all going the other way.

A defenseman deflected the shot into the netting. Liam's line came off for fresh skaters—all but Russ, who stayed on for a second shift because Russ could skate thirty minutes a night.

Liam could get hung up on what that might mean about his stamina in other areas another time. Like later tonight, when he was alone in his hotel room.

Finally a mad scramble in front of the net had the whole bench on their feet, leaning over in excitement to see if the puck would go in. Russ took a shot from the point—but no, it hit the crossbar with a *ping*. The bench groaned in agony. Next to Liam, Hughesy thumped his stick against the boards.

And then—Liam couldn't see exactly *what* happened, a chaotic bounce, a flubbed attempt by one of the Firebirds to clear the puck—but then it was in, and the horn went off. It might be a fluke, but it put the Caimans on top with three seconds left on the clock.

Liam's body surged with energy until time ran out. Then his muscles went lax and jelly-like, and every piece of his equipment suddenly weighed twenty pounds.

He still couldn't keep the grin off his face. Even reading the reply from Bernadette—*I would love that, but I'm going to be out of town for work that weekend*, followed by a string of sad faces—couldn't bring him down, since he actually believed her.

Somehow Liam got out of his gear and trudged into the visitors' exercise room. If he didn't do his cooldown routine, everything would seize up and he'd feel like garbage. But while Russ and Baller casually went through sets of butt kicks and box shuffles, Liam barely had the energy to do supine pigeons, where he lay on his back on a mat on the floor, made a P shape with his legs, and hooked his hands around the back of a thigh to bring it up to vertical.

"I'm going to die," Hughesy said next to him. He was doing iron cross, which was still more work than Liam could manage, but Hughesy'd only played ten minutes. "I'm going to throw up, and then I'm going to die, and then I'm going to sleep forever."

Liam let go of his thigh and sprawled out like a starfish. "How can you talk so much?"

Someone nudged Liam's left foot. "Don't stop. You'll cramp."

Laughing hurt. Liam made himself open his eyes and squint up at Russ, backlit against the ceiling. "How would I tell?" He'd played plenty of games before, and he would have said he'd put his all into every one of them. But tonight he must have found another level of play, because he'd certainly found another level of exhaustion.

"Come on. I'll help." Russ knelt on the mat between Liam's ankles.

Liam's battered, bruised, adrenaline-crashed body decided it had some energy left after all. He took a deep breath from his diaphragm and prayed to a God he didn't believe in that Russ wouldn't notice if he got a semi.

"I am a wuss," Liam said as Russ coaxed him to cross his left ankle over his right knee.

Russ put his warm hands on his calf. "Lift."

Liam lifted in self-defense. If Russ pushed on the back of Liam's thigh to help him, he'd have a stroke when all his blood pooled in his dick. He kept his eyes on the ceiling so he wouldn't have to look at Russ. "I feel like I get steam rolled."

After a second, Russ cleared his throat and moved his hands away. "Not surprising. You played twenty-two minutes."

Liam almost lost his grip on his leg. Russ steadied him behind the knee, and every muscle between Liam's thigh and his navel tensed in hopeful anticipation. His skin tingled with hyperawareness. "I did *what*?" He'd sat for so much of the third—there was no way. Defensemen in the pros often played upwards of twenty-five minutes a night, but he didn't expect to get that kind of ice time until he had more experience.

Well. Preseason was good experience, actually.

"Higher," Russ instructed. "Foot parallel to the ceiling." This time he didn't let go.

With a grimace, Liam complied. The stretch felt good. His heart rate slowed as his body moved back into rest mode.

Most of his body, anyway.

"We only brought six D on the trip," Russ continued. "You probably won't play as much next game. If they play you like this with the Thoroughbreds, you might want to take an ice bath after. Helps with recovery."

Liam flushed with warmth at Russ's casual assumption that Liam would get a contract. "Remind me why I wanted to become a professional athlete?"

Russ tapped the side of his leg and moved back. "You said something about it being easier than writing a book."

Finally Liam released the stretch. He put his feet flat on the floor with his knees bent in hopes that it would camouflage any conspicuous bulges. "It probably pays better too."

Russ reached down to give him a hand up. "Come on. It's time for second dinner."

WITH ONLY one game left in the preseason, Liam knew his days were numbered. Any minute now the team would reduce the training camp roster.

He thought he'd done well, considering. He'd played his best. He'd listened to his coaches and to Russ.

But he also knew he didn't have as much experience as some of the other players.

Practice at their home rink had been over for a good half an hour, with Liam dawdling around the lobby and hoping someone important would ask him to come upstairs and sign a contract, when he decided he couldn't put off leaving any longer. He'd have to go back to his Airbnb and wait for his agent to call.

So of course that was when he heard footsteps approaching from the elevators.

"—have you onboard."

"I appreciate the opportunity."

Liam's heart sank. That was Carl's voice.

So. Now he knew.

And now Mr. Singh, the team GM, and Carl were going to *see him* hanging around like a dog waiting for table scraps.

Liam had had better Fridays.

"We'll see you next week."

There were vague goodbyes, which Liam tuned out as he panicked. Should Liam take off to the bathroom or something, try to make some kind of discreet exit? Or—

"Oh, hey, Liam." Carl smiled. Of course he was smiling—he had a job. "You're still here."

"Uh, yeah. My mom called and she gets mad if I take calls in the car," he lied. Whatever. Carl never needed to know the truth.

Carl kept smiling. "It's good she cares about you. See you later."

Or not, Liam thought. "Yeah. See you."

His fingers had only just closed around the strap of his bag when Mr. Singh said, "Liam, is that you?"

Liam steeled himself and turned around. "Hi, Mr. Singh."

"Just the man I wanted to talk to. Do you have a few minutes?"

Was Liam going to have to pretend to be gracious about not earning a spot on the team? That sounded terrible. But he pasted on a smile and agreed anyway. "Sure."

"Come on, please, come upstairs."

Liam sucked it up and followed.

"Look who I found," Mr. Singh said when he opened the door to his office again.

Seated on the other side of the desk were Bruce, the Caimans' coach, and Erika, the agent Liam's college coach had put him in contact with.

"I'm glad I caught you. Much nicer to do this now than have to call you back in after you'd left."

Call him back in?

"Great day for me." Erika smiled as Mr. Singh gestured Liam to the only remaining seat on that side of the desk. "This wasn't supposed to be a surprise, but Bruce convinced me."

Liam sat, mind whirling.

Mr. Singh leaned forward across his desk. "I'll cut to the chase, yes? You've had a great preseason, Liam. You've got a lot of potential, you work hard, and you really impressed your coaches… but you're inexperienced. Ultimately we've signed Carl Ericsson to be our seventh defenseman."

Liam nodded numbly. "Right. I understand."

"But we'd like to keep you, get you some more experience, and see how you develop. How would you like to start the season in Lexington with our AHL affiliate?"

LIAM BLANKED out a lot of what happened next, but he was able to put together the pieces afterward from his conversation with Erika at their celebratory dinner.

Mr. Singh laid out what the team was offering, and then Erika asked for time to confer with Liam and somehow convinced him they should ask for two years instead of one, as well as a signing bonus "since you're a college student and presumably have no savings, and you'll need to put a deposit on an apartment and buy furniture and eat more than just ramen."

Liam had to admit that that sounded good, even if he felt ungrateful asking for more, since the AHL salary was already more than he'd make at any other entry-level job.

"And you'll need a cushion in case you're injured and can't play," Erika pointed out, and yeah, Liam hadn't thought about that. That made sense.

Apparently this was why people had agents.

In any case, by six o'clock that night, Liam was officially a member of the Caimans organization on a two-way contract, which meant he was starting his pro career as a Thoroughbred but could be recalled to play for Miami at any time if someone got injured.

By eight o'clock, he was ready for bed. Erika took him out to dinner… or maybe Liam took Erika out to dinner, depending how you looked at it. Liam ate his body weight in chicken and pasta and started to doze off before dessert. Happily, he perked back up again when the server brought him a brownie the size of his head.

When he finally got back to his Airbnb, he was grateful Erika had insisted on dropping his rental car at his place before they went out, because he was exhausted. For the first time in weeks, he felt like he'd be able to catch up on all the sleep he'd missed when he was keyed up about his future. Not even the crappy Airbnb mattress could foil him now.

But before he could faceplant on it, his phone exploded.

Are you serious? Marie-Jean had written in the family chat. She'd included a screencap of a tweet from the Caimans' official account. *You became a professional athlete and we found out from Twitter?!*

Everyone else had piled on in the excitement, with equal measures of congratulations and chastisement.

Oops. Liam probably should have called his family after the meeting with Mr. Singh, but he hadn't thought of it. He'd been too busy with the emotional roller coaster of going from thinking he was leaving empty-handed to getting a pretty good deal that could set him up for life.

Sorry! he replied. *I haven't touched my phone since I found out. I thought they were going to cut me.*

Well, anyway, congratulations. That was from Bernadette.

We're proud of you, honey. That was from his mom.

Of course, then Bastian sent, *What, no room in the big leagues? I'm just kidding. Well done.*

So that put kind of a damper on Liam's mood, but whatever. Bastian was too self-centered to be any good at team sports.

Liam was feeling way too good—and tired—to be grumpy about it. Besides, tonight he had a date with Zillow.

He fell asleep with his phone three inches from his face, midway through an email about an apartment.

Belanger Best In Show in Thoroughbreds Debut

The Lexington Thoroughbreds opened their season with a decisive shutout win against divisional rivals the Jacksonville Lightning.

The Thoroughbreds potted 5 goals and goaltender Ivan Havriuschenko stopped all 28 shots in the 5–0 victory. Captain Mathieu Delancy had a hat trick, and center Jonas Nieminen had a goal and three assists.

Rookie defenseman Liam Belanger also had a goal and an assist in the match and was integral in breaking down the Lightning's offensive attempts.

The Thoroughbreds play again at home on Thursday before leaving for a road trip.

First Period

LIAM SIGNED a lease on the first Lexington apartment he saw. It had a dishwasher and a parking spot and was only ten minutes from the Thoroughbreds' arena. He didn't need anything else.

Except a car to park in that parking spot, of course. It pained him, but he went with a moderately priced SUV instead of a luxury brand.

He did get the sunroof and the expensive speaker package, though. He might be an adult with a real job, but he wasn't going to forget how to have fun.

At least he was sleeping soundly again, one mattress upgrade later. Hell, a leaky air mattress would've been a step above the torture device at his Airbnb. Boxed memory foam felt like the ultimate indulgence, even if it took three days for his apartment to stop smelling like rubber.

Or, he guessed, it could've taken longer, but after that Liam wasn't home to know about it, because the Ponies headed out on a road trip.

When he signed his two-way deal, he hadn't realized how much his preseason time with the

Caimans had spoiled him. The Thoroughbreds didn't fly—not unless they made it to the Calder Cup Final, when they'd have to fly to play the Western Conference champs. Instead, they traveled by bus.

A lot.

Liam had spent a lot of time on buses in college, so he was no stranger to catching a few z's with his mouth open while cruising down the highway. But in those days they'd had two games a week, and they'd almost always been back-to-back—a Saturday and Sunday game in Ohio, and then two games at home the next week.

Now he was playing three road games a week and might be gone for two weeks or more. He'd lost count of the number of hours he'd spent on a moving tin can that smelled like feet. The AHL life was grueling.

On the plus side, he got a ton of ice time.

On the other plus side, he'd been wrong about how his teammates viewed him and each other. He thought there would be cutthroat competition, but the whole AHL system was set up to get every player the training, support, and experience they needed to succeed in the Big Show, and everyone from the coaches to the players bought in.

Liam's new captain was Mathieu Delancy, a thirty-two-year-old forward who'd been up and down between leagues for over a decade, with a handful of NHL goals under his belt and one Calder Cup championship.

They'd met at the Caimans' training camp, obviously, but in Lexington, before their first game, he made it a point to take Liam aside and get to know him.

"So. Confession time."

Oh no, was Liam's new captain a religious nut? Before he could do more than blink and open his mouth, Mathieu continued.

"Guys end up here for three reasons. They're not talented enough, not lucky enough, or they haven't worked hard enough. Can't do anything about the first two, but if you're lucky we can fix the third." He shrugged. "You won't make the Show until you admit where you're slacking and start working on it."

Liam could've chafed at the insinuation, but Mathieu was right. If he didn't face up to his shortcomings, he'd never overcome them. So he squared his shoulders, looked his captain in the eye, and said, "Forgive me, Father, for I have sinned. It has been two weeks since my last leg day."

Mathieu laughed. "Okay. We can work on that. But first, we've got a game to play."

And play they did. Hell, it might've been the best game Liam had *ever* played.

"Oh, you're going back up," Mathieu said afterward as he handed over the puck that had scored Liam's first professional goal. "Just gotta get a few more pounds on you first, I think."

Mathieu had scored a hat trick and didn't seem to think *he'd* be getting called up anytime soon. "Any pointers?" Liam asked, and Mathieu put him under his arm and steered him toward the trainer and the nutritionist.

When he had his leg-day-and-weight-gain plan in hand, he opened the family WhatsApp and shared a picture of himself with his first professional goal puck. Bernadette reacted with the flame emoji. Clearly she was the best sibling.

Do they put these games on TV? his mom wanted to know.

Liam's mother hadn't even watched his hockey games when she was his chauffeur to and from; she always brought knitting or a book to read. But better late than never, right? Liam said, *Sometimes. I'll look into it.* The internet was full of wonders.

He also got a message from his college coach, and another from Brett, who'd been his D-partner. Mo messaged too. Liam figured the guy would forget about him—out of sight, out of mind, and he had his own league to follow, his own teammates to encourage. It was nice to know he was paying attention.

He didn't get a message from Russ, but did Russ even have his contact? Liam wasn't sure, so he tried not to dwell on it.

Along with the obvious downsides—less money, less glory, way more time sleeping upright in a moving bus—Liam's AHL experience in Lexington had one surprise plus side. He hadn't expected to find a hotbed of liberal thinking in Kentucky. And maybe he hadn't, by his own standards, but Lexington was home to one of the biggest gay bars in the US, and there were multiple Pride organizations in town. If Liam ever had the energy to have sex again, he could probably find a willing partner.

But first, a road trip.

RUSS SET his tablet on the table for the call, because his whole family were hand talkers and he'd thrown his phone across the room too many times to risk it. "Hi, Ma."

"Hi, honey." His mom smiled brightly at him. She still had a red imprint on her face from her lab goggles; she must be working on something interesting. These days she usually didn't work weekends. "How's… oh, I can't keep track—"

"Quebec," Russ told her with a laugh.

"Quebec," his mother sighed wistfully. "The food…."

Russ grinned. "I know."

"All ready for your game tonight?"

She asked every week, and Russ answered the same way he'd answered for over a decade. "I'm always ready." He even had a spare mouth guard, which he'd double-checked after the last game they played because Jonesy took a stick to the face and broke a tooth. He scratched at the edge of his hairline. "So listen… I want you guys to come down when I play game one thousand." Before she could object, he went on quickly, "I know it's hard to take time off, especially when you don't know exactly when it'll be—"

"Russell. Of course your father and I will be there." His mother's brow creased with a frown. "Why would you think we wouldn't?"

"I know. Sorry. It's just I know it's also a pain because we don't know when it'll be for sure." He could get injured and miss a few games, get the flu…. He could even get suspended, although that hadn't happened in a few years.

"I'll save my vacation days," she promised.

Which prompted him…. "Do you think Grandpa would want to come? And Andi and Gia?"

Now her expression folded in on itself. "Gia… could be a problem, depending on the timing. How many games is this?"

Russ did some quick math, his heart sinking. "Nine hundred and fifty-two."

"So forty-eight games left, three games a week, that puts us at sixteen weeks, add another because there won't be any at Christmas…."

"Middle of February," Russ said.

His mom shook her head. "Gia's due in March. She won't be able to make it."

Shit. His parents might not want to come either, if it came down to it. Gia would need the support. It was a good thing Russ loved his sister, or he might be resentful about it.

His disappointment must've shown, because his mother clicked her tongue at him. "I'm sorry, sweetie. But there's a good chance Andi will be able to go, since her reading week will be around then."

So would her exams, but if he had to Facetime Gia anyway, he might as well Facetime Andi too. "It's all right. They can't do anything about it." That didn't stifle the disappointment, though. "What about Grandpa? Do you think he'll come?"

"I bet he would love to. Why don't you ask him in person, though? You're in town in a few weeks, right?"

"I already reserved tickets for everybody." Even Gia's fiancé, who was a Winnipeg fan. Russ couldn't complain since he'd grown up one too.

"You should ask him then."

"I will. Anyway, tell me what I'm missing back home. Are you going to get to do that project you've been talking about?"

His mom filled him in on work and family gossip. Andi was stressing over her first big midterm; Gia couldn't wear her favorite shoes because her feet had swollen. The city had commissioned Dad to do another mural downtown. Ma's work had given the go-ahead for her to put together an official proposal for a project—one of the strains of bacteria she was studying had shown a propensity to eat plastic, which wasn't why they were interested in it but had potential applications in other industries.

After years of practice, Russ's mom did a decent job explaining without making him feel like an idiot, but by the time the conversation ended, he was shaking his head and wondering how Liam managed. At least Russ had moved out before Gia finished elementary school. He didn't know how he'd have managed when she started talking about higher-level mathematics. Now she was an actuary, which meant she did the kind of complex calculations that told insurance companies how much to charge Russ's NHL team for his health care premiums. Andi had only just started university and claimed she wanted to be a social worker, but everyone else in the family figured she'd never be satisfied long-term with helping one person at a time when she could go into politics and influence policy instead.

Russ had his money on a law degree before she turned thirty.

Liam hadn't been able to move out before his siblings started postsecondary education. He had to just live with it.

Then again, he'd gone to college too, so maybe it didn't bother him. Russ should ask him about it. Actually Russ should touch base with him, period. He knew Liam had gotten a goal in his first game and was playing well, but he hadn't talked to him.

He felt bad about that. If Liam were up with the Caimans, he'd be Russ's rookie, and it would be fine and normal for Russ to text him.

But Liam was with the Thoroughbreds, and Russ *couldn't* text him. He didn't have his number. He purposely hadn't asked for it. Part of him knew that having that open line of communication to Liam would open the doors for... well, for Liam to keep flirting outrageously. Russ wasn't going there.

Eventually Liam would get called up, and Russ could step in and do his mentoring thing. And that was it.

A knock at the hotel-room door helped him shove those thoughts down into the depths of his subconscious, where they belonged. He opened it to find Yeti waiting with a frown. "You know what room Jonesy's in?" he asked. "He's not answering my texts."

Give the man some privacy, Russ thought. "Maybe he's talking to his wife," he offered. "Or jerking off."

"Or talking to his wife while jerking off, yeah." Yeti didn't look less concerned. "He always texts before naps, though, and he didn't do that either."

The only way that should've rung alarm bells was if Yeti and Jonesy were the kind of codependent D-partners that couldn't pick out suits without coordinating.

They weren't codependent. They weren't even D-partners. The texting routine was pure superstition. No one on the team had more complex rituals than the two of them. Which meant that if Jonesy really had missed texting Yeti instead of experiencing some kind of cell coverage malfunction, something was actually wrong.

Russ kind of hated that he knew that.

"He's across the hall," he said.

Jonesy didn't answer their knock. No one in the team group chat had heard from him, and he wasn't at dinner.

"Okay, now I'm panicking," Russ said. Had someone sneaked into his hotel room and murdered him? Did he fall in the shower and hit his head?

"I'll go get a key."

As Jonesy's D-partner, Russ got the unenviable job of going inside. Team took care of team—no reason to bring in the coaching or training staff yet. This went unspoken. If Jonesy'd simply overslept, or if his phone was dead, or whatever, the coaches didn't need to know. If it was something else—substance abuse or mental illness—team leadership could assess the best way to deal with it to preserve his privacy. They'd have to bring management in, but they could give Jonesy options on how to go forward.

The door clicked open. "Jonesy?"

The room was dark, and the air smelled close and sour. "Jonesy?" Russ repeated. He turned on the light on his phone. It would be rude to turn on the overhead light if he was sleeping, even if he should definitely get up.

"Rabbits," Jonesy mumbled. "Errywhere. Fluffy lil… rodents."

At least he was alive. Although apparently he was drunk or high or having a very strange and loud dream.

Russ approached the bed. The sour smell was coming from Jonesy. Shit, was he sick? It *smelled* like he was sick, like sweat and… something.

"Jonesy," he repeated. "Wake up, buddy, we got a game to get to."

Jonesy rolled over. "Russ?" He squinted. His face looked funny. "What're you doing in my dream?" A pause. "And how come you don't have a tail?"

The smell hit Russ like a truck. God, what *was* that? Was that—? He carefully panned the flashlight up Jonesy's chin to his mouth.

The right side of his face where he'd lost the tooth was swollen and furiously red. From the dampness on his face, he definitely had a fever—one bad enough that he was hallucinating.

Fuck.

Russ brought his phone to his ear and speed-dialed their coach. "It's Russ. Jonesy's tooth is infected bad. He needs to go to the hospital."

Then he hung up and looked back over his shoulder at Yeti, who was silhouetted in the doorway.

"Somebody needs to go find Carl and tell him he's playing tonight."

DUE TO a nasty storm system that left the interstate looking like a climate disaster movie, the Thorough-breds pulled into the motel outside Scranton two hours behind schedule. The rain had pounded so hard even Liam hadn't slept on the bus, and his eyes felt like sandpaper when he finally opened the door to his room.

On autopilot, he dropped his bag next to the bed. Fuck brushing his teeth. He just wanted to pee and wash his face and then crawl into bed and sleep for as long as his body allowed.

In the past month, he'd stayed in some shady places. One of them he'd slept with the light on and the desk chair shoved in front of the door. In Wilm-ington, Liam's television cut out every time the guys doing construction across the street used their jack-hammer. He'd dealt with weird smells, A/C units that made more noise than a jet engine, mattresses that could have doubled as concrete slabs, and water pressure so bad he'd resorted to pouring cups of wa-ter over his head to rinse the conditioner out of his curls. This place seemed tame in comparison. Sure, it had last seen a décor update in 1996, but it was in a quiet, noncreepy area and all the hallway lights worked. Liam was elated—

Until he flicked on the bathroom light.

He stared.

He flicked the light off again and turned around.

Then, just to be sure he'd really seen what he thought he saw, he went back into the bathroom and turned on the light.

Still there.

"Okay," he said out loud to himself. "I am not equipped to deal with this right now." He closed the bathroom door, grabbed his toiletry kit from his suitcase, and went across the hall to Mathieu's room.

"Oh God, what do you want?" Mathieu said before he even opened the door. When he did, he seemed surprised to see Liam and even more surprised by the toiletry bag. He blinked at Liam in exhausted confusion.

"There's shit on my bathroom floor," Liam explained.

Mathieu's brow creased. "Like... stuff?"

"Like an actual turd." Liam had moonwalked into a parallel dimension where this kind of thing happened, or something. "Can I sleep on your floor?"

"There's no way."

Fuck. "Please?" Liam was ready to beg.

"No, I mean, there's no way there's really a piece of shit on your floor."

Liam had thought the same thing, so he couldn't blame Mathieu for being skeptical. He sighed. "Do you want to see it?"

"Obviously."

So Liam went back across the hall, Mathieu in tow. He didn't bother going toward the bathroom himself. He just gestured and let Mathieu see the carnage for himself. Liam didn't need to see it again. It was seared into his mind for all eternity.

It wasn't like someone had smeared feces all over the room or anything. At least that would have been obviously intentional. That was the baffling part. It was one medium-sized, kind of dried out piece of poop, sitting right next to the toilet on the floor.

Liam could not figure it out. Surely someone hadn't just failed to realize they'd missed the bowl? He knew some people preferred to hover when using public toilets, but this was taking it a bit far. Besides, there was no impact mark. Wouldn't it have gone *splat*?

But then how did it get there? The other option was, what? Someone reached into the toilet bowl, pulled out a log, and placed it on the bathroom floor on purpose?

The questions would haunt Liam until his dying day.

"Holy shit," Mathieu said.

"I doubt it." Immaculate conception was a stretch. Immaculate excretion was out of the question.

"What the fuck?"

"So can I sleep on your floor, or what?"

Mathieu closed the door. He had the look of a man who had seen some shit, on a bathroom floor, in an otherwise clean but nondescript hotel, at quarter past two in the morning. "Fuck no," he said. "You want to sleep on the floor in a place where that floor might have been shat on?"

Put like that, no. Liam might never sleep again.

"We can share the bed." He said it with an air of finality as he ushered Liam toward the door. "And tomorrow we're going to have a come-to-Jesus with whoever's in charge of hotel reservations."

"I'm an atheist," Liam said automatically while Mathieu unlocked the door to his room.

"Figure of speech, bud." Mathieu nudged him toward the bed. "Come on, seriously, I'm shattered. You better not snore."

Liam didn't have the energy to snore, or even the energy to argue. He crawled into Mathieu's bed and made sweet, sweet love to the hotel pillow, thanking God Mathieu wasn't one of *those* straight guys.

The coaching staff had managed, possibly through blackmail, extortion, or magic, to get their practice time pushed back to ten thirty, so at least Liam managed a half-decent night's sleep. And after the past month of conditioning, he could have a good practice even with the sleep deprivation.

He thought that morning's skate was one of his best yet, so his stomach sank when the coach called him into a borrowed office afterward. Maybe he hadn't been performing up to expectations? Had he not paid enough attention during drills? Or maybe this was about the penalty he'd taken the other night—

"Breathe, Belanger, you look like you're going to pass out."

"Sorry," Liam squeaked. Then he reminded himself to do the breathing as instructed. He did feel better.

Coach shook his head, and Liam hoped that meant the apology was unnecessary. "Look, kid, I'll be straight with you. I like your work ethic. You're not all the way there yet, but you get better every game. The Caimans front office called last night, but they couldn't get through because of the storm. One of their guys is sick and they asked me to send up a defenseman. I picked you."

Holy *shit*. "Thank you!" Liam accidentally shouted. "I mean, uh, thank you, sir. I won't let you down."

"Don't get too excited," the coach warned him. "You might not play."

Right—Liam would be backup, there to rotate in if someone got hurt or as relief. Of the twenty-three players allowed on a team's roster at one time, twenty could dress for a game, and that included the goaltender and a backup. That left eighteen spots usually filled by twelve forwards and six defensemen, but three extra players would travel on road trips to fill in.

At the beginning of the season, Liam had hoped he might be one of those extras, but Carl got the spot he wanted. Now Carl would be playing and Liam... would hopefully not spend the entire time he was with the Caimans riding pine, but even if he did, his bank account would thank him.

Plus, it wouldn't suck to ogle Russ from up close again.

"Liam? Hey. Earth to Liam."

Whoops. "Yes, sorry, I'm... I'm just processing. I won't let you down." Did he say that already?

Coach shook his head. "Don't let *yourself* down, kid. We sent someone to the hotel to get your stuff."

Oh jeez. "Um, that thing on the bathroom floor isn't mine."

"Kid, I'm not even going to ask."

That was probably for the best.

RUSS'S BODY played the game in Ottawa, but his mind was with Jonesy in the hospital. He wasn't the only distracted one on the team either, and they finished the game with a 4–2 loss.

In the locker room after, the team was due for a chewing out, but Coach opened with "Jonesy's fever is down. They've got him on IV antibiotics for the infection. Doctors want to keep him overnight, but they're going to fly him back to Miami in the morning."

A murmur of good-spirited relief went around the room.

Then Coach got down to business and reamed them for not keeping their heads in the game, which they deserved. He ended with, "That's it for tonight. Hit the bikes and get some sleep."

Russ inclined his head. "Coach."

Bruce turned his way. "What's up?"

Shit. Russ wished he'd found a way to ask privately, because now he felt like the whole room was watching him. He didn't want his temporary linemate—Carl, tonight—to feel like Russ was in a hurry to replace him. More importantly, he didn't want anyone to think he was too eager to see Liam again.

"Did we call someone up?"

"Belanger's going to meet us in Toronto."

Mo put his chin in his hands and affected a dreamy voice. "Aww, Russ, your rookie's becoming a man."

So much for that faint hope. But Russ rolled his eyes, and no one made further remarks.

They had a day off in Toronto before the game, and Russ turned off his phone for a few hours to give himself some real time away from the team. In the morning he had his edges done by the guy he saw when he was in Toronto in the summers for training. The weather was still nice this early in the season, so after that he walked through High Park and admired the leaves changing colors. It felt good to be outside alone. As a bonus, fewer people recognized him when he was by himself.

After one last deep breath of surprisingly fresh fall air, he switched his phone back on. He was supposed to meet Mo for a late lunch in Kensington Market, assuming he'd picked a place by now.

But some of the other players on the team had been up to different shenanigans this morning, and the group chat had blown up in the hours he'd been gone.

Baller had added Liam to the chat late last night with the invitation, *Ok, rookie, welcome to the Show. Let's see your NHL debut suit game.* This morning Liam had responded with a photo.

Put succinctly, he needed help. Russ knew with one look that his suit had once belonged to his older brother. The navy color had no personality, and the cut didn't do anything for him.

Russ was saved from feeling guilty for not reacting with appropriate horror in time, because Baller had done so three hours ago. *Absolutely not. You are gay and French-Canadian and you live in Florida.*

You are allowed to have color, pattern, AND style. What's your room number, we're going shopping. You can't disgrace us like this.

To his embarrassment, Russ felt a pang when he saw that plans were already underway, but it was probably for the best. Liam didn't need a whole new venue for his flirting—or an audience, for that matter. Besides, they didn't have a ton of time and he didn't actually want to go shopping. Better to leave Liam in the hands of Baller and his husband, who had tagged along on this trip to see family.

But he couldn't just not contribute to the conversation. He needed to make his position known. *If you show up in that suit I will fine you.*

Then, because it was inevitable now, he added Liam to his contacts.

He hesitated a minute over sending a message, but he felt guilty enough for being out of contact with someone he was supposed to be helping. His internal conflict was his own problem; he couldn't make it Liam's.

Good to have you on board, he said. *Heard you've been tearing it up in the A.*

He didn't expect a reply right away, but he got one—*Aww Russ have u been keeping tabs on me?* followed by a heart emoji.

Of course Russ had. It would have been irresponsible not to. And yet it felt like admitting it would imply more than it was.

He wrote back with a screencap of Liam's stats and added *and a fight. If you call that a fight.* Liam had gotten into it with someone who had twenty

years and forty pounds on him and had his ass soundly handed back on a platter. He was lucky he hadn't
been injured.

Maybe u can show me how u do it.

So much trouble. Russ switched over to his chat
with Mo and called an Uber to take him to lunch. He
could worry about Liam later. Let Liam stew over
being left on Read.

Knowing him, it wouldn't faze him in the least.

Russ did his best to put it out of his mind. This
was a day off; he could start his official mentoring
duties tomorrow. He enjoyed lunch with Mo, even if
his taste was a little more hipster than Russ usually
went for.

It was Russ's turn to sit out at table tennis in the
hotel recreation area when his phone buzzed with a
picture message from Baller later that afternoon.

Your rookie is a natural, he wrote, under a
shot of Liam making a ridiculous model pose. His
cream-colored dress pants called all kinds of attention to his ass and thighs. The pale pink shirt fit Liam's playful nature miles better than the awful thing
his brother had passed off on him, and from his grin
and the sparkle in his eye, he knew it. The gray jacket had a subtle plaid pattern with pink threads woven
in. He looked good—grown-up. Happy. Confident.
Sexy.

Like he was waiting for Russ to come along and
mess up his perfect outfit.

Russ had no idea how to reply. He didn't even
know what he wanted to say. That Liam wasn't his
rookie? He was. Russ had claimed him right off the

bat, and he didn't want to give him up just because Russ found him inconveniently attractive. That Liam was a natural flirt? Everyone knew that already, Liam not least of all.

Fortunately the next set of pictures went to the group chat instead, so Russ could ignore the one Baller sent him personally. These included Hughesy, who must have tagged along on the shopping trip. He hadn't yet learned his angles but was apparently game to take half a dozen photos with Liam looking like an ad for a yacht club. Possibly one that provided young male companionship. This impression only strengthened in the last two shots, which included Baller and Gabe in the middle, with a pretty young thing on each side.

Mo wasted no time capitalizing. *Yo, when did your husband start a side gig in high-end escorts?*

You know what these retired guys are like. Gotta keep em busy somehow.

Christ.

Then, a moment later, Baller added an unimpressed emoji. *Hey Russ. What's the fine for rookies hitting on my husband?*

If you didn't see that coming, I can't help you, Russ sent. A beat passed and then he added, *Trouble, you're punching out of your weight class.* In some strange alternate universe where Gabe had never met Baller, he would eat Liam alive.

Not that Russ wouldn't, given the chance. He'd make sure Liam enjoyed every second of it too. If he thought he could keep teasing Russ the way he did with no consequences, well… he'd learn a very slow, thorough lesson. Russ couldn't decide if he'd rather give Liam a taste of his own medicine for a few weeks or just give him what he wanted and blow his mind that way.

He could even do it with a clear conscience, if Liam got enough ice time with the Caimans to prove he was worth keeping around.

But he probably wouldn't get to play, and even if he did, chances were he'd be heading back to Lexington before long. Russ might be able to scratch the itch, but it'd be like scratching a mosquito bite. In the long run, it would only make the situation worse.

For a fleeting moment, he imagined what it might be like if it didn't—if Liam had made the team right out of training camp and Russ took him up on one of his invitations, if he'd taken Liam home with him, not as his rookie, but as something more than that.

But he knew if he did, he wouldn't want to let him leave again. The kid was a sunbeam in a room with no windows.

It didn't matter, though. Even if Liam made the team, and even if he wasn't too young for him, they barely had a short-term future, never mind a long-term one. Russ would be leaving the team soon, gone to the highest bidder or the best Cup prospect—but only for a couple of years before his body got too old for the game and he had to hang up the skates and his mom guilted him back to Winnipeg for retirement. Liam had another year here and then the NHL would be his for the asking for another decade. Every team with any sense would make him an offer.

The funny thing was, he could imagine Liam with his family. Russ's dad was an artist, so he'd appreciate Liam's quirks and the fact that he'd bothered to get a BA in a "soft" subject like French lit. Russ's sisters would give him endless shit for picking up a white boy ten years his junior, but the second they heard Liam deliver one of his endless cheesy pickup lines, they'd fall head over heels.

Russ's mom…. He didn't know. She'd tried so hard to set him up with a local boy. She might not appreciate him having a built-in reason not to come home to her.

Russ shook himself out of his thoughts. He was getting maudlin in his old age if he was contemplating the logistical nightmare of dating another hockey player, even theoretically. Clearly he needed to hit a club and find someone to distract him for a few hours.

Not tonight, though. Tonight Russ needed to do his duty as Liam's mentor and alternate captain and plan his welcome-to-the-Show celebration.

LIAM LANDED in Toronto at two o'clock in the morning with nothing more than his hockey gear and the road-trip clothes he'd had with him. He checked into his room—blissful clean sheets and a comfy mattress and a mound of quality pillows he would never again take for granted—and passed out for seven hours.

When he woke up he had a new WhatsApp group and a request for suit pics. An hour after that, he was in a cab with Hughesy, Dante Baltierra, and Gabe Martin on his way to buy something more appropriate.

He would have been disappointed—part of him had hoped Russ would be the first one to extend that kind of invitation—but Baller made it impossible.

"This is his favorite kind of mission," Gabe confided under his breath as Baller shepherded them down the sidewalk toward the fashion district, which was just a handful of blocks from the team's hotel.

"Walk, walk, fashion, baby," Baller said. "Hurry up, we can't keep Tom James waiting."

Liam was pretty sure he couldn't *afford* Tom James, but that turned out not to be an issue either. With Hughesy monopolizing the change room, Liam finally had a chance to look for a price tag on something. But when his eyeballs bugged out, Gabe clapped him on the shoulder and said, "Breathe. It's his treat."

No one had ever treated Liam to anything with that many zeros. "Does this make you my sugar daddies?"

He jumped half a mile when Baller laid a hand on his other shoulder. "We don't use the D word in this relationship, kiddo." Then he pushed Liam toward the racks of jeans and sweaters. "Now let's find you something casual for dinner."

There were worse ways to spend a morning than as his hockey idols' personal dress-up doll, even if Baller kept handing him more and more outlandish things to wear.

Finally, with a fondly exasperated expression, Gabe pulled Baller away from the changing room curtain and handed Liam a pair of pants and a deep green V-neck. "Trust me."

Liam trusted him. He put the clothes on. The sweater clung to his shoulders and waist and highlighted his hazel eyes. After all his working out, the jeans hugged his thighs and ass and were borderline indecent. But they must have been specially made for hockey players, because he moved with ease, no straining of seams.

Liam had to admit he'd never have picked this out for himself, but he looked hot.

"Trouble! Time's up, I want to see!" Baller pushed the curtain back and raised his eyebrows. Then he whistled. "Gabriel, look at this. Baby's got back."

Liam had never been able to cultivate that hockey player physique in college—he couldn't just eat and work out all the time. He had to do homework. Now eating and working out *was* his homework, and he was getting straight A's. He preened.

Baller snickered and shook his head, almost to himself. "He's gonna burst a vessel."

Who is? Liam looked at Gabe, who seemed satisfied but only said, "You'll do."

"Or get done," Hughesy chirped. "We don't judge."

Baller high-fived him.

"You should wear that to dinner," Gabe suggested while his husband paid a bill that gave Liam heart palpitations.

It seemed like the least he could do—and then he was so exhausted that a midafternoon nap almost made him late. Liam woke up to pounding on his door and opened it to find Baller on the other side. He blearily wiped his eyes. "Time's it?"

"Time to get dressed." Baller patted his cheek. "Chop chop."

Liam stumbled into the bathroom to wash his face. By the time he dragged on his new jeans and sweater, he was mostly functional.

Gabe must've gone back to Ottawa to be with his family, because he was nowhere in sight when Baller ushered Liam into the back of a cab.

And then pulled a black ski mask out of his sleeve and cheerfully tugged it down over Liam's face, backward, so he couldn't see anything. "Don't worry, we did the hazing rituals back in Miami."

"Oh good. I feel much better," Liam deadpanned. At least he didn't have to worry about the hat ruining his hair. That was a lost cause when he slept in.

Baller patted his shoulder.

Liam knew he was lucky. To get the chance at the NHL at all, yes, but also that someone on the team had taken a personal interest in him. He had no right to be disappointed that it was Baller and not Russ.

Only a few minutes later, the car stopped and Baller tugged him out. He left the makeshift blindfold in place until the bright fall sunshine gave way to an interior air-conditioned space. Liam followed gamely where Baller led, straining his ears for clues, but wherever they were, it was silent.

"You're not going to murder me in here, are you?"

Without warning, the blindfold whipped off.

Cheering erupted. Liam blinked to focus his eyes and found himself in a crowded private room at a restaurant with Baller beside him. In front of him were the team's other captains, with Russ holding a beer in each hand.

He passed one of them to Liam, then touched the edges of their glasses together. "Welcome to the Caimans, rookie."

Liam had to be imagining the elevator eyes, right? And the slight flush in Russ's cheeks? That was probably a trick of the light. Liam was absolutely going to flirt his ass off, but Russ wasn't *interested*. "Thanks."

"Okay, okay, quit hogging him." Mo nudged Russ over and took Liam under his arm to present him to the rest of the room. "Boys—let's welcome the new kid, eh?"

So this was why Liam needed a fancy new outfit.

"This is a lot of trouble," he said quietly when the appetizers had been cleared away. "Do you do this whenever someone gets called up?"

Next to him, Mo snorted. "Nah, we usually wait 'til after you actually get to play. But the next game's in Winnipeg and Russ'll probably be with his family, so he wanted to do it early in case."

Liam hadn't gone to college for nothing; he could read between the lines. Russ had planned this, or at the very least, moved it up so he wouldn't miss it.

That was as good as a personalized shopping trip. And it was probably better Russ hadn't taken him to get a suit, because if Russ had dropped a few thousand dollars on clothes for him he definitely would've felt like a sugar baby. And then he would've batted his eyelashes and asked how he could repay him.

It was a nice fantasy, even if in reality, Liam would like a little more even footing. He shook himself out of it—there was a time and a place—and focused on the here and now. "So hey… is there gonna be steak?"

FOR ALL the trouble Baller and Gabe went to with his wardrobe, Liam didn't dress for the game in Toronto. But he had a great practice and even got to play as Russ's partner for a few rushes, and when the team won the game, he got to go out with them afterward to celebrate, and then sleep in his nice cozy clean hotel bed. Because he'd gotten in so late, he didn't even have to share a room with Hughesy, though they'd be bunking up in Winnipeg.

Whatever. Hughesy had to be a better roommate than the actual mouse Liam had seen at that place in Charlotte.

They had practice again in Winnipeg. This time Liam spent most of his time paired with Yeti while Carl worked with Russ. He practiced on the second penalty-kill unit, which was something he'd done a lot of with Lexington, but he didn't expect to be given so much responsibility with the Caimans.

Of course, it didn't mean anything unless he actually got to play—

"Good practice," Russ commented as they filed off the ice.

Liam looked over at him, helpless to stop his smile, which was weird. He wasn't a teenager with his first crush. He was a twenty-two-year-old with a very quenchable thirst. He should be smiling at Russ on purpose, with a suggestive leer and a double entendre and possibly the same elevator eyes Russ had given him the other night.

Sadly, Liam wanted to hear he was good at hockey even more than he wanted to hear a pickup line. "Think so?"

"I don't say things I don't mean."

They were halfway through the post-morning skate meeting when Yeti's D-partner's phone chirped.

Under normal circumstances Russ would've fined him—Liam had seen it happen a couple times in the preseason—but he must have a special exemption or something, because while no one commented, everyone turned expectantly in his direction.

He looked at his phone and his eyes went huge. "Tammy's water broke."

So that explained why no one cared about his phone.

When the ruckus of congratulations died down, Coach said, "Go get on a plane." Then he looked at Liam. "Looks like tonight's your night, Trouble."

In Liam's daydreams, he made his professional debut on home ice, either for whatever team signed him or in Montreal or Quebec City. His family would be there cheering him on. It was an event they'd anticipated and planned for.

In reality, there was no way his parents could make it to Winnipeg in time for puck drop unless they got on a private jet, which Liam couldn't afford. But he was excited enough for himself that it almost didn't matter. He snapped a photo of his jersey and sent it to the family group chat with the note that he was making his primetime television debut at nine o'clock Eastern Time. *Watch for number 22*, he added.

Maman complained that that wasn't enough time to order a customized jersey. Papa said he'd take her to the SportChek and then Michaels, and she could make do until they could get the real thing. Marie-Jean sent a thumbs-up and a *good luck!!*

Bernadette cursed her lack of sports channels and followed that with a screenshot from Google Maps—*sports bars near me*. Liam hearted the picture.

Bastian didn't say anything, even though the little ticky marks showed the message had been delivered. Maybe he was busy.

Either way, Liam was grateful for the grind of the AHL season. Despite his excitement, his body knew it needed to rest. It didn't matter that Hughesy mumbled in his sleep in the next bed; Liam shoved his face into his pillow, took two deep breaths, and woke up three hours later with his blood singing.

"Mind if I take first shower?" he asked.

Hughesy rolled over and pulled the pillow over his head. Liam took that to mean *go ahead*, with an option on *please tell me you're not going to be like this every time you wake up*.

Which, definitely not—Liam and mornings had a long-running feud—but he might be obnoxious until he got sent down again.

At team dinner he tried to buckle down and fuel up, but he couldn't contain his excitement; his leg kept bouncing under the table.

Finally Russ—who was here now but hanging out with his family after—put his hand on Liam's knee.

Liam felt like a cartoon thermometer about to explode. Had that part of his leg always been hard-wired to his dick? Or did Russ just have some kind of shortcut? He cleared his throat and batted his eyelashes. "Sorry."

But Russ didn't seem to be looking for an apology. His gaze was as heavy as his hand, which spanned an awful lot of Liam's leg considering how big Liam's thighs were getting. For what seemed like an eternity, he didn't move and didn't break eye contact, and all the while the back of Liam's neck got hotter. Now his dick was getting hard. If Russ didn't look away soon, he was gonna notice, and then... well, okay, Liam was twenty-two, so he had an excuse, but—

Finally Russ's lips curled into a knowing smirk. Yeah, he noticed. And he maybe did it on purpose. When he pulled his hand away, his fingers slid an inch or two up Liam's inseam. "It's fine," he said.

Totally nonchalant. That asshole. "But you're shaking the table."

"Sorry," Liam said again. His voice cracked. "You can tie me up if you want." Oh for fuck's sake. He was supposed to be cool. "To get me to stop fidgeting, I mean."

Across the table, Baller was coughing into his plate while Mo thumped him heartily on the back. Russ ignored them and glanced sidelong at Liam. "Let's save that for a last resort."

Fuck that. Liam was saving it for his spank bank.

WARM-UPS FELT surreal. Liam had never played with the full team on NHL ice or against another regular season NHL roster. Every bright light and camera seemed focused on him, and he *loved* it.

Who cared if he was playing third line? He was in the NHL. He'd made it.

The Caimans were up against Winnipeg, in Russ's hometown, and he was clearly a local favorite, judging by the number of children pressed up against the glass and holding signs.

Not only children, Liam amended when he caught sight of one bearing Russ's jersey number and the motto *U might be a defenseman but U can score on me any time.* He snorted to himself and followed the sign up to the man holding it—

Except it was a woman, of course. Because Russ wasn't out. Which was none of Liam's business and definitely something he was not going to spend time thinking about right before his first professional hockey game.

Instead he flipped a puck over the glass—yes, fine, something he'd practiced—and into the waiting arms of a small child who clutched it and jumped up and down. Liam winked and waved at them and then forced his mind onto the game.

Miami and Winnipeg didn't play each other often enough to have a rivalry, but the last time they'd played—the season previous—had ended with the Caimans blowing out the home team 7–2 and multiple injuries on both sides. Liam expected a tough, fiercely fought game, if not one with actual *fighting*.

He got it. By the middle of the first period, he had a scrape on his chin from a trip that might or might not have been intentional, a bruise on his shin from a slash in the crease, and a whole new level of focus. But he was playing on his off side with Yeti. He had a left-handed shot, and his brain and body wanted to stick to the left side of the ice for that advantage, but Yeti was a lefty too.

The first period ended scoreless. In the locker room after, Coach looked at Liam and shook his head. "Trouble, you're doing well. Switch with Carl, see how you do."

A trainer put some more glue on the cut on Liam's chin. As soon as they filed out to take the ice for the second, the sting faded into white noise in his brain. Every time he cornered sharply, the blood pulsed through the sore spot in his leg, satisfying, like worrying a loose tooth.

Winnipeg got possession after their goalie deflected a shot from Baller, and suddenly they had a three-on-two with Liam and Russ holding the line. Liam had half a second to guess what they'd do, but he didn't guess. He knew. He stick-checked before the forward could pass and the puck shot onto Russ's tape.

Now Winnipeg was on the back foot, but the Caimans' forwards were as tired as they were. And maybe Russ was too, because he didn't bother trying to work the puck into the crease. He took a shot from the top of the circle.

Ping. 1–0.

In the group celly after, Mo rubbed Liam's helmet. "Nice moves, Trouble."

Liam was still grinning about *that* when Russ grabbed his hand and shoved something in it. The puck.

Russ smiled. "First NHL point. You should keep it."

His first NHL point—on Russ's goal. Liam liked that more than he should. "Thanks."

The game went to overtime, but not for long. Russ, Baller, and Mo had the first shift, and Russ forced a turnover twenty seconds in. Mo and Baller did their double act to put the puck over the goalie's right pad, and that was it.

A win *and* a point in his first-ever game. And he'd played first line most of the night.

They were going to have to scrape Liam off the ceiling.

But before he could get to the locker room, their PR liaison grabbed his elbow. "Media wants you."

Liam grinned wider. It was a good day to do his first postgame interview.

RUSS FINISHED his media duties while Liam was still flirting his ass off with the reporters. After a quick cooldown and a shower, he met his family outside the locker room.

"You put on a good show for us," his mother teased when he swept her into a hug.

Russ kissed her cheek. "You're easily impressed."

His dad was next. "I think you might have some artistic talent after all." He smiled as he slapped Russ on the back. "What do you think? Synchronized goal-scoring? Could be the next big thing."

"I'll keep that in mind for my retirement."

"Okay, okay, old man, get out of my way." Andi shoved Dad over and claimed her own hug. "Talking about retirement at your age. Please. You love this dumb sport and you might as well play it forever."

Russ was glad she'd taken to wearing her hair natural, because it gave him a convenient way to hide his wince. He didn't know what he'd do when he retired—that vague *spend time with my family* idea only went so far—but right now thoughts of his professional future just brought up the big question mark that was which team he'd end up on next.

"That dumb sport paid your way through Europe," he reminded her.

When she pulled back, her expression was sly. "I said you should play forever, didn't I?"

Russ rolled his eyes and moved on to Gia. "Hey, sis. Looking good. How's the baby treating you?"

"Like I'm its personal chef and butler," Gia said wryly and turned her face up for a kiss. "Orange creamsicles and pickles at two thirty in the morning. I ask you, Why?" She patted her stomach. "Must take after its daddy."

"We all know he's got no taste." Russ shook hands with her fiancé.

"I forgive you for beating my team," Jason said dryly.

"Wasn't asking forgiveness, since I'm not sorry."

"Hey now," said a voice over Russ's shoulder. A sharp chin followed it, digging into the meat above Russ's clavicle. "He didn't get that goal single-handedly."

Russ must've broken the seal at dinner—Liam was going to be twice as ridiculous now and probably handsier too. Russ was going to enjoy winding him up, just not in front of his parents. He smiled in spite of himself and shoved Liam off him. "I'm sure you told the media you did all the hard work."

Liam elbowed him back. "Hey, that pass was perfect."

"Unlike most of your passes." Russ's parents would assume he was giving Liam shit about hockey, not his deplorable pickup lines. "This trouble-maker is Liam. Liam, my family."

He waved. "Hi, I'm Russ's rookie." Someone called for him down the hallway, and he looked over his shoulder, then turned back to Russ's mother.

"And I have to go or they're going to drink Winnipeg dry without me. Nice meeting you!"

Russ's sisters watched him go with no small measure of amusement.

"He's like a puppy," Andi said.

"He's charming," said Russ's mom with a shake of her head.

Russ snorted. "And he knows it, which is why we call him Trouble." He paused. Now that he had a moment to gather his thoughts, the family was noticeably two shy. "Where are Gramps and Tony?" He'd left enough tickets at the box office for everyone to sit together in the VIP section.

Conspicuously, no one answered right away. Was his grandpa sick?

Andi looked at Russ's ma. His ma looked at Dad. Uh-oh.

Dad cleared his throat. "Oh, they're meeting us at the restaurant. They went ahead to get the reservation on time."

His ma was looking everywhere but at Russ. He had a bad feeling about this. "Tony loves VIP access, though." Tony was the younger man his grandfather had been seeing for the past year or so—well, he was younger than Russ's grandfather, anyway. Russ didn't know him that well, but he liked him. The guy was a big sports fan, though he was more into football.

Before his ma could come up with an excuse, Gia rolled her eyes and said, "Oh for—Russ. Ma found out Tony has this cousin—"

Oh for fuck's sake. She'd hinted all summer that Russ should make time to meet the guy, but Russ hadn't bitten and eventually he'd escaped to Toronto to do his off-season training, hoping that would be the end of it. Obviously not. "Ma!"

"What?" his mother sniffed. "He's a nice man. And we worry about you all by yourself in Florida—"

Russ was barely *in* Florida half the time, and he spent most of his waking hours with twenty-five other guys. "I'm not alone. And we've talked about this. I am capable of handling my own love life."

"When is the last time you introduced us to someone, hm?" she challenged.

It had been two years ago, and she'd hated Mike on sight. Russ still kind of thought that was because Mike was from Florida and she worried he might lure Russ away permanently. Either way, he'd learned his lesson—they'd had a big fight about it and Russ had told her if she couldn't say anything nice, he'd simply leave her out of his romantic life. "You know why that is." She might've been right about Mike in the end, but he certainly wasn't going to tell her so.

Finally his dad stepped in to defuse the situation. "Look, no one has been promised anyone's hand in marriage. Let's just go to dinner and have a good time, all right? You can pretend he's not there, if you want."

"Even though it'd be very rude," Russ's ma added pointedly.

Gia, Jason, and Andi all looked like they wished they'd gone with Gramps and Tony and whoever this mystery guy was, so they didn't have to witness this.

Fuck it. Russ sighed. He didn't get to see his family much during the season, and he didn't want to ruin the night. "Okay, I'll come to dinner. But this is the last time this happens, Ma. I'm serious. I'm not looking for a boyfriend, and I'm definitely not looking for a long-distance one." One no doubt intended to get Russ to consider Winnipeg as a potential candidate for his next NHL contract.

"Of course," his mother said right away. She might be a meddling busybody, but she loved him. He knew that. She wasn't *trying* to drive him nuts. "I'm sorry, sweetheart, I just—"

"Ma," Russ cut her off gently. She pursed her lips, and Russ sighed again. "Let's just go have dinner, okay? And if any of the trainers ask if you saw me eat dessert, no you didn't."

Gia brought her hands together in a firm clap. "Right! You heard the man. Now that we're all agreed, let's find Tony and Gramps and get some dinner before Russ decides to eat us instead."

Belanger Notches Point in NHL Debut
By Rocky Sanderson

Rookie defenseman Liam Belanger earned his first NHL point tonight, notching the singular assist on linemate Russ Lyons's first-period goal.

Belanger signed a PTO with the Miami Caimans in September and inked a two-way, two-year deal at the close of training camp. A native of Saguenay, Quebec, Belanger grew up watching the Quebec City Nordiques as Dante Baltierra made his NHL debut. Now he's on a team with him.

"It's really surreal, you know?" Belanger says in the locker room, all smiles. "Sometimes I still wake up and think, 'Can this be my life?'" The smile turns into a laugh. "And then I look down and see all the bruises and I'm like, yes, it's real."

Caimans fans have a bright reality to look forward to. Tonight's assist came after a beautiful stick-check on Winnipeg forward Cliff Masterson. Not many seasoned defensemen would have been able to pull that off.

"I've been working hard to be the best player I can be," he says. "I know I've got a lot of work to do still, but I've been lucky because Russ is great at teaching me the ropes. It's special to have my first point be on his goal."

Watching the replays, one thing seems certain: Belanger got his first point tonight, but it won't be his last.

LIAM GOT to stay with the team for one more game after Winnipeg—a home game in Miami—though with Jonesy back on the ice, he didn't play.

But he did get to go out with the team, and even watching the Caimans win from the press box had him buzzing like a live wire.

Baller had scored the game-winner, so he got to choose the venue for their postgame celebration.

"Hell yes," Baller said. "Put on your dancing shoes."

Liam switched out his dress shirt and jacket for a fitted polo before they left the rink, because he liked them too much to risk them, but the pants made his ass look too good to give up. This might be Liam's last chance to hang out with the team this season. He had to look his best. Tomorrow he'd be on a plane back to Lexington to meet up with the Thorough-breds—back to dodgy motels and bus trips.

But tonight, he got VIP seating and bottle service.

Going back to the Ponies wouldn't be the worst. The experience Liam was getting there was turning him into the kind of player he'd dreamed of being—quick, dependable, creative. But Lexington didn't have a hot gay defenseman to flirt with.

If Liam was getting straight A's in Eating, Sleep-ing, and Working Out, he had less of an idea what he was making in Flirting with Russ. But the flirting was sort of its own reward. It made Russ smile, and Russ was handsome when he smiled, and Liam liked attention from handsome men. That was enough. Something had happened recently, though—some-thing that made the tension between them crackle hotter than ever. Russ kept flirting back. Liam didn't know if he'd intended it to scare Liam off or if he wanted to follow through, but Russ should know by now that Liam didn't back down from much.

Obviously Liam intended to double down instead, which was why he made sure to slide into the booth in the VIP section next to Russ. When Hughesy piled in next to him, if he moved over a little closer than necessary, Russ didn't complain. He just shot Liam a look that said he knew what Liam was doing and that he wasn't going to crack so easily.

Game on.

Liam batted his eyelashes and fist pumped internally when Russ rolled his eyes and some of that guardedness fell away. There was no point if Russ didn't at least pretend to make it a challenge.

At the end of the table, Mo stood up and lifted a bottle of champagne. Liam couldn't hear what he said over the pounding beat of the music, but it didn't matter. He cheered anyway and so did the rest of the table.

Liam leaned into Russ's space, close enough to breathe in the warm scent of him. Unfairly sexy—more intoxicating than any alcohol. Just because Liam was still pretty sure Russ would never take him up on one of his offers didn't mean he wouldn't jump at the chance if Russ proved him wrong. "He's even better at pep talks than you are."

Russ's laugh reverberated in his chest. "Not a high bar." One of the bottles made its way to their end of the table, and Russ held it over Liam's glass. "Drink?"

Perfect opening. Liam gave his best saucy smile. Whatever was going through Russ's mind,

Liam intended to distract him from it. "Thanks. I *am* kinda thirsty."

"Trouble," Russ said with a shake of his head. Liam wasn't sure if that was an accusation or an admonition or both, but either way, Russ was still smiling.

He kept smiling even as he wrapped his hand around the wrist of the hand that held Liam's champagne glass to steady it. Liam was sure the way Russ rubbed his thumb over Liam's pulse point was completely accidental.

Russ poured a generous helping and then pulled his hand away again. So much for watching his intake. "Cheers."

RUSS DID his best to put the incident in Winnipeg out of his mind. He knew his parents. His ma meant well. After their awkward dinner—Tony's cousin turned out to be a nice guy with whom Russ had exactly one thing in common, aside from the obvious, and that was that he deeply regretted being roped into a blind date—Russ let it go. It was done, his ma apologized (reluctantly, with caveats), Gia and Andi spent six minutes in the sibling group chat alternately blaming each other for not telling Russ and suggesting that if he wanted to get their mother off his back he could just start oversharing about his sex life.

This is why we can't have nice things, Andi said after Gia made that suggestion. *By nice things*

I mean another brother-in-law to bring me presents at Christmas.

Yeah, I don't think those are the "nice things" Russ is worried about. Gia followed this with the eggplant, peach, and water droplet emojis. Russ blamed pregnancy hormones, the effects of which Gia had already explained in more detail than Russ ever needed from his sister.

For his own peace of mind, he muted the chat. He didn't want it spoiling his night out.

He would focus on driving Liam out of his mind instead.

He hadn't expected Liam to get the chance to play hockey, but now that they were on more even footing, Russ had another game in mind. He'd keep upping the ante on Liam's flirtatious bluffs until Liam either folded or called. If he folded, Russ could go back to playing hockey unmolested by a rookie trying to get into his pants. If he called, Russ would give him what they both wanted. Win-win. Sure, there was basically no chance of anything long-term working out, but that didn't mean they couldn't have a little fun.

Besides, Liam was so easy to wind up. Russ liked that. It was sexy to have that kind of effect on someone. And his flirting was hilarious, vacillating wildly between sincere and so sincerely terrible that Russ had no choice but to stop taking himself too seriously.

To be honest, it was difficult to take *anything* seriously when, after the family-style meal they'd ordered arrived, Liam turned to Russ with a sweet doe-eyed expression, put his hand on Russ's upper back, and tilted his head to ask, "Can you grab my sausage for me?"

Russ didn't claim to be an expert in French grammar, but that little "slip" was a bit of a reach to let slide. "Really?"

Liam's façade broke, and he grinned. "Too much?"

"You wouldn't know what to do with yourself if I grabbed your sausage." Russ passed him the plate of bratwurst. He talked a big game, but that's all it was— talk. All it would take was a few words, a little teasing, and Liam would probably come in his pants.

Liam paused. Then he shook his head and helped himself. "Probably not," he finally said with a gusty sigh. "Bet I could figure out what to do with you, though."

That little shit. "You wouldn't have to." No way was he letting Liam drive.

Russ turned to check out Liam's reaction and found him flushed, with his mouth slightly open. He had a smear of ranch dressing at the corner of his mouth, a hundred times more suggestive than anything he'd done on purpose. After a moment he realized Russ was staring and shook himself out of it. "What?"

Goddamn it. Russ gestured at his own face. "You've got a little something."

Liam thumbed at the corner of his mouth. "Oh, um. Thanks." He licked the dressing off, totally un-self-conscious and without bothering to try to make it sexy.

The tiny flash of pink tongue made Russ's neck break out in a sweat. The champagne must've gone right to his head. Of course, there was always the possibility it wasn't the champagne and Russ was having a midlife crisis that made him lust after impressionable young rookies who didn't know what they were getting themselves into.

That thought made him want to switch to hard liquor.

Instead he reached for another helping of pasta. Maybe he could drown his thoughts with carbs.

Happily, when faced with a smorgasbord, the attention span of a twenty-two-year-old rookie gave Russ a reprieve from having to plan his next attack. He concentrated on his own dinner while Liam chatted with Hughesy and told a hotel horror story that made Russ want to call his union rep.

He barely registered when Jonesy took the seat across from him. "Hey. Asshole."

Russ looked up.

Jonesy did a double take. "I've been trying to get your attention for twenty seconds and 'asshole' is what does the trick? Where's the bartender?" He eyed Russ's mostly full glass of champagne, then looked up and down the table exaggeratedly. "Where's your beer? Oh my God, are you pregnant?!"

Russ flipped him the bird. "Funny."

"I'm not laughing." Jonesy glanced sideways in both directions and then must have judged the completely open table setting to be enough privacy, because he said, "You've been weird since you got back from Winnipeg."

"You've been weird since birth."

"Don't change the subject." Jonesy leaned closer across the table and lowered his voice to something just audible over the throbbing of the club music. "Did something happen with your family?"

Russ rolled his eyes. "Another setup attempt."

Jonesy made a sympathetic face. "Trying to give you a reason to settle down in the Peg, eh?"

Ugh. "Don't call it that."

"What, settling down?"

"The Peg." No one said that.

"Whatever. That's the problem, though, right? Mom and Dad want you to commit to a life in the frozen north?" Jonesy plucked a roasted potato off a serving tray and ate it.

When it became clear Jonesy wasn't going to drop the subject, Russ huffed. "That's half the problem."

Jonesy raised his eyebrows. "What's the other half?"

"That I have to go somewhere that's not Miami." Erika had called before tonight's game. Contract extension talks with the Caimans were basically a no-go. That meant he'd get traded before the deadline or hit the free agent market in the summer.

"Oh." Jonesy didn't ask for clarification. They'd all been through it before. "Shit, man, do you need a drink? I need a drink. I think Baller ordered a couple bottles of tequila."

Of course he did.

"He's just sipping it like an old-man weirdo." Never let it be said that Jonesy didn't know how to redirect a conversation. "Is that a thing people do? Like it's whiskey?"

Russ let him do it. "If it's good tequila."

"Are you guys talking about me?" As if his name had summoned him, Baller set down a bottle of tequila in the middle of the table, along with his own rocks glass and a handful of shot glasses. "I've graduated beyond Cuervo. Of course it's good tequila."

"—wait, you *slept with Mathieu?*"

This squawk from Hughesy derailed anything anyone might've said to Baller, who glanced at Jonesy and then Russ and then plopped down across from Liam and raised his glass to his lips.

Russ had frozen at the words and only moved again when Liam huffed and said, "I slept *in his bed* because of a literally shitty hotel room. It wasn't a porno."

Hughesy had apparently just been giving him a hard time, because he made a face and then asked, "Does he snore?"

"How do I know? I'd sleep through a hurricane."

The kid really was kind of a disaster.

Baller said, "Anyway, I brought shot glasses because I know you're all too sad to sip tequila." He paused and pulled one glass back toward himself. "Not you, Hughesy, you're too young."

Hughesy looked at the beer in front of him, then back at Baller, then carefully pulled the bottle out of Baller's reach like he was afraid Baller might try to take it away. "You're not my dad."

Liam snickered.

Baller shot him a look, but he was clearly fighting a smile. "That's enough out of you, rookie." He pushed a shot glass toward him across the table.

Liam tapped his fingertips against the glass. He glanced sideways at Russ, scrunched his nose, then predictably suggested, "Bottoms up?"

Hughesy's head thunked against the table, and Russ sighed but raised his glass anyway.

Baller toasted to Liam. "I like you, kid."

Liam beamed, and they knocked back the tequila—all but Baller and Russ, who figured he should at least try tasting it. He had to admit it was way better than Cuervo, even if it felt strange to sip from a shot glass.

"It's better on ice," Baller told him. "I mean, technically it's better ice-cold and not diluted, but they don't keep it in the freezer here, so." He thrust his glass at Russ. "Here. You take this. I need your rookie on the dance floor."

"Hell yeah you do!"

Before Russ could move out of the way, Liam was half in his lap, climbing over him to get out of the booth. Russ put his hands on Liam's hips to steady him before his brain registered what was happening. Suddenly Liam's knee was between Russ's legs and he was leaning on Russ's shoulder. The pads of his fingers skimmed the sensitive skin at Russ's collar, and the heat of him seemed to sear into Russ's skin. For a moment, the front of his pants was just inches from Russ's face, like an invitation for Russ to consider how closely tailored they were, or how thick Liam's thighs were.

He did both.

"Sorry, sorry, *merde*." Liam laughed and finally half fell out of the booth, so at least his crotch wasn't in Russ's face anymore. Only Russ's hands on his waist saved him from faceplanting. His obliques flexed under Russ's fingers. "I got it. I'm good."

I bet you are. "You're a disaster." Russ rubbed his thumb in a soft circle under the hem of Liam's polo and then pulled his hands away. He glanced up at Baller. "Try not to let him maim you."

"Don't worry, I'm not fragile."

Anyone who had thrown a check on him knew that.

"I'm coming too." Hughesy scrambled out the other side.

Russ watched them go with mild trepidation, sure Jonesy was about to make some observation about Liam's flirting or Russ's reaction to it. Instead Jonesy poured another splash of tequila in Baller's abandoned glass. "So are we getting drunk tonight or what?"

Russ *could* get drunk to make himself forget his infuriating lack of control over the direction his life had taken, sure. He pulled the glass toward himself.

On the other hand....

He took a sip—it really was good tequila—and let his gaze drift to the tangle of bodies on the dance floor.

The pulsing strobe lights gave the scene an anonymous vibe—the changing direction and color made it difficult to make out the edges of people's bodies, the lines of their features. But Russ had no trouble picking out Liam, who was dancing with his hands stretched toward the ceiling, his head tilted back, totally unselfconscious. Free. Other dancers touched him, pulled him against them, even spun him around under their arms.

No, not just other dancers—other men. One man in particular, now—tall, with tousled hair, broad shoulders, and glinting mischievous eyes. The light played over his skin like a lover's fingers as he slid his arm around Liam's waist and splayed his hand on his stomach.

On the other hand, alcohol might make Russ forget about his lack of control, but it wouldn't give him any back.

With Liam…. With Liam he might find a measure of what he was looking for. Russ had never gotten to dance like Liam was now, unconcerned and anonymous and joyful. What good did all his planning do him if he kept denying himself simple pleasures along the way?

Liam certainly seemed to be enjoying himself, and Russ had never looked at him and thought, *He'll regret this later.*

"Actually," he told Jonesy, "I think I'm going to dance."

Before he could change his mind, he slid out of the booth and onto the dance floor.

The sea of bodies swallowed him up. Russ let it take him and didn't worry about who he was dancing with or what might happen if someone recognized him. He just moved. He had a good sense of rhythm. And he *liked* to dance. He let the music carry him away from unproductive thoughts of the future that he couldn't control. Instead he focused on what he wanted *right now.*

And what he wanted right now was—

"Hey, hot stuff," someone said from behind him. "Come here often?"

Russ wanted to call the game.

He turned around and pulled Liam toward him, not quite close enough to touch. "Usually I wait 'til I get home."

Liam laughed, loose with just enough champagne and not enough inhibitions, and put his hand on Russ's hip. "Such self-control."

"Comes with the experience." If Liam could touch, so could Russ. The tequila and the club lights and the scent of booze and sweat made him brave, or maybe just reckless, and he slid his hands into Liam's back pockets. There wasn't much room for them in there; Liam's ass took up most of it.

Liam half stumbled into him, either because he was surprised at the touch or because the tempo of the music changing caught him off guard. He steadied himself with his free hand on Russ's chest, and a wild flush spread across his cheeks.

That, Russ thought immediately. *I want more of that.* More of Liam looking at him like that, surprised and turned-on and curious.

A shaky breath Russ felt more than heard, Liam's chest hitching against his own, and then Liam licked his lips. "Experience getting picked up in clubs?"

More. When Liam didn't move his hand, Russ pulled him closer, moving him to the beat of the music. He smirked at the question. "Something like that."

The flush deepened, and Liam swallowed. This close, Russ couldn't help noticing his eyelashes, how ungodly long they were. Liam wasn't fluttering them now. He let Russ lead. "I haven't seen this side of you before."

He liked it, though. That much was obvious. "I'm full of surprises." Even for himself—*especially* for himself. Half their team could be watching right now and Russ just didn't give a fuck. How could he when he had Liam pressed against him? When he had finally allowed himself the freedom to do what he wanted?

The brush of Liam's half-hard cock through their pants stirred a wild creature in the back of Russ's brain. It awoke and spread its wings with a roar. Liam might have started this game, but Russ was going to finish it.

He pulled his left hand out of Liam's back pocket and moved it low on his hip, slipping his thumb just under the hem of Liam's shirt and brushing it over the soft, warm skin of his stomach.

Liam's hand clenched against his chest, and Russ *felt* it when his dick jerked. "Russ." His voice was hoarse, barely audible over the pulsing music. "What are you doing?"

Giving us what we both want. "What's it feel like I'm doing?" He slid his thumb in and down, until it tucked under the waist of Liam's pants.

Liam licked his lips again. "It feels like you're about two minutes from trying to get me to cream my pants on the dance floor."

Fuck. Some of Russ's common sense kicked in then, because he *did* want that, but he wouldn't cross that line.

At least not tonight.

"You could also wait until we get home," he suggested. "I'll even let you take your pants off first."

Liam flattened his hand against Russ's chest and slid it upward until his thumb rested in the hollow of Russ's throat and his fingers touched his collarbone. "I'm not complaining." He blinked once, slowly, like he was having a hard time keeping his eyes open. "But um, what… what happened to, ah, 'what will people think if they see you trying to fuck me'?"

"You got called up." He'd played well. Everyone had seen it. No one could take that away now. It was only a matter of time before he made the NHL full-time. "And now you're going back down—"

"Presumptuous," Liam said, but his voice was breathy.

Trouble. Russ smiled and tilted his head. "Am I wrong?"

He watched Liam's throat work as he trailed a hot gaze down Russ's body. "I'm willing to negotiate."

Yeah, Russ thought so. "As I was saying. You're going back down. So it won't affect our working relationship."

"Well. I'd hate to go without a proper seeing-to." Liam's breath hitched when Russ slid his thumb lower. "I mean seeing off."

Russ chuckled. "You want to get out of here?"

Liam took half a step back and then slid his arm through Russ's, leaning against his shoulder. "I thought you never ask."

Second Period

Liam didn't know what sex god had smiled upon him, but he hoped that whatever happened next pleased them immensely.

He wasn't drunk—at least not on alcohol. Lust buzzed thick in his veins like the most potent cocktail and made his pulse pound and his mouth dry.

He couldn't believe this was happening.

God damn it, he should've jerked off before the game. The last time he'd taken someone home was over the summer, just before he went to training camp in Miami. He'd been kind, good-looking, and forgettable, which was sad since it wasn't like Liam had a high standard. Most of Liam's experiences had been crammed in between school, games, and practice—hand jobs and blow jobs at parties or on the road with heteroflexible teammates.

Opportunities for more involved activities had been limited, which sucked because Liam was young and horny and probably at, like, peak attractiveness. He'd literally dreamt of all the fantastic sex he could have when the only thing on his agenda was playing hockey, but most of the time he was exhausted, and the AHL life was not glamorous. Even Liam didn't want to *see* the rooms he slept in, a lot of the time.

All these factors resulted in three thoughts that cycled through Liam's brain on repeat. One, he was so keyed up he was going to come like five seconds after Russ touched his dick. Two, if Russ was any better than just competent at sex, he was probably going to set some kind of benchmark Liam would be jerking it to for the rest of his life. And three, if Russ put those two things together and realized Liam had been—how had he put it? Punching out of his weight class?—Liam was going to die of mortification.

Be cool, Liam, he thought. If his fingers were a little sweaty as he stabbed the call button for the elevator to take them to his floor, well, that was just from the heat of the club. Obviously.

Then Russ touched the inside of Liam's wrist with big, warm, beyond-competent fingers, and *cool* went out the window into the Miami night. Liam snapped his head up and found Russ watching him intently, head slightly tilted.

Like he was assessing if Liam was having second thoughts.

Liam was absolutely having second thoughts—and third, and eighth, and twentieth thoughts—but not about his decision to go home with Russ. He just couldn't decide what he wanted to do *first*.

But it was probably a bad idea to say so out loud in a hotel lobby, so he just flicked his eyes at Russ's lap and wet his lips.

Russ tightened his grip fractionally in warning, then pulled away again, dragging his fingers across Liam's palm in a way that made Liam shudder.

This elevator needed to show up, stat.

Finally the doors dinged open and they stepped inside.

The doors closed behind them.

A beat of silence. Then Russ said, "If you changed your mind—"

Hell no. Liam did not get this close to Russ's dick to go home without seeing it. He surged forward and slammed his mouth into Russ's.

It wasn't graceful or particularly good. What it was was desperate. After an eternal second of too many teeth and too little softness, Russ made an amused noise against Liam's mouth and brought his hand to Liam's jaw to angle his head.

All of a sudden it was like he was licking the pleasure center of Liam's brain. An embarrassing sound escaped him as his lips parted and Russ slid his tongue inside. Sparks zipped up Liam's back and down his chest, and he shuddered as Russ pushed him against the door.

Oh God, Liam hoped he didn't get some kind of manhandling kink from this. Getting hard anytime someone checked him would be inconvenient.

Then Russ tore his mouth away and started biting a path from Liam's chin down his jawline toward his ear.

Ding.

For a second, Liam thought his brain had made a game-show sound effect—*right answer!*

Then the elevator door behind him shifted and he almost fell out into the hallway.

Russ caught him by the waist before he could, and they froze that way, halfway out. Liam looked around so he wouldn't have to look at Russ; at least no one had seen them.

"You're steadier on skates," Russ commented a beat later.

Say that after you've kissed me while I'm wearing them. Liam righted himself and grabbed Russ's wrist. "Let's find a soft place to land."

Russ's laugh echoed down the hallway.

It only took Liam two tries to get the hotel room door open, which didn't make up for almost falling over because Russ was kissing him, but he pretended it did. Liam tossed the key card in the general direction of the desk and turned around to pull Russ along with him.

He caught his shoe on the pajama pants he'd left on the floor and almost went over backward onto the bed.

This time, instead of catching him, Russ lifted and shoved. Liam landed with a bounce in the center of the mattress.

Russ toed out of his shoes. "How have you lived this long when you're this clumsy?" He climbed up onto the bed, stalking over Liam's body like an apex predator.

Liam splayed his legs and tilted his hips up and his head back—*eat me.* "I was hoping I'd trip and fall on your dick?"

Russ settled his muscular ass right on top of Liam's crotch. Liam's erection kicked in approval. His boxers were already sticking to his skin, wet with precome. "My dick was in the other direction." He seemed to be enjoying giving Liam shit.

Unfortunately Liam was enjoying it too. "What you want me to say? Evolution made me gay for a reason." Russ quirked his lips and shifted his weight on Liam's lap. Liam shuddered as another pulse of precome escaped. "Uh, if this is doing it for you that's awesome, but unless you actually want to make me come in my pants, maybe we get naked now."

Russ stopped wriggling, but his gaze went sharp and calculating. He dragged it down Liam's body to the place their bodies met, as if he was trying to see through his clothes to know just how close Liam was to making a mess of himself.

"You first, then." Russ got up in one fluid motion, so quickly it made Liam dizzy. In the same moment, he pulled Liam off the mattress so he was sitting and slipped his hands under his shirt.

"Yes, that's what I'm saying." Liam obediently raised his arms. Russ skimmed his palms over Liam's nipples as he pulled the shirt off, and electricity zinged through his body. "Tabarnak, uh, maybe I should do the pants." While keeping his hands away from his dick.

Russ paused with his hands on the hem of his own shirt. "Did you have too much to drink for this?"

"I had a glass of champagne and *one tequila shot*," Liam protested, offended. "I'm embarrassingly horny, not drunk." Then he stopped and thought for a second, because he'd really believed Russ would never sleep with him in a million years, and he'd die if it turned out the shoe was on the other foot. "What about you? You don't get roofied or something, did you?"

"By one of our teammates, who were the only other people in the VIP section with us who had access to our drinks?"

Wow, he didn't have to be rude about it. Liam let it go because Russ had taken his shirt off and he was busy staring. Russ had broad shoulders and a narrow waist, and his dark skin gleamed as if beckoning Liam to lick a line right down his chest to the waist of his pants.

"Liam?"

Liam belatedly realized he was palming his dick through his pants. He dragged his hands to unbutton his fly and his eyes up to Russ's instead. "Are you always this nice to guys you fuck?"

"Hey." Russ stood next to the bed and dropped his pants. "I'm nice."

Holy shit. "Parts of you sure are." Liam had caught glimpses in the locker room, obviously, but Russ naked and Russ naked, hard, and looking at Liam were totally different things. His perfectly proportioned dick curved up against his stomach from a patch of neatly manscaped hair. Liam swallowed. "Can I suck it?"

Fuck. He didn't mean for it to come out sounding like that, somehow straddling the line between conversational and pleading. Actually, he hadn't *meant* to say it at all, even if his mouth was already wet with anticipation. If he'd been thinking about it, he would've gone for something sultry and suggestive and less... less....

Naïve.

For a second, he worried Russ would mock him. Why Liam should care about that when that was basically their status quo, he didn't know, but he did. But no smart remark came. A flicker of an expression crossed Russ's face, too quickly for Liam to identify before it disappeared under his usual affability. "Take your pants off first."

Right. Pants. The sooner he took them off, the sooner they would stop strangling his dick. Liam raised his hips and pushed his pants down, heedless of the catch of elastic over his hard-on. His cock slapped against his stomach, leaving a wet smear.

He got his pants as far as his ankles before he remembered about his shoes, and how fitted the cut of the pants was. By then he was stuck, ankles basically tied together by his own eagerness and lack of foresight. If there was a lesson in that, Liam refused to learn it; he was too embarrassed. He couldn't learn under these conditions.

Maybe because he could tell Liam was actually mortified, and not just embracing his normal surface-level cringe, Russ didn't comment. Instead he knelt—*God*, he was handsome, and naked, and radiating body heat like a furnace—at the foot of the bed and put his hand on one ankle. "Should've told you to do these first."

Liam was twenty-two years old. Pretty much everything turned him on. But the way his cock jerked at the touch of Russ's hand on his ankle made him feel like a swooning Victorian maiden. For a hot second, he worried he'd developed a fetish about having his feet touched, but then Russ put his other hand on his knee while he was working the shoe off, and nope, false alarm, it was a Russ thing.

His relief didn't last, because while the touch felt good, it also *tickled*. Liam kicked reflexively and would've popped Russ right in the mouth if Russ didn't react so quickly. "Easy." He steadied Liam's calf. "Should I stop?"

Did Russ think Liam was trying to fend him off all of a sudden? "No, sorry. Ticklish."

Russ quirked his lips and trailed his fingers lightly over Liam's bare calf. Liam twitched again, and the pressure tightened until it didn't tickle anymore. "Got it." He worked Liam's other foot free, and then Liam was naked, with Russ on the mattress between his feet. He shivered in the air conditioning. "I'll use a firm hand with you."

"Uh," Liam said. He wasn't sure what Russ meant by that, but it sounded hot and it distracted him from the unexpected wave of vulnerability.

That feeling fled completely when Russ squeezed his ankle and asked, "You still want to suck me off?"

Oh God, yes. He loved giving head and he knew he was good at it, and he'd feel like they were on more even footing with Russ's dick in his mouth. "Yeah. Yes. Please."

Okay, so he sounded like a stunned virgin, but fuck it. Russ was looking at Liam with a heated gaze that was somehow also calculating, so Liam wasn't going to worry about it.

Definitely not once Russ raised his hand to Liam's cheek and thumbed his lip. "How do you want me? On the bed? Or standing?"

Liam's brain ran through a montage of filth—scenes of him kneeling with Russ above him, or lying on his back on the bed with Russ fucking his throat, or getting Russ splayed out like Liam was now and getting to touch him and look at him and take his time. How was he supposed to pick one? "Yes?" he said again. Russ was going to think he'd forgotten how to speak English. Liam was starting to worry he'd forgotten how to speak, period.

But Russ took the answer in stride. "Come here and kiss me first, then."

He didn't have to ask twice. Liam scrambled onto his knees and met Russ's mouth with his, shivering at the pleasure that zinged through him. He steadied himself on Russ's broad shoulder, the skin hot and smooth under his palm. Russ maneuvered Liam where he wanted him, half straddling Russ's thigh on the bed, Russ's thumb in the divot of his hip a grounding pressure.

Russ kissed like he'd happily do it all night, unrushed and thorough, a deep, hot exploration of Liam's mouth that left Liam hard and dizzy. Then Russ pulled back and retreated to just a tease, flicking his tongue against the seam of Liam's lips until Liam's pulse roared in his ears.

He was breathing like he'd just skated a double shift when Russ pulled his mouth away and brushed his thumb over Liam's lower lip again.

Liam felt that touch on his nipples and the head of his cock. Without meaning to, he licked his lips and caught the pad of Russ's thumb. Russ's gaze caught his and held it captive. "On your knees next to the bed."

Liam slithered downward before his brain processed the words. He rested his hands on Russ's thighs.

Russ pulled him forward with a hand on the back of his neck.

Liam went.

Russ's musky scent filled his nose, and then his dick filled Liam's mouth. Liam made a soft sound that made him flush all over again—something pornographic and needy—but he pushed the way that made him feel to the back of his mind and focused on Russ.

He'd thought it would be more difficult.

Not because he didn't want to get his mouth on Russ like this, explore the salty taste of him on his tongue, feel the rasp of the hair at his groin on his cheeks and chin. But because he'd wanted it so much, and been so certain it would never happen, that it seemed like the reality should have left him quaking with nerves like he had been a moment ago.

Liam leaned into the warm, firm guidance of Russ's hand as he bobbed on Russ's cock, taking him as deep as he comfortably could and then pushing deeper, deeper every time. Yeah, he knew how to give good head, but he should've been more nervous. He couldn't be, though. Russ was as steady here as he was on the ice—a fixed point to navigate with.

Not that Liam was going anywhere. His lips tingled where they were stretched around Russ's cock, and spit slicked his face and mouth.

Liam swirled his tongue over the head, pulled the foreskin back with his right hand, and moaned when Russ carded his fingers through his hair. "Feels good."

It felt *amazing*. Liam closed his eyes and savored it. He dropped his hand to his lap to stroke himself, and Russ thumbed at the hinge of his jaw and gently pulled him off. "You like this?" he asked. His voice was hoarse, like he'd been the one with a cock down his throat.

I'm literally jerking off about it right now. Liam licked wetness from the corner of his mouth and forced himself to meet Russ's eyes. Russ's gaze was dark and heavy—hot but also searching. "Yeah," he rasped.

"Come up here. I want to touch you."

He was helping Liam onto the bed almost before Liam could respond. They fell back on the mattress together, grasping at each other, fused at the mouth. The first brush of Russ's cock against Liam's made him gasp and bite Russ's lip. In response, Russ growled and nudged his thigh between Liam's, and God, now he was leaking on Russ's leg and it felt incredible.

But that wasn't good enough for Russ, who seemed to want to destroy Liam completely. He kissed down Liam's chest until his mouth was between Liam's nipples. Then he scored his teeth along Liam's sternum to the right until he scraped over his areola. A whiny huff escaped Liam's throat, so Russ repeated the teasing bite on the other side.

"Oh fuck."

Russ made a thoughtful noise against Liam's skin. "Work to do first." He raised his head. "You have lube, right?"

Liam's dick twitched against Russ's stomach.

Russ smirked loudly.

"Yes," Liam said. "Shut up. In the drawer." He didn't care if his hotel room was a disaster otherwise, but he didn't want the cleaning crew having to see his sex stuff. Russ could get it himself. Liam was paralyzed by lust, and also by Russ being on top of him.

He expected a retort, but instead Russ leveraged himself into a whole-body lean that put every beautiful line of his body on display and had his cock dangling over Liam's like a baited hook. Too bad Liam had lost his voluntary muscle control, because he missed his chance to get his hands on it.

A moment later a bottle of lube and a box of condoms dropped next to Liam on the mattress and Russ settled back between his thighs. Hallelujah.

"Can't help noticing." Russ picked up the half-empty bottle in one hand and the unopened package in the other. His face was doing a great job walking the line of *this is hilarious* and *don't take it personally*. He shook the box. "One of these things is not like the other."

Liam had bought the economy size in a fit of unfounded optimism. "If you saw the places we stay on the road in the A, you don't make that judgy face."

Russ laughed and dropped the condoms. "You sure you're up for this?" He gestured to his dick—unnecessarily, Liam felt, although he didn't hate having an invitation to look. "We can do something else."

This was the weirdest one-night stand Liam had ever had. "I can take it," he said defiantly.

"Yeah, but are you going to spend a lot of time sitting on a bus in the next twenty-four hours?"

Liam had a flight back to Lexington the next day, which meant the team was playing at home, but he didn't know how long for.

That was future Liam's problem. However—"Maybe just go slow."

"Slow." Russ's eyes glinted as he dragged his gaze down Liam's body. "I can work with that."

Liam had bitten off more than he could chew, but that didn't mean he wasn't going to swallow. "Not *glacial*," he complained. "You can touch my dick again now."

Russ laughed again, like he was somehow surprised that Liam was the same in bed as he was on the ice. "Impatient much?"

Liam gestured at the condoms. "I bought those in August."

Finally, *finally*, Russ put his hand on Liam's ankle and pushed his foot toward his ass. "I'll take that as a yes."

"It's a—"

Russ clicked open the lube.

"Yessss," Liam finished as a slick finger rubbed his hole.

A second later he felt Russ's lips on the head of his dick. Russ kept the pressure of his mouth light and teasing, just enough to have Liam arching and panting for more.

Then he pressed his finger into Liam's hole, and Liam's brain overheated.

It had been a long time since anyone touched him like this. Actually, *no one* had really touched him like this; the few times Liam had been fucked, he'd opened himself up, partly because they hadn't had a lot of time for foreplay and partly because he didn't trust his partners' experience.

Russ knew exactly what he was doing. He fucked his finger gently in and out, rubbing against Liam's passage in a way that made him ache for more.

"Good?" Russ rumbled.

An embarrassing *uh* escaped Liam's lips. He arched his neck into the pillow, savoring the intrusion, pinned between Russ's mouth and his hand.

"Good." Russ sounded smug.

"Check your—" Liam gasped when Russ nailed his prostate. "—ego."

"It matches my dick."

Liam was midlaugh when Russ slid a second finger into him. The stretch turned the sound into a groan as Liam's body adjusted. Russ had big hands, and his fingers felt amazing, but he missed Russ's mouth on his cock. When he hitched his hips, though, Russ only made an amused sound and pinned his arm across Liam's pelvis.

"Taking it slow, remember?"

Liam flopped an arm over his face. "You're a sadist."

Russ curled his fingers just right and pressed a wet, openmouthed kiss to the base of Liam's cock. Desire pooled heavy in Liam's belly. "Be dumb to spend this much time working you open if I was into hurting you."

The casual way he said *working you open* fried half the remaining neurons in Liam's brain. "Get outta here with your logic."

Russ did not get outta there with his anything. He stayed right in there with his fingers, driving Liam crazy with pointed thrusts, each one angled to drag over Liam's prostate until Liam was grateful Russ had taken his mouth off his dick, because he was sure he'd come at the slightest touch.

Two fingers graduated to three, which was uncomfortable enough to take the edge off. The pace of Russ's thrusts slowed suspiciously, and Liam lifted his head to give Russ a look. "Don't," he warned. He could practically taste Russ's offer to back out and blow him or whatever. Which Liam would be into, or onto, at some future date, but tonight he had his heart set on Russ's dick.

Russ responded by thrusting deep again, this time with a twist against Liam's rim that had him practically choking on how bad he wanted more. "'S good," Liam gasped around a tongue that suddenly felt too thick for his mouth. "Russ. C'mon. Fuck me."

Incredibly, Russ didn't protest. He only withdrew his fingers—horrible; the sudden emptiness made Liam feel like he was losing his grip on reality—and reached for the box of condoms. "Pretty sure you can't return these once I break the seal—"

"You *suck*," Liam said as Russ finally ripped the box open.

"Maybe, if you're still up for it later," he agreed over the slick sound of latex unrolling. The whole thing was unfair. Liam was lying unspooled on the bed like a ball of twine the barn cats had gotten at and Russ was kneeling between his legs making dad jokes about sucking his dick. It shouldn't be allowed.

But he didn't have time to complain, because then the head of Russ's dick was pressing between his cheeks, so close to where Liam desperately wanted it. "You good like this?"

In response, Liam hooked his ankle around Russ's ass and pulled him forward. No way was he waiting for Russ to pick a different position. "Fucking *fuck* me."

Russ fucked him.

Liam had maybe been a little hasty getting to this point. Russ's cock was thicker than three of his fingers, and longer, and the stretch of him stung Liam's rim and ached deeper in. But it felt good too—full, delicious—and when Russ bottomed out, the brush of his balls against Liam's ass made Liam clench down reflexively, and—

"Fuck," Russ groaned roughly, stilling with his cock pressed deep.

"Ungh," Liam agreed. He curled his hands into the blankets, then raised them to Russ's hips.

Russ shifted just enough to push all Liam's buttons. "Can I—?"

If he didn't move, Liam would kill him. "*Yes.*"

When Russ drew back, the sudden emptiness made Liam hiss. But the thrust back in had his breath hitching in his throat, and after that he lost track of it, meeting every movement with his own.

Russ had promised slow, and he delivered. Liam's mouth opened for a series of formless vowels that fell from his lips with every painstaking stroke of Russ's length. Pressure built low in Liam's stomach, and his dick drooled against his abs, half hard at first but filling with each passing breath. Finally the pleasure grew too much and Liam let go of Russ's hips and wrapped a hand around himself, chasing an orgasm he knew would wreck him.

"God, you look—" Russ increased the pace. Liam couldn't tell if he was losing control or trying to make Liam lose his. "So good."

"Yeah," Liam said without processing the words. His gaze went from Russ's eyes to the head of his own cock peeking out from the top of his fist.

Then Russ said, "Can you…?" and dragged Liam toward him, pushing his own knees forward, until Liam was *in Russ's lap* with only his shoulders touching the bed and Russ was so deep inside him he was splitting open.

Like this, he didn't have any leverage, couldn't do anything but jerk off and take it while Russ pinned Liam on his dick and made him see stars. "Oh fuck," Liam said. "Fuck, fuck—"

More words followed, maybe a third of them English. Liam trembled on the edge of release for what felt like forever. Finally Russ slammed home and nailed his prostate *hard*, and Liam erupted all over his own hand and chest, his hot release sliding toward his throat with the angle of his body as he clenched down on Russ's thick cock.

"*Jesus*," Russ groaned, and his hips jerked one more time and then stilled. Liam *felt* it when he came, and a mewling noise escaped him as his own softening erection twitched one final time.

Holy fuck.

After a moment of silence broken only by their heavy breathing, Russ carefully eased Liam off his lap and pulled out.

Liam didn't have the presence of mind to hide the wince, but it wasn't bad. Well worth it. He flailed one-handed and managed to drag the box of tissues off the bedside table.

The cleanup, too, was quiet. Liam didn't notice it until he'd finished wiping come out of his belly button, and by then it was getting awkward. He rolled onto his side to toss the Kleenex into the wastebasket under the desk.

When he rolled back, he had a strip of condoms sticking to his body. Snickering, Russ peeled the foil packets away from Liam's still-sticky body and shook his head. "I don't want to disappoint you, but I don't think I can go forty-nine more times tonight."

Liam crawled up toward the pillow and stuffed it under his head. "What kinda work ethic is that, Russell?" He tsked. "Setting a bad example for the young, impressionable members of the team—"

"You're the one who made an impression on my member," Russ said solemnly.

Liam recoiled, laughing. "That's terrible."

"Oh, I don't know. I didn't mind it." Russ disposed of the condom and then lay down on his side on the bed next to Liam. "Seemed like you enjoyed yourself too."

"It was all right," Liam deadpanned. Russ definitely did not need his ego stroked.

"Yeah? You got notes?" Russ pillowed his head on his hand. "Wanna go over the game tape?"

Liam made a face at him. "I think maybe I should do my cooldown routine first." He needed a shower. "If you join me, we can make a start on the rest of the forty-nine."

"Let's not overdo it. You've got a flight tomorrow." Russ stood up and pulled Liam to his feet. "I have an off day, though. You want to top?"

Oh shit. Liam had never topped, and now he wasn't going to think about anything else for the rest of his life. "Seriously? Because your ass is life goals, but you don't exactly give off 'come fuck me' vibes."

Russ put his hand on Liam's shoulder and steered him toward the bathroom. "I'm feeling spontaneous."

"I love being spontaneous." Liam tried, without success, to look over his own shoulder and Russ's to get an eyeful of the goods, and would've walked into the doorframe if Russ hadn't stopped him.

"Eyes forward, Trouble," he said with amusement.

"Get in front of me, then."

After that everything got very hot and steamy, in the literal and figurative senses. Russ's body was hard and slick against his in the shower, and he kissed like he skated, confident and firm, like he could do it all night.

They were still damp when they stumbled back to the bed. Russ might have offered to let Liam fuck him, but he was definitely still calling the shots, which Liam was grateful for because he could concentrate on the mechanics and not losing it immediately. He ended up on his back with Russ riding him, stretched above him looking like every future wet dream Liam would ever have. His body was hot and slick around Liam's cock, and when they got the angle right, Russ's eyes fell to half mast.

Not surprisingly, Liam didn't last long. But he didn't leave Russ hanging; as soon as he caught his breath, he slithered down the bed and sucked Russ's dick into his mouth.

"That's two down," he said afterward, lying with his head pillowed on Russ's thigh as they recovered. He held up the depleted strip of condoms.

Russ snorted and halfheartedly dragged Liam up the bed by his hair. "What made you buy a box that big?"

"They're cheaper. I was being economical." Liam collapsed next to him on the mattress and tried not to think about the tip he was going to have to leave Housekeeping. "I didn't have a lot of time for hot sex in college. There was, like, homework and stuff. So I think, 'I'm a professional athlete now. Professional athletes get laid all the time.' Except then I'm mostly on a bus or tired or both."

"Tragic," Russ said solemnly.

"Right? At least college guys are not that picky about who touches their dick. I can't believe it was easier to get laid then."

Russ made a thinky face, scrunching up his nose and eyebrows. Like that, with his hair pushed around by the pillow, he looked younger. Or maybe Liam just thought he did because Russ was acting younger, more carefree, tonight. "I'm afraid to ask."

That was okay; Liam never needed prompting to run his mouth. He wiggled over on his back so he could talk with his hands. "First time I got fucked, it was this guy on my team. He was obsessed with trying anal and his girlfriend wasn't having it. So when she break up with him and he spent three days ranting about it, I said he could fuck me if it would make him shut up."

Russ looked at him in vague horror.

"What?" Liam said, spreading his hands. "He was hot and convenient and I was horny. It was not a sacrifice."

Russ shook his head against the pillow, placating. The horror dissolved into mild amusement. Liam liked how changeable he was, that he let Liam tell him how to feel. Liam was a grown-up now and had been then. He didn't need anyone's pity. "Okay, sorry. And? Was it everything he dreamed of?"

Liam snickered. "Only if his dream was during a nap. He last like two seconds."

This time Russ's laugh seemed to sneak up on him, because there was surprise in his face when it overtook him. "Not a banner night for you."

"Meh." Liam shrugged. "I wanted to know what it felt like. I got what I wanted." But he needed to get to the root of Russ's objection, so he added, "Not everyone needs their first time to be *special*."

He could tell by the twitch of Russ's lips that that hit had landed. Yep. Liam had been bang-on.

"I'm not a kid. I don't need…." What were they called in English? "Those public service announcements?" He didn't think that was right, but he couldn't be bothered to think about it any further. "About how I should feel cherished—"

"Liam." Russ grabbed one of his hands out of the air to stop his gesturing. "I get it. I didn't mean to offend you."

Was Liam offended? Oh… he kind of was. He tried to unruffle his own feathers. "I don't like being treated like a kid."

"I wasn't trying to," Russ said.

Liam narrowed his eyes. Russ had literally called him *kid* on multiple occasions, which was fine when they hadn't just fucked each other's brains out. "Sure."

Groaning, Russ let go of his hand and rubbed his forearm over his face. When he took it away again, he looked embarrassed. "Seriously. I'm just…." His cheeks were actually turning a little bit pink. Liam was fascinated. "I'll fuck you like a porn star, but I'm a romantic, okay?"

"Oh my God," Liam said. Big, tough, stoic Russ—a romantic. A hearts and flowers guy. Breakfast in bed. Back rubs. Candlelit dinners. Liam could see it. "That's adorable."

The flush deepened. "Shut up."

Liam did not shut up, but he did forgive Russ immediately. "So, wait. Was *your* first time special?"

He could tell he'd surprised Russ again by the way his features froze just for a moment. The embarrassment was fading now, replaced by something softer and more introspective, but when he answered, he seemed surprised by that too. "Yeah, actually."

Liam rolled onto his stomach and pillowed his head on his arms. "You gonna tell me about it?"

Russ flicked him between the eyebrows. "No. I don't kiss and tell."

Well, that was just rude. "Russell! I told you mine!"

He shook his head again, smiling. "Sorry. Not just my story to tell. Besides, you have to let me keep some secrets."

"Ugh, fine." That probably meant he'd slept with someone in the hockey community and he didn't want Liam to be weird about it. Maybe Baller's husband— they would've been on Team Canada together at some point, right? Before Gabe was out?

Yeah, Liam probably shouldn't think about it too much. That really *could* get weird.

Russ tapped his nose. "You should sleep. You have an early flight."

"Yeah," Liam sighed. "Back to reality." He didn't mind, though. It would be good to get back to playing every game instead of mostly sitting. He rolled onto his side and stretched up his arm to flick off the light. "Night."

It didn't occur to him that Russ might want to get up and go home until several seconds later, when Russ mumbled back, "Good night."

But he didn't get up, so, whatever. Clearly he didn't care where he slept. Liam just hoped he didn't get upset if Liam's packing woke him up in the morning.

RUSS FIGURED he'd close his eyes for a few minutes until Liam fell asleep, then gather his stuff and walk back to the players' parking garage at the arena so he could go home.

But somehow he slept until nine, when he woke up to an empty bed, bright sunlight streaming in around the edges of the curtains, and an overall ache like he'd just skated the game of his life.

There was two hundred dollars on the night table. Helpfully, Liam had written, in block print FOR HOUSEKEEPING. SORRY. Russ shook his head. The kid really was something else.

Liam was obviously gone—though Russ found a sock and a T-shirt he must've forgotten in his haste this morning—but checkout wasn't for another hour, so Russ took a long, hot shower before dressing and letting himself out of the hotel room.

Last night hadn't turned out the way he'd thought it would.

Okay, so he hadn't exactly been *thinking* about how things would go. Not with his upstairs brain, anyway. Russ had been wild with the need to find something he could control, and Liam had offered himself up so nicely. He was young, attractive, en-thusiastic about sex, and just as enthusiastic about making sure Russ knew he was available for the tak-ing. It wasn't complicated. He'd assumed that the sex would be hot, but also that it would be all they had in common.

In reality....

Russ jangled his keys against his palm as he walked down the sunny Miami street.

In reality, the sex hadn't been at all what he ex-pected. It was *good*, hot. Liam had been everything he hoped for. But it was also… worrisome. Too ca-sual? Too friendly?

Too comfortable, maybe. Russ hadn't expect-ed to laugh so much. He hadn't expected Liam's half-empty bottle of lube and giant unopened box of condoms, or the face Liam would make when de-fending himself, or that Russ would want to stay not just for round two but also for Liam to fuck him.

But the whim had struck him, and he hadn't been able to get the idea out of his head, and he'd thought, well, he could still be in control. That had been different too. He didn't regret any of it. He was just… thinking about it harder than he needed to.

Maybe he should get laid more often.

By now he'd reached the parking garage, and he waved at the attendant as he walked by the security booth on his way to his truck.

"Crazy night last night?" Patti asked as he passed.

Russ had to laugh. She had no idea. "You could say that."

It wasn't unusual for the guys to leave their cars at the arena overnight when they went out after a home game. Russ was usually one of the first to swing by and get his, but everyone else must've called it an early night, because his was the only car left in the lot.

He didn't think anything of it until he showed up for practice the next day to find Mo and Baller waiting for him in the locker room, uncharacteristically early.

Too late, Russ realized he'd walked into a trap.

"Hey." Mo looked up from the meticulous work he put into taping one of his sticks. "You disappeared on us the other night. How much trouble did you get into?"

Baller snorted. "I think you mean how much of Russ did he get into Trouble."

At least they hadn't asked how much of Trouble got into *him*. "Hi to you too, assholes." Russ dropped his bag at his stall and kicked his slides under the seat. "Is this an intervention? Do I need a lawyer?"

"Not for me," Baller said cheerfully. "Queers who live in glass houses shouldn't throw stones. I'm here to celebrate you becoming a real boy." He picked up a paper noisemaker from the bench next to him and blew on it. It unrolled into a penis shape, incongruous with the sad whistle sound. At least until it deflated again—then it was pretty appropriate. "Congratulations on finally hitting that."

Jesus Christ. "How long have you had that thing?"

"A while. I didn't think it would be this long before Trouble got called up."

Russ decided he was better off not asking for clarification. He turned to Mo instead, suddenly uneasy. He didn't think he'd done anything wrong, and clearly Baller didn't either, but Mo was the captain and the only straight guy among the three of them. He might have a different view.

Mo finished taping the handle, snapped the adhesive off the roll, and then met Russ's eyes. He rolled his. "If anyone thought you were the type to take advantage, you wouldn't have a letter on your sweater."

The tightness in Russ's shoulders eased. "Okay. So what's with the ambush?"

"We're here to talk to you about your car's extended warranty—"

Without looking, Mo tossed the tape at Baller. It would've hit his chest, but he caught it. "I wanted to see if you'd made any coming-out plans, since apparently you're picking up guys in public now."

Fuck. "Can we have an intervention about Liam instead?"

Mo's mouth twisted wryly. "No."

Russ sighed. "Can we do it somewhere that's not the locker room ten minutes before morning skate?"

Beaming, Baller said, "Thought you'd never ask. Come over for lunch, I'm doing tilapia."

Russ glanced at Mo, who shrugged. "He's the coming-out expert."

Before Russ could make up an excuse, the door opened to admit Yeti and Jonesy. "Fine," he sighed. "But you better have beer."

For all the churning Baller and Mo had stirred up in his brain, Russ had a good practice. His body felt good. And maybe he had needed a night to burn off some sexual energy, because he was even in a good mood. He fined Yeti a hundred bucks for spraying Axe body spray in the locker room afterward and spent ten minutes catching up with Jonesy about his ongoing dental saga—Russ made a mental note to floss more often and buy a second backup mouthguard—and then walked out of the room with Baller and Mo, resigned to his fate.

They passed the coach and a couple of the front-office guys on their way out to the car, and Russ felt a different kind of tension. He hadn't heard anything from Erika about a trade, but that didn't mean it couldn't happen. The Caimans were cap strapped, and they had a lot of money tied up in their defensive core. With players like Carl and Liam waiting in the wings—young, decent, and cheap—they could afford to offload some veteran talent and free up some cap space.

Or room to acquire another high-powered forward like Baller just in time for playoffs.

But Russ couldn't control that. He needed to focus on the areas of his life that he could. Which, right now, meant how he treated his body—what he put it through and what he put in it, and also apparently who, when he got out of bed, when he practiced, how much time he spent with friends. All of those were within his sphere of control, and controlling those elements let him master his own emotions.

Generally speaking, spending time with friends was good.

Spending time with friends who wanted to work-shop your coming-out plan could go either way. Russ didn't regret going home with Liam, and he'd dismissed the possibility of a public outing in the moment, but in the bright light of day…. Yeah, he'd be pissed at himself if this ended up being how he came out to the world. Especially in a contract year.

Twenty minutes later he pulled into Baller's driveway and parked next to a golf cart. He eyed it as he got out of the truck, only for Baller to say from the garage, "Gabe's request." He smacked the button to close the door. "He said if I was going to expose him to Florida Republicans, he at least wanted to live on a golf course."

Russ shook his head. "Your husband is a strange man."

"Eh." Baller shrugged. "He also stipulated we gotta get out of here before the kiddo's in school. Which, fair. C'mon, I'm cooking outside."

Russ followed him around to the back, where there was a fancy outdoor kitchen complete with a mini fridge full of Modelo and Stella Artois. Interesting choices. He grabbed a Modelo and helped himself to a patio chair while Baller fussed with his grill.

Mo showed up just before Baller plated their meals, and they sat under the pergola to eat. Baller was a good enough cook that Russ forgot he was there to be emotionally supported. He finished his plate and a second beer before they set the dishes aside, at which point Baller said, "Okay, so let's talk about closets."

Damn it, he should've stuck to a single beer, but it was hot out here. Probably all part of Baller's master plan. Russ groaned. "Closets are dumb. Everyone I care about in my life knows I'm gay. I should've ripped the Band-Aid off ages ago. But…."

For a second, Baller paused, head tilted, like he was reevaluating. Then he reached for the pitcher of water on the table and poured them both another glass. "Go on."

"But you know how it is."

Baller nodded. "Yeah."

Mo was frowning. "How what is?"

"We're already 'other' to some people," Baller said, gesturing to himself and Russ. "Hockey's pretty white. You might not have noticed."

"Yeah, despite the fact that *I'm* actually the minority in this current situation, I do actually have eyes."

Baller eyed him. "The categories are not 'white' and 'not white,' so your math is flawed, college boy. But that's not the point. Which is that it's one more thing that makes us obviously different from what people traditionally think of when they think of NHL players."

Mo looked like he was still digesting the math, but he chewed on this too. "Okay. Right. So coming out means lower salaries, fewer opportunities, potential clashes in the locker room."

Russ shrugged. "Yeah. My parents would love for me to sign with Winnipeg, but I know the coach is racist, so I wouldn't sign there unless I had no other options. And like, I could tell my parents that, but...."

Again, Baller nodded and Mo looked lost. "But what?"

For a second, Russ struggled with how to put it into words. "It's not like racism isn't a fact of their lives or anything, because it is. But that doesn't mean it doesn't hurt you when you come across it. So my choices are hurt my parents with that or by telling them I don't want to play in Winnipeg."

"Also not the point right now," Baller said. "Although actually what if you just told them the coach is a homophobe instead?"

That wasn't the worst idea he'd ever heard.

"Anyway. Coming out." He paused and then said, "Let's stop here and get ice cream."

Russ couldn't tell if he was being softened up or if Baller was indulging his own sweet tooth.

When they had full bowls in front of them, Baller said, "What if it's not about what everyone else thinks?"

Mo *oofed*.

Russ pulled his ice cream bowl close to his chest like a shield. "You could've pulled that one a little."

"Like ripping off a Band-Aid, dude." Baller picked up his spoon. "You wouldn't be the first, is all I'm saying. You got some internalized homophobia you want to unpack?"

Mo aimed a kick at him under the table, but it went wide and grazed Russ's shin instead. He grimaced in apology. "Less jargon, more supportive feeling words."

Russ was going to get a headache. He shoveled in a spoonful of ice cream. "I'm not ashamed of being gay."

Baller shrugged. He had a smear of ice cream at the corner of his mouth. "Okay."

"I'm not!"

"So what is it, then?"

How could Russ explain something he didn't understand? What *was* the root of the issue? He poked at his melting dessert. "I'm supposed to set an example."

For a moment there was silence. Then the clink of stainless steel on ceramic. Finally Mo said, "Uh… you are? You work hard. You help your teammates. You do charity and shit?"

"Yeah, but like…." He huffed. "My personal life is kind of…." He had friends, but other than Mike a couple of years ago, his dating history was spotty at best.

Not that that was anyone's fault but his own.

Baller blinked and raised his eyebrows as something seemed to occur to him. "Are you worried about people finding out and thinking you're out sexing up rookies or something 'cause you're not a safe married gay?"

Shit.

"Why would he be worried about that?" Mo's voice was mystified. "That sounds *awesome*."

Baller shot him a look. "Help less."

"I mean." Russ closed his eyes, shoveled in an enormous glob of ice cream, and then mumbled through the ensuing brain freeze, "I definitely do not want people thinking I'm not married because I've been fucking my rookies."

"You did mentor a lot of them," Mo acknowledged. Then, "Wait, you only fucked one, right?"

Russ turned an incredulous gaze on Baller. "Why did they make him captain?"

"Don't look at me. I just got here." He finished his bowl and set it on the table. "Look. There's not a wrong way to be queer, all right? Married, celibate, unrepentant slut—none of those things means setting a better example than the others. You don't think Liam's setting a bad example by being out and slutty on main."

"Liam's not a slut."

Baller and Mo looked at him expectantly.

Russ was not going to explain about the box of condoms. "I mean, he'd probably like to be."

"*The point is,*" Baller went on, "you're a good role model the way you are. Management gave you the A. Guys look up to you—the real you, not the you you think you have to be."

"Wow." Mo shook his head. "Why *did* they make me captain?"

"Don't try pawning off your responsibility on me. I'm a father. I have other priorities." Baller collected the empty bowls. "Okay, truth bombs away. You get a choice of a hug from me or cat or baby cuddles."

Russ was definitely being handled now, and he wanted to complain about it, but it felt nice that his teammates wanted to understand what he was going through, and he did kind of want a cuddle, so he followed Baller inside in search of Mario.

THE MORNING he left Miami, Liam packed as quietly as he could. In truth he hadn't expected Russ to still be there when he woke up, never mind to sleep through Liam's alarm, but there was no question of him pretending; he had passed out facedown with one asscheek peeking out from under the blankets.

He hadn't expected Russ to text him afterward either, but that afternoon he got a picture on WhatsApp—a shot of a round black-and-white feline curled up in Russ's lap, unfortunately obscuring the most interesting bits.

Omg did u get a cat? Liam asked.

Nah this is Baller's cat Mario.

U should get a cat. Liam had always wanted a pet, but now that he finally had his own space, he was often on the road for weeks. Didn't seem fair. At least Russ didn't have to worry as much about travel time.

Russ didn't reply, and Liam figured that was that, and they'd go their separate ways. Which sucked, but he wasn't going to sulk about it. At least not where anyone would notice.

Besides, he had hockey to play.

His first game back was a personal best, with a goal, two assists, and three takeaways. He didn't want to attribute it to the effects of his night with Russ, but at the very least, he could say it hadn't hurt.

Well. It hadn't hurt his *game*. He'd been a little sore on the flight, but that felt like a small price to pay.

After the win, Mathieu stood to bestow the unofficial MVP award. "Tonight's prize goes to a guy who obviously missed the shit out of us while he was in Miami." The locker room hooted as he plonked the trophy—a rhinestone-studded cowboy hat—on Liam's sweaty curls. "Attaboy, Trouble."

Liam tipped the hat in acknowledgment. The PR intern snapped a picture for the team's Instagram.

After any other home win, they probably would've gone out to celebrate. But they had an early call tomorrow to get on the bus for another road trip, so Liam went home and microwaved a freezer meal.

While he waited for it to heat, he flipped through the messages on his phone. Bernadette must've been following the game on Twitter, because she'd congratulated him for each point he'd earned and again for the win.

Then she'd sent the picture of him in the hat to the family group chat.

Marie-Jean reacted with the heart emoji, as per usual. His parents sent generic words of encouragement, but at least they left room for Liam to believe they meant it.

Bastian said, *Wow, did they make you stand on the street corner after the game?*

Between the angle, the postgame flush, and the rhinestones, Liam *did* look like an underage prostitute, but Bastian was still a dick for saying it.

Apparently Liam was always going to be the runt of the litter as far as he was concerned.

When the microwave beeped, Liam sat at the kitchen counter to eat his dinner, scrolling through his phone with his left hand and shoveling forkfuls into his mouth with his right. It was better not to pay too much attention to a microwaved dinner.

He was considering sending Russ another message—would that be too pushy? Clingy? Liam didn't want to be a clinger—when Russ sent a screencap of the Thoroughbreds' Twitter. *Nice hat. Suits you.*

Relieved for the distraction, Liam smiled around a mouthful of salt-flavored noodles and typed out a response. *Yeah? You don't think it's too dignified?*

You had a 3 point night. How much more dignity do you need?

That made him smile wider. *Aww u been checking up on me?*

Wanted to make sure you could still skate.

Sure. Liam would buy that. *Can you?*

Russ sent him a middle-finger emoji.

Hmm, maybe Liam should've checked to make sure Russ wasn't scratched before he sent that. He pulled up Google, peeked at the Caimans' stats, and was gratified to see Russ had had a completely normal game—twenty-eight minutes, four shots on goal, one assist—though the Caimans had lost 3–2.

When he closed out of that window, his search results mocked him.

Cap-Strapped Caimans Dangle Lyons, Jones as Trade Bait

Liam closed the search results before he could be tempted to click the article. He didn't need to think about Russ dangling anything.

… He didn't *need* to, but it certainly wouldn't ruin his evening.

Get some sleep, came Russ's next text, two minutes after the emoji. *And remember to hydrate.*

He was always so bossy. Liam didn't mind it in bed, or in person when he had Russ physically fussing over him to soften the blow, but it wasn't the same over text. *Not ur rookie anymore, u can't tell me what to do.*

The last thing he expected was for his phone to ring. He was twenty-two years old. People didn't *call* him. That was weird. "Hello?"

"Hey," Russ said, casual. Like calling Liam after eleven o'clock at night was a thing he did on the regular. "Did I catch you at a bad time?"

No, just a bad mood. "Um… no, I just finished second dinner." He almost added that he'd been about to go to bed, but he didn't want Russ to think he'd been following Russ's orders. Or… something.

"Good." Why did he sound so relieved? Liam felt like he'd missed something important. It was weirding him out. In a kind of good way, because he'd obviously rather have Russ's attention than not, but still. Finally he said, "Is everything okay? You uh… I kinda feel like I touched a nerve." While Liam was still recovering from his surprise that Russ noticed that from a text message, he added, "You didn't even say I can't tell you what to do when we're not in bed."

In spite of himself, Liam had to laugh. "Okay, yes. I... my brother was a dick earlier, treating me like a kid, and I saw your message and...."

"Got it." Another pause. "Sorry we ruined your night."

Aww. Wasn't that cute? "Nah, you didn't," Liam said. After all, if they hadn't made Liam cranky, Liam wouldn't have Russ on the line now. "It's nothing, forget it."

"Family stuff isn't nothing." The sound of a door closing. "I mean, since we're sharing...."

It seemed like this wasn't going to a sexy place, but Liam was intrigued anyway. He got up from the island and lay down on his couch instead, pointing his toes and arching his body into the stretch. "You have family beef too?"

A soft, self-deprecating laugh. "I don't know if it's beef. Ah, you know how my fam came to the game in Winnipeg?"

Nope, completely forgot about literally meeting them. "Yeah."

"So my grandfather came too, and his boyfriend. But they didn't come down to the VIP area with everyone else, because they also brought Tony's cousin." He paused. "Who my mother was trying to set me up with."

Liam bristled with a fleeting touch of jealousy, but he vaguely remembered Russ saying something about that, back when they were locked in Mo's kitchen half a lifetime ago. "Again?"

"Old habits," Russ said. "I mean, it could be worse, right? They could be assholes."

"You can be an asshole and not be a homophobe," Liam said. "I think. Lots of ways to be a dick."

Russ exhaled dramatically. "I don't think they're dicks. They just want me to sign in Winnipeg next season and they're pulling out all the stops to make it happen. If Gia makes me her kid's godfather or something, I'll know for sure."

Liam had conveniently forgotten that Russ's contract was coming due in July. Now he'd like to forget again. It didn't seem fair that they'd probably only get to play a handful of games together. "Why?"

"We're not religious."

Right. "Oh."

"Yeah. Anyway, so I was in my head about that a little, and I think Jonesy noticed and went running to the dads—"

"Aren't you older than they are?"

"Whose side are you on?" Russ rumbled, but he sounded a little amused, at least. "Anyway, Mo and Baller tried to give me therapy, and *that* led into some heavier stuff about what it means to come out of the closet. Or to still be in one. Which, I'm glad they care, and I know Baller gets it, but he's also...."

"Like... too good at being himself?" Liam tried.

"Yes!" Russ burst out. "I love the guy, but can he have his shit a little less together? He's disgustingly well-adjusted."

"I bet his parents hugged him *just the right amount*," Liam said darkly.

Russ howled. "God, you're so right. Oh man. I feel bad because my parents are mostly great, but…."

"Maybe he's secretly psychotic," said Liam, who loved his parents but considered them firmly middling. "Like…." He squished his feet between the arm of the couch and the seat cushion. "I don't know. He alphabetizes his pantry."

"Deeply disturbed," Russ agreed. "Only buys the orange juice with pulp in it."

"Sorts his books by color."

"Drinks decaf."

Liam muffled his giggles in a throw cushion before suggesting, "Irons his underwear."

"Wears socks during sex."

Oh, now Liam couldn't let that pass. "Hey, what's wrong with that? What if his feet get cold? I'm in bed with a guy, I want his full attention on me, not on the fact that he can't feel his toes."

"I don't think you have to worry," Russ said. "You're pretty good at keeping a man's attention."

Before Liam could divine whether that was a come-on, there was a clamor in the background. "Hey Russ! Did you get lost out here?"

Liam frowned. Had Russ gone out after the game? That wouldn't be unusual, even after a loss, but Liam couldn't place the voice.

Russ quieted, though the tone suggested he was actually speaking louder, his words coming through the speaker as though muffled, like he was holding the phone against his chest but not making much effort to conceal what he was saying. "Did you finish your victory drink already? Give a man some privacy. For all you know I'm peeing on the wall out here."

"Bullshit, I bet you haven't pissed on a wall since juniors. Fine, keep your secrets, but I'm ordering a mai tai."

Liam still didn't know who the guy was, but now he was burning with curiosity. Obviously Russ wasn't out on a date—like, you didn't hook up with a guy, then go on a date with someone else and call your hookup during it. Well, *some* guys might, but not Russ. "You make interesting friends."

"Past Russ made some choices about Team Canada bros for life." That narrowed down the field, but it wasn't Gabe either, and the implication of *victory drink* was someone from the other team.

Finally Liam put the pieces together. "Are you drinking with Max Lockhart?"

"We're in Miami at a locals kinda place. Technically Max Lockhart is drinking with me."

Had they slept together? Probably not, like, recently. Everything Liam knew was second- or third-hand, but Lockhart's rival-turned-fiancé seemed like the possessive type, and Lockhart struck Liam as the kind of guy who enjoyed that immensely. But they could've, years ago.

"Stop trying to figure out how to ask if I've fucked him." Russ sounded amused. "I gotta go buy this guy another drink, apparently. Maybe try to get him to shut the fuck up about his future husband. And you have to—" He cut himself off.

"I have to get a good night's sleep because I have to get up early again for another bus trip," Liam admitted. "Have fun with Lockhart."

"Not *that* much fun," Russ promised.

They hung up.

For a few minutes afterward, Liam stayed on his couch, still tucked into and around the cushions like an animal making a burrow. He didn't mean to get snippy with Russ, but he was glad he had. Even if talking on the phone was super 2001, it was better than texting. Who knew?

Finally Liam stretched on a yawn and peeled himself off the couch. He really did need to get some sleep.

NOVEMBER INCHED toward December, and Miami edged out of hurricane season without a major disaster. Russ would give it another month or two before he donated the items in his emergency kit to a food bank and replaced them with new ones for next season.

Meanwhile, he needed some distractions from the uptick in trade talks.

Erika had promised to keep him in the loop, and he knew she would. She was great at her job. But Russ still felt the possibilities hanging over his head, and he hated that. Instead of dwelling on it, he tried to concentrate on the things that made him happy, even if most of the time that boiled down to ordering dessert after dinner and occasionally binge-watching *Storage Wars* without feeling bad about it afterward.

Unfortunately, one of the side effects of not wanting to have awkward conversations with his family was that he had conspicuous holes in his schedule where that used to be. So when someone from front office contacted him about the celebration for his thousandth NHL game, he was grateful. It gave him something positive to focus on—something whose details he could, to some extent, control.

But he did still have to think about where he might end up next. About a week after his night out with Max, Erika emailed a list of potential teams with her noted pros and cons. Russ was mulling it over when Jonesy called. Like most of the team, Jonesy was a texter, so Russ picked up with a vague sense of alarm. "Hey."

"Hey." Jonesy's voice held a thread of tension. "You want to come over?"

Russ had been a hockey player and, maybe more importantly, an adult male, long enough to hear *I need to talk to somebody* in the question. "You want me to pick up a six-pack on my way?"

He'd enjoyed the Modelo at Baller's, so he grabbed that and then made his way to Jonesy's.

Jonesy lived inland far enough not to get too much of a breeze, and the weather was mild enough for jeans and a T-shirt. Russ let himself in through the back gate and found Jonesy in a Barcalounger by the pool, shades on. His hair had, for the first time in memory, actually deflated, which was worrisome since it wasn't even hot out. Whatever product he used could defeat helmet hair.

Russ put the beer in the cooler, sat on the adjacent chair, and put his phone in Do Not Disturb mode. "Okay. Who died?"

He immediately regretted it—he'd feel like such an asshole if someone actually passed away—but Jonesy only flipped him off and then held his hand out for a bottle, so Russ figured he was safe. Jonesy took a sip and said, "Columbus."

Russ swallowed the tightness in his throat and chased it with the beer. "Constantinople."

Jonesy snorted and fumbled his beer, which foamed over the top of the bottle and coated his hands. Cursing, he set it on the small side table and sat up straighter. "What the hell, man? Constantinople?"

"Thought we were saying random place names that started with C."

"God." Jonesy pressed the cold bottle against his forehead. "Fuck off." But his hair had perked up a little bit. Maybe it was just dehydrated. "I asked for a trade."

"Kinda figured." Without talking to Russ about it, which stung. He probably hadn't talked to Mo or Baller either. "Why? I'm going to assume it's not personal, since I'm here."

"Ah… family thing." He put the bottle down and rubbed a hand over an eyebrow. "Look, I don't want to tell the whole team, all right, because not all of them are going to get it and I don't want anyone demonizing Abby."

Abby was Jonesy's wife. She and their four-month-old son were the lights of his life, which was why no one gave him a hard time for ducking out of postgame celebrations. Russ sat up too and turned toward Jonesy. "Is she okay?"

"She's—yeah, she's all right. It's just a lot, you know? I'm gone all the time and we've got a kid now, and you know the first few months are hard…." He shrugged, and for the first time Russ took note of the dark circles under his eyes. Maybe *hard* was an understatement. If he hadn't been sleeping well, no wonder he'd let that infection go unchecked. "And we have a nanny, but that's not what she needs, you know? She needs her family. And they're in Columbus. So I talked to my agent and front office and said, I mean, obviously we don't have control, but if there was an opportunity…."

Jonesy had a full no-movement clause and a big contract. Under normal circumstances, trading him would be difficult. It just so happened that Columbus was one of those teams that had trouble meeting the cap floor—the minimum a team could spend on salary. Plenty of room to take him on.

It sucked to lose him, but he had a family and they had to come first.

But a quiet, selfish voice at the back of Russ's head whispered that with Jonesy's contract out of the way, the Caimans had room to keep him if they wanted.

He pushed those thoughts away. Jonesy didn't ask him here for Russ to get in his own feelings. "I'm sorry I didn't know Abby was having a tough time. We should've been there for you guys."

"Nah, man, she didn't want anyone to know." Jonesy gave him a wry look, and they both pretended he didn't sound a little choked up when he gestured around them and said, "I'm gonna miss the Florida weather, though."

Just like they both ignored the dampness in Russ's reply. "Wow, I'll miss you too, asshole."

They hugged it out because that was what brothers did, and then the baby monitor squawked. "That's my cue," Jonesy said. "You wanna meet the kid?"

Why did everyone want Russ to hold their babies all of a sudden? If the universe was trying to tell him something, it was barking up the wrong tree.

Tyson was cute, though, even red-faced and squalling. He was basically a little round blob except for his arms, which had muscle definition like he'd been working out next to his dad in utero or something.

"Abby used to say she was carrying an MMA fighter," Jonesy said when Russ commented. "But I dunno, I mean, he's already got hockey ass."

Russ winced as Tyson hit a new pitch and decibel. "I think he's leaning more toward a career in opera right now." He could definitely see why Abby wanted some help.

While Jonesy fed the baby, Russ took a look around the kitchen. He loaded and ran the dishwasher, then took out the garbage. After that, he peeked into the fridge, got another garbage bag, filled it, and ordered dinner to be delivered.

Then he poked his head into the nursery. Jonesy had Tyson in his lap and was staring down at him with abject adoration as Tyson waved his superbaby arms in delight.

Before he could help himself, Russ said, "You're a good dad."

Jonesy looked up sharply.

"And a good husband." As a team, Columbus was going nowhere fast, and Jonesy had to know that. But he had his priorities right.

"Fuck off," he said quietly. "Don't make me cry when I'm holding my kid."

Russ offered a half smile. "I don't have kids, but something tells me it won't be the last time." He shook his head. "We're gonna miss you around here."

"*All* the way off," Jonesy amended. He had actual tears on his face now.

Time for Russ to leave him to pull himself together. "I've gotta take off. Dinner's coming in about an hour, though; make sure to let them in."

Tyson squealed and managed to capture Jonesy's finger, which he immediately pulled into his mouth. Jonesy shook his head. "Thanks, man. I'll miss being your D-partner."

"Same."

"Oh—Russ. One more thing."

Russ paused in the doorway, one eyebrow raised.

Jonesy gave him a cheeky, if watery, grin. "It's Istanbul now."

Asshole.

For once, Russ turned off the radio in the car on the drive home. He wanted space to think. As he drummed his fingers on the wheel, he ran through the revelations of the past two weeks.

Not long ago, he would've sworn he was happy. He loved his job, his team, his house. He didn't like the uncertainty of his future, but everyone dealt with some level of that in their lives. He'd thought he was doing so well.

But watching Jonesy with his kid, listening to the way he talked about Abby… something about that resonated. Russ had always wanted to be a role model. His parents had raised him right. And being in the closet didn't jibe with that, not really. The thought of being in a relationship with someone and not being able to openly say that he cared about them turned his stomach.

Russ wouldn't want to be with someone who kept *him* a secret, after all. He wanted what Jonesy and Abby had—a relationship that meant putting his partner first, a shared home, someone to come home to and build a life with. Russ didn't know what that might look like for him, but right now it seemed more important to admit that he wanted it. Now, or soon, and not two years from now, or five years from now, or when he retired.

He wanted hockey *and* a love life. He deserved that. And he knew he could have it—other queer guys in the league made it work. If Russ was going to learn anything good from his current situation, it was that it was never too late. His grandfather had found love again. Russ could have that too.

The only trouble was finding someone to have it *with*.

He pulled the truck into his garage, grabbed his phone from the cupholder, and turned notifications back on.

As usual, the team group chat had a handful of new messages, but none of them would be important. Jonesy's trade wouldn't be announced to the team at large until tomorrow, when it became official. Russ's mom had sent him a text asking if they were on for their usual chat time tomorrow.

Russ left it on read.

And then he had a message from Liam—a blurry, badly lit photo of the interior of a bus. *Someone took their shoes off please come fine them I'm going to suffocate.*

Oof. Whoever committed that offense deserved far more than a fine. *See you and raise you. Got to smell jonesy's kid's dirty diaper today.*

Did u have to share a bus with it for 7 hours?

Seven hours? *Aren't there laws about that kind of thing?*

Liam replied with a crying emoji.

Russ was about to console him that he wouldn't be in the AHL forever, but he had to pause. What would Jonesy's trade mean for Liam? Would the team call him up full-time? Or would they trade Liam and another prospect for someone with more experience?

It probably depended on what management thought about the team's chances at a deep playoff run. The Caimans held the number two spot in the division, but the season wasn't even halfway over. Would management go all-in and try to win it this year? Making a decision like that this early was a gamble. Or would they take the extra cap space and try to keep more of the team's core together, and hope Liam could find a role on the team sooner rather than later?

What would Russ do if they did?

Fuck it. He was a grown man. He didn't *have* to plan for every contingency just because that was what he'd always done. Best not borrow trouble.

Or Trouble either, for that matter.

Hang in there, he said. Then he went inside to think up an excuse to text to his mother.

Caimans Recall Belanger From Thoroughbreds
By Rocky Sanderson

With the trade of veteran defenseman Riley Jones to Columbus, the Miami Caimans have recalled defenseman Liam Belanger.

Belanger, 22, has 17 points in 23 games with the Lexington Thoroughbreds. He made his NHL debut in Winnipeg, where he played 17 minutes and recorded one assist.

The cap-strapped Caimans get some relief by offloading Jones, whose $8m AAV deal now comes off the books and makes room for trade-deadline acquisitions or off-season signings. It also drastically alters the picture of the future of the Caimans' defensive corps. Veteran Russell Lyons is a pending free agent this summer. Word from the Caimans' front office is that the team is looking to go young and cheap on defense, and rumor has it that a contract for Lyons is not in the cards.

With talented younger skaters like Carl Bjorklund and Liam Belanger waiting for their shot, Miami's front office may just be willing to roll the dice on losing another veteran defenseman.

THIS TIME the Caimans sent Liam back to Lexington to pack before he joined the team in Miami.

He hadn't expected Jonesy to get traded. He'd been with the team forever, and of the two of them, Russ seemed the more likely candidate to offload. But Liam wasn't complaining. He was packing.

Workout clothes, jeans, polos, all his suits, three pairs of dress shoes, two pairs of sandals. Check. Bathing suit, sunglasses, sunscreen. Ten pairs of underwear. Three handfuls of socks, most of which had partners. Tablet and phone charger, check. Toiletries—toothbrush, toothpaste, bodywash, shampoo, conditioner. Check.

Forty-eight condoms and a new bottle of lube, which made him laugh when he added them to his suitcase.

The travel pillow he used on the bus would come in handy on the plane. Passport and wallet. Check.

He put his bags by the door and surveyed his apartment. It usually looked like a bomb had gone off, but now he'd packed all his personal things, so it was just vaguely dusty. The throw pillows were squished. His bedsheets lay in a heap on the floor because he'd rooted through his bed in order to find the lube.

It didn't look like Liam's apartment any more than any of the hotel rooms on the road did. Which, actually, that was gross. He should treat his space better.

He glanced at the clock on the microwave. He had twenty minutes before his Lyft would arrive to take him to the airport. So he could… do something about the state of his apartment. At the very least, he didn't want to come back to find his fridge full of mold and his cupboards full of mice or something. The fridge had been awful the first time he came back from a long road trip with the Thoroughbreds.

It took four minutes to get all his dirty dishes in the dishwasher and start it. Then another five to empty the fridge of perishables and ten to drag the trash down to the bins. That left him just enough time to go back upstairs, get his bags, and look around one last time.

It wasn't a bad apartment. Not exciting, but it was the first place that had really been *his*, even if he hadn't spent that much time here.

Even if he was hoping he'd never live here again.

Here goes nothing. He took two steps out the door and locked it behind him. That spot on the Caimans' roster was his to lose. No pressure.

GETTING CALLED up felt different this time. He was even on a different floor at the hotel, in a room with a kitchenette—something better suited to a long-term accommodation.

The Caimans had a home game tomorrow and then another road trip—Texas and Tennessee, followed by Tampa on the way home. Liam's sister might come to a game, since she had a conference in Nashville the weekend they played there. Of course, Liam might not dress.

But he shouldn't get ahead of himself. He needed to focus on the task in front of him.

At least he didn't have to worry about how he was getting to the game tomorrow since the hotel was walking distance from the arena.

He did, however, need to figure out how to get to practice today. The practice rink was out in the suburbs, and he didn't have time to rent a car. He could take another Lyft, if he made sure to order one that would have enough trunk space, or....

He thumbed open the team WhatsApp. *So hey... whats the best way to get to practice from the hotel if you don't have a car yet? Asking for a friend (the friend is me)*

With twenty-plus people in the chat, it didn't take long for an answer to come through. *Put on your big boy pants and ask someone for a ride.*

Liam flushed—duh, obviously, he could do that, except he hated that it made him feel like he was fourteen—but before he could get around to it, Baller jumped in.

You know better than to give him an opening like that.

Then Hughesy: *Can we not talk about his opening.*

At least Liam didn't feel like a baby anymore. He was saved from having to defend himself and his butthole when Russ said, *$100 each for sexual ha-rassment. Y'all need Jesus.*

Liam was pretty sure Russ was an atheist, but it was the thought that counted. Or something.

A minute later Mo volunteered to pick Liam up, so that solved his transportation problem. As for the problem brought on by some smartass making a comment about riding… he probably had just enough time to take care of that before Mo arrived.

What he didn't have time for was processing the doubts that crept in afterward. Would Russ treat him differently now that they'd had sex? So far the texting they'd done seemed to indicate no, or at least, not differently in a way Liam wouldn't like. But that was different from seeing Russ in person, hanging out with him as part of the team.

I don't kiss and tell, Russ had said. Between that and his enthusiastic fining, Liam didn't have to worry about him defaming Liam's character with completely true tales. He'd probably act like nothing ever happened.

Liam opted not to consider why that felt worse.

Forty minutes after his text, Mo pulled up in front of the hotel and Liam went down to meet him. Mo drove a sleek convertible with a flat black paint job, and today he had the top down and the music up. Liam grinned as he climbed in the passenger side. "Nice car."

Mo revved the engine and grinned back. "Thanks."

By the time they got to the rink, Liam looked like he'd gone three rounds with America's Next Top Hair Metal Stylist. He caught his reflection in the glass doors as they went inside and cast Mo an accusatory look, but Mo only clipped his sunglasses to the front of his T-shirt and said, "Come on, it was worth it. Besides, it's going under a helmet anyway."

"Yeah, but not before people *see* it." Hopefully they'd be early enough that he could avoid that.

No such luck—they pushed open the locker-room doors and the heckling began immediately.

"Well, well, would you look what the cat dragged in. Backwards, through a hedge." Baller held out his hand for a bro-five. "Good seeing you again."

"Aww, Mo, didn't anybody tell you not to put rookies in the dryer? Their heads shrink."

Liam slapped hands with Hughesy too, even as the veterans kept chirping. "Hey Yeti, don't look now, but I think your hairline's receding."

His timing was good—the room was quickly too busy razzing Yeti to pay attention to Liam, who'd moved on from Hughesy and now stood face to face with Russ.

Their eyes met and caught for what couldn't have been more than a few seconds, even if it seemed like some kind of time warp. In the past couple weeks, Liam had somehow forgotten the effect Russ had in person—tall and broad, radiating warmth, with the smoothest skin Liam had ever seen on a man. At some point since Liam last saw him, he'd decided to grow a beard, trimmed to just a few millimeters and with edges sharp as razorblades.

Liam needed a moment.

Fortunately his body responded automatically when Russ held out his hand for a slap, and then followed the natural progression in for a bro hug without input from his brain. Russ smelled good too—some kind of sandalwood or something. Was that his aftershave? Liam refused to believe he smelled like that naturally. It was new, so maybe it was beard oil.

After a too-short eternity, Russ released him. Liam mentally awarded himself a hundred points for not protesting.

Then Russ said, eyes dancing, "You know, I think I have a fro pick around somewhere. You could've asked for help."

I want to exfoliate my thighs with your beard. To his relief, that didn't bubble out his lips when he opened his mouth. Instead he said, "I dunno, couldn't even be bothered to give me a ride to practice. How'm I gonna expect you to help with my hair?"

He didn't realize until he said it that he was *disappointed*. Oh fuck, was he going to be, like, needy and shit now because they had sex once? Okay, technically twice. Liam was too proud to be that guy.

A furrow appeared between Russ's perfect eyebrows. Then he cocked his head. "So that thing about asking—"

Yeah, damn it, he had a point. Liam made a face at him and went to his stall to get dressed.

He'd proven he was worth giving a chance at a permanent spot on the roster. Now he had to prove he deserved to stay.

COACH PUT Carl on Russ's line for practice. Russ had plenty of experience and could adapt to playing

with just about anyone, but he wished he had Liam
as his partner instead.

On the other hand, not playing with him meant
he sometimes got to *watch* Liam make magic on the
ice—when he wasn't actively attempting to prevent
that magic from happening.

Russ normally thought of creativity as a trait of
forwards, not defensemen. But Liam found opportunities to turn defensive plays into offensive strategy.
When he forced a turnover, he knew exactly how to
get the puck into a scoring lane.

His time in the AHL had given him experience
and confidence. If Russ felt some kind of way when
Liam bodied Hughesy off the puck behind the net and
sent a slap shot down the ice to clear the zone, well,
it wasn't a real game, so it didn't matter. He should
probably settle down about it. Hughesy wasn't that
heavy anyway.

To finish off the practice, Coach had them run
man-on-man coverage defending breakaways. They
didn't usually use that defensive style—it didn't allow for the freedom to take advantage of mistakes
and it relied too heavily on even matchups that
weren't always possible. But if the team got caught
during an awkward changeover or something, they
might end up with one-on-one.

Which meant every skater did the same drill re-
gardless of their position, so you could end up with
a forward trying to stop a defenseman's shot, or two
forwards or defensemen against each other.

Russ loved drills like this because they were different and because they usually only lasted two or

so rounds before people started getting silly. On his first turn, he slipped past Hughesy only for Sparky to stonewall him. Then he had to defend while Liam took his shot.

That would've been fine. Russ's ego would survive if Liam got past him. But he didn't think it was fair that Baller and Mo pulled him aside before his turn and gestured down the ice, obviously offering suggestions.

"Hey! No cheating!"

Mo made a face at him. Baller winked and then patted Liam on the shoulder.

Russ narrowed his eyes, loosened his stance, and focused on his opponent.

Liam was a beautiful skater. His body moved naturally on ice, and that economy of movement made it difficult to guess what he'd do next. Russ let himself ease slowly back toward the net as he waited for the break—at some point Liam would have to decide to go left or right to try to get around Russ.

Instead, Liam rushed straight toward him, well within Russ's reach. It was so unorthodox Russ lost a fraction of a second's reaction time to his surprise, and only pulled his stick in close to knock at the puck when Liam was practically on top of him.

The puck kicked off to the right, but Russ had only gotten a piece of it—the danger wasn't over yet. Liam raced after to collect it, and Russ chased him into the corner and pinned him to the boards. "You didn't really think that would work."

Liam dug at the puck, but Russ had trapped it against the side with his skate. "Fuck off. It almost work."

Maybe, but Russ didn't have to admit it out loud. He flattened Liam a little more, ignoring the gut punch familiarity of the scent of his sweat, and kicked the puck backward to Sparky as Liam *oof*ed out a breath.

"Horseshoes and hand grenades," Russ said sweetly. He swatted Liam's ass and started back toward the line.

But then he stopped. Mo would attack Liam next, and turnabout was fair play, right? He caught Mo and Baller's laughing faces and turned around to give Liam some advice.

"He'll either try to make you look stupid by flipping the puck over your stick, or he'll break wide to your right looking for the shot from the circle. If you fake a charge, he'll probably break early."

"I thought you said no cheating!" Baller yelled down the ice.

"I'm educating my rookie!" Russ shouted back without breaking eye contact with Liam. He lowered his voice again. "Just a fake, all right? Be ready to hang back and go right."

"You're not trying to make me look dumb?" Liam scrutinized his face.

"Why would I do that?"

"I don't know. Rookie hazing?"

Russ didn't put up with rookie hazing, at least not the kind that might embarrass them skills-wise. The last thing they needed was their players having a crisis of confidence midgame. "I'd have to fine myself." He tapped his stick on Liam's shins. "You got this." Unless Mo anticipated his advice, but Russ doubted it. If Russ *hadn't* stopped to offer a suggestion, Mo would've gone along the boards and tried to get around Liam with a quick one-eighty—Mo could turn on a dime.

Sure enough, Liam feinted forward and Mo tried to go wide to the top of the circle. But Liam was already shadowing him, lightning-quick. He shot his stick out for a poke check Mo didn't see coming, and suddenly Liam had the puck and nothing but clear ice between him and the net on the other side of the rink.

Do it, Russ thought, and grinned when the puck hit the back of the net. He whistled. "Attaboy, Trouble."

Liam bowed to a smattering of applause, but when everyone else's attention shifted away from him, Russ caught him looking at him speculatively.

He should probably try to set things right. Whatever else happened, Liam was still his rookie and likely to be his teammate for the foreseeable future. Earlier in the locker room he'd gotten the definite impression that Liam was upset Russ hadn't offered to drive him to practice.

Maybe he should've. It would've given them a chance to talk before they had to interact with the team.

But that could get uncomfortable. Russ had wanted a few more minutes to live in the illusion that he could have sex with his teammate with no consequences.

He'd spent a lot of his life regretting not doing things he wanted. It just figured that he'd also have regrets about the things he had done. Except *regret* wasn't the right word, given how many thoughts Russ was having about doing it again.

Practice finished. Time was running out on Russ's opportunity to offer Liam a ride—an actual, non-euphemistic ride, during which they could talk.

"Hey." He caught Liam as they filed down the tunnel toward the locker room. "Give you a lift back?"

Liam glanced at Mo, who was three steps ahead of them, and then said, "Not a ride?"

"A lift," Russ reiterated wryly. He'd brought this on himself. He deserved it.

Liam debated for a moment. "Fine."

Russ showered quickly, the skin on the back of his neck prickling like someone was watching him. He half expected to turn his head and see Mo giving him the side-eye or Baller miming a blow job. Neither happened.

The walk out to the truck was awkward anyway. It was a cool day for Miami, overcast, which meant Russ had no excuse to put on his sunglasses. He sucked it up and went without. "You're at the Marriott again, right?"

"Yeah."

Great. He unlocked the truck. They got in.

Awkward.

Russ started the truck and put it in Reverse. He still hadn't come up with a conversation opener. He should've stuck to texting.

Finally Liam blurted, "Are you going to say 'it's not you, it's me'?"

Russ startled and slammed on the brakes before turning to glare at Liam.

Liam kept a straight face for all of three seconds before one of their teammates honked—Russ was blocking their exit—and then he snickered.

This damn kid's nickname had become a self-fulfilling prophecy. Russ put the truck in Drive and exited the parking lot. "I wasn't going to lead with that." Even if it was sort of the point.

"What, you were going to butter me up first?" Russ couldn't read his tone, and traffic was heavy; he couldn't afford to look over.

"It's not either one of us," he said instead. "You're going to be with the team for a while, it looks like. We should keep things professional."

"Good thing we got all that sexual tension out of the way already."

Russ snorted. They'd hit a stop light, so he took the chance to glance over. Liam was smiling a little, like he was daring Russ to tell him he was wrong.

He was definitely wrong, and the look he was giving Russ, with his crooked little dare-you grin and eyes full of mischief, was designed to show it. "Good thing," Russ agreed, heavy on the sarcasm, and Liam laughed.

Well, that was the worst part over. Now for the rest. "Mo and Baller know we slept together."

The temperature in the cab dropped a few degrees. "Oh?" Yeah, Liam was not impressed. Russ didn't blame him. He hadn't wanted this for the kid either.

"I told you I don't kiss and tell." He made the turn onto the next street. "Mine was the last car left in the players' lot the next morning. They only act stupid. They put two and two together."

"Oh." Now Liam sounded sheepish. "I could have woke you up, eh?"

Russ shrugged. "It might not have mattered. Depends when they left that night." He drummed his fingers on the wheel. "They're not going to say anything to anyone else. Or give you grief about it."

"You must have something good on Baller if you can make him shut up."

Yeah, right. "There is nothing to get on Baller. He is an open book. Sometimes he reads himself out loud." Russ shook his head. "But he's not a dick."

"He's *kind* of a dick," Liam pointed out after a beat.

Russ grinned at the windshield. "But he's not mean about it. Just obnoxious."

"There was a guy on my college team who don't use headphones to listen to videos on the bus."

Every day Russ found a new reason to be glad he hadn't gone to college. "And nobody beat his face in?"

"He was the goalie."

Goalie weirdness could only be accepted and not fucked with. "Brutal."

"At least I can use my own headphones. It was better than smelling Miller's socks. Oh!" Russ put his blinker on to pull into the hotel. "I forgot to tell you. Speaking of socks."

Russ slowed the truck to a stop and glanced over. "Speaking of *socks*?" What kind of subject change…?

Liam ran a hand through his hair. "Um, I accidentally took yours when I left that morning. Sorry."

"I wondered what happened to those." Russ had walked to his car in shoes with bare feet. "Now you tell me they were some kind of kinky sex trophy?"

"Oh my God!" Liam yelped. "I packed in the dark so I don't wake you up. It was an accident. You asshole."

Winding him up was too much fun. "Uh-huh. Sure. And why haven't you mentioned it before now?" Russ shook his head. "Sock-related sex crimes."

"Fuck off," Liam laughed. "If you're so worried about your socks, come up and get them. I brought them to give back to you."

Russ pulled into the parking lot. "I will. Gotta make sure you haven't defiled their virtue."

"There are two of us in this truck. Only one of us makes socks into a sex thing."

They got out, and Russ locked the truck as they walked into the hotel. "You better have washed them."

Liam pressed the button for the elevator. "No, they still smell like your feet," he deadpanned. "That's why I took them."

Fucker. Russ shouldered him into the car. "I knew it. Deviant. You're nasty."

Liam elbowed him in the gut and stabbed the button for the tenth floor. "If you don't want to know, don't ask."

The doors closed. Russ should put some distance between them; they were still standing close enough that their elbows brushed.

The last time they'd been in this elevator together had gone a little differently.

Russ didn't move. Liam didn't either.

The doors opened, and Liam led the way down the hall. Russ took the opportunity to get his perspective back. When he got too close to Liam, the only thing he could think about was getting closer still.

Besides, hanging back gave him a nice view. Russ shouldn't touch, but that didn't mean he couldn't *look*.

Although Liam had only checked in that morning, you wouldn't know it from his hotel room. His suitcase was open on the luggage rack, items spilling out onto the floor and scattered on every surface. And the bedclothes were mussed.

Russ pulled his eyes away from the bottle of lube on the side table. "Wow. Are you sure you just got here this morning?"

Liam flipped him off and dug in the suitcase with his other hand. "Shut up or help me look."

If Liam didn't care about Russ digging through his stuff, Russ didn't either. And the faster he got out of here, the better. He was already having flashbacks to their night together. Even the bedspread pattern was the same.

Looking at the bed—or the night table and the lube sitting on it, bold as anything—was probably more dangerous than pawing through Liam's

suitcase, which from the look of it had been organized using the same system Liam had used to unpack it.

This was dumb. Russ could just buy new socks.
Instead—

He pushed aside a pair of underwear and revealed Liam's giant box of condoms just as Liam
made a triumphant sound. "Ha—found them!" He
turned to Russ, holding his trophy. "One pair of jerk-
off socks—"

Russ's hand had picked up the box without input
from his brain. His eyes met Liam's.

Liam's eyes went to the condoms.

It was still heavy, Russ's brain supplied. Part of
him wanted to open it and see how many were left.

The bigger part of him wanted to open it and get
to work using the rest.

Liam licked his lips. "So about that sexual
tension—"

"Maybe we should—"

They both stopped. The air in the room grew
thick.

Fuck, this was so stupid. Russ found himself
saying, "I mean, just to make sure it's gone—"

Liam kissed him, fast, furious, desperate. Russ
scored his teeth over Liam's lip. Liam gasped into
his mouth.

Russ dragged himself away, chest heaving. Liam's flush spread from his cheekbones to the neck
of his stretched-out T-shirt. His dick tented the front
of his shorts.

Russ doubted he looked much different. Could Liam see the way Russ's pulse was beating too fast in his throat? Were his pupils as wide as Liam's?

Liam's gaze dropped to Russ's crotch.

"Fuck it," Russ said, and the next second they were pulling off their shirts before crashing together, tumbling toward the bed.

Just one more time. Then they'd have it out of their systems for good.

LIAM LOVED playing in the NHL.

He loved the fans and the bright lights and the thrill of sharing the ice with the best players in the world.

He also—and this could not be overstated—loved Russ's cock.

The AHL had been great for him. Without Mathieu to bully him into making leg day his new religion and plenty of ice time to whip his game into shape, Liam wouldn't be here. But getting laid made his life *so much better*. He should convince Russ that preemptively taking care of any sexual tension was the way to maintain their professional relationship.

Based on the enthusiasm Russ had shown sucking his dick yesterday, Liam didn't think he'd have trouble talking him around.

Probably he wouldn't have to talk very much at all. He might have to invest in some soothing lotion for his thighs, though. Liam's life was very hard.

When he stepped out onto home ice in his Caimans gear for the first time, he felt more alive than ever. Russ had said a rookie lap—the first loop of the ice that teams usually had a first-time player do by himself—didn't count as hazing, but even if it did, Liam wouldn't have minded. He hadn't gotten this far in hockey because he hated attention.

He didn't crack the starting lineup, but he was playing on the team's second defensive line in his second-ever professional game, after sleeping with Russ for the second time.

So yeah, he skated the hell out of that warm-up lap. He soaked in the cheers from the fans as the organist played a punk-distorted version of "Crocodile Rock."

He stood by the bench for the anthem, eyes on the pint-size singer who filled the building to the rafters with her voice, and let himself get goose bumps. It wasn't his anthem, but it *was* his barn now. His team. His place.

Then the puck dropped and the game was on.

By midway through the first period, Liam could tell the game would be a slog. The visiting Fuel were playing the second half of a road back-to-back, having been in Tampa the night before.

The Caimans had no excuse; they were sinking to the level of their competition. They didn't have to stay sharp to keep the Fuel from scoring when the Fuel were dull and slow. The puck cycled in and out of the offensive zones, turnover after turnover with barely a shot on goal to show for it. Liam winced when Russ and Carl's failed pass resulted in yet another loss of possession for the Caimans. Only the fact that the Fuel's forwards made the same mistake saved the team from disaster.

Behind the bench, Coach paced back and forth, his temper growing noticeably shorter. Liam couldn't blame him.

Finally, late in the second period, Liam corralled a wild bounce at the blue line. He didn't have a passing lane open. The team had been out of position all night. In the back of his head, he could hear every coach he'd ever had, from Timbits league up to today, telling him to take his time. But after the shit-show of the day, his trigger finger was itchy.

He blasted a shot at the net and almost fell over when it went in.

The stands erupted in cheers. A half second later Liam crashed into the boards, propelled by 170 pounds of screaming Hughesy. Yeti, Mo, and Baller followed, quieter and with less enthusiasm, which Liam's spine was grateful for.

"What a rocket!" Hughesy whooped.

Mo knocked his helmet against Liam's. "Making the rest of us look bad."

Liam's grin felt like it could split his face open. Maybe now the game would break—they could get some momentum and start putting more shots on goal.

And then the linesman blew his whistle and announced the goal was under review for being offside.

Liam chewed his mouthguard while the replay went up on the jumbotron.

Fuck, he hadn't been aware of his footing. He'd skated backward farther than he thought while chasing the puck.

No goal.

If a goal might have energized the team, this call did the opposite. Liam felt worse about the game than he had before the shot.

The third period ended with a 1–1 tie, both goals ugly accidents that had no business ending up in the net. If Liam had paid money to watch this game, he'd want a refund.

Overtime ended without resolving anything. Liam's legs ached from chasing the puck all over the ice, which was what happened when you turned the puck over every two goddamn seconds. He hoped he didn't have to attempt a shootout, because he already knew how that would go. He'd take three strides and the puck would go straight into the goalie's glove.

Fortunately it didn't get that desperate. Mo and Baller both scored in the shootout to only one goal for the Fuel, so they didn't have to go past three rounds.

"Thank fuck," Coach muttered behind the bench. "Trouble, Mo, you've got media tonight. Everybody else hit the showers. And for the love of God, pray you don't play like this in Nashville."

RUSS SHOWERED off the bad game. They happened a few times a year, and he wouldn't get anything out of stewing over it. At least he didn't have to talk to the press today.

Between their flight to Nashville tomorrow and their generally poor showing, no one was going out tonight.

By the time Mo and Liam finished with media, half the team had left. Russ had gotten sucked into a conversation about smoking meat—amazingly not a euphemism—with Baller, so he was only half dressed when they walked in.

"Oh fuck," Baller interrupted himself, snapping his head up. "I gotta get home so I can record this week's bedtime stories for the kiddo."

Russ knew better than to ask why he had to rush home for that, instead of recording them on the road; there was probably a convoluted answer that would come packaged with an overshare about Baller's sex life, like "We almost traumatized our toddler once so now we only use the Dedicated Kid iPad with her." Sometimes it shocked him that he'd only been friends with the guy for a few months and knew so much about his personal life.

Then again, Baller had a lot of personal life, and he was vocal about it. If he'd been married to a woman, Mo would've called him a wife guy—he might talk shit about Gabe's golf habit, but even that came out flavored with adoration. He was equally wild about their kid. He even seemed to enjoy spending time with his in-laws. Russ wondered if the guy ever had a bad time or if he'd just gotten lucky across the board.

It wasn't that Russ was jealous. Jealousy was an ugly emotion. But lately when he looked at Baller and Gabe and their life, he felt a tug deep in his chest, like a muscle that had come loose and was looking for something to attach to.

Russ had been so lost in thought that the locker room had emptied around him without him noticing. Christ, maybe he needed to get laid more if he spaced out like this thinking about *settling down*. This kind of thing didn't happen to guys who were getting their dick wet on the regular.

He got up from the bench and reached for his pants—he'd sat down partway into getting dressed—only to realize the shower was still running.

Was Mo still in there, getting all pruney as some kind of penance for their game? Russ had caught him like that once or twice before, but usually when something had gone more catastrophically wrong, with an injury or a lost playoff game. Something higher stakes than this.

Russ put the pants down and shoved on his slides before walking back into the showers.

It wasn't Mo standing under the steaming spray, half drowning himself to wash away the sting of the loss.

It was Liam.

Fuck, of course it was—getting your first professional goal in a game like that only to have it taken away minutes later, and then giving an interview about it. Russ was lucky it was water he was wallowing in and not a bottle of whatever cheap bottom-shelf liquor Quebecois youth poured themselves into when things went to shit. Everclear? Boxed wine? In Winnipeg during Russ's youth, it had been Wild Turkey.

His stomach still turned at the thought, a decade and a half later.

"Hey, Trouble, are you—"

Okay, Russ meant to finish. But his legs had carried him around the chest-height half wall, and now instead of just the top of Liam's back, he could see all of him, every lean muscle glistening under the caress of the spray as he ran his hands back through his hair.

Liam turned around, eyes closed, and found something more interesting to wrap his fingers around.

And then the fact that someone had spoken to him registered, his eyes opened, and he looked at Russ in a combination of embarrassment and invitation.

Suddenly Russ was glad he hadn't finished getting dressed. He watched him with want curling in his stomach and cataloged all the ways he could take him apart.

A moment later he had Liam's mouth under his, his wet skin against Russ's. Liam stumbled back against the wall, hissing when his shoulders touched the cool tile.

Russ pushed his thigh between Liam's and wrapped his hand around Liam's cock. Even in the water, Russ could tell he was leaking, the slick of his precome sliding under Russ's thumb when he rubbed a circle over the head.

Liam moaned and tried to deepen the kiss, but Russ pulled back, teasing the seam of his lips with his tongue the way he was teasing Liam's cock—never enough pressure to satisfy, just enough to keep him hungry for more. He kept his own dick pressed tightly between their bodies so Liam couldn't rush him.

Was this the stupidest thing he'd ever done? Maybe. But it felt incredible, and Russ intended to savor every second.

"Oh God," Liam gasped when Russ raised his left hand to pluck at a nipple. The sensitive flesh peaked and pebbled in the damp air. "Why won't you fucking—*touch me*?"

"I am touching you," Russ murmured. To prove his point, he slid his hand down and fondled Liam's balls before trailing his fingertips up his cock again.

A trail of French invective dripped from Liam's lips. Russ recognized some of it. Liam had a dirty mouth. He groaned and shoved Russ's boxers down while Russ teased him.

"Fuck," Liam gasped. He bucked his hips, pushing up against Russ's weight as though it might convince Russ to tighten his grip and stroke him off. His cock had leaked so much between them that their stomachs were slippery with it. "Calisse, tabarnak, t'encule-moi."

Oh, Russ knew that one. "Not in the locker room." Although damn if the idea of fucking Liam there didn't make him hot—knowing Liam would think about it every game, every practice, every intermission.

Liam tilted his head back against the wall and scrabbled at the tile like he thought his legs might go out from under him. "Please. I need to come."

Good enough. Russ tightened his hand just enough and leaned down until their lips brushed again. "So come," he breathed into Liam's mouth.

Liam's body shook as he strained to get what he needed. Russ took pity on him and kissed him again, barely more pressure than he was using on his cock. With his other hand he pressed up on the sensitive skin behind Liam's balls, the firmest touch he'd used on Liam all night.

Liam made a broken, gasping, wretched moan into Russ's mouth, and then his legs really *did* give out, and he sagged into Russ's arms as he came. Russ tightened his grip to stroke him through it as his chest heaved and he chanted, "MonDieucalisseputain*fuck*."

Finally, when the twitching seemed more uncomfortable than anything, Russ stopped. He brushed his nose against Liam's. "Told you I could handle it."

"You're *mean*," Liam managed after several seconds of ragged breathing. He sounded impressed.

Russ held his hand up to the spray to wash off Liam's come. "Judging by the evidence, you liked it."

Liam wet his lips. His lust-blown eyes followed the last drops as they slithered down Russ's wrist to his elbow. "It was all right," he rasped, laced with mischief.

Then he knelt between Russ's feet and put his mouth on Russ's dick.

Russ should stop him. Actually Russ shouldn't have come in here in the first place, and he definitely shouldn't have gotten close enough to Liam to touch. But if jerking him off had been *bad*, this was unforgivable—fucking his cock into his rookie's mouth in the team shower after a game, where anyone could walk in. Russ stayed as quiet as he could, turned to face the door to the locker room in the impossible hope that he'd have the time and mental fortitude to pull Liam off his dick before anyone could come around the half wall and see him.

At least Liam's noises were barely audible over the sound of the water… and muffled by Russ's cock. He blinked wet eyelashes up at Russ and swallowed around him like he was making a point, and Russ cursed and fisted a hand in his hair, holding him down on his dick as he came.

Fuck, that tile had to be hell on his knees, which were worth way too much to be treating like this. Russ braced himself on the wall and hauled Liam to his feet.

"See?" Liam wiped the corner of his mouth, but the smirk stayed firmly in place. "That's how you be nice to someone."

Russ nudged him toward the door. "I'll keep that in mind. And now it's my turn to be nice to you by telling you to go home and get some sleep." He paused and looked down at the red circles on Liam's patellas. "And maybe ice your knees."

"Maybe I just crawl into the ice machine." Liam rolled his shoulder as they went back to the locker room, and for the first time Russ noticed the bruise running down his side.

Russ hissed. "That from tonight?"

Liam craned his neck to look over his shoulder and down his side, which was darkening from pink-red to light purple. "Yeah. Kipriyanov got me in a corner."

Russ had given and received worse bruises. He'd seen teammates with livid blue-black lines from an opponent getting a grip on their pads and digging the edges in, hidden in a corner. Hockey was a contact sport; bruises were part of the game.

So he had no excuse for the flush of anger that went through him at the thought of someone leaving a mark like that on Liam. Russ had a worse bruise from a game last week.

But stranger still than the desire to butt-end Kipriyanov next time they were in Indy was the urge that followed on its heels—to take Liam home with him, make him a late second dinner, and rub arnica gel on his side before putting him to bed.

To *sleep*.

And now the realization was dawning on him, as they dried off and dressed—thank God Russ always had a spare pair of underwear in his bag—that he wanted to sit close enough to Liam to touch him.

After a few weeks of letting himself do what he wanted, Russ found it difficult to go back to rigid self-denial. He settled for sitting in the corner next to Liam, close enough that he could feel the heat from Liam's knee radiating into him without their skin touching.

What had he done? Maybe his original MO had flaws, but it kept him from putting his dick in a teammate. It kept him from doing crazy things like getting off in his workplace.

It kept him from wanting to settle down with someone totally unsuitable.

He needed to get out of here. More specifically, he needed to go home and get his head right. Figure out how to get himself out of whatever trouble he'd gotten into—damn it—without making things awkward with Liam.

"You wanna walk me home?" Liam asked a moment later with a suggestive lift of his eyebrows.

Yeah, Russ thought, followed by *fuck*. "Better not. Still have to pack."

Liam mock gasped, one end of his tie in each hand. "And here I thought you were the responsible one."

"I'm in a rebellious phase." One that he needed to get over. Russ shrugged into his jacket and tucked his own tie into his pocket. "See you tomorrow."

Hopefully by then Russ would have an idea how to handle this.

IT DIDN'T matter how much sleep Liam got. He was never going to be a morning person. But he had been blessed with the ability to catch five minutes of sleep just about anywhere, including in his car before practice and in crowded airport terminals—not that he had to deal with many of those these days since the team chartered a private plane.

Of course, the ability wasn't always a blessing.

A sharp elbow poked him in his bruised ribs. "Dude, wake up. You're drooling on me."

Liam flinched and sat up so quickly his neck twinged. His chin was wet too, so Hughesy hadn't been exaggerating. He wiped a hand over his face and grimaced. "Sorry."

"S'okay." He looked at the damp spot on his shoulder and then shrugged it. "Uh, so like, don't take this the wrong way, but I've got some cortisone cream in my bag if you want to use it."

Did cortisone cream prevent drooling? "Uh?" Liam's brain hadn't woken up all the way.

Hughesy pointedly rubbed his thumb over his jaw line. When Liam automatically raised his hand to do the same, he got it.

Russ's beard had felt amazing on his skin last night, but this morning his skin was objecting with raised bumps that were probably red and irritated-looking. A little sore too.

"Sometimes I forget I can't use, like, anybody else's soap," Hughesy said. "'Cause my skin will try to peel off my body." He paused for what felt like an unnaturally long time until Liam realized Hughesy was giving him the opportunity to claim he also had bad reactions to cleansing products. "So I always have cortisone, in case."

That was sweet of him. "Thanks, man, yeah, I should probably take care of that." *Before someone else on this team puts Russ's beard and my beard burn together.*

Hughesy dug the tube out of his carry-on, and Liam smeared cream on his face, then used the selfie camera on his phone to make sure he'd rubbed everything in. "Thanks again."

"It's cool." He zipped the pocket back up, then looked over, a little shyly. "Us new guys have to stick together."

Liam didn't hate that idea, especially if Hughesy was going to save him from embarrassing himself. "Exactly. And I gotta at least try to look respectable tomorrow."

"I dunno," Hughesy said dubiously. "I don't think I have enough cortisone for that."

Liam shoulder-checked him, but he was grinning. He'd never had a *little* brother. This year was just full of new experiences. "Asshole."

"Nah, you love me." Hughesy mugged. "You got someone important coming to tomorrow's game? Although I guess not if you've got, you know." He drew a wide circle around his own mouth, like someone applying clown makeup. Shit, so he did know it was beard burn. Liam's ears went hot.

"Shut up. My sister, yeah. She's in town for work." *She'd* even texted *him* to ask if he wanted to meet up before the game, because she was going to be in Nashville and wanted to support him. Liam was still bewildered that he hadn't had to ask.

"What's she do?"

Today, a certified professional athlete, Liam felt proud instead of like the underachieving younger sibling when he said, "She's a rocket scientist."

Hughesy's eyes widened. "Wait, for real? Dude. That's sick. Like, not a lot of people have cooler jobs than us. Imagine if you could buy a ticket to *her* work for a day."

Oh yeah, a whole evening spent watching someone do math. "She doesn't actually get to *go* into space," he pointed out.

Hughesy's face fell. "Oh." Then he perked up again. "Is she hot?"

"Gross. First of all she's like forty years old—"

Bernadette was thirty-seven, but she wasn't here to defend herself.

"That's cool! Like, a cougar, right?"

In the row behind them, one of the team's veterans made an outraged noise.

"She's a lesbian," Liam said, furiously grateful for that fact. "I think she's bringing her girlfriend."

"Sick! Is *she* an astronaut?"

"I have no idea." They hadn't been dating that long, and Bernadette didn't bring her love life into the family group chat much. Liam didn't blame her. His mom had two settings—*I'm just not sure they're right for you* and *they're not going to wait around forever.* In her eyes, only her darling Bastian had married at an appropriately young age, and the other three were shaming her with their lack of commitment.

Liam couldn't speak for Bernadette or Marie-Jean, but he was enjoying extremely uncommitted sex, even if he'd only had it with one guy recently. But that one guy was Russ, so that was fine. Was a random hookup going to be funnier, better in bed, or cooler about Liam's idiosyncrasies? Not likely.

His conversation with Hughesy lasted until the plane landed, and then Mo abducted Hughesy—"Secret forward things, Trouble, you wouldn't understand"—and dragged him to the back of the bus with the cool kids. Liam rolled his eyes and found a seat in the middle section, took his phone out of airplane mode, and blinked in surprise when he saw he had a message from Marie-Jean as well as one from Bernadette.

They both wanted to know if he'd heard from Bastian, which was weird since Bastian barely liked him. Liam responded that he hadn't and added *???*

Never mind, Marie-Jean replied.

Can't talk now, in a conference, said Bernadette.

Typical older siblings closing ranks. He'd get information out of her later. Maybe.

RUSS COULD admit to himself that he'd made a few mistakes lately. If the first one was sleeping with Liam, so were the second and third.

Now he was facing down a fourth mistake—convincing himself a relationship was possible and also a good idea.

All things considered, it was probably best if he put some distance between them while he hit the reset button on his brain, before that potential mistake became a reality. Even if Russ's days with the team weren't numbered, Liam was twenty-two—not the stage of his life where he was looking for a life partner. Not if the jumbo box of condoms was any indication.

So Russ sat with Mo and Baller at breakfast, and only stewed a little when he noticed Liam had passed out on Sparky's shoulder at the next table.

That night when they walked into Nashville's arena, a camera crew caught Liam reuniting with his sister. Russ tried to hurry by—on top of avoiding Liam, he knew the older-sibling side-eye and would prefer to escape that too, even if Bernadette had no reason to suspect him of defiling her kid brother— but Liam grabbed his sleeve. "Russ, hey." He dimpled. Russ should fine him for that. It was playing dirty. "This is my sister Bernadette and her friend Lakshmi."

It would be rude to keep walking now, so Russ stopped and shook hands with both of them. "Nice to meet you. Thanks for coming out." Bernadette had the same pale skin, freckles, and short, wavy brown hair Liam did. Her date—Russ didn't know if she was married or if this was a work colleague—wore a Nashville jersey and had her long, shiny dark hair in a braid. He paused and gave Lakshmi a wry smile. "Even if you didn't get the memo about the dress code."

Bernadette had the same dimple as Liam too, but on the other side. "She grew up here. I guess hockey fandom is genetic?"

Russ wondered if the NHL would consider offering courses in making small talk when you wanted to run away. "Are you staying in Nashville after the game?"

"Yeah, we don't leave until tomorrow afternoon."

Liam perked up. "You want to come out for drinks after?"

Bernadette and Lakshmi agreed to consider it, and then Liam and Russ had to go get ready for the game and the two women walked off arm in arm. "She still has to teach me about offsides," Bernadette laughed. "Bonne chance, boys!"

Russ didn't know if luck figured into it.

Nashville was rested and the Caimans were tired. From his perspective, it wasn't a great game for Bernadette's first taste of her brother's career. Then again, the fact that neither team got a lot of scoring chances meant that defense was doing its job.

Albeit, in tonight's case, in a somewhat lackluster fashion.

Despite multiple practices, Russ could not get any chemistry going with Carl. If there were two possible strategies to take, Russ took one and Carl took the other. They were professionals, and tonight at least that meant they could make their passes connect, but in terms of generating offensive opportunities, they were dead in the water.

The Caimans lost in the final minute of overtime, 2–1, on a flukey bounce Russ had a hard time feeling sad about. Sometimes weird shit happened. At least they'd gotten a point and the game ended before it went to a shootout.

A dumb loss in a poor game was usually reason enough for everyone to keep to themselves in the locker room, and Russ was no exception. Tonight it provided the perfect cover for going back to his room without socializing with his rookie.

There was just one problem with that plan—his weakness for Liam's sad puppy-dog eyes. Liam's freckled, dimply face should smile all the time. Gloomy Liam was against the natural order.

"Couldn't pull off the win," he mumbled to his knees, quiet enough that only Russ could hear.

By this time he had to be used to losses. The Thoroughbreds had played some real stinkers this year. Losing in front of your family hit different, though, especially if they'd traveled a long way to see you. Double for Liam, who already felt over-shadowed by his siblings' accomplishments.

Russ couldn't leave him to his own devices. He nudged Liam in the side. "You can still go out with your sister. Maybe just the hotel bar, so it's low-key? You wouldn't be able to talk at a club anyway."

That cheered him up a little. "Yeah, that's a good idea maybe." He turned those puppy-dog eyes on Russ. "Will you come? Keep me from being a third wheel."

Trying to cheer Liam up had definitely been a mistake, because Russ could not say no to that face. He cursed himself as he agreed.

At least the hotel bar was a good option, as Bernadette and Lakshmi's conference was at the same hotel the team was staying at. Liam even managed to keep his eyelids open most of the time.

Lakshmi turned out to be Bernadette's girlfriend, though they were keeping it quiet at work for now.

"Mostly because everyone we know will say 'I told you so.'" Lakshmi smiled at Bernadette, then at their hands, which were linked on the tabletop.

Something half-dead panged in Russ's chest. But unlike the other times he'd felt it, this time it didn't go away when he shoved it down. Maybe it had never gone away. Maybe he'd just gotten better at pretending he didn't feel it.

Next to him, Liam shifted and their knees brushed under the table. That didn't help either. "Have you told Mom and Dad?"

Bernadette and Lakshmi exchanged glances. "Not yet," Bernadette said after a moment. "They've got a lot on their plate right now."

"Does this have something to do with why you asked if I talk to Bastian? Because, like, we never talk."

Another exchanged look. Suddenly *Russ* felt like a third wheel. He cleared his throat and met Lakshmi's eyes. "You want to come with me to get another round? I could use an extra set of hands."

Fortunately Lakshmi picked up what he was putting down. "Sure."

They waited at the bar for the bartender to notice them, not in any particular hurry. Lakshmi sat on one of the stools and turned toward Russ. "So. He's really okay here? I know things aren't what they used to be, but Bernadette worries." When Russ didn't catch on, she raised her eyebrows. "About Liam being gay in pro sports?"

Right, because Lakshmi had no idea Russ was gay. Because most of the world thought he was straight. "Not everyone is as awesome as we are, but yeah, he's as safe as he can be in a game where people regularly try to take your head off." The silence stretched for a moment while they waited for the bartender to help a customer at the other end of the counter. Russ felt compelled to fill it. "I didn't get the impression they were that close."

"It's complicated, I think. She's fifteen years older than he is. They barely lived together growing up, you know?" She drummed her fingertips on the bar. "Does he talk about her much?"

Russ knew a fishing expedition when he heard one. He wouldn't betray Liam's trust, even if he believed Lakshmi had good intentions. "No comment."

She lifted an elegant shoulder and smiled. "I had to try."

"But… he was really happy she decided to come to the game."

Lakshmi's smile widened. "We're pretty happy too."

Russ could see that. She and Bernadette exuded a warmth with each other that the people around them could feel. It was like watching someone eat your favorite meal, steaming hot and mouth-wateringly fragrant, while you sat starving two feet away.

Why was this suddenly so overwhelming? Russ had spent plenty of time around happy couples. Someone on the team was always getting married or having a baby. And sure, he'd occasionally felt a little twinge of envy, but this?

Suddenly his hunger had a focus, and now it wanted to consume him. Even now, waiting at the bar for their drinks, he was watching Liam out of the corner of his eye. That sweet, funny, troublesome pain in Russ's ass tweaked his protective instincts.

But what business did Russ have pursuing a twenty-two-year-old? If one of Russ's sisters tried to date someone born a full decade before them, they'd hear Russ yelling about it in the next county.

There was no question about it now. Russ needed space from his personal ray of sunshine before he got burned. The only control he had now was damage control. It would suck, but eventually he'd be okay. And maybe then he could go out and look for an appropriate partner—someone who didn't make him feel like he was getting away with something he shouldn't.

AS MUCH as Liam appreciated Russ giving him the opportunity to have a heart-to-heart with his sister, he would've appreciated a distraction more.

"What about Bastian?" he asked when Lakshmi and Russ had cleared out. The switch to French happened automatically, a small extra layer of precaution.

Bernadette fidgeted with a package of sweetener that had fallen out of the dispenser. "Okay, so he's having some drama with Mom and Dad. It's about the kids."

"They're okay, right?"

"They're fine. It's Mom who's having a fit."

That was probably worse. Liam leaned forward in concern. "Is this why he's been such an asshole lately?"

"Oh yeah. She's on the warpath. Which is absurd." Bernadette shook her head. "Turns out after the baby's baptism, she found out Bastian and Marielle gave the kids her last name."

Liam sipped his drink. "So?"

"So she had a crisis because it's Belanger Farms and the kids are Dad's only grandkids. They're supposed to take over one day."

In Quebec you couldn't change your name when you got married—or for a whole host of other reasons. "*Mom's* not even a Belanger." Her last name was Tonnellier. "Who cares? Calisse. I thought someone had cancer or something."

She snorted. "No. Anyway, she's been wailing about the family legacy. If she starts asking you if you're ever going to hire a surrogate, you'll know why."

Fuck. Liam hoped she wouldn't try to convince him to knock someone up. "I'm not having a kid just so the farm can have an heir. Rename the farm. Or don't. It doesn't matter. This is dumb."

"Oh, I agree. Marie-Jean thinks she's *actually* pissed at Marielle because she asked Mom to call first before coming over instead of just waltzing in, but she can't admit that because it's psychotic."

When Bastian and Marielle got married, his parents gifted them a share of the business and a plot of land to build a house on, not far from the one where his parents lived. Liam was so glad he didn't live at home anymore. "Mom needs some serious boundaries. Jeez."

"Yeah." She mashed her straw into her ice cubes. "Anyway, that's what happened. But then—and like, you know our family is ridiculous when, right?—they all had this big come-to-Jesus moment, and Bastian and Marielle told Mom and Dad they're pregnant again. And if Mom's willing to respect the 'call first' boundary, they'll give the next kid the Belanger name."

"What the fuck." He shook his head. "First of all, why? Second of all, like... I feel for Marielle. Isn't the baby only like six months old?"

"Oh my God, right? Like I want to send Bastian a box of condoms or a Fleshlight or something."

"Maybe we could get Marielle into pegging."

Bernadette cackled. "God, you're funny now that you're an adult. We should hang out more."

Liam stared at her, flushed with unexpected warmth. "You wanna move to Florida?"

"'Cause it's such a hotbed of LGBT freedom?" She smiled and shook her head. "Nah. But maybe we can go on vacation or something together in the offseason?"

"I would—yeah. I'd really like that." He smiled.

Bernadette smiled back. "Cool."

He laughed. "Cool," he echoed.

Russ and Lakshmi must've taken that as their cue to return, because they did, each carrying two drinks. Russ slid a beer in front of Liam and kept the other, while Lakshmi passed Bernadette a daiquiri.

"Oh, fancy," she said. Lakshmi kissed her cheek. "Thank you."

"This round's on Russ, actually."

Of course it was. Get dragged out to drinks with Liam, his sister, and his sister's girlfriend; then pay for them. That was Russ all over. And he'd made it seem like it was an excuse to give Liam time to talk with Bernadette alone. "Thanks."

Russ gave him an awkward smile. "You can get me back next time."

Liam had been thinking he could repay him some *other* way, like on his knees in his room up-stairs for example, but he probably shouldn't get too lost in that fantasy in front of his sister. Or anyone else.

He put the thought on the back burner and enjoyed the rest of the visit. But when they'd finished their round and dropped Bernadette and Lakshmi off on their floor, he suddenly found himself alone in the elevator with Russ again.

This had worked out well for him the last two times.

But when he looked at Russ to get a read on how he might react, he was tucked into the corner of the car, leaning against the back wall, eyes closed, jaw set.

Maybe tonight wasn't the time.

Liam didn't like the expression Russ wore, not for his own sake but for Russ's. He'd rarely seen Russ lose composure. He was usually so focused on the team and helping others that Liam had started to think of him as superhuman.

Which was stupid of him and a disservice to Russ. But if Russ was looking out for everyone else on the team, who was looking out for him?

Someone should.

Liam shoved his hands in his pockets. These pants, at least, had room for that. "Hey… you okay?"

Russ ran a hand over his face, then over his hair. "Yeah, fine." He shook his head. "Just a long couple of days, you know?"

"Yeah." Nobody liked back-to-backs, especially on the road. But something told Liam there was
more to it. He took a stab in the dark, trying to walk
the line between supportive and nosy. "Is everything
okay with your family?"

Something in Russ's face closed off. "Yeah. Why?"

"I don't know, I just thought…." He shrugged.
"Sometimes when I see other people with their fam-
ilies it make me think about mine."

The elevator ticked up another floor. Finally
Russ closed his eyes and let out an audible breath
through his nose. "You're too sharp for your own
good sometimes, you know that?"

"Um." Liam had asked, but he hadn't actually expected an honest answer. Not that he thought
Russ was a liar, but he'd played on hockey teams his
whole life. In his experience, nobody talked about
shit if they could help it. "Sorry."

Russ snorted. "Not your fault. Consequences of
my own actions."

"That's the worst."

Liam had the satisfaction of making Russ laugh,
even if just for a second. "It really is."

"Yeah." He couldn't have said what it was about
the mood between them. It felt fragile, like an ending. Liam grasped for something to say to bring back
the ease they'd had before—fuck, before they slept
together—but the elevator doors opened onto their
floor before inspiration struck. He was out of time.
"Um, I think I'm going to go to bed." He stepped off
and to the left, in the direction of his room. Part of

him hoped Russ would offer to come with, change the mood.

And part of him thought that maybe that was the problem to start with.

"Same." Russ's lips barely twitched up at the corners, and he jerked his head in the other direction. "Night."

Liam went off to bed with the unsettling impression that Russ had been trying to tell him something but didn't know how to say it.

BREAKFAST BROUGHT Russ a repeat of yesterday's pain, this time in a different form.

He set his alarm for early, knowing Liam liked to sleep late and wouldn't roll up until breakfast had nearly finished. He got coffee and put his order in for an omelet.

He'd managed to eat a single bite when Mo and Baller sat down at his table.

"Hi," said Baller.

Mo said, "This is an intervention."

Russ forked a piece of omelet. "Fuck off. I told you I'm fine."

Baller nodded seriously. "I know. It's not that we don't believe you—"

"It is," Mo put in.

"—it's just that you're full of shit." Baller picked up a piece of toast. "You spent the whole night with him."

Russ definitely had not. "I slept in my own room. Alone."

Mo winced. "Bro, you're not helping your case. We meant you hung out with him and his sister and ignored the rest of us all night."

Baller elbowed him in the side. "Not that there's anything wrong with that if it's a sometimes thing and you're honest with yourself about it."

"But we all know it's not a sometimes thing and you're deep in denial. Anyone can see your moony eyes from space. Hence the intervention."

The omelet was getting cold. Russ might as well play along or he'd never get to eat. He shoveled in a mouthful and asked, "What kind of intervention activities are we talking about?"

"Day drinking at a distillery tour."

Russ couldn't imagine anything worse than getting drunk in public while Mo and Baller embarrassed him to death.

He also couldn't imagine saying that out loud.

Before he could reply, Baller continued, "I'm a terrible neutral third party, but I'm very good at playing devil's advocate. Not that you're the devil, except maybe in the horny sense? Anyway, since the intervention is about your big gay crush on Liam, as the *other* queer person on this team, I call lawyer privileges."

Russ hoped the tasting portion of the tour started early. "I'm thirty-two years old. I don't get *crushes*."

Baller clapped him on the shoulder. "Go with me on this. Anything else I call it is going to sound worse."

If this was what it was like having Baller in his corner, he'd hate to go up against the guy. Sometimes he still couldn't believe this circle-jerk of frat boys had made it to adulthood.

Either way, he didn't mind having an excuse to blow Liam off for the day. Last night's revelations had left him feeling like a broken tooth with an exposed nerve. He didn't want to poke at it at all, but since the poking was inevitable, at least he could do it out of Liam's presence, with alcohol as an anesthetic.

To Mo and Baller's credit, they left the subject alone throughout the tour—probably because their other option might out Russ, but he still appreciated getting to enjoy part of his day off. They'd chosen a newer microdistillery that made small-batch whiskey. The tour wrapped up with a Q and A with the five co-owners, a group who'd met in college, and then segued into lunch and tastings. The whiskey-barbecue pulled pork melted in Russ's mouth, and the applewood-aged bourbon made an excellent whiskey sour.

But that was where Russ's good fortune ended, because once the food arrived, their tour guide disappeared and Mo closed in.

"First off—" Mo paused to lick barbecue sauce from his thumb. "—I want to apologize for getting it backwards. Clearly it was your ass I should've been worried about." He paused and then corrected himself, "Your ass's heart."

Baller made eye contact with the server to ask for another round.

"And maybe your ass. I shouldn't assume."

Baller wordlessly slid his glass toward Russ, because he was a gentleman and a scholar. Russ downed it.

"Also, I don't want to be that guy who's like, more concerned about the age of the people you sleep with than, say, the people Sparky sleeps with."

The server dropped off their round of drinks and left with a wink at Mo. She'd written her number on a napkin.

When she was out of earshot, Mo continued, "It's totally only about age because Sparky doesn't sleep with people he works with."

"To be fair, we don't *know* he's having sex with Liam again." Baller picked up a french fry and used it to punctuate his point. "Until we open the door to the supply closet, it's Schrödinger's sex. They're both fucking and not fucking."

"We're not fucking in supply closets," Russ grumbled. "I have some restraint." *Unless the team showers are involved. Then, not so much.*

"Trouble doesn't." Mo reached for his drink.

"Okay, hold on, I'm calling time-out." Baller held up a hand. "We need to clarify the problem. Is it that they're fucking and work together, or that they're fucking and Liam is twelve years old, or that they're fucking and Russ is going to get his feelings everywhere?"

"This is you helping?" Russ hissed.

Baller patted his knee. "I'm just here for immoral support. But seriously, I promise two queer guys can fuck without making it awkward. Plus queer relationships sometimes have bigger age gaps than your typical heteros, so while I *could* tell Russ not to fuck his much-younger teammate, that's definitely not what I told Gabe and I'm concerned the hypocrisy might be fatal."

Mo made a face at his drink for the hundredth time. "I'm not worried you're taking advantage of Liam," he said. "He's an adult who knows what he's doing, and I know you wouldn't... whatever. It's not about the age thing, except for the part where the age thing might result in you getting your dumb heart broken."

"Okay, well, *as I've been saying*." Finally Russ could put an end to this nightmare. "I'm not going to sleep with him anymore, so you can all relax and go back to minding your own."

Mo acknowledged this with a nod and a tip of his drink.

Russ was just about to allow himself to slump in relief when Baller ruined everything by saying, "Sorry, devil's advocate again, but did you tell Liam that?"

Fuck. "No. But he'll get the idea eventually."

"Oh sure, sure." Baller wiped liquid from his top lip. "Eventually. But like. My dude. Hands up if you had sex with another pro athlete when you were twenty-two." He raised his own hand. No one else did. "Yeah, so the sex is probably amazing, and as Liam is twenty-two, his brain is ruled by his dick, and he's going to keep asking to have it again unless you give him a good reason why not."

... *Fuck.*

"Not that I think he'd push if you gave him one," Baller went on as Russ took a long drink. "And maybe even if you didn't. But if he thinks you had simple, uncomplicated, no-strings sex—which he definitely does—then he probably assumes it's still uncomplicated."

Which it was not.

"I'm just saying. If you're going to keep turning him down and you'd rather just do it once, be honest about why."

Russ would rather pull his toenails out, but he saw Baller's point—the subtext that said, *If you let him ask over and over, you're going to say yes.*

Russ knew he could only say no to Liam so many times. He sighed. "You're probably right."

Baller patted him on the back. "I totally am." He paused. "Maybe wait 'til you're sober to do it, though."

Mo nodded sagely. "Smart man. I knew I liked you." And then something on the wall caught his eye and he brightened. "Oh shit, did you guys know this place has karaoke?"

SINCE THE Caimans had a day off, Liam got to eat breakfast with his sister and Lakshmi before their conference started.

Then he was at loose ends. He'd hoped he could sneak in a few hours of fun with Russ, but Russ was doing a distillery tour with Baller and Mo. Which was fine. Whatever was going on with Russ, he probably needed a day with friends. Friends who were not Liam.

Friends who also had not invited Liam on said excursion, even though Liam was well over legal drinking age, unlike, say, Hughesy.

Ugh, maybe the point was Liam needed to spend time with his other friends too. Liam sent a text and then tossed his phone on the bed to wait for a reply.

This was ridiculous. Instead of staring at his phone and waiting for it to buzz with a notification, he got up and packed so he wouldn't have to rush tomorrow.

He'd just finished zipping his suit bag when his phone went off. Thank you, Hughesy.

Did big russ ditch u or smth?

Liam winced, both because it was true and because he deserved that for only wanting to hang out with Hughesy as a second choice—even if Hughesy wouldn't blame him if he knew half of Liam's motivation was orgasms.

He decided to lean into the problem and hope Hughesy accepted that as an apology. *He said we should see other ppl!!!* He added an exaggerated crying emoji for effect.

Harsh, Hughesy replied. *Guess I can find room in my schedule. U have a plan?*

Liam sent a screenshot from TripAdvisor. *Underground donut tour?*

Fuck yes meet u in the lobby in 10!!!

Sparky and a couple of the other guys ended up tagging along too. After all, who didn't like donuts? So that was Liam's day sorted.

Truthfully he didn't know what to expect from an underground donut tour, other than the opportunity to stuff his face with fried dough. At the second stop, he got into a heated debate with Hughesy and Yeti over the maple-bacon donut when he wrinkled his nose at the syrup. "This is *not* like Maman used to make."

He expected them to laugh, and they did. But it turned out they didn't get the joke. Yeti shook his head in confusion. "What are you, some kind of maple syrup snob?"

Liam shrugged. The syrup had been overprocessed; it tasted burned. "I mean, I guess? I grew up on a sugar shack—a maple syrup farm. Didn't I tell you that?"

Apparently not, if Hughesy's face was any indication. "Dude. That's fucking sweet."

Yeti draped an arm over his shoulder. "Pun intended?"

Liam sighed and picked a pineapple upside-down donut tester instead. Russ would've gotten the joke.

He didn't see Russ, Mo, or Baller until the bus to the airport the next morning. They all wore sunglasses onto the plane, which said a lot about their whiskey tasting. Considering Liam had eaten his body weight in donuts, he couldn't throw stones.

Hopefully it didn't slow him down for the next game.

Mindful of his resolution—he needed to branch out to spending time with teammates beyond Russ—he grabbed the seat next to Sparky for the flight and spent the trip annihilating him at competitive Tetris.

They landed, went to the hotel, and had a nap. Rinse, repeat. Liam would've lost track of which city they were in, except Tampa was kind of an obvious one.

Tampa was cool because it was kind of close to home, so they had a decent-size crowd turn out for autographs on their way into the arena. Some of the guys went straight past without signing, but most of them made time for a few. For Liam, the novelty of people wanting to see and talk to him hadn't worn off, even if most of them didn't recognize his face, so he spent ten minutes signing things and taking selfies before Baller yelled, "Trouble!"

Liam finished signing a Caimans hat for a girl who looked about thirteen. "That's me," he told her. "Thanks for coming out."

A few feet away, Baller had just finished putting Sharpie all over the letters of one of the Caimans' Pride Night jerseys. "This one needs your touch too."

"Yeah, of course." Liam smiled at the guy holding it and scrawled his name next to Baller's. Then, as Hughesy went past, he reached out and tugged his arm. "Hughesy! Got a sec for a fan?"

"Could you have signed your name any bigger?" Hughesy grouched to Baller, but he was laughing as he squished his signature into the serif on one of the numbers. "Your ego is out of control."

"It's proportional," Baller said loftily, and the fan snorted so loud Liam worried he might've swallowed his tongue. Baller winked, and then Sparky came up and had a Sharpie thrust into his hand.

The signing had clearly evolved past out queer guys, so Liam thought nothing of calling out, "Hey, Russ!"

Russ was passing by on the opposite side of the aisle cleared for the players, so he had to backtrack. "What's up?"

Then his eyes went to the rainbow jersey, and his expression flickered. For a moment Liam worried he'd made a mistake, but then Russ got control of his face and plucked the Sharpie from Liam's hand. "You let this guy sign?" he asked the fan, who looked like he might spontaneously orgasm as the back of his jersey filled up with his team's autographs. "Look at that signature. Chicken scratch. So unprofessional."

"That's Hughesy's," Liam said.

The fan shrugged at Russ, cheeks flushing pink. "It seemed like a good opener for asking for his number."

Oh, Liam liked this guy. "Settle for a selfie? Russ, can you take a pic?"

Russ twitched when the fan made the pass at Liam, but Liam didn't think the fan noticed. He capped the Sharpie and handed it back. "Sure."

Liam leaned as close as he could for the shot, even slipped his arm around the fan's shoulders as they held the jersey up together with the opposite hands. "Thanks for coming out," Liam said as Russ handed the guy's phone back. "Hopefully we get the win for you, eh?"

"Hey, thanks." He smiled. "Bonne chance."

And he made an effort to speak French! Liam blew a cheeky kiss and then turned and walked into the arena.

The game got chippy the moment the puck dropped. Liam wasn't surprised—Tampa was their biggest rival.

It was the most physical game Liam had played, and he spent a good portion of it getting his ass handed to him along the boards. But he didn't give up the puck often, he didn't let the hits slow him down, and he laid his fair share too. Every time a penalty went uncalled, it fueled him to play harder, faster, better. Tampa was sharp. Liam needed to be sharper.

The Caimans were up 1–0 courtesy of Hughesy when Liam got into it in the corner with one of the Tampa players. Liam had the puck protected between himself and the boards, while his opponent crowded behind him trying to work it free.

"Getting kinda friendly," Liam complained when the guy used his full weight to try to force Liam into the plexiglass.

"I'm a friendly guy," he shot back.

Liam figured they were close enough to hide a tiny little sin and made judicious use of his elbow to create some space. His opponent's breath whooshed out and Liam worked the puck out to Russ. Easy-peasy.

Everything went a little bit sideways in the second. Just before the puck drop, Liam noticed the fan with the rainbow jersey in the stands behind the Caimans' bench and gave him a wink. The guy held his hand up to his ear in a "call me" gesture.

Russ caught it too, and he raised an eyebrow at Liam. "You sure you want to encourage him?"

Liam rolled his eyes. "Come on. It's harmless." He didn't even know that guy's name.

Russ chewed his mouthguard. "Whatever." Maybe he was still cranky from his hangover.

Liam didn't have time to think about it. He needed all his energy and focus on the game, which got progressively rougher. Hughesy lost a tooth to an errant stick five minutes into the period, Russ went to the box for a hit that wasn't any worse than twenty others, and Liam drew a slashing penalty in front of Tampa's net that left him limping well into the third.

The Caimans eked out a 2–1 win to close out the road trip. Even better, in Liam's opinion, was they got to go home afterward, and it wasn't even a long flight. He stepped onto the tarmac in Miami and felt a weird kind of relief to be back.

That was new to playing pro hockey. He'd never had that feeling in college. He didn't feel that way when he visited the house he grew up in, where his parents still lived.

In Lexington he'd be sleeping in his own bed, in the apartment he'd picked out, with the nice sheets that cost the same as a car payment, rather than in a no-tell motel or a nicer one that happened to be located next to a busy highway or an airport, and that itself had been bliss.

In Miami he was still in a hotel, but at least it was a nice hotel that had a lot of his own stuff in it and a mattress softer than a puppy's tummy.

Too bad he didn't have anyone to share it with tonight.

As if on cue, Russ walked past him, making a beeline for his car.

Outside of work, Liam hadn't spoken to him much since that moment in the elevator in Nashville, and it bothered him. Yeah, he enjoyed spending time with other guys on his team, but he was sure Russ was avoiding him. He'd even seemed annoyed with Liam tonight for no particular reason.

Honestly, it sucked. Liam felt… he didn't know. *Used*? That seemed too strong a word for a friend he'd had a couple hookups with. *Hurt* fit, even if he didn't like to admit it. Liam didn't consider himself a delicate person, but he *did* think he was pretty fun to hang out with. He was a good friend. He was approachable. If Russ didn't want to spend time with him anymore, the least he could do was tell Liam to his face.

Before he could talk himself out of it, he switched directions and followed Russ to his truck.

He didn't even have his mouth open to say anything when Russ said, "Now's not really a good time, Trouble."

Well fuck him very much too. "Yeah? When's a good time for you? Maybe next time we're in the team showers together?"

Russ flinched like Liam had slapped him. Good. Liam wasn't going to be the only one hurt. "Would you keep your voice down?"

"Why?" Liam retorted. "You don't want anyone finding out we fucked a couple times? Newsflash,

Russ. Everyone fucking knows." If Hughesy had figured it out, there was no way the rest of the team was
in the dark. Which made Liam's position that much
more awkward. Now everyone would think he was
the loser rookie who'd gotten butthurt because his
older teammate lost interest.

Russ closed his eyes. In the fluorescent parking
garage light, Liam could make out every furrow of
his brow, the grim set of his mouth... the bags under
his eyes. "I'm not airing my shit out here." Suddenly
Liam registered the exhaustion in his voice—exhaustion that had been there when he'd said this was a bad
time. The expression he'd glimpsed in an elevator not
long ago. There was a mechanical clunk as the truck
doors unlocked. "If you want to talk, get in."

Liam's anger melted into something nebulous.
But he needed to know what was going on, get this
sorted out.

He got in the truck.

Russ said, "I owe you an apology."

He said it to the steering wheel, which might've
been funny if it weren't so fucked up. Liam had a
strange vision of Russ yanking too hard to the left and
then lovingly washing the truck to make up for it.

"Yeah, you do," Liam said after a beat when
Russ didn't elaborate. "Do you know what for?"

"I shouldn't have slept with you."

Liam had half expected that, but it still stung
like antiseptic in a cut. "Which time?"

Russ flinched again, but he took a deep breath
afterward and straightened his shoulders. "Look, it's
not.... This is on me. I just need some space, okay?"

What the fuck. They weren't even together and Russ was breaking up with him. This had to be some kind of record.

Liam experienced the uncomfortable sensation of his body pulling him in two directions at once. His stomach was trying to sink through the floor, while his heart was in his mouth. He wasn't sure what he'd done, but he'd fucked *something* up.

And he was *upset* about it. More upset than he should be about the end of a friends-with-benefits arrangement, even if Russ was being a dick about ending it.

He crossed his arms over his chest even though it was warm in the truck. Russ hadn't started the engine, and the windows were starting to steam. Kind of ironic, given the usual implications of steamed-up car windows. But he couldn't dwell on that, or on the twisting emotion in his stomach, because he could not afford to fuck up his relationship with the team. "I didn't mean to make anything awkward, and I'm not trying to change your mind. I just want to know, did I do something?"

Russ leaned his head back against the seat. "No, you didn't do anything wrong."

With some effort, Liam took a deep breath and forced his organs back where they belonged. His stomach unclenched a little, and the tightness in his lungs eased. "Okay." Another deep breath. Nope, the tightness was coming back, bringing panic with it. "So you're just like... not into it." Liam was a big boy. He could deal with that.

"Liam."

Okay, he had overestimated his ability to cope. He forced a shaky smile. "I get it. You don't have to explain."

Russ groaned. "Yes, I do. I just don't want to."

Liam was pretty sure he didn't want Russ to explain either. He'd rather go back to his hotel room and pull the blankets over his head until he could face Russ again, like maybe in a week. "It's fine. I'll just go—"

"I can't have casual sex with you anymore—"

Liam pawed at the door handle. "Yeah, you made that clear—"

"—because it's not casual, for me." Russ looked like he would rather be anywhere else. "I'm not going to make it weird on purpose, I just need some space. Like I said."

Liam's lungs suddenly stoppered, and he froze.

Holy *shit*, Russ had feelings for him.

Warmth washed through him, starting in his cheeks and chest and radiating outward, pushing back the panic and humiliation. Unfortunately that left a vacuum in his brain, so the thing that came out of his mouth was "Wow, this is what you're like when you like someone?" He was lucky his self-preservation instincts kicked in before he added *please get some therapy*.

Russ looked miserable, which, yeah, Liam was not making great grades in Adult Communication either. He didn't want Russ to be miserable. He wanted Russ to have the same stupid-making head rush Liam had, and a too-fast pulse, and maybe even some butterflies. But also he needed Russ to know martyring himself was dumb, so he hurried to add, "If you opened with that we could have skipped the worst parts of this conversation."

Russ made skeptical eyebrows. "The worst parts for *who*?"

Liam didn't answer. He had that blissful feeling again, that going-to-go-home-to-my-own-bed feeling, and he let it wrap around him like a blanket. Metaphorically, since the truck was hot as balls. "Like. Say we rewind the conversation. And instead of making me feel like an asshole for not being good enough, you say, 'Hey, Liam, I like you. Can we have less-casual sex instead?'"

Sometime in the past few minutes, they'd turned their bodies toward each other, and now they were face to face across the center console. Russ met his eyes. His cheeks were flushed now, even if his voice was still serious, like he wasn't quite ready to commit to hope. "Hey, Liam," he parroted. "You're too young for me and the Caimans aren't going to renew my contract at the end of the year, but do you want to start a doomed relationship anyway?"

Russ was really good at making things more complicated than they had to be. Objectively speaking, he was a catch. Kind, funny, hot… really good with giving advice. Generous with his time. Absolute force of nature in bed. Maybe Liam wasn't actively looking to settle down, but he didn't think Russ counted as settling. "*Calisse de Crisse*, you don't have to put a ring on it. We can just see what happens. Maybe in a week it turns out I can't stand your snoring and you have all this angst for nothing."

"I don't snore," Russ protested. But the corner of his mouth turned up, so at least Liam had knocked a little bit of sense into him. "You're saying we have the power to fuck this up all by ourselves and don't need to borrow trouble."

He was saying they'd both be a lot happier if Russ stopped what-ifing himself to death. "I never need to borrow trouble. I have my own."

The smile turned up a couple more degrees. "Nice of you to share."

"Hey." Liam found himself flushing when Russ's fingers brushed over his on the center console. "You're not the only one who can be nice."

"I guess not." The last of the tension eased out of Russ's shoulders, and he briefly laced his fingers through Liam's. Then he squeezed and returned both hands to the wheel. "So. Want to come home with me and see what happens?"

Liam reached for his seat belt. "I thought you never ask."

THIRD PERIOD

WHAT HAPPENED was Russ woke the next morning with an armful of naked rookie. Liam's curls tickled his nose. Under Russ's arm, his chest rose and fell in a slow, rhythmic, almost hypnotic way, like it was trying to lure Russ back to sleep.

But his brain had kicked on, and he might as well let it do its thing before Liam opened his eyes and decided they should do something about the erection poking him in the back.

So. Apparently Russ had a boyfriend now.

He'd definitely decided *against* sleeping with Liam again. He'd intended to step back and get some objectivity. Russ had never believed in failing up, but that was before he failed at not having sex so badly he'd ended up in a relationship.

He liked waking up with Liam just as much as he liked going to bed with him, and not necessarily in a sexual way. Russ had grown up in locker rooms and with a loud, big family and siblings who used to use him as a climbing gym. Ever since he realized his sexuality, he'd been policing himself with the team, hyperaware that any touch could be miscon-strued. He didn't have to do that with Liam anymore. The liberty to look and touch was heady. The touch itself… he felt like he could get high from it. It was going to be difficult to keep his hands to himself—never mind the rest of his body.

Subconsciously, Russ pressed his face to the back of Liam's neck and breathed him in. He didn't smell like anything romantic, just sweat and skin and sham-poo. For a second, Russ was convinced he smelled maple syrup, and he imagined Liam dabbing some be-hind his ears to remind him of home or something. He smothered a laugh in Liam's shoulder blade.

This was probably going to end in disaster, but Liam was right. Relationships ended for any number of reasons. No one had the luxury of going into one knowing it would last forever. At least with Liam, he knew their days were numbered from the get-go. That didn't mean he wouldn't enjoy it while it lasted.

"Mmm." Liam stretched, skin sliding along Russ's as he breathed in deep. After a few lazy sec-onds, he turned to look over his shoulder and met Russ's eyes. "Morning."

"Mmm," Russ agreed. It was a pretty good morning. And from the way Liam was moving—pulling Russ's hand lower, tilting his hips back—it was about to get better. "So?"

He wrapped his hand around Liam's dick. Liam hissed in pleasure and arched into the touch. "So?"

Russ thrust against his ass and rubbed his beard against the sensitive skin beneath Liam's ear. "Do I snore?"

"How can I know?" Liam laughed as he turned in his arms. His morning accent was thick like maple syrup. "You fuck me until I'm unconscious."

Russ nipped his lower lip. "That so?"

"Mmm," Liam affirmed. The freckles on the bridge of his nose crinkled when he scrunched his face into a teasing grin. "And then you wake me up again so early. It's very rude. You should make it up to me."

"Oh yeah?" Russ slid his thumb over the curve of his ass.

"Ouais." He walked his fingers down Russ's chest, over his stomach. "You can help me go back to sleep."

When he put it like that, it seemed like the least Russ could do.

Afterward, he left Liam dozing in bed and got up to start his off-day workout. The weight room beckoned. Sometimes he struggled with the boredom of it, but today the routine came easily. His mind was clear. His body felt good. And it *was* an off day, so he didn't have to push himself. His body needed time to recover too.

Russ paid an exorbitant fee to heat the pool in the winter, so after weights, he dove in and did a handful of laps. Muscle memory kicked in and carried him through the water without conscious thought.

Maybe he should start every off-day workout with Liam in his bed, if it put him in this kind of mood.

Liam was still in bed when he got out of the pool, but Russ had seen the kid at team breakfast and knew he'd wake up hungry and in need of caffeine. He rinsed off in the downstairs shower and dressed in a pair of shorts from the laundry room. Then he started the coffee maker and poked his head into the fridge to see about breakfast.

He was so distracted by his stomach that when his phone rang, he didn't look at the call display. He'd put his earbuds back in after his shower so he could listen to music while he cooked, so he just tapped to answer. "Hello."

"Oh, so you're not too good to talk to your mother after all."

She sounded like she was teasing, but Russ detected something in her tone that spelled bad news for him. Whether that was suspicion, annoyance, or hurt, he couldn't tell yet. "Hey, Ma. I was just about to call you."

"Mm-hmm." Apparently she knew better than to believe that. "You mean you were about to blow me off like our last two calls?"

Russ closed his eyes and sent up a silent prayer to the gods of men with nosy mothers that Liam stayed asleep for another half an hour. "Ma...." He closed the fridge and leaned against it. What could he say? He *had* been avoiding her. He had no intention of telling her why over the phone. That left apologizing vaguely with just enough detail that she wouldn't push with questions. "I'm sorry. I've been going through some things with the team, trying to figure out my future...."

She humphed. "That's a reason to *call* your mother, not avoid her."

Not when I'm avoiding you because you're part of the problem. "I know, Ma, I just…. You know I'm not good at talking about stuff."

"Much to my chagrin," she agreed, less sharply than she could have. "Your dad and I raised you better."

Russ rubbed his chest. His parents had always emphasized the importance of talking openly about problems. It hadn't come naturally for Russ. How could he admit to struggling while still being the role model they expected him to be for his sisters? Once he'd gotten into elite hockey, it only became more difficult. Hockey players just didn't do that.

In any case, Russ might be her child, but he was an *adult* child now. "I'm grown. I'm allowed to keep things to myself until I'm ready."

Hopefully she would at least appreciate the fact that he'd internalized the lesson about setting boundaries.

She sighed, and the fight went out of her voice. "Yes, you are. And you're also allowed to tell your mother she fucked up and she's the reason you haven't been talking."

Shit. "Ma…."

"No, sweetheart. I need to apologize. You've told me to back off before, with trying to help you meet someone, and I never listen. I'm sorry."

"I know you just want me to be happy." He still wasn't ready to tell her about Liam—she loved him, but she would be *so* judgy about Russ getting into a relationship that was doomed from the start.

"I do. But you'll find someone in your own time." Her tone gentled further, and she chuckled to herself. "I admit, for a while there I thought you had met someone and you were off in the honeymoon period, and maybe that was why you were so upset about the setup."

Just when Liam came down the stairs and said, "Pour l'amour du hockey dis-moi qu'il y a du café."

Russ turned around and caught Liam's gaze, which went from barely conscious to *oh shit* in a fraction of a second. He furiously mouthed apologies while Russ braced himself and crossed his fingers that his mother hadn't heard.

Naturally his mother had batlike hearing. "Russell Lyons, do you have company at this hour? Maybe I was right about you meeting someone after all?"

Russ grimaced an apology at Liam. "It's Trouble, Ma. He doesn't have an apartment in Miami yet."

"Of course. Well, it's nice of you to let him stay with you. Are you sure that's not making things harder? You're already worried about your future with the team…."

Crisis averted. Russ breathed a silent sigh of relief and directed Liam toward the coffee maker. "He's a pretty good distraction, don't worry. Having him around helps."

"All right. I suppose at the very least he'll keep you busy, with a nickname like that."

"You have no idea." And hopefully she never would.

Liam glanced back from pouring himself a mug of coffee. He winked and lifted the cup along with his eyebrows. Russ nodded—he could use some too.

"That's probably for the best," she laughed. "Since he's a roommate and not a guest, though, I won't feel guilty about monopolizing your time this morning. You owe me that much. Besides, I haven't gotten to give you an update about my latest research project."

There was no way to get out of it without risking her wrath. "Just give me a second to go into the den so I can give you my full attention."

"Okay. I'll wait."

Russ couldn't believe he'd gotten away with it, but he wasn't going to take this gift for granted. He muted his phone and leaned over to kiss Liam's cheek as Liam passed him the mug. "Thanks. I've gotta take this. Think about what you want for breakfast?"

"Oh, five-star service." Liam copped a feel, straight-faced. "I'll be here."

Russ bumped his hip and retreated to the den to pay his penance.

True to her word, his mother kept him on the phone for twenty minutes catching him up on her life, Gia's pregnancy, and Andi's first year of university. Russ had already seen his dad's plans for the mural—his dad hated wearing his hearing aids at home, so they texted more than speaking on the phone—but he let his mom tell him about it again anyway. Grandpa was moving out of Russ's parents' house and in with Tony. If nothing else, the holidays would be a little less cramped.

Finally she let him off the hook, and Russ hung up. He let out a long breath, lay back on his couch, and stared up at the ceiling. He hated that he'd met someone he actually liked and didn't even get to talk him up to his family.

Unfortunately, Russ couldn't hide in the den about it forever, because he'd promised breakfast.

He heaved himself to his feet and opened the door to the den only to be assaulted by the scent of frying butter.

"I think I'll make breakfast," Liam said cheerfully from in front of the stove, "except I grew up on a sugar shack, so I only know how to make pancakes."

Russ had to admit they smelled fantastic, and they were fluffy and bubbling away on the tops. They beguiled him. Liam was making him pancakes in his own kitchen. So… he wasn't mad?

Maybe he was just really hungry?

"You don't have maple syrup, though. Just the nasty sugar stuff. So I'm having mine with jam."

Russ got the impression he was more miffed about the lack of maple syrup than Russ hiding him from his mother. But he should still apologize, right? He might not have a ton of experience in relationships, but he knew this was a minefield. He'd seen enough TV shows. "I'm sorry about my mom."

Liam gave him a perplexed look. "Why? It's good that she calls you. *My* mom never calls."

Could Russ really be getting away with this? "I just mean… I'm not trying to keep you a secret or anything, but…."

"We haven't even been on a date. You think I'm texting my mom how big your dick is?"

Russ sincerely hoped not.

Liam lifted the edge of a pancake, judged it perfectly browned, and flipped it. "We need protein. Do you have bacon or something?"

Finally Russ decided Liam really didn't care, and opened the freezer to look for pork.

RUSS MIGHT'VE liked to spend the next few days in a sort of new-couple bubble, but he knew he shouldn't dive into things so quickly. Liam was young, Russ was teetering on the edge of a major trade, they worked together, everything was new….

He didn't know whether to be proud or embarrassed at how easily Liam talked him back into bed.

But *after* that, Russ squared his shoulders and did what he had to. He dropped Liam off at his car and then went about his usual day-back-at-home routine—he got his edges done, put in an order with his grocery service, and dropped off his dry cleaning.

He got the rest of the day to decompress and recalibrate after the road trip, and then the next day, practice.

Russ got there early and tried to ignore the odd sensation in his stomach. He'd played in the NHL for more than a decade. He had no business having nerves for a practice.

But he'd never had a practice with a teammate who was also his boyfriend and who the rest of his leadership team had expected him to break off a casual sexual relationship with either. So. Oops?

He probably should've texted Liam, figured out how they were going to play this. Appearances to the contrary, Baller was not an idiot and was going to clock the change in dynamic in about half a second. But he *might* let them get away without making a press release to the entire team.

But *so how are we going to handle this with the team* felt like a serious conversation to have with someone he'd only been officially dating for a day and a half, and it also might send Liam running for the hills, so he kept the talk light.

Well. If *come over after practice?* counted as light. Liam had replied with a string of eggplant emojis, so Russ figured it did.

In any case, everything would be fine. Unless they broke up and things got super awkward, or Russ got traded and Liam decided a long-distance relationship was too much work.

Fuck, didn't *Russ* think a long-distance relationship was too much work? The plan was that this was only temporary, right?

He firmly put the questions out of his mind and focused on hockey.

By the time Liam arrived—with a dried smear of what looked like toothpaste on his chin, because he was a disaster if left unsupervised in the morning—the locker room was full, so Russ didn't have to worry about it much. They locked gazes and Liam grinned at him and gave him the elevator eyes, because Russ was stripped down to his compression shorts, but everyone else was busy doing their own thing and no one commented.

Practice was practice. Liam and Yeti couldn't read each other any better than Russ could read Carl.

But despite the challenges, and aside from a few errant looks, on the ice, Liam behaved like a total professional, as though their discussion had never happened. The D-core might be in rough shape, but Russ thought their personal life was in the clear until Mo snowed up next to him between rushes. "So. You talked to him?"

Russ didn't look over. "Everyone on this team is so fucking nosy."

"So it went well, then."

It wasn't worth flipping him off with the gloves on, so Russ shot him a poisonous look.

"I'm being serious. This is remarkably not awkward. I'm impressed."

"What's not awkward?" Baller asked from Mo's other side. Why did he always appear at exactly the moment when Russ needed him to go away? Did neither of them have work to do? Where was their coach?

Damn it, he was talking to Sparky and Liam. No help from that direction.

"Russ calling off the sexcapade with Liam. I thought he'd be, like, grumpier."

Russ stared stonily at the boards across the ice. He could feel the weight of Baller's gaze on the side of his face. *Don't look at Liam. Don't look at Liam. And absolutely do not smile.*

"Bro," said Baller after three seconds of scrutiny. "You had one job."

"And I'm doing it," Russ protested. Unlike some people he could name.

"Wait," Mo said to Baller, "what's going on? What do you know?"

"For starters, I know that hickey on Trouble's neck wasn't there when we got back from the road trip."

"I didn't leave a hickey," Russ said, probably way too loud. At least not above the collar, jeez. What was he, fifteen?

Baller smirked. On the other side, Mo turned to face Russ more fully.

Oh. Shit.

"Busted."

Russ resisted the urge to bury his face in his hands. For one thing, he didn't want hockey glove smell near his face. "I said I'd talk to him and we'd stop having casual sex." He'd rather not look either of them in the eye, so instead he examined the rafters. Someone should probably dust up there. "I did both of those things."

There was a brief pause while his teammates digested this.

Then Mo said, "Did you just 'well, technically' sleeping with your rookie?"

"Only the same way you're sleeping with Shelly."

Before Baller could weigh in, Coach blew the whistle. "Lyons!"

Russ snapped his head up. "Yes, Coach!"

"See if you and Carl can generate any more chemistry than Trouble and Yeti."

Baller coughed loudly. Russ shot him a quelling look. "Yes, Coach!"

HAVING A boyfriend turned out to be awesome.

Beyond the regular sex—something that improved Liam's mood immeasurably—it meant having someone to hang out with and a place to do it. Russ could cook, so Liam was saved from the endless monotony of hotel and restaurant meals, at least when they were at home. Plus Russ's house was way nicer to hang out in than Liam's hotel room, not only because it often contained Russ, but also because he had a bigger TV and a better sports package, a grocery service, and a weight room, and he didn't mind bringing Liam's dry cleaning in with his own. As if he hadn't been Liam's hero *before*.

On the road he had different advantages. Mostly they consisted of a strong shoulder to lean on during breakfast before the coffee kicked in and a team veteran to pointedly announce to guys who outranked Liam that "you're in his seat" when he came back from getting his round at the bar.

Of course, Liam had to endure Baller's attempts to mortify him with sex tips masquerading as safety education until finally he asked if Liam had any questions. Liam waited until Baller took a sip of beer to say, "Yes, how many dates do you go on before it's okay to ask someone to fist you?"

Baller didn't spray all over the table, but he did glare at Liam with chipmunk cheeks for a few seconds before he could swallow. "Well played," he said, and they changed the subject to the Firebirds' penalty kill.

Not everything went smoothly all the time. They dropped the final game of Liam's first full road trip to the New Jersey Monsters 5–1.

He'd taken a bench minor in the second, for which Mo gave him shit. "Guess BC doesn't teach their undergrads to count to six"—that Harvard asshole. Then in the third, Liam had a fantastic open shooting lane to the net and absolutely hammered it, but the Monsters' goalie got his stick on it and it deflected *halfway back down the ice*, which resulted in a breakaway and goal for the other team.

Three more unanswered goals followed it. Considering Liam played defense, he took that personally.

"Great teams get blown out sometimes," Mo told them in the dressing room after. "We just have to learn from our mistakes and put it behind us."

The Caimans' mistakes this game included poor puck possession, poor puck protection, taking too many penalties, and failing to create scoring chances. On top of several instances when he'd passed when he should've shot, Liam had taken another question-able penalty, gotten pissed off about it, and then got slapped with an unsportsmanlike for arguing.

With regular losses, they usually ate second din-ner together, as a way to brush off bad feelings. But with nasty ones like this, most guys preferred to suf-fer alone or break into small groups with people who would forgive them if they snapped.

Liam definitely felt like snapping.

Russ, Baller, and Mo usually spent their time talking to anyone who'd had a particularly bad game. Liam glanced around their conference room as everyone gathered, and took stock of how things were breaking down. Mo had his arm around Sparky, their goaltender, and two dinner boxes in his other hand. Baller made eye contact with Russ and jerked his head toward Hughesy.

So that left the rest of the team for Russ, Liam guessed. He should probably grab a meal and go eat it in his room, then try to get some sleep. Mechanically, he lined up at the meal service table—he had no idea what was on offer—and took a hot aluminum tray. He didn't even want to eat. He *did* want Russ's attention, but like, Russ had responsibilities. He couldn't be putting Liam first.

No matter how much Liam wanted him to.

He was just getting into a good sulk when a big hand clamped down on his shoulder. "Come on, come eat dinner in my room."

The loss might have bruised Liam's spirit, but he'd only thought it ruined his appetite. As soon as they sat at the little table in Russ's room, he was ravenous. The problem was trying to get food in at the same time as he got the venting out.

"I just don't know what's worse, you know?" He shoveled in a forkful of pasta and swallowed it. "That move Hedgewood did when he went around me like I was a fucking pylon—"

"Eat slower," Russ said. When Liam glanced up from his dinner and met his eyes, they were wide. He looked vaguely ill. "You're going to get indigestion. And he's done it to better players than you. You'll learn from it."

Liam didn't acknowledge him other than to make a face, but he did chew his next bite. He didn't want to make himself sick. "Or that bullshit penalty the ref gave me. *Or* that I cost us the game for arguing."

"We were down already," Russ said flatly.

Sure, but an extra two minutes shorthanded didn't *help*. Liam flushed at his dinner. "We could've come back if I hadn't killed our momentum—"

"Trouble."

Liam stopped with a piece of chicken on the end of his fork and looked up.

Russ met his gaze evenly. "You're the newest guy on the team. You think you're so bad at hockey that twenty guys who've been playing longer than you had perfect games but still lost 5–1 because, what? We can't win when you're not at your best? Check your ego. We can lose without you."

Wow. Phrased that way, Liam had to admit he sounded kind of self-absorbed. He blinked. "I guess you *can* give a pep talk."

"I can give you a verbal smackdown, is what," Russ said, long-suffering. "Finish your dinner— *chewing*—and I'll go over game tape with you before bed."

Game tape. Heh. Liam smiled into his pasta.

Russ's socked foot kicked him under the table. "And stop thinking I'm such a geezer for saying 'tape' instead of 'video.'"

When they'd finished dinner, Russ cast the game to the TV in his room. The angle from the dining table would've killed their necks, so they kicked off their shoes and sat on the bed, propping themselves up on pillows.

"You did that a lot this game," Russ said when the screen showed Liam dropping the puck back for Mo. Looking at it objectively made Liam wince— anyone else would've gone for the top shelf. "Be a little selfish, please. Were you still thinking about that flukey bounce from earlier?"

Liam felt like a kid who'd been caught with his hand in the cookie jar. "No?" he tried.

"You're a bad liar. Shit happens. Shoot the damn puck."

Advice that boiled down to *get out of your own head* was tough to take. No amount of physical conditioning would solve that.

They restarted the game, and a few shifts later Russ paused on a play of Liam backchecking toward the Caimans' net. "See, this here. You're out of position. You need to trust your teammates to have their man."

Liam groaned. "Yeah. I was so sure he was going to pull that move—you know the one, where he does the little—" He spun his finger in the air. "And I thought, if I came up on the left—" It had seemed so clear in the moment.

"Yeah, but it was Hughesy's job to react if he did that. And you left that passing lane wide open."

"Ugh." He smothered a groan in a pillow. He *had* done that. He knew better. Coach was going to bench him, and he'd deserve it.

Russ carded fingers through his hair. Liam wondered if he knew that made him feel better or if it was just a coincidence. "You just do your job. Let everyone else worry about theirs."

"Yeah, I got it," Liam said, still into the pillow. Then he pulled it away from his face. "Can we watch the second again?"

He was fully aware Russ should tell him no. They needed to go to bed—and actually sleep, not fool around for an hour and exhaust what remained of their energy. Not that a 5–1 loss put Liam in any kind of sexy mood.

But apparently Russ was a sucker for Liam, because he skipped back to the second period.

He didn't move his hand from Liam's hair, though, and a few minutes later, Liam fell asleep to the sound of Russ's voice.

WITH ANY other partner, Russ would've wanted a plan for telling the rest of the team they were dating. Okay, so Russ wanted a plan now too. Unfortunately, the one time he managed to bring up the subject, Liam reminded him of their adventure in the locker-room showers, and Russ quickly forgot all about it.

In any case, it would've been a moot point after their game in New Jersey, because Liam came down for breakfast wearing Russ's T-shirt, sat next to him, and stole a sip of his coffee. Sparky and Hughesy watched silently while he buried his face in Russ's shoulder and announced, "I owe you a new toothbrush."

Like ripping off a Band-Aid, Russ thought. Not much point pretending Liam was just his rookie anymore. He smiled—morning disaster Liam was too endearing to do otherwise—and figured if they were found out, he might as well just do what he wanted, so he pressed a kiss to the top of Liam's head and said, "Did you forget you were in my room?" Considering the places Russ had had his tongue, and vice versa, sharing a toothbrush didn't seem too terrible.

"No." He raised his head just enough to meet Russ's eyes. His own were still half closed with sleep. "I accidentally drop it in the toilet."

In that case, he definitely owed Russ a new one.

"Is this finally happening?" Sparky asked. "Is it my birthday?"

Oh Lord.

"Where've you been?" Hughesy said. "This is, like, old news."

Wait, how long had he known? Russ glanced down at Liam to ask him, but he'd lost consciousness again. Russ reached around for his coffee mug with the arm not currently hosting his boyfriend.

"Oh my God. Mo! Baller! Yeti!"

Russ contemplated his breakfast. How much could he eat one-handed while this circus played out? He switched fork hands and speared a piece of sausage as his teammates assembled.

Sparky gestured toward Russ and Liam. "It's time."

"Me first." Baller elbowed Yeti aside. "So, Russ—have you been keeping out of Trouble?"

"Think he's more likely to be in deep trouble." Mo paused. "Or deep in Trouble."

"Don't you think you're asking for Trouble?"

"You can't really blame him, you know, kid like that, nice place like Miami…. Trouble in paradise."

"Do you always meet Trouble halfway?"

Russ let it all wash over him as he finished his breakfast, Liam still half dozing against his arm. Obviously everyone had been waiting for this moment, and they needed to get the puns out of their systems.

It was all getting repetitive and predictable, winding down, until Hughesy asked thoughtfully, "So does Trouble really come in threes?"

Liam raised his face from Russ's shoulder. "I do on a good night."

Russ couldn't help a self-satisfied smirk at that as their teammates busted up laughing. He passed Liam the rest of his coffee. "Now that that's over with," he said dryly, "I'll be fining anyone who recycles a joke, so I hope you enjoyed yourselves."

Their teammates drifted back to their breakfast, leaving Russ with Liam and Hughesy as Sparky got up to do his post-game-day guided meditation.

"Sorry," Liam said after he'd gotten about half the mug in him. "That could have been more planned."

"No, you were right. They already knew anyway." Baller had probably been stockpiling puns. He nudged Liam in the side. "You should hurry up and get some food before you miss your chance."

Most of the team was already drifting off to get their things, but Russ wasn't surprised when Baller joined them instead as Liam returned from the buffet.

"Did he take you on a date yet?" Baller had procured a single-serving box of Froot Loops and was munching it like popcorn.

Liam made a noise of consideration around a bite of scrambled eggs. "You know, I think I haven't been on a date since high school."

Baller must've seen Russ's eyes bug out, because he snorted into his cereal and then stood up.

"I think my work here is done. Bye, kids. Try not to miss the bus."

Much as he didn't like being manipulated into doing things, Russ had to admit Baller had a point. Besides, it galled him that no one had taken Liam out and shown him a good time, even if it also secretly pleased him that he'd get to be the first. Sue him; he was a complex guy with complex emotions.

Plus it wasn't like he wouldn't have done it without prompting. He just might've waited until they were back on home turf and he had a better idea of what to do.

He nudged Liam's foot under the table. "So, what are you doing next off day?"

To HIS credit, when it came to hockey, Liam took Russ's advice to heart. He shot the puck. He kept his head in the game, trusted his teammates, and played the Caimans' system near perfectly. He didn't take risks that had low chances of paying off.

So it sucked that the team couldn't buy a win.

Even though their forwards stepped up, no doubt as stung from the rout as Sparky and the defensive core, the team dropped the next two games 5–4 and 4–2. Losing at home was one thing, but losing on the road—losing *stupidly* on the road—demoralized them.

With morale in the tank after the third loss, Russ got a summons from Mo before they even made it back to the hotel that night.

Liam didn't even pick his head up off Russ's shoulder. He'd gotten tripped in the final frame and gone sprawling awkwardly on the ice. No penalty, because you could never count on the refs to see something when you needed them to. The combination of frustration, hurt, and embarrassment made him grumpy on the ice, but now the adrenaline had fled, leaving him... well, cuddly. They'd gotten a few teasing comments about it, but chirps made up at least half of a hockey team's communication, so when Mo made a joke about Russ's new barnacle, Russ had flipped him off and told him he was just jealous Shelly didn't get to travel with the team.

"Let me guess," Liam mumbled now. "Duty calls?"

"Nah. It was Mo."

He couldn't see Liam's smile, but he felt the movement of his face against his arm. It was a strange sort of intimacy, to feel what someone else was feeling like that. "Was that a dad joke?"

"Are you calling me old?" Russ asked, feigning offense.

"Are you trying to ask if I have a daddy kink?"

Russ reached around with his far arm and poked Liam in the side until he yelped.

"I swear to God I will take over as fine master and bankrupt you for flirting on the bus," Sparky grumbled from the seat behind them.

"We can make out instead," Liam offered sweetly.

"Gross." Sparky kicked the seat.

Russ figured they deserved it.

At the hotel, Mo and Baller commandeered a small conference room for their dinner and brainstorming session while Russ detoured to his hotel room to raid the mini bar. He returned with a few small bottles and all the snacks from the fridge.

Baller immediately abandoned his dinner in favor of a chocolate bar. "Russ Lyons setting a bad example? I'm telling the nutritionist."

Russ pulled his own dinner toward himself. "Snitches get stitches."

"Baller, don't tease your brother. Russ, violence is not the answer." Mo opened a can of beer. "So, we need something to shake us out of our funk, and we're not at home, so beach volleyball is out. Ideas, go."

When Mo was mid-sip, Baller suggested innocently, "Circle jerk?"

Mo glowered but didn't spray beer everywhere, which was fortunate since Russ was sitting across from him.

"He said 'shake us out of our funk,' not 'get covered in spunk.'" Russ speared a slice of roast beef. Mo's glare kicked up a notch. "Barbecue?" Russ could feel his planned date day with Liam slipping away, but the team had to come first.

Baller snorted. "I believe in the healing power of food and everything, but we were gonna eat barbecue anyway."

Well yeah, probably.

"We could get massages," Mo suggested.

"I don't think it counts as team-building unless we're massaging each other," Baller pointed out. "See my earlier suggestion."

Russ shot him a quelling look. "What else is there to do around here? Batting cages? Paintball?"

Mo wrinkled his nose. "Do you not have enough bruises?"

Point. "Okay, so not paintball. But batting cages would still be good. Home-run derby?"

"Mmm." Swallowing a mouthful of beer, Mo reached for a bag-of-chips chaser. "Maybe. Is it too much like work?"

"It's not very team-y if it's a home-run derby, is it?" Baller mused. "I mean, hitting the ball over and over is not a team sport. Even if it would be cathartic."

"Paintball was better," Mo agreed. "Except for the bruise part. Laser tag?"

Russ sent off an email request to book a place last-minute. They finished up the meal and took care of their mess, and then Russ went up to his room and got ready for bed.

Meanwhile he needed to let Liam know what was going on so he didn't get blindsided by their date getting rescheduled. Russ texted him one-handed while brushing his teeth. *Need to cancel tomorrow. Team bonding. Rain check? I'll make it up to you.*

He didn't get a reply, but Liam fell asleep fast—he'd probably stuffed his face and then passed out with his shoes on.

The mental image had Russ smiling, which made brushing his teeth kind of difficult. He spat and rinsed and wrapped his hair and was halfway to his bed when someone knocked on the door.

He expected Mo or Baller—had he forgotten something in the conference room?—but it was Liam. Russ shouldn't be surprised. The kid had basically agreed to date him to continue getting access to Russ's cock. "You could make it up to me now," he suggested, leaning in suggestively.

What a loser. Russ pulled him inside and didn't bother fighting back a smile as he threaded his fingers through Liam's soft curls. "Did you have something in mind?"

Liam closed his eyes to near slits and tilted his head into Russ's touch. "We do have a day off tomorrow… unless your legs are too tired?"

Now that was just uncalled-for. Russ tightened his grip a bit. "Only one of us has been playing twenty-eight minutes a night for the past ten years, Trouble. I think my thighs can handle you."

Besides, a small voice in the back of his mind piped up, he'd only have so many more chances. Either he'd get traded before the deadline or this would be his last season with the Caimans.

"We'll see," Liam teased, and then squawked when Russ bodied him onto the bed.

As much as Russ would've liked to go slow, he knew how that would feel—like he was drawing things out in bed because he didn't have control over their expiring time together. He didn't want that bittersweet taste in his mouth tonight, and anyway, neither of them had the patience or the energy. In three minutes he had Liam naked and squirming on his fingers, cursing in two languages and asking for more.

Russ didn't make him wait. He slid in deep and fast, spurred on by Liam's nails in his back and the sharp, bitten-off noises that escaped his mouth with every thrust, occasionally accompanied by declarations of how much Liam loved Russ's cock.

Something about Liam's enthusiasm for getting fucked spoke right to Russ's lizard brain, whispering that he could keep Liam just like this always, ready to take Russ's cock whenever Russ felt the urge, and that still wouldn't be enough for Liam.

It did things to Russ's ego… and his libido.

Liam was already reaching for his dick, hard and red and leaking prettily all down the length. Russ watched with a gaze that felt heavy and then leaned down to lick a wet kiss into his mouth. When Liam strained to meet him, Russ pulled back and put his hands on Liam's hips to yank him into his lap. The angle let him get even deeper, sheathed in perfect tight heat.

"One day we're going to see if you can come on just my cock." He doubted Liam could—surely it would've happened by now—but the thought of keeping him strung out on Russ's dick and not letting him touch himself made Russ feel crazed with lust. The way Liam would beg for him, until he couldn't anymore and he just had to *take* what Russ gave him—

Apparently Liam thought it sounded fucking hot too, because he gasped and erupted in his own hand, shooting all over himself like he hadn't come in days.

That brought Russ to the edge too, and he swore and put his hand in the center of Liam's chest to keep him still while Russ finished, pounding into his hole with his stomach clenched and his mouth half open in pleasure.

His orgasm hit low in his stomach and punched through him, racking his body until his muscles trembled and his lungs screamed for oxygen. He half fell forward before catching himself on nerveless, clumsy hands, somehow no longer braced on Liam's clavicle.

Liam mumbled something that sounded exhausted and reverent, though Russ's brain was too fried to decipher if it was English. With some effort, he pulled out and off and sank gracelessly to the bed.

"Fuck," Liam added a second later.

Russ wheezed out an incredulous laugh. Liam had a way with words all right. Maybe he *should* write that book. "Yeah." Grimacing, he pulled off the condom and wrapped it in a handful of Kleenex. By the time he'd finished, Liam's eyes were closing.

Russ nudged his thigh with his knee. "Come on, up. Clean off before bed unless you want to wax your trail with your own jizz tomorrow."

Liam groaned but made no indication of getting out of bed until Russ prodded him a second time. "Liam. If we clean up now, we'll have more time to fool around in the morning."

That got him a laugh and a pair of bright, suddenly alert eyes focused on him. "Your pep talks are getting better."

Russ could've pushed him out of bed, but he got up and yanked him to his feet instead. "Guess I just needed to find the right motivation."

By the time they crawled between the sheets, Russ had locked his thoughts about their losing streak and the precariousness of his own future deep in that box at the back of his mind. Liam was kind of magic like that. Russ curled around him and pressed a kiss to the back of his shoulder. Barely a few breaths passed before sleep took him.

GROWING UP in a backwoods Canadian town, Liam had had his share of adventures—snowshoeing, snowmobiling, snowboarding, tobogganing, fishing, hiking, ATVing, pond hockey. If you could do it outside, he'd been all over it.

He'd never played laser tag.

"How many left?" Sparky whispered in the dark. He and Liam were huddled behind one of the many half walls, hiding and listening and waiting for Russ, who'd gone out to scout the enemy and hadn't reported back.

Liam bit his lip and tried to think. They'd broken into four teams, two of just forwards, one of just defense, and a mixed team that included the goalies. Liam, Russ, and Sparky were on the mixed team, currently facing off against one team of forwards.

"Hughesy and Mo, for sure." Baller had been hit in the first minute and wouldn't be living that down anytime soon. "And maybe—"

Sparky put a hand over Liam's mouth. Someone was coming.

Liam nodded his understanding and raised his gun a fraction of an inch. Sparky withdrew, gestured with his head toward an adjacent wall, and crept across toward it. This way they'd have a decent chance of catching whoever it was in their crossfire.

The footsteps came closer. Hesitated. Then—

Tap tap tap.

Liam exhaled and lowered the weapon as Russ came around the corner.

"So? What's the situation?"

"Not good. Just the three of us left. Forwards have five. Fucking Hughesy's a ringer."

Shit.

"Plan?" Sparky asked.

Russ looked at Liam. Liam looked back, eyebrows raised.

Finally Russ said, "Liam, how many did you hit?"

"Four."

Russ had hit two, Sparky five; why the fuck was he a goalie? Clearly he'd missed his calling.

Russ shook his head. "Guess that makes me the bait."

They set the trap with Liam behind a corner in an L-shaped section of hallway. Sparky folded himself into a sort of sniper's nest a bit farther down. Russ had seen Mo and Hughesy in the far back side of the maze and their other teammates a little closer on the other end.

"Wish me luck," he said. Then he headed off to try to lure someone out.

Liam did his best to keep still and silent, even though his thighs were cramping. He shifted minutely, watching to his left, even though he knew he had left himself exposed on the right side. Sparky would cover him. Hopefully.

It felt like forever before he heard the cartoonish sound of laser-tag fire. Russ shouted in triumph, and then—

Thundering footsteps. Liam raised his gun.

Russ ran past and ducked down a side tunnel, zigzagging like mad to try to escape being hit. As soon as he had, Liam poked his head out from the cover and aimed. *Zapzapzap.*

"Aww, boo!" Mo complained, but he was "dead," so he didn't get to say anything else.

They used a similar tactic to get everyone but Hughesy, since Mo couldn't warn them. Unfortunately, the third time was *not* the charm, and Sparky got hit.

That left Russ and Liam against Hughesy. By now he must've figured out what they were doing, so they couldn't use their trick again.

Worse, Mo had gotten in a glancing hit during Russ's trap, so one more and Russ was done for. Plus, Hughesy was small and fast, and Liam didn't know if he'd been hit at all.

"Team one—last man standing," announced the prerecorded voice on the loudspeaker.

Russ and Liam exchanged looks. "Think he'll run?"

Liam snorted. "No. That bloodthirsty maniac coming for us."

They blinked at each other in the near darkness for another moment before they heard footsteps.

"Maybe *we* should run?" Liam suggested.

"Yeah," Russ agreed and grabbed his arm.

They ran.

Well, sort of. The maze was designed to hide people, but also to trap them, and several times they turned a corner only to find a dead end. They'd half run into each other, laughing and swearing under their breath but never letting go of each other's hand.

They managed to stay far enough ahead to have time to turn around—until suddenly the right at the end of a long stretch of hallway turned out to be a spiraling dead end.

"Putain," Liam said. They were going to have to face Hughesy head-on. He'd have cover; they wouldn't.

Then Russ said, "I have another idea," and knelt on the floor.

Liam blinked at him, because what? "We just start dating, what are you doing?"

Even in the dim lighting, he could see Russ roll his eyes. "Get on. Piggyback ride. *Hurry up*, he's coming!"

Well, that explained why Russ had his back to him. Liam climbed on—

And Russ charged down the hallway toward Hughesy, both of them firing. Jesus Christ, how was Russ moving this fast with Liam on his back? Liam clung to Russ's hips with his thighs and steadied his left arm around his shoulder. With his right, he aimed the laser gun at Hughesy's chest plate and pulled the trigger.

Zap. Zap. Zapzapzap.

The light on the front of Hughesy's vest flashed and beeped.

The one on the front of Russ's wailed. Fatal hit. He wasn't allowed to hold Liam up anymore.

Liam rolled off and crouched to the floor, still shooting. If he lay close to the ground, Hughesy wouldn't get a good angle, and maybe—

Hughesy's vest let out a scream.

"Winner! Team two!" announced the PA, and Liam rolled over onto his back and raised both hands in the victory V.

"The champion!" he yelled.

Russ pulled him to his feet, rolling his eyes. "And so modest too."

"And his *hero*," Liam added, fake swooning into Russ's arms. "The chivalry. The self-sacrifice. The… *ferda*." He patted Russ's chest plate.

"That sounds so wrong with a French accent," Hughesy complained.

Liam shot him the finger without taking his eyes off Russ, who was still holding him like a superhero. "I don't have a French accent."

Somehow Russ didn't even smile at this blatant lie. *Such* a gentleman. Liam swooned for real this time.

"Okay, now get off the course," Mo yelled. "It's Three and Four's turn. Watching you make out is *not* part of the team-building exercise."

Russ snorted and nudged Liam into moving toward the sidelines. "You should've heard Baller's ideas for team building."

Liam snickered. "Seriously, though. Why the self-sacrifice?" Russ had the same competitive spirit as every other professional athlete.

"It's a team sport, Trouble. You're a better shot than me." He shoved Liam toward the lounge where the "dead" waited on leather couches. Earlier, the big-screen TVs had been showing the match, but now they were playing video games while teams three and four suited up. "Have some pizza and don't read too much into it."

Liam wasn't reading into it so much as he was thinking out loud. He kept thinking as he grabbed a slice of pizza and wormed his way onto the couch between Russ and Hughesy.

Russ was the kind of guy who'd literally put his team on his back and carry them to victory. As a boyfriend, he seemed to enjoy spoiling Liam. That was just who he was, and he never expected anything in return—at least not anything more than someone to play cribbage with by candlelight when the power went out, because he was secretly ninety years old. (And a romantic. Liam hadn't forgotten. He knew for a fact Russ had a backup generator. He just didn't run it until the next morning unless he had to.)

The point, Liam thought as Russ slid an arm over his shoulders without pausing his conversation with Baller, was that Russ looked after other people. He deserved someone to look after him too.

Liam could barely take care of himself half the time, but if he could learn to love leg day because it gave him NHL hockey, he could practice being a good boyfriend too. The payoff would definitely be worth it.

RUSS DIDN'T know if it was the team-building, the extra day off, or something else, but when the team filed onto the ice for the last road game of the trip, they felt *loose*. In the warm-up shootout drill, Baller pulled a ridiculous behind-and-between-his-own-legs shot that somehow went in. Sparky looked at his stick in betrayal, then took off out of the crease after Baller and mocked a fight with him until Baller ended up turtled in the net, laughing. When he got up again, Liam ran the drill as though he was the goalie.

Baller dramatically missed the save, and Liam cellied like he'd just won Olympic gold.

"Aww," Mo said at Russ's shoulder. "The kids are all right."

I love my stupid team, Russ thought fondly, and decided not to point out that both Sparky and Baller were older than Mo. But the moment was bittersweet. Who knew how much longer it would be his team?

Before he could get too deep in his own head, Coach blew the whistle and roped everyone into order, but he was laughing too. Either the good mood had caught on, or the coaching staff had had their own kind of relaxing day off.

Russ didn't think much of it until Coach called for everyone's attention in the locker room before the anthem. "Right, okay, we're going to mix up the lines a little tonight. Hughesy, let's try you at 2C, okay? Baller, you take his left wing. And Carl, Trouble, switch places. Let's see how Liam does with Russ."

There was a chorus of "Yes, Coach!" when he finished. Russ was so pleased to get to play with Liam instead of Carl that he had to focus on not smiling too broadly. He didn't want to offend Carl—it wasn't anyone's fault they didn't have great chemistry—but he also didn't need anyone chirping him for his happiness where Coach would hear. *Plausible deniability*, he'd told Russ once. *It makes the world go round.*

Liam hadn't gotten that lesson. He was practically bouncing in his skates as they stood at center ice for the anthem.

"Calm down," Russ murmured out of the side of his mouth.

"Can't," Liam said, grinning. ".... Partner."

Russ pretended to snort, but he knew from the way Liam bumped his shoulder that Liam didn't buy it.

True to his word, Liam did not calm down. The rest of the team followed his lead, and right from the puck drop, they were cracking. From the first faceoff, the Caimans dominated the play, jumped on every loose puck, and shut down every opportunity the Tartans had for a goal.

Russ and Liam clicked almost seamlessly. Russ checked, Liam blocked shots, and together they cleared the defensive zone. It had taken a year of playing together before Russ and Jonesy could read each other that well.

"You two are buzzin'," Mo commented on the bench. "Keep it up."

Russ knew exactly what would happen if they did—and he was right. The Caimans went up 2–0 by the end of the first, and he and Liam were on the ice for both goals. But that wasn't what Russ was angling for. The way Liam was playing tonight, going hard in the corners, throwing his body around, getting his stick on everything? It was only a matter of time.

Russ didn't jinx it by saying so out loud. He just thanked the years of experience and conditioning that let him keep up, and waited for Liam to find the right spot at the right time.

The second period slipped by, and each team scored, but Liam didn't find the twine. Russ thought maybe he'd been wrong and it wouldn't be tonight after all. Then, in the final moments of the game, the Tartans squeaked a goal under Sparky's pads. Newly energized, they pulled the goalie.

Russ and Liam were stuck on the bench when it happened, unable to do anything but watch helplessly as Carl, Yeti, and the three forwards got hemmed in with no opportunity to change. He could see their energy waning as the Tartans grew increasingly frantic.

With forty-three seconds to go, the Tartans scored again to tie it.

No, Russ thought. No fucking way. Not after the way they'd played tonight. Not again.

The stoppage in play gave the Caimans the chance to put fresh legs on the ice. Mo put on his grim captain face and said, "Fuck overtime."

Russ couldn't agree more.

Sometimes the wheels came off a game like this and a team got demoralized. It didn't happen to the Caimans tonight.

Russ and Liam hit the ice with Mo, Baller, and Hughesy, and snapped into action. Hughesy won the faceoff. Baller's pass to Mo made a clean zone entry.

But this late in the game, the ice was garbage. A flukey bounce ended with the puck on a Tartan stick.

Not tonight. Not when they'd been so close, when they'd been playing so well.

Russ stepped in on the guy and stick-checked him. A little wrist action and the puck was sliding across the chewed-up ice right to Liam.

And just like he hadn't for the past three games, Liam didn't hesitate. He pulled his stick back and let loose with a slap shot that rang as it hit the bar at the back of the net.

The sound was all the sweeter for the buzzer that followed it.

Russ swept Liam into a celly, whooping as their teammates crashed in around them. He hoped like hell someone grabbed that puck, because he didn't want to let go of Liam's pads.

"Hell of a time for a first goal," Mo said with a pat on the shoulder.

Russ smiled in a way that felt far too intimate for the setting, but he didn't care. "Knew it would be tonight."

Liam beamed. "This means I get to pick the bar, right?"

Belanger First Star of the Night as Caimans Crunch Tartans
By Rocky Sanderson

The Caimans ended their three-game losing streak with a 4–3 victory over the Ottawa Tartans last night.

Despite the close score, the Caimans dominated the play, outshooting their opponents 43–18. The final goal came off the stick of rookie defenseman Liam Belanger, who played a personal-best 27 minutes. The goal was Belanger's first in the NHL.

"Obviously it was a great time to get that," Belanger said after the game, all smiles as he posed with the game-winning puck. "Big thanks to Russ for the perfect setup."

Tonight was also the first time Belanger paired with veteran Russ Lyons for an entire game. Together they were on the ice for an impressive 57 percent of the team's attempted shots. Lyons, whose six-year contract with the Caimans expires this season, is set to play his thousandth NHL game early in the New Year.

"He's a big role model for me and playing with him, he [makes] it easy to score. Hopefully I get to play with him a lot more now. We'll see what Coach says."

The Caimans play their next game in Miami on December 18.

BACK HOME, Liam and Russ attempted to schedule their date twice more. Sadly, their jobs had other ideas. They had three games crammed into the remaining days before the Christmas break. The one night they were both free and not too tired to leave the house was after a brutal game against Tampa in which Liam got pancaked into the glass so hard the whole right half of his face was purple.

"Maybe I don't show my face in public," he said, looking at his reflection. "I might scare children."

Russ poked his head into the bathroom and winced. "Yeah, I'm going to get you an ice pack." There he went, taking care of Liam again.

Liam touched his cheek. *Ow.* The ice pack sounded good. "So... not going out. I should order something in? Dinner and a movie?" He followed Russ out of the bathroom and into the kitchen.

Russ pulled a gel pack out of the freezer and gave him a wry look. "Netflix and chill?"

Smiling hurt, so Liam pressed the cold to his face. "Pizza, barbecue, or Chinese?"

The Caimans carried the momentum from the last game of their road trip right up until the break. Coach kept Liam and Russ paired together, though they rotated between first and second defensive pairing, which Liam appreciated because he needed a lot more leg days before he'd be able to consistently keep up with Russ's minutes. The new pairings suited everyone better. Liam even got some time quarterbacking the second power-play unit.

So it shouldn't have come as a surprise when management called him into a meeting before the last game before the break. The GM and Coach Bruce shook his hand but didn't bother offering him a seat—apparently it wouldn't be a long meeting.

"Thanks for coming in," the GM said, smiling. "I know you've got warm-ups to get back to, so we won't keep you, but I always like to do this in person."

Liam blinked. "Do what in person?"

The GM chuckled and shook his head as though Liam were being coy. "Modest, eh? That's the game, I guess. Start looking for an apartment, kid. You're staying in Miami for the foreseeable future."

Coach must've understood Liam's expression to mean *that's great, but so what?*, because he added, "He means we're not paying for your hotel anymore, Trouble."

Oh. *Oh.* Liam grinned. "That's—wow, thank you, sir!" Although looking for an apartment in Lexington had been bad enough, and that had been before the regular season started. Not that Liam spent a lot of time in his hotel room anyway….

Coach cleared his throat and gave Liam a significant look. Liam wasn't yet fluent in Coach's significant looks, but this one read pretty clearly that if Liam was thinking about how much time he'd spent in Russ's bed instead of his own, he'd better not say as much in front of the GM. Which, like… fair. His bosses did not need to know about his sex life.

"You've earned it," the GM said. "Great job. Keep it up. Now get out of here—you've got a game to win."

"Yes, sir."

It seemed fitting that Liam got his first power-play point of his career that night, and that the team went out to celebrate. And that Liam and Russ continued their celebration afterward at Russ's place.

Unfortunately that meant that by the time Liam and Russ got out of bed the next morning, Liam had an hour and a half to catch his flight and no time to clear his stuff out of his hotel room.

He hopped around the bedroom, cursing as he put on his socks, while Russ calmly scrolled through his phone because he'd packed two days ago and didn't have a flight until noon.

"They could've told me sooner," Liam complained as he zipped his duffel bag closed. He didn't even *have* a suitcase at Russ's; half his things had just migrated naturally one at a time. "Then I could've been ready."

"They probably figured you'd be going back to your hotel to sleep last night," Russ pointed out.

Ugh, why did he have to be so reasonable? Liam frowned at the floor. Was that his sock or Russ's? "I guess I could call the hotel and like, give them my credit card so they don't kick me out of my room while I'm gone." Was his credit card still current? He was due for a new one soon, but it might've gotten sent to Lexington.

Shit.

Russ dropped his phone on the bed. "Liam. Deep breaths."

Belatedly, Liam realized he was on the verge of panic. With a huff, he threw himself onto the mattress next to Russ. "I'm a shitty adult." Despite his resolution, not only had he not figured out what taking care of Russ the way Russ took care of him even looked like, he'd failed to be an independent adult yet again.

"You're a little disorganized," Russ allowed. "Do you have your passport?"

That, at least, Liam could keep track of. "Yeah."

"Good. Give me your hotel key."

Liam opened his eyes and turned to look at Russ.

"I'll drop you at the airport and go pick up your stuff before my flight. I'll leave it in my car and you can get it when we're back."

You couldn't have offered three minutes ago, before my heart rate hit 150? Liam let out a huge breath. Of course Russ was here to save him. "You're trying to win an award for best boyfriend ever?"

"I'm trying to get my boyfriend to the airport on time so I don't miss my own flight." Russ softened the blow by pressing a kiss to the top of Liam's head like he was some kind of adorable but misbehaved pet. "Come on."

The departures lane at the airport was too public for a kiss goodbye, but considering the situation, Liam didn't think he had any grounds to complain. "Thanks for the ride," he said instead and tried not to think about why it felt so awkward and stilted. "See you after."

He thought Russ must've caught the vibe he was feeling, because his voice was soft and sweet, almost apologetic, when he said, "Safe flight."

Liam couldn't help smiling at him, even though he didn't have time to draw it out. "Yeah, you too. Don't forget you owe me a date when we get back."

For a brief moment, Russ covered Liam's hand with his own. "I won't."

Liam had to book it to his gate, but he didn't have a checked bag anyway and there was plenty of room in business class for his carry-on.

His seatmate was an older woman knitting something in bright pinks and purples. The project spilled across her lap and into a bulging bag at her feet. When Liam finally sat down, panting slightly, she looked up at him and flashed a knowing smile. "Long goodbye?"

Caught out, Liam laughed and leaned into the seat. "Long good morning."

He was asleep before takeoff.

RUSS'S SISTER was enormous.

"Don't you dare say it," she warned him darkly as he gathered her into a hug.

"Say what?" he asked, releasing her. "My little nephew is getting so big."

Gia slapped him on the back of the head, but she was grinning. "You're such a jerk."

That jerk had bought his nephew an entire nursery set for Christmas, and he wasn't even making an appearance for another two months. Russ accepted the abuse because she didn't mean it and growing an entire human was more physical work than he'd do in his entire life. "Love you too, sis."

The break over Christmas never felt like a vacation. It was too much traveling and too many family events squished into too little time to be relaxing. But Russ appreciated the opportunity to relax with his loved ones, even if they were the nosiest people in the universe.

"Andi's seeing some boy from one of her classes, but she won't bring him around for dinner," his mother complained during cleanup the first night.

She was probably afraid Ma would try to give him a blood test at the table. "She will when she's ready."

At least everyone was too invested in Andi's love life, Gia's pregnancy, and Tony and Gramps's home renovations—and giving updates about the neighbors, their coworkers, and all the cousins and aunties—to dig into Russ's private life.

It should've been too busy and crowded for Russ to have time to think and sleep, never mind miss anyone, but he found himself imagining Liam ribbing Tony about being a sugar baby at seventysomething, and smiling more wistfully than he had a right to.

Russ might have a few days off from playing, but there was never any rest from his agent, who had kicked into high gear planning Russ's thousandth-game celebration with the team. The game would fall just before the trade deadline, so she was also running down a list of teams he'd prefer to go to. It looked different than it had a few months ago, with several good teams out of playoff contention due to injuries and a few surprises creeping up in the standings.

Russ didn't have any control over where they sent him. He didn't have a no-movement clause. But he'd been with the team long enough that he had some good will built up; they'd probably at least try to send him somewhere he wouldn't hate. Besides, right now the most likely teams to acquire him would be ones lining up a deep Cup run.

Not for the first time, Russ felt a pang of regret about his last contract negotiation. The Caimans had offered a limited no-movement clause with a lower annual salary. He could've taken that and had some control over his future. But in the end, he'd figured a trade was a trade, and if he couldn't keep himself in one place, then where he went didn't matter.

Or it hadn't then. Now he couldn't help but think about how much he liked Florida. Not the weather, which was too hot and prone to hurricanes, or the politics, which were just that side of batshit fuckery. But he did like the beach and the food, and if he couldn't share a team with Liam, then sharing a state with him was the next best thing. If he couldn't stay in Miami, Tampa wouldn't be so bad.

The Caimans were never going to trade him to Tampa, though, even if Tampa could afford him, which they couldn't.

"Hey." Andi kicked his shin under the table. "Quit brooding about your job and do your part eating dessert."

All things considered, Russ was glad to get back home, finally, after a six-hour delay leaving Winnipeg due to a snowstorm. He pushed open the front door and trudged up to his room, gritty-eyed and exhausted, at two in the morning, knowing he had to be at team workout tomorrow at ten.

There was someone in his bed.

That was—weird.

He'd known Liam would be there, of course. He'd been texting with him since the storm rolled in. Liam hadn't booked a hotel or an Airbnb yet, and it wasn't like Russ wasn't used to having him around.

It was still strange to crawl into his bed when someone else had already warmed it.

He was taking off his belt when Liam inhaled deeply and half rolled over. "Hey. You made it."

"Finally," Russ agreed. He tossed his jeans on the chair next to the bed and peeled off his shirt. "Good break?"

"Mmm," Liam mumbled into the pillow. "It was nice."

Russ had to nudge him over—he'd gravitated to the middle of the mattress. "Go back to sleep."

He was wasting his breath. From the deep sigh Liam let out, he was already well on his way. Russ pulled the covers up and was surprised when Liam rolled over next to him and flung an arm across Russ's chest. Apparently Liam had missed him too.

Russ brushed a kiss into his curls and closed his eyes.

LIAM HAD expected that the first day back after the break would have a laid-back vibe. Something that let the guys ease out of their personal lives and back into their professional roles. The fact that the trainers had scheduled a gym workout instead of an on-ice one, he thought, reinforced that.

Liam had been wrong before, but usually being wrong wasn't this embarrassing.

He handled the physical part of the workout fine. Mathieu had converted him—Liam wanted to play professional hockey, so he never skipped leg day. The yoga, the bikes, the wind sprints, the agility exercises—he could handle all of those. Maybe he couldn't keep up with the guys who'd been doing it for years yet, but he was closing the gap. He had made a lot of progress in a few months.

The weights, though. Liam didn't know what the fuck was going on with the weights.

He lifted them no problem. Bicep curls, leg presses, chest presses, bench presses. Sure, his muscles went hot with exertion, but Liam knew that feeling. Liam *liked* that feeling, or he'd never have made it this far.

The way his shorts stuck to his crotch, though. That was new.

At first he didn't notice. He was working out; workouts got sweaty. Plus, he lived in Florida and Florida humidity could braise you in your own skin. Liam's clothes stuck to him all the time. It wasn't exactly a revelation that it happened while he was doing bench presses.

Then he switched to deadlifts, and he needed the mirror for that because he didn't have the right muscle memory to keep his form correct, and suddenly the problem became more apparent.

There was a wet spot on the front of Liam's shorts. It looked like he'd been playing with himself all morning instead of working out.

His cheeks burned. God, what if someone *noticed*? Hockey teams weren't known for their discretion when it came to avoiding embarrassing topics. And like—okay, it had been a few days and he was *horny*. He'd had to share a room with Bernadette over Christmas, and he hadn't exactly had a lot of alone time to take care of his needs, but this was ridiculous. Right? He wasn't even hard, really, just….

Clearly he should have set an earlier alarm for this morning and had a proper reunion with Russ before going to the gym.

He was debating how to cover his problem when Baller sidled up next to him. "Tough being away from your man, huh?" he said empathetically.

Liam wanted to die. Of course he'd been caught by the worst possible person. "This has never happened to me before." If Baller decided to call attention to him—

He clapped Liam heavily on the shoulder, chin wrinkled in a regretful sort of frown. "Sorry about this.

"Sorry about—"

Baller raised his water bottle in his other hand and squirted Liam in the face. Ice-cold water hit his nose, his eyelids, his hair. His chest. Then his crotch.

To his horror, Liam shrieked.

Finally Baller stopped and gave him a cheeky grin while Liam glared, dripping from his eyebrows. "Heard you're getting kicked out of your hotel," he chirped loudly enough for everyone to overhear. "Welcome to the big leagues for real."

Liam raised the hem of his shirt to wipe his face, and also to give himself time to compose his expression. Baller's reason for squirting him was flimsy—he'd had plenty of proper welcomes to the team by now—but he'd given Liam an explanation for his shorts being wet and made sure everyone knew what it was. "You're the worst."

The conditioning coach shouted across the room, "Baltierra, you're supposed to be doing jump squats!"

"Hundred bucks for distracting the rookie," Russ added.

"You're welcome," Baller told Liam under his breath. "Next time don't let him make you go so long without, yeah?"

Good grief. "He didn't *make me*," Liam hissed, sure he was scarlet. He stopped short of admitting he'd had to share a bedroom with his sister. His honesty had limits. Although—"Wait, are you saying this has happened before?"

"Not to me," Baller said beatifically. "Known a couple guys who wear two pairs of compression shorts, if you know what I mean. Oh, and one guy on my last team could come from a good core workout. He never did those with the team for some reason. Great abs, though, as you can imagine."

Jesus. "And I thought there wasn't privacy in the AHL."

"Baltierra!"

"Whoops, gotta go. Remember what I said."

When Baller turned away, Liam unfroze enough to grab a towel and dry off properly and added *buy more compression shorts* to his to-do list. Obviously having more sex was the desired outcome, but it was better to be prepared.

After the workout, they had a team meeting, which Liam bravely paid attention to. At least there was food, so when it was over, he and Russ could go back to Russ's place and deal with Liam's situation.

Or so he thought, but they'd only been in the truck for thirty seconds when Russ's phone rang. The call ID on the truck screen read ERIKA OR-RICK—his agent.

Liam felt like he'd been punched in the chest.

Cursing, Russ stabbed the button to send the call to voicemail.

An awkward silence descended in the cab.

People's agents talked to them about a lot of things—sponsorship deals, charity gigs, interest in international tournaments. A call from an agent didn't necessarily mean a trade. And sure, Russ's contract was up at the end of the season, the trade deadline was only a month and a half away, and Russ had been up-front that he didn't think the Caimans could or would re-sign him.

But that didn't mean anything.

What maybe did mean something was the way Liam's stomach hit his knees when he saw the call display. But as much as he and Russ had an exclusive relationship, Liam had always known it had an expiration date.

He'd just… inconveniently forgotten.

Liam licked his lips. Should he say something? *What* should he say? Should he ask if Russ was being traded? They'd been careful to tiptoe around the topic.

Finally he managed, "Um… should you have taken that?"

Russ exhaled. "I'll call her back later."

That didn't make Liam feel any better.

"Let's focus on our date," Russ said after a moment. As attempts to lighten the mood went, it was obvious, but it worked anyway. "Thursday night?"

"Done." Assuming Russ was still around on Thursday to go with him.

Russ covered Liam's hand on the center console. "Hey. One other thing, actually." He rubbed his thumb over Liam's wrist, eliciting an involuntary shiver. The man had enormous hands, and he knew exactly how to distract Liam with them.

"Hmm?"

"Why did Baller really spray you with the water bottle?"

Oh God. Now *that* was an effective distraction. Liam raised his other hand to his mouth to try to stifle the mortified laugh that came out. "Um."

Russ turned Liam's hand over and rubbed down the center of his palm. "Did he decide you needed a cold shower?"

Calisse. "I *did* need a cold shower." Liam sank low in his seat. "It's just been a while, I guess, okay? I'm not used to that."

Around them, traffic thickened; they were navigating the intersection of two busy thoroughfares. Russ didn't comment until he'd merged into the flow. Then he cleared his throat. "So you're saying he was, what, helping camouflage your boner?"

Fuck it. He asked. The least Liam could do was give him a taste of what Liam had gone through. "Did you know that sometimes your dick will start, like, leaking during exercise?" he said. "Especially if it's a few days since you have an orgasm."

Russ swallowed audibly.

"And then you're working out with your team, and everyone is very in shape," Liam went on without mercy. He'd only been thinking about going home with Russ at that point, but let him be a little jealous. "But you said we don't have time to fool around this morning."

The speedometer needle edged toward the right.

Liam wondered what would happen if he told Russ what Baller said about his old teammate. Probably they'd get in a car accident. He decided not to risk it.

"My parents turned my old bedroom into a study," he went on. "So over break I shared with Bernadette. No privacy, you know?"

Russ's hand spasmed around Liam's. "So you're saying you haven't gotten off since—"

"Since before the break."

Russ inhaled deeply and held it. Liam watched it shudder back out of him again. "Here's what's going to happen."

The sudden drop in his timbre made the hair on the back of Liam's neck stand up.

"We're going to get home and you're going to go into the gym."

They'd just finished a workout and Russ wanted to go back to it? Except, no, he couldn't. Not with the heat in his voice.

"You're going to take off your shorts. Leave the shirt on. Sit on the weight bench and wait for me."

Liam had no idea what Russ had in mind, but his cock was already into it. He rubbed his palm on his thigh. "And then what?"

Russ pulled into the driveway and slammed the truck into Park. "Do it and find out."

Liam didn't need convincing. In the weight room, his hands shook in anticipation as he shoved his shorts down. He felt ridiculous with his erection jutting out from his body, but maybe that was part of the point?

Either way, he didn't have to wait long. A moment later Russ appeared in the doorway with an old towel slung over one shoulder. His gaze was hot when he beckoned Liam over to him.

The kiss set all Liam's nerve endings firing, but Russ kept his hands almost entirely to himself, only ghosting teasing passes over Liam's shoulders, then brushing his palms against the sensitive skin of Liam's thighs and ass. Liam shuddered and tried to press more firmly against him, but Russ grabbed him by the shoulders and held him still.

When Russ finally broke the kiss, Liam's cock was drooling all over again and his lips felt beestung from the scrape of Russ's beard.

He still hadn't caught his breath when Russ raised something into his field of vision and asked, "You ever use one of these?"

Liam's breath hitched. The toy was vaguely penis-shaped, so its purpose was obvious, and while Liam had used a dildo before, he didn't think that was what this was. For one thing, there was a ring attached at the base that looked like it would go around his dick. "What is it?"

Russ pushed a button on the base and the end of the toy moved, emitting a low humming sound as the bulbous tip rotated. "Prostate massager."

Liam was going to die. He swallowed. "No."

"You want to try it?"

"God, yes."

Russ kissed him again, another light, teasing caress of his lips and tongue, as though he thought Liam might spontaneously combust if he touched him harder. Liam thought it might be a possibility.

This time when the kiss broke, Russ trailed his hand down Liam's neck, brushed over his Adam's apple, and thumbed his nipple through his shirt. "Come here, then."

Russ laid the towel on the weight bench and straddled it before beckoning Liam to do the same. But when Liam made to face him, Russ shook his head. "Other way, Trouble. I want you to be able to see what I'm doing to you."

Liam didn't realize what he meant until he turned around and saw his own reflection, Russ standing behind him, pressing kisses to the side of his neck.

He was right—he did look dumb with his shirt on and his cock hard. Especially with Russ fully clothed behind him. But he could hardly complain about it when Russ flicked open the lube and slicked his fingers. And he certainly couldn't find the words to protest when Russ slid those fingers between Liam's cheeks.

All the while, he never stopped the movement of his mouth. Wet kisses to the side of his neck. The score of teeth on the cartilage of his ear. When Russ pushed inside him, he sucked Liam's earlobe into his mouth and Liam's knees tried to buckle.

Russ held him steady with his other hand on his stomach. "Easy."

He really was.

Liam let out a shuddery breath and accidentally met his own eyes in the mirror. They were hazy, and a flush spread across his freckles. His dick bobbed against the hem of his shirt. The soft fabric felt like even more of a tease.

Russ didn't spend a long time stretching him open. The toy was slender anyway, and it wasn't like Liam needed help getting turned-on. It seemed like only a handful of seconds had passed before Russ was sliding the silicone ring over Liam's cock. Even the fleeting touch had Liam curling his hands into fists so he wouldn't buck into it.

Then he felt the tip of the toy at his hole. Liam's body offered almost no resistance. He wanted this. He wanted Russ to show him what his body could do.

When the toy was seated, Russ moved his hands to Liam's hips and pulled him slightly backward. "Okay. Now sit down."

Liam sat.

The movement made the toy shift inside him, and suddenly it felt a lot bigger than it looked.

"Fuck." He groaned and leaned back against Russ, who'd sat behind him.

"Look at that," Russ murmured. He reached around Liam's body to pull the hem of his shirt up so his cock was exposed. Clear fluid had leaked all down the sides and was still seeping from the tip. "No wonder you put on a show at the gym. You're just too full, aren't you?"

Liam swallowed. This was *not* going to take long. "Russ—"

He didn't even realize he'd moved until Russ said sternly, "Hands on your thighs."

Liam yanked his hands away from his dick and dug his nails into the flesh of his quads.

"I know you don't want anyone else to see you like this." Russ smoothed his palms across Liam's chest over his shirt and then pushed his chin up so he was watching himself in the mirror again. He looked like some kind of needy slut, sitting there with his cock out and dripping, Russ behind him but barely touching him.

Russ pulled back Liam's foreskin and swirled his index finger oh-so-lightly over the top of his dick, coating it in liquid. "This is only for me. So we're going to make sure to get all of it. Right?"

"Right," Liam said. He only had a vague idea what he was agreeing to, but he felt amazing. He would've agreed with anything Russ said. Russ would take care of him, just like he always did.

"I'm going to turn the massager on now," Russ told him. "It's pressing right against your prostate, isn't it? That's what it's supposed to do."

The humming noise started, and the toy in Liam's ass rotated away from his prostate, then back over it, slowly, slower than Russ had ever fucked him. Liam's mouth dropped open and his erection jerked.

"Does it feel good?"

It felt like Liam was on the edge of orgasm already, but he wouldn't get there without touching himself. He didn't know if he could answer out loud, so he nodded, every muscle in his body taut with anticipation.

"See how wet you're getting?" Russ touched his cock again, too lightly to offer any kind of relief. When he drew his fingertips off the head, a string of viscous clear-white fluid followed. "The toy's gonna help you pump all of that out."

Oh God. Russ turned up the speed, and Liam jerked, desperate to get a hand on himself. He wanted to come. He needed it.

Russ caught his wrist before he could touch his dick. "Not yet," he said. He bent down next to the bench and picked something up from the floor. He pressed it into Liam's hand.

It was a five-pound weight.

Liam's bicep twinged. He couldn't. Could he? He curled his fingers around the grip.

"Twenty reps with each arm," Russ murmured into his ear. "Nice and slow, Trouble. No cheating. Form counts or you can start over. And then I'll make you come."

Liam wet his lips.

He lifted the weight.

Pleasure arced inside him. The contraction of his abs as he curled the weight toward his shoulder heightened his awareness of the toy inside him. His cock leaked and jerked with pleasure, hypersensitive. He was so wet that the chill of the air conditioning almost hurt.

Ten reps in and he needed a break, not because his muscles ached but because he couldn't concentrate on his form. "Can I switch arms?"

"Whatever you need," Russ assured him. "You're so fucking hot like this, Liam. Show me how much you want it."

It took all his concentration to get through twenty reps on his left arm. Russ made him watch himself in the mirror; the hem of his shirt was soaked and so was the towel underneath him. The fluid leaking from him now was thicker, pulsing out of him in globs. His balls were drawn up tight to his body, but he couldn't come.

"Ten more, right arm," Russ said encouragingly. Liam could feel the line of his hard cock pressed to the small of his back. "Almost there."

Liam's arm was shaking by the time he got to the tenth rep. He barely had the presence not to drop it on their toes as Russ pulled him back tight against him and made good on his promise. The setting on the toy kicked up another notch, and it pounded inside him as Russ took him in a loose grip, just two fingers and his thumb.

A pathetic sob broke free of Liam's mouth. All that teasing and Russ was going to make him come like this, with a touch so light it was almost worse than nothing.

"Come on, Trouble," Russ commanded into the side of his neck. "I want you to come."

He tightened his grip just enough.

Liam's body went nuclear. His balls throbbed as his cock pumped waves of thick fluid out of him, hot spatters landing on his chest and legs. His ass clenched around the toy inside him, drawing out his pleasure to unbearable levels, until he finally had enough control of his vocal cords to say, "Shut it off, fuck, please."

Russ fumbled for a moment until he found the remote to turn the toy off. "Can you stand?"

Liam made a noise that meant *absolutely not*, and leaned forward on the bench instead, bracing his hands in front of him so Russ could pull the massager out. He eased it carefully over Liam's sensitive cock before setting it aside.

Liam's hole felt swollen and used and empty, and lust was still singing in his head. His body wanted to collapse in a heap on the soft gym mats.

He almost tripped over his tongue to say, "You should fuck me."

Something clattered to the floor behind him. The toy? The bottle of lube? Russ rubbed his thumb over Liam's opening. "I didn't bring down any condoms—"

"*I don't care.*" Liam didn't have anything communicable, and Russ would never put him in danger.

"Fuck, okay. Get on the floor."

Liam didn't bother trying to stand. He half fell off the end of the weight bench and braced himself on his hands and knees.

His desperation could have embarrassed him, but Russ didn't even take off his shorts. He just shoved the elastic down and slicked his cock and shoved right in, so perfect Liam could've cried.

Russ thrust in hard and fast, forcing Liam to his elbows. His spine wanted to liquify. He didn't think he could possibly come again—he couldn't have anything left in him—but he wrapped a hand around himself anyway.

Russ nailed his prostate. "Like this?"

Liam managed only a bitten-off whine and tightened his grip. When he let his head drop, he could see his cock disappearing in and out of his fist, driven by the pistoning of Russ's hips against his ass.

"You're so good for me," Russ rasped. "I want you to come again. Can you do that?" His thumb skirted the edge of Liam's hole.

Liam bit his lip and fell into another orgasm, his dick twitching. But almost nothing dripped over his fingers. Scattered, desperate vowel sounds dropped from his lips as his body clenched and shuddered.

"God, did you—?" Russ's rhythm stuttered.

Russ had wrung him dry. "You said you wanted all of it. Now it's my turn. I want all the come inside me to be yours."

"Fuck!"

Russ's thrusts stuttered, his nails digging into the flesh of Liam's hips, until one brutal shove had Liam collapsing to the mat with Russ behind him.

Everything was hot and wet and sticky and glorious. Liam breathed heavily against the vinyl-covered floor. It was possible he was drooling.

"Liam?" Russ asked a moment later.

"Ouais," Liam said brainlessly.

This hadn't been what he *intended* when he made that resolution to take better care of Russ, but it seemed effective.

The flop of fabric, and then rough terrycloth on the sensitive skin of his backside, followed by a gentle sweep of Russ's fingers. "You okay?"

Liam stifled a hysterical giggle. Was he okay? He rolled over. Everything hurt in the best way possible. "No. Not a good enough word."

He was *so* skipping everything but leg day next time they were in the gym, though.

Russ's cheeks were flushed, and Liam thought it was only partially exertion. "I thought maybe I went a little too far."

"You warned me." Liam's legs didn't want to stand and his abs sure as fuck didn't want to do a crunch to get him to sitting, so he was forced to reach out a hand for Russ to pull him up. "You say 'I'll fuck you like a porn star, but I'm a romantic.' I took it as a promise."

Russ snorted and caught Liam when he swayed. "And a challenge? That was pretty filthy."

"Mmm," Liam agreed, self-satisfied. "I learn from the best." He leaned his head on Russ's chest as Russ stroked his back. Now that the endorphins were wearing off, real life started to seep back in, and he remembered the dismissed call from Erika.

Russ sure knew how to distract a guy.

"We probably have to talk," Russ said after a moment during which neither of them moved except for the gentle sweep of Russ's hands over Liam's back.

Liam swallowed. "Probably." This was part of taking care of Russ too. He looked up, forcing himself to be brave. "But I think I need a shower first."

WHEN RUSS got out of the shower, Liam was already on the couch, flopped on his back in a clean pair of shorts that might be Russ's, scrolling through his phone.

Looking at him almost hurt. He'd made himself so at home in Russ's space, and he fit Russ's life in a way he had no business doing—he should've been too young, too immature, too *something*.

But the only things that came to mind were *too late* and *too bad.* He'd gotten himself into this mess and now he had to figure out the least painful way out of it for both of them.

Russ tapped Liam's ankle so he'd make room, and Liam pulled his legs up so Russ could sit. "Doom-scrolling?" Russ nodded at the phone.

Liam made a face. "Is that how you say 'apartment hunting' in English now?"

Apartment hunting. Because if Russ was gone…. "I think so, yeah." He put his head on his hand on top of Liam's knee. "Anything good?"

Liam dropped the phone on his chest. "No idea." He wiggled his feet, and Russ moved his hand to let Liam stretch his legs into his lap. "Did you call Erika?"

Even Liam wouldn't let Russ escape this conversation. "She left a voicemail. I haven't listened to it yet."

Nodding, Liam curled his legs toward himself and half sat up. "Do you want me to leave?" he asked finally.

Russ really didn't. "No." Not that having him here would make a difference one way or another. He wouldn't feel better about whatever Erika had to say, or worse. But if Liam was here, if the put his phone on speaker, at least he wouldn't have to repeat it.

"Okay."

"Okay," Russ echoed.

He played the message.

"Russ, it's Erika. I just got off the phone with Harold Lindemann in the front office. They've worked out the details. If you don't want to hear by voicemail, hang up and call me back." She paused. "Okay, so you probably won't be surprised, but we didn't get anywhere with extension talks. They've been shopping you around, and they've got a deal with the Altitude. The trade's going to be finalized after your thousandth game."

She went on a little after that, but Russ stopped listening. Colorado. Not a bad team. He could do worse.

He hung up before the message ended.

Only then did he realize he'd twined his fingers with Liam's.

He let out a long breath.

"So that's it, then?" Liam's brow furrowed. "You've been with this team six years and that's it?"

"That's how it goes." It sucked that Russ had to comfort him. Russ was the one whose life was getting upended. But Liam was so young. He'd never had to deal with a trade before. "Lots of guys get less warning." Liam would get less, if they traded him.

A squeeze of his hand and then Liam withdrew his fingers. "Sorry. I didn't mean to make it about me. It just feels...."

"Businesslike?" Russ suggested. He scrubbed his hands over his face.

"Maybe." He shook his head. "I guess it just don't make sense to me. You're the heart of the defense. How are they going to replace you?"

Oh, kid. "They already have."

Liam blanched. "I can't—I'm not—"

He would. Russ had known it for months. "Not yet, but they've seen your potential. The team's got a lot of gas in the tank yet. Plenty of time to train up a younger model." One with an offensive creativity Russ had never developed.

He'd expected to feel bitter, and he did, but not in the way he'd anticipated. Mostly he wanted another four years on the ice with Liam, wanted to get to be the one to teach him all he could. To make him into the player Russ knew he could be and to play alongside him while he did it.

Maybe they could see each other in the offseason. A couple months together. It wouldn't be the same, but—

"So that's it," Liam repeated. He'd gotten to acceptance faster than Russ thought he would. "Two weeks." He paused and seemed to steel himself for the hard question. "We gonna break up?"

They should—make a clean break, let things heal over instead of dragging it out. Russ should end it. But he didn't want to.

Instead he copped out. "Kind of a two-person decision."

Liam flopped over on the couch, suddenly boneless, and rested his head on Russ's chest. "When we started this, we knew this would happen. I think that would make this easier, but it doesn't." He glanced up briefly, eyes accusatory but understanding. "You promise me sex and exclusivity. Not feelings."

Feelings. Russ swallowed, throat dry. "Sorry."

Liam put his head back down. "I believe you."

In thirty-two years, Russ had made great friends. He had a good relationship with his family most of the time. But no one had ever shown the kind of blind faith Liam did. "You shouldn't."

He could feel the curve of Liam's smile through his shirt. "I will if I want to."

That much Russ knew. "I guess we're not breaking up, then."

"Guess not," Liam agreed. He flipped over and pushed against the arm of the couch until his head was in Russ's lap and he was staring up at him. "I tell you what, though."

"Hmm?"

"This better be a really good first date."

That seemed fair. The whole relationship thing had been Russ's idea in the first place. The least he could do was treat Liam to the first date he deserved.

"I promise. I'll even include weird getting-to-know-you questions and awkwardly ask if I can see you again after."

Liam smirked. "You're assuming I don't put out on the first date."

But what kind of date did Liam want? Fine dining? Something with too many forks and expensive wine? Russ liked good food as much as the next guy, but when he mentally tried to squeeze Liam into the picture, it came out wrong. Awkward.

Something more casual, then. Except that they were teammates, and they ate together at casual restaurants all the time, both with and without the other guys.

So… not food? What kind of a date didn't involve food?

Russ was mulling it over on the way back from practice—Baller and Gabe had absconded with Liam to take him apartment hunting—when a roadside advertisement caught his eye, and he smiled.

Perfect.

"Oh my God," Liam said when they pulled into a haphazard parking lot Thursday night. There were no marked lanes or spots, just a flat stone-chip surface in front of a long warehouse. "Serious?"

He put the truck in Park. "Would I tease you?"

"Yes." He gestured at the sign. "But really. You give me shit about the mechanical bull at the country bar, but ax throwing is okay?"

Grinning to himself, Russ pocketed his keys. "I mean, I wasn't planning on telling anyone about the ax throwing, but if you'd rather not—"

"Hey, no takebacks." Liam hopped out of the cab. His shoes crunched on the gravel. "I should have worn flannel. I feel underdressed." He was wearing shorts and a polo because Russ told him the dress code was athletic-casual, and a snapback because, Russ suspected, he desperately needed a haircut. His hair had gone past the curly stage and was bordering full-on fluffy.

"You'd roast in flannel," Russ pointed out.

Liam bumped his shoulder as they walked into the building. "Stop trying to use logic."

If the host at the reception podium recognized them, she didn't let on. Russ mentioned his reservation, and she checked it off her chart with a smile and said, "You're in arena thirteen. Come with me."

Handy Jack's Ax-Throwing and Finger Food occupied a warehouse-style building on the outskirts of the city. Stalls with thick plywood walls lined one side, and pub tables were set up at the open end, almost like bowling lanes. The other half of the building housed the kitchen, restrooms, a larger seating area, and a few pool tables, which Russ assumed was backup for when people drank too much craft beer to handle axes.

"Have you been here before?"

"Nope." Russ smiled. "First time."

"Me too," Liam put in.

"Great. Okay, so I'll go over the waiver with you, and we'll do a quick safety lesson, and then we can start on the technique. Do you want to put in an order of food before we get started?"

Their nachos arrived just as Brittany handed Russ the ax and waved him toward the target. "So just like we talked about, we're going to start with a two-handed throw. You'll want to bring it back behind your head and then release when you're at about eye level. Once you've got a throw in, we'll look at how you're hitting the target and we can adjust farther or closer based on that."

Russ's first throw hit the target handle-first and fell anticlimactically to the floor.

"Aww," Liam said from a safe distance. "Better luck next time."

Russ shot him the finger.

"Okay, so you're going to want to take a half step back for your next throw." Brittany indicated a mark on the floor, then set Liam up for his first practice throw on the adjacent target.

For someone who was still twenty pounds lighter than Russ, Liam looked like a natural with an ax in his hand. Maybe that should've given off serial killer vibes, but Russ was too busy appreciating the way his shirt rode up and his shoulders filled out his sleeves to notice.

Then the ax *thwacked* into the target and stuck, almost perfectly centered.

"Holy shit," Brittany exclaimed.

Liam grinned.

Russ knew that grin. "You said you'd never done this before," he accused.

"No. I say I've never been here before." He plucked a chip out of the bowl and dunked it. "I grew up on a sugar shack. With *tourists*. We have one of these at home."

Of course he did. "Cheater," Russ accused.

Liam crunched down on his snack, smug.

Brittany looked back and forth between them and then shook her head. "Looks like you've got a professional to help you out. You guys want to put in an order for something else and I'll leave you to it?"

Suffice it to say that the date didn't go exactly how Russ intended. He spent a lot more of it than he planned watching the lines of Liam's body unfurl as he sank the ax into the target again and again. Now that the secret was out, he'd switched to a one-handed throw.

Russ had expected ax throwing to be fun, not sexy. He should've known better. Of course it was both, with Liam.

By the time their meals arrived, it was obvious Russ had no chance at beating him. If Liam decided hockey wasn't for him, he could probably take up professional ax throwing. Russ had the vague impression that he ought to feel emasculated, but he was just kind of turned-on. Maybe Liam should top tonight.

"So," Russ said as he peeled the checkerboard wrapper from one half of his burger and affected a first-date kind of interest, "ax throwing. You do that a lot?"

Liam picked up a french fry and hummed at it. "What's the word? I dabble."

What a little shit. "My fault for forgetting where you grew up, I guess." He shook his head.

"If it make you feel better, my mom's burgers are not this good." Then he narrowed twinkling eyes. "Wait, if this is our first date, you're not supposed to know where I grew up. Creepy. Did you Facebook stalk me?"

"You mentioned it earlier," Russ protested, laughing. "But okay. I promised first-date small talk, so... do you have any brothers and sisters?"

Liam nodded around his burger. "Like five hundred. You?"

"Just the two sisters. And a nephew on the way, next month." Which Liam already knew. Russ bit into the burger. It was juicy and perfect and he kind of wanted a moment alone with it.

From the laugh tucked into the corner of his mouth, Liam had noticed Russ's reaction to the burger, but it seemed his first-date manners didn't let him comment. "My turn to ask a question, I think?" He picked up another fry. "What do you do for work?"

Really? Russ swallowed a bite. "Hit people."

"Not with that aim," Liam said cheekily, and Russ kicked him under the table. "*Miss* people, more like."

Russ had missed a check the game before and ended up on his ass. He'd be getting shit for it for at least another week. "It's true that my aim is better with a different tool."

Liam muffled his snort in his dinner, but he kept his knee pressed against Russ's under the table.

Russ's turn for a typical first-date question, and he spent a moment thinking about it. He still felt like he'd done something wrong, that he'd swindled

Liam into a relationship somehow. That couldn't keep up if he was across the country; they'd both be miserable. But he'd tried to give Liam an out, and Liam wasn't biting. If Russ pushed that, Liam would be pissed. He didn't like to be told he didn't know what he wanted.

Which meant that this time it was Russ who didn't know what Liam wanted, but he could fix that. "What're you looking for in a relationship?"

If Liam noticed that the question was more serious than the others, not a silly game anymore, he didn't call Russ on it. Instead he took a sip of his beer and tilted his head in thought. Then he said, "I wasn't, you know? Looking." He ducked his chin toward his chest, but after a moment he straightened again. "But sometimes it's like—a set play doesn't go to plan, but suddenly the puck is on your tape and nobody between you and the goalie, right?"

Russ wanted to agree, but he couldn't get any words out. They all seemed to be stuck in a chest that had expanded to accommodate a sudden rush of warmth and emotion.

That turned out to be for the best anyway, because Liam wasn't finished.

"And it's… responsibility, if you find someone who makes you feel like that." His cheeks were red, and he was half talking to his plate, which was fine because if he made too much eye contact Russ was going to lunge across the table and kiss him. "Like, you can be who you are, and that's enough, but they also see all the things you could be, things maybe you can't see yet."

Russ inhaled shakily, light-headed. He wanted a sip of his drink, but he didn't think he could manage any kind of movement and keep up the casual veneer.

"And they want to help you be that person." Finally Liam took a break and met Russ's eyes. He was bright red now, but still bold—braver than Russ could be. "The only thing that could be better, maybe, is it needs some balance, right? I need to take care of them too."

It was definitely Russ's turn to talk, but it took him a moment to get past the frantic pounding of his heart and make his mouth work. "I think that's really… smart," he said carefully. "But people don't need the same things in relationships. Some people"—like Russ—"need someone to make them… let go a little bit. Enjoy the moment." He would have missed out on so much if he'd let himself brush Liam off as an impossibility. "That's just as important."

Liam's pleased little smile seared itself into Russ's psyche.

But the moment had gotten too heavy for public, and Russ found himself self-conscious. On the one hand, they should've had this conversation in private. On the other, he couldn't imagine having been brave enough to talk about it without the veneer of a fake-but-not-really first date. So he reached for his own french fries, gestured toward the cages with the targets, and added, "Even if it means losing at your own game."

Liam bumped their knees together again. The contact sent warmth radiating through Russ's body, more comfort and companionship than anything. Or so Russ thought until Liam leaned closer over the table and looked up at Russ to ask through lowered lashes, "So where do you see yourself in half an hour?"

God, he was perfect. Russ broke into a laugh and looked around for their server. "Hey—can we get some takeout boxes?"

They spilled out into the parking lot, almost giddy, their shoulders bumping with every step. Russ's hand itched for Liam's, and for once in his life he let himself take it. Maybe someone would see them, recognize them. Maybe he'd get outed in a way he couldn't control. But he could handle that as long as he had Liam next to him.

Besides, the only light came from the flickering floodlamps outside the entrance. It was too dark for anyone to see anything. If Russ wanted, he could *kiss* Liam right here, outside, and no one would ever know.

He was thinking about doing it when he heard the skid of tires on gravel.

There wasn't anything particularly threatening about it. He couldn't have said what made him turn and look over his shoulder. By the time he did, the truck was careening around a line of parked cars, almost on top of them.

Russ had just enough time to let go of Liam's hand and shove him out of the way before the grill hit him and everything went dark.

Overtime

LIAM DIDN'T realize what happened until he lifted his head and felt the sting of gravel on his face.

Then suddenly he was scrambling upright toward the dark shape on the ground in the parking lot.

The truck had hit a parked car a few meters away and stopped, alarms blaring. People trickled out of the building, pointing, saying things Liam couldn't parse over the ringing in his ears.

He skidded to his knees next to Russ, heart in his throat, and fumbled one-handed for his phone. The screen had cracked, but it still worked. He put it on speaker and dialed 911.

God, he couldn't see anything. Was Russ bleeding? Was he dead? He wasn't talking. Liam put a shaking hand in front of his face and felt breath on his fingers. So he was alive.

The strength went out of his thighs, and he landed on his butt.

He couldn't have said how long it took for the ambulance to arrive. Brittany came out with a first-aid kit, and some other employees kept the crowd back. Someone shoved a bottle of water into his hands.

There were lights and sirens, police and ambulance. They wouldn't let Liam ride with Russ. He got his own ambulance, even though he was fine. Wasn't he fine?

"They're probably gonna give you a CT scan at the hospital," one of the EMTs told him. "Just in case. You hit your head."

Something told Liam that wasn't the first time she'd said it.

So he went to the hospital. He got a CT scan. A nurse, or maybe a social worker, offered to call someone for him, but who was Liam going to call? The person he most wanted to talk to was in the hospital too.

Shit. Who would Russ call? His agent? Liam couldn't call Russ's agent, even though she was also his agent. That wasn't his place. He definitely couldn't call Russ's parents. Hell, he didn't even want to call his *own* parents. But someone from the team, maybe? Yes. He should call Mo. Mo would know what to do.

It took him three tries to click the right contact. He pulled the shock blanket the EMTs had given him tighter around his shoulders in the curtained-off bed in the ER and raised the phone to his ear.

After that he pulled his arm back under the blanket and stared at the wall for a little while.

What was happening with Russ? Would the doctors even tell him? *Could* they tell him?

Liam flicked a loose bit of gravel off his shirt and wondered how long it would be before a doctor came to see him about his test results. His head didn't really hurt, but the cuts and scrapes stung with antiseptic, and he had a whole new collection of bruises and a vague impression that he was going to be really sore tomorrow.

"Trouble?" A metallic screech as someone jerked the privacy curtain aside, and Mo burst in, wild-haired and red. "Jesus, are you okay? What happened?"

Where could Liam begin? He wet his lips. Oh. He was cut there too. Finally he managed, "He pushed me out of the way."

All the color drained from Mo's face. "Liam, where's Russ?"

He shook his head. The rest of him shook too. "They won't tell me. I don't know anything. The truck hit him pretty hard." Had Liam had blood on his hands when he got in the ambulance? Was it Russ's, or his own?

Mo swore. "Okay, look, I'm—I'm Russ's medical POA, because his parents are nosy and he, uh, he said he needed another hockey player to make those decisions if he couldn't, because we know what's important. So I'm going to go find someone to talk to me, and then I'm going to come back and talk to you. Okay?"

That seemed like a reasonable suggestion. At some point a doctor would return and want to talk to him. Mo's plan made sense.

Like hell Liam was going to stay here and wait to find out what happened to his boyfriend.

He slid off the bed. "No. I'm coming with you."

"Jesus," Mo said again. "Kid, you look like you're gonna fall over."

"Did that already." At least they'd let Liam put his own clothes back on after his CT scan, so he didn't have to wander around the hospital with his ass hanging out. "Just don't let me faint in front of anyone who looks like a hockey fan."

Mo didn't look happy about the situation—his face had that constipated expression he got when they were down two goals with five minutes to go in the third—but he obviously knew Liam had made up his mind, because he didn't argue. "Fine. But if you end up needing a wheelchair to get around safely, we're done and you're back in here. I'm not getting sued because you were stubborn."

Who exactly did he think was going to sue him?

Never mind, Liam didn't care. "Deal."

It took less time than he thought it might for Mo to find the right person to talk to and prove he had the authority to hear about Russ's condition, which was great because Liam had been wrong. He wasn't going to be sore tomorrow. He was sore now.

The doctor gave Liam a look, but maybe she saw in Mo's posture that he was just going to tell Liam whatever she told him anyway, because she gestured toward a sitting area in a quiet section of the third floor and waited pointedly until Mo made Liam sit down.

"Mr. Lyons is pretty banged up," she said, and for a second Liam's hearing cut out. *Pretty banged up* was not *critical condition*. *Pretty banged up* was not *dead*. *Pretty banged up* was what happened to them when they played Washington.

He didn't hear the next few sentences in real time, but his brain processed them after the fact: the impact with the truck had broken three of Russ's ribs and his collarbone, he had contusions all along the right side of his chest, and one of his ribs had punctured his lung. But miraculously, he didn't have any head trauma, and he'd escaped a spinal injury.

Liam hadn't even considered that option—that Russ might survive never to walk again. He was grateful Mo had made him sit down, because imagining what that would do to Russ sucked all the oxygen from Liam's lungs.

Then the doctor said, "He's awake now, and he's been asking for… Liam?"

Liam tried not to look too much like someone's boyfriend. Outing Russ while he was in the hospital seemed bad. "I was with him when the truck hit him."

The doctor blinked at him, then looked at Mo.

Liam didn't realize he'd spoken in French—that maybe he'd been speaking French since Mo showed up, or maybe since their phone call—until Mo translated, "They were together when the accident happened."

"Ah." The doctor's expression softened. "In that case, I think I can overlook the fact that this young man should obviously be in another part of the hospital for a few minutes. But a few minutes *only*. After that I need you to bring him back where he belongs so he can finish getting checked over and Mr. Lyons can get some rest. Do we need to get a translator in?"

Mo shook his head. "No, he speaks English. I think he's just rattled."

Rattled. Liam had a very mature, emotional, intimate conversation with his boyfriend and then watched him get hit by a truck.

"Sorry," he said, making sure it was the right language this time. "It's been a long night."

She smiled kindly. "I imagine so. Five minutes, all right?"

She might as well have been talking to a brick wall, because Liam walked into the room like he hadn't even heard her.

He didn't know what he expected—some kind of horrible soap-opera scene, with Russ looking tiny and wrapped up in gauze and the grim specter of mortality hanging over them both.

This wasn't that. Sure, the monitors were annoying, and all Russ's exposed skin—of which there was a fair bit, because they'd taken his shirt off to bandage something on his chest—was mottled blue and red and purple. But the tiny hospital bed only served to make him look more enormous than usual. Maybe they were out of regular-person-size beds. Maybe they'd given him a kiddie bed by mistake. Either way, there was no room for Liam to sit next to him on it, which sucked because the only chair was over by the wall and he didn't have the energy to drag it closer.

He moved the water glass off Russ's bedside table and sat on that instead. "Hey. How, ah, how are you feeling?"

Russ turned his head to look at him and gave him a vague, haphazard grin without quite focusing on Liam's face. "Like I got hit by a truck." The grin widened, but his laugh cut off abruptly.

So much for no head trauma, Liam thought, but then he saw the IV in the back of Russ's non-slinged arm. Russ's brow furrowed and he narrowed his eyes as he asked, "Why do you look worse than I feel?"

It was Liam's turn to abort a laugh into a gasp, because yep, he'd definitely pulled *something* in his side in the fall, and that hurt. "Probably because you have morphine."

Without meaning to, he caught Russ's hand.

"Probably." Russ leaned back into his pillow. He was sitting up in the bed, if by *sitting up* you meant *leaning in a very stoned way*. "You're okay, though?"

Liam made a strangled noise. *You literally got hit by a truck. Stop asking how I am.* "I've taken worse hits during a game." Of course, he usually had padding and a smooth surface to fall on. "What about you?" Fuck, he already asked that. "You look… uh…."

"I look like shit," Russ said cheerfully, and oh yeah, he was high as a kite. "We match."

Liam snorted and then squeezed his eyes closed. "I'm glad you're okay."

"Me too."

THE LONG night got longer. Liam finally saw a doctor, as well as a police officer who wanted to take his statement, as though Liam had seen anything. At some point Gabe Martin showed up to take him home.

"Sorry, Mo called Dante," he explained, "but he only gets so much time with Reyna."

What was he doing with her? Liam wondered. It was like three in the morning.

But he was too tired to care.

Gabe brought him home and showed him the guest bedroom, and Liam got as far as taking his shoes off before he passed out on top of the covers and slept for ten hours.

When he got up, Baller was in the kitchen, dancing around with his daughter on his hip as he wiped down the countertops. "Oh, you're up. Saved you some lunch. Didn't we, Reyna?"

Liam sat down in front of the plate, suddenly ravenous. There was something he was supposed to do today. What was it? He picked up the sandwich. "Did I sleep through practice?"

Baller gave him an odd look. "They canceled it. They do that when someone gets hit by a car."

"Oh." He blinked. "Does that happen a lot?"

"No."

"Oh." Something furry rubbed against Liam's ankles, and he looked down to see a tuxedo cat twining around his legs.

"Eat," Baller reminded him. There was a huge bottle of Biosteel by his plate too, which Liam grimaced at, because it tasted disgusting even if it was supposed to be better than Gatorade for performance.

"Hydrate. You probably have to get evaluated by the team docs later. Did you check your phone?"

It had to be dead by now. Liam shook his head.

"Eat," Baller said again. "I'll find you a charger."

The charger turned out to be a curse rather than a blessing. Word of the accident had filtered onto the internet and from there to Liam's family. He had thirty-odd text messages and seven missed calls, and he hadn't gotten any further than plugging his phone into the charger in Baller and Gabe's guest room before it rang in his hand.

He had to lie down on the bed in order to have a conversation without hunching over, and that nearly ended up with him falling asleep on the group call while Marie-Jean gave him pointers on dealing with the bruising.

His mom was asking if he was sure he was okay for the tenth time when Baller stuck his head in. "Mo's here. You have to leave in ten."

Thank God. "I have to go. Doctor's appointment," Liam said. Not that he was looking forward to that, but at least he didn't have to spend the next two hours reassuring his mother he wasn't dying.

After he hung up, he got a text from Marie-Jean. *Glad you're ok. Sorry mom's making it about her. Feel better soon and I'll help run interference when I can. Xxx*

To LIAM'S surprise, coaches wanted to sit him a game to make sure he didn't have lingering injuries. Truth be told it would've been difficult for Liam to say if he did, since he basically felt like a walking contusion.

Mo had come to pick Liam up for the appointment, because apparently no one trusted him to drive. He slung his arm around Liam's shoulder. Even that hurt. "Don't worry. We can play six D, no problem."

The words threw Liam so much that he stopped walking toward the car.

Mo stopped too. "Trouble? Too soon?"

"No, I just, um." Did Mo know Russ was supposed to be traded? Surely he must. Russ and Mo were close, and Mo was the captain. "I guess he won't be going to Colorado."

Maybe he wouldn't be going anywhere even after the season.

Mo winced, and Liam wondered if Mo was thinking the same thing—that this might be the end of Russ's NHL career, a few games shy of his thousandth. Forced retirement over a stupid injury in a stupid parking lot with a stupid drunk driver.

A stupid accident.

But no. No way. Russ was too hardworking and stubborn to let this be the end. Liam put the thought out of his mind.

"I guess not," Mo agreed.

The silence between them suddenly felt oppressive, and Liam couldn't take it anymore. "Can you drop me off at Russ's?" He'd had enough of being babysat. Liam was fine. Russ was the one who was still in the hospital. If no one was even going to let Liam get on the ice for another few days, he could make himself useful by spending time with his boyfriend, and for that he needed to pick up his car.

"Yeah, kid. Sure."

ONE THING about being a professional athlete—your team doctor would make house calls while you were in the hospital.

Dr. Chapel pulled up a chair next to Russ's bed. "Hey, Russ. Been a rough weekend for you so far, huh?"

Russ had been weaning himself off the morphine. It made his head fuzzy and he hated feeling like he wasn't in control of himself. An addiction would be worse. Besides, he needed to be able to think clearly when talking about his injuries and recovery.

Unfortunately, now it hurt when he breathed. He had some over-the-counter pain relievers to take the edge off, but the soreness and misery didn't help keeping his mind focused.

At least he'd gotten to see Liam for a short time last night. "I've had better."

Dr. Chapel had an incredible poker face. Russ had always wondered if that was part of med-school training. "I'm sure you have." He set a folder on Russ's bedside table where Liam had sat. "Have you spoken with your doctors here about your prognosis?"

He shook his head. "Just the basics. They said six weeks' recovery for the ribs. Collarbone is more wait-and-see." Six to twelve weeks was a pretty big window.

Nodding, Chapel opened the folder. "I've got printouts of your X-rays." He smiled a little at Russ's bemused expression. "I know, very old-school. But it's easier to hand you pieces of paper than have you hold my tablet."

Russ took the printout, which showed his shoulder. Even to his untrained eye, the break was obvious. No wonder it hurt like a son of a bitch. "No offense, doc, but this doesn't mean much to me."

"Fair enough." Chapel took out a pen and outlined the fracture. "There's the break, as you can see. In terms of placement for healing, it's borderline. It might heal just fine without surgery, or it might not. I've suggested a follow-up X-ray in two weeks to check on the progress, and we can decide what to do from there."

Great. Add another two weeks onto his recovery time. Not much Chapel could do about it, though. Or was there? "If there's doubt, why not just do the surgery now?"

"Well, there's the complicating factors of your other injuries. I don't want to suggest operating unnecessarily on someone who's just had a collapsed lung."

Russ thought about how many TV dramas he'd seen with people being intubated for surgery and wondered what that would feel like with broken ribs. "Right. That makes sense."

"And then there's the potential for tissue damage." Chapel put the printout back in the folder. "Modern medicine is very good, but there's risks with any surgery, and there's a lot of connective tissue in your shoulder and chest. While surgery may help the bone heal better, it could cause additional trauma to the muscles that would add to the recovery time."

Additional trauma. To the muscles in Russ's arm, chest, and shoulder. He needed the bone to be strong for making and taking checks, but he needed the muscle in good shape to control and power his shot.

Either way, *additional trauma* didn't sound good. "Bottom-line it for me."

Chapel closed the folder and leaned forward in the chair, clasping his hands between his knees. "I'm less worried about your ribs, but the clavicle is a complicating factor. Best-case scenario, you're going to miss the rest of the season. If you're very lucky, you might be able to start no-contact practice in mid-March."

Russ exhaled slowly. The regular season ended in early April. The Caimans were on track to make the playoffs, but that could change. Still, plenty of guys took the time to heal up their injury and come into the playoffs fresh and well rested. It *could* be an advantage.

Anyway, Chapel hadn't finished his predictions. Russ braced himself, feeling something hollow in the pit of his stomach. "And worst-case?"

"Worst-case, you'll be dealing with limited strength and range of motion in that arm permanently. You might never heal well enough to play in the NHL again."

Even though he'd prepared himself to hear them, the words hit him like a crosscheck in the broken ribs. He was thirty-two. He'd known his career had an expiration date and that it wouldn't be long. Probably another three or four years. Six if he was very lucky.

But he'd had plans—play his thousandth game. Come out after that. Spend the summer training with Liam wherever he wanted, and let his parents be mad they didn't have the chance to try to set him up this year.

"Russ? I want to stress that's a worst-case scenario, not necessarily the most plausible. It's early in the healing process. You have access to the best doctors, surgeons, and physiotherapists in the world. Every variable we can account for—"

Russ inhaled sharply. He didn't want to be placated. He'd asked for the unvarnished truth. "I got it, doc, thanks."

Chapel must've gotten the impression that Russ wanted to be left alone, because their meeting didn't last much longer. The doctor let himself out with a promise to touch base with Russ in a few days to see how he was handling things and to make a plan with the physiotherapists for exercises Russ could do to keep his strength and conditioning up. He had the feeling it would mean a lot of nothing, as far as his usual workouts went. The hospital staff wanted him to work on breathing deeply.

If that was all he could manage for six weeks, he'd lose his mind.

It was only an hour after Chapel left that his nurse came in to go over his discharge instructions. It turned out that a bunch of cracked ribs and a punctured lung weren't enough to keep you in the hospital if you didn't want to be there. Russ got a printout of dos and don'ts, a handful of prescriptions, an appointment for a follow-up, and then a cab home.

Erika had sent a meal service by to stock the fridge, and a care package of high-protein snacks waited on the kitchen table, probably from Mo. Those would come in handy since a lot of his meds had to be taken with food.

There was a small bouquet of flowers too. Russ glanced at the card and snorted. *Next time please don't get your ribs broken just because I hate Colorado.—E.* She'd never let that influence how well she did her job, naturally, but every once in a while she let something slip.

All thoughtful gestures, but none of them meant much right now. Where was Liam?

Never mind. Russ needed to eat something so he could take his next set of pills. He didn't feel hungry, but that was probably the last of the good painkillers wearing off. One of the prepared meals would do fine.

The instructions said to pull the cellophane off before he put the tray in the microwave.

How the fuck am I supposed to do this one-handed? He could barely get his fingers around the edge of the cellophane. Maybe if he wedged the tray under his other arm…?

He'd just managed to rip off the world's tiniest, most insignificant piece of plastic when the side door opened.

"Oh holy shit, you scared me." Liam dropped his keys on the end of the counter. Other than a little road rash on the side of his face, he was unscathed. Some of the weight lifted from Russ's shoulders, even as some other nameless thing twisted in his stomach.

None of it mattered when Liam hugged him, first because he had Liam in his arms—well, arm—again, proof he was safe and sound, and second because—

"Ow."

"Sorry! Sorry!" Liam let go of him and backed away. "Um. Hi." His cheeks were pink where they weren't purple with the bruise. Unthinking, Russ raised his good hand to touch the edge of a cut.

Liam caught it and laced their fingers together. "I didn't realize they let you go home already. I would have come to get you. Well, I would have if I hadn't just gotten home myself."

Home. Russ cleared his throat. "Turns out you can sit on your ass at home just as well as in the hospital."

"Yeah?" Liam put on a very bad fake curious expression. "How come you're standing up, then?"

Russ rolled his eyes. "There's actually nothing wrong with my legs."

"Or your ass?" Liam said innocently.

Brat. "I need to eat so I can take my meds. Ergo, standing." He gestured at the meal tray. "Except a career in professional hockey did not prepare me for opening this thing one-handed."

Without needing to be asked, Liam reached for the meal and opened it easily. "Good thing your house rookie went to college." He put the tray in the microwave and hit the button. Every movement spoke of nervous energy. While the microwave whirred, he clenched and unclenched his hands at his sides. "You know, when I said it would be nice if you needed me for stuff, this isn't what I meant."

Something in the way he stood reminded Russ of last night. Thanks to the morphine, his memory of it was hazy, but he remembered Liam's hand in his.

Kid was barely holding it together. Russ held out his good arm to try to coax him closer. "Hey…."

Liam winced. "Sorry. Again. You got hurt and I'm the one who's…."

"Shut up and hug me," Russ instructed. "Gently this time. Hands below the waist."

This time Russ held on longer, inhaling the smell of Liam's hair and soaking in the warmth of his body. He must've showered wherever he stayed last night, because he didn't smell like his usual shampoo. "I'm okay," Russ said, willing Liam to believe it even if he didn't know if he believed it himself. "All right? I'm fine. The worst thing that will happen is maybe I get a little hungry while waiting for you to open my dinner for me."

Liam shuddered slightly in his arms. "You scared the shit out of me."

Russ closed his eyes. The sound of the truck's engine came roaring back to him, and goose bumps

rose on his back and shoulders. "I scared the shit out
of myself."

Finally the microwave beeped, and Russ reluctantly pulled away. He really did need to eat. "You
hungry? Erika sent me more premade dinners than I
could eat in a year."

"Am I hungry." Liam managed a small smile.
"Dumb question."

IN THE aftermath of the accident, any thoughts Liam
had about finding an apartment took a firm back seat
to everything else. All at once he realized how much
looking after him Russ had really done. With his arm
in a sling, Russ couldn't drive—not until his collarbone healed enough to let him use the arm. He also
couldn't do many tasks around the house. How was
he supposed to chop anything for dinner? Or take
out the garbage when that required both lifting *and*
bending, both of which would hurt his ribs?

So it was an adjustment period. Liam felt more
than a little guilty. Here he'd thought he was finally
evening out the division of labor, and it turned out
Russ had been doing all the work right in front of his
face and he hadn't noticed.

From now on, that changed. Liam was going to
pull his weight, and he wasn't going to take Russ for
granted. He made himself a chore list on his phone,
and every time he came across a task that wasn't being done, he added it.

At the end of the first twenty-four hours, he found himself very grateful Russ had a lawn service, a pool service, and a cleaning service.

With Russ out of the lineup, Liam expected some shuffling to the team lines. It would make sense for someone with more experience to take over Liam's spot for a while, since he didn't have Russ to shore him up. He figured he'd get bumped down, and he'd made peace with that.

Instead, Liam's first practice back, Coach looked at him and said, "Belanger, you're moving to the first power-play unit. We'll try Yeti as your partner again, see how it goes now that you've got some more experience under your belt."

So Liam got *promoted* instead. That made guilt churn in his stomach as he remembered the way Russ had looked at him when he'd said he was getting traded. *How are they going to replace you?* Liam had asked.

They already have.

It looked like Russ had been right.

Yeti bumped his shoulder as they filed onto the ice for practice. "Big skates to fill."

"Oh yeah," Liam said. "No pressure."

Yeti tapped his stick on the back of Liam's legs. "You'll be fine."

They had one more home game before they hit the road. Liam took care of as much around the house as he could think of—stocked up on groceries, ensured Russ had someone to drive him to his doctor's appointments, ran the dishwasher and emptied it. He peeled the corners up on a bunch of different ready-made meals so Russ could finish the job one-handed.

"I was a functional adult before you came around, you know," Russ reminded him as Liam hefted a load of laundry into the dryer.

"You were a functional adult when I'm still learning to spell my name." Liam yanked open the drawer next to the washing machine. "We're out of Bounce sheets."

"I'll add them to my functional-adult grocery delivery order."

Okay, so maybe he'd gone a little overboard. Russ was more capable than Liam was giving him credit for, and anything he really couldn't do, he could afford to have someone do for him. But what was Liam supposed to do? Just sit there and feel guilty for being healthy? "Am I being crazy?"

Russ held up his finger and thumb an inch or so apart. "Little bit. It's cute, though." He reeled Liam in with a hand on his shirt and kissed him quickly.

That was another thing Liam would have to get used to. Until Russ's chest and lungs healed better, marathon kisses were off the table. Or bed. Or wherever. Liam didn't have any business complaining, even if he did spend a few minutes every morning daydreaming about it in the shower.

Which, speaking of showering and getting ready—"Shit."

"Hmm?" Russ asked.

Liam leaned his forehead against Russ's chin. "I forgot to pick up my dry cleaning."

Russ snorted and pulled away. "Come on. There must be something you can wear. Can't have you showing up to your new job without looking the part."

They eventually settled on a polo shirt under one of his jackets, which Mo thought looked douchey and Baller thought was cool. Liam was just glad he made it to the arena on time.

Before the game, the media wanted to talk to him not only about his new role but about the accident.

"What can you tell us about the driver of the vehicle?"

That one Liam had been briefed on. "Not very much, sorry." As far as he knew it was still under investigation.

Another reporter picked up the thread and ran in a different direction. "Can you give us an idea how Russ is coping?"

Liam didn't want to get too deep into it. He knew Russ's family were nosy, and even though it was an open secret that Liam lived with him, he didn't want to call attention to it in case that caused other problems. So he just said, "He doesn't like to sit still, and I think he misses getting to bully me in practice, but otherwise he's good."

"How are you feeling about taking on more responsibility with the team?"

"Ah, well." Liam tugged at his earlobe before he could remember not to fidget. He hated the fact that he'd taken Russ's place. It would've been bad enough if he'd gotten traded. This was worse. But he didn't want to sound ungrateful. "Of course I'm happy to help out, to have a chance to show what I can do. Whatever I can do to help us win games."

Now all he had to do was go out on the ice and deliver on that promise.

The game was against the New Jersey Monsters, who'd won the Eastern Conference Championship the year before and had creamed the Caimans earlier in the year. Needless to say, the Caimans anticipated a tough game, especially since they were missing their number-one defenseman.

Liam dialed into Coach's pregame plan and tried to block out everything else.

Under normal circumstances, Mo saved his captain talks for when he needed to get the team in line—if they were playing badly or taking dumb penalties. Occasionally, if they were having a *great* game, he'd chime in with something like *let's finish strong, boys* to remind them not to get sloppy.

Today, Coach ceded the floor to Mo and Mo said, "We're winning this one for Russ," and that was that.

Hughesy drew a penalty in the first forty seconds. Liam thought the call was suspect, and the Monster going to the box for hooking certainly thought so too, but either way, it meant Liam was officially on the ice as part of the first power-play unit for the first time. He skated out behind Mo and Hughesy, Baller at his shoulder.

"Just like in practice," Baller said. "Except you can hit them harder. And feel free to go for the slap shot."

Liam snorted. "Thanks."

The dumb advice loosened his shoulders, and it worked. It wasn't like this was his first time QBing a power play. He'd done it plenty in college and before. He knew what he was doing.

The puck dropped and Mo snapped it back to Liam, who took up his position near the blue line, where he could see the entire offensive zone. His teammates fanned out in a semicircle around the net, with the Monsters in between, boxing them out, trying to anticipate Liam's moves.

Liam sent a no-look pass to Hughesy, watching the Monsters to see what they'd do. One of them might react too quickly to a feint, or too slowly to a pass. The skater guarding Mo seemed like the jumpy type—he reacted before Liam moved.

Now Liam knew where to apply the pressure.

When the puck cycled back to him, this time he went to Baller. Across to Hughesy again, who sent it up to Liam.

Liam took a stride toward the net and waited for the defenders to collapse on him. Sure enough, Mo's man moved too fast. Liam slipped the puck between his skates and his stick and right onto Mo's tape for a top-shelf goal.

"Yes!"

The Caimans converged on their captain for a hug. Mo slapped the back of Liam's helmet until their visors bumped. "Nice read, rookie."

"Learned it at college," he said cheekily. "They don't teach you that at Harvard?"

Mo shoved him toward the bench. "Let's go get our high-fives, asshole."

They got their high-fives.

Coach waited until Liam was back on the bench to tap him on the shoulder. "Way to step up, Trouble."

Liam's grin didn't leave his face for five minutes.

By the time the third period started, the Caimans were up 4–1. The energy of a rout in progress buzzed under Liam's skin, kept his skating sharp and his focus strong. The Monsters' frustration came through in hard hits and uncharacteristically desperate plays, but the bruises only fueled Liam further. Every check he took—hell, every check he *made*—knocked the breath out of him a little more than usual, given his already banged-up body.

But the pain kept his head clear. He forced three turnovers and drew a penalty for roughing, and all he had to do was have possession of the puck in the offensive zone.

The icing on the cake came with a minute left in the third, when the Caimans were on their fourth power play. Liam had taken point again, and he was looking for the right window to make a pass. Instead, a shooting lane opened and he thought—*I'm going for it.* He put everything he had into the slap shot, which squeezed between the goalie's glove and the crossbar.

The arena roared.

"Okay, all right," Mo laughed in the group celly. "You can do it all, we get it. Jesus, what got into you?"

You said we were going to win it for Russ.

The thought took some of the wind out of his sails. It would've meant more if Russ were here, if

Russ had seen that goal, if Russ were on the ice to congratulate him.

But Russ would be waiting for him at home, so it could've been worse.

After the game, everyone wanted to go out, but as soon as Liam left the ice, the energy left him and his body remembered that it had had a close encounter with a gravel parking lot a few days ago.

"You go without me."

Baller gave him a knowing look, but Hughesy booed. "Come on. You got first star of the night."

Another honor he wished Russ had been around for.

"I'm exhausted. Look at this." He pulled up his Under Armour to reveal the cuts and bruising that decorated his body from hip to shoulder. The road rash on his right leg was already exposed. "I'm going to bed."

"Leave him alone, he wants to get laid," Baller said, bullying Hughesy toward his stall.

Liam's face flamed. He didn't know what would be worse—if Baller meant that, or if he knew the truth and was covering for Liam to get the guys off his back.

"I'll suck his dick for him," Sparky offered, because you could always count on a goalie to be a shit-disturber. "Least I could do, after that blocked shot in the second."

The blocked shot had been a mistake on Liam's part. It had hit him in pretty much the only unbruised part of his body, his upper left thigh.

"Thank you, but I'll pass. Have a drink for me."

He knew he'd made the right choice when he pulled into the driveway and realized he barely remembered the drive home. Yawning, he locked the car and shuffled into the house, hoping Russ was still awake.

Nope—passed out in the armchair in the living room. The TV was off; Liam had no idea if he'd managed to make it through the game.

Probably not. He'd have texted if he watched it.

Telling himself it was childish to be disappointed, Liam touched Russ's shoulder. "Hey. You want to go to bed?"

Russ inhaled quickly, but it turned into a cough, which turned into wheezing and a wince.

"Sorry," Liam said.

Russ shook his head and got his breathing under control. "It's okay. What time is it?" Then he seemed to realize, and his face fell. "I missed the game."

"Looks like you needed your beauty sleep," Liam offered. "Do you need to take any pills before bed?"

"I'm fine." The words came out sharp, and Liam wondered if he'd overstepped, but then Russ sighed and said, "Sorry, I was having a shitty dream. I should go back to sleep."

"Good plan. Let's go do that."

They climbed the stairs to go to bed. Liam ducked into the bathroom to brush his teeth and wash his face while Russ pulled back the sheets.

When he entered the bedroom again, Russ was lying on his back. Liam hadn't realized how accustomed he'd become to a good cuddle before going to sleep until broken ribs made it impossible. He

slipped into bed, telling himself the distance between them was in his head. He didn't want Russ to
injure himself further just so Liam could feel cared
for. Liam was an adult. He—

Russ's hand found his on the mattress, and he
squeezed.

Liam melted a little. Adults needed reassurance
and affection too. "Tell me about your game tomorrow?" Russ rumbled.

Liam squeezed back. "I will," he promised.
"Night."

RUSS WAS going out of his mind.

If he took the painkillers, he felt fuzzy and grog-
gy. If he didn't, he was snappish and in pain. He was
simultaneously bored stupid and exhausted all the
time. His body didn't like prolonged periods of in-
activity, and he was so used to physical exertion that
he had a hard time falling asleep without having put
in a day of exercise. So even though his body needed
rest to heal, he didn't sleep well.

He couldn't even distract himself doing things
around the house, since he was supposed to keep his
arm in the sling for another week and a half. It galled
him that he needed Liam to open his premade dinners. He couldn't drive, couldn't work out, couldn't
even tie his own shoes.

At least he lived in Florida, where flip-flops and
deck shoes were in season year-round.

After a week, the doctors gave him the all-clear
to walk back and forth across the shallow end of his

pool, as long as he didn't submerge himself past his navel, so at least he'd have *something* to do while Liam was away.

Then there was the other stuff.

The night Liam came home from his game to find Russ asleep in the armchair, he'd been in the middle of a stress dream about the accident. He tried to move faster, tried to dodge out of the way, but the truck was always just behind him. In the dream, the lights were brighter than reality, and at the last minute, Russ turned around and they blinded him.

He'd had the dream a few times now. Sometimes the truck went after Liam instead, and Russ would wake up in a cold sweat to the sound of Liam's bones crunching at the impact.

He'd given his statement to police the day he got out of the hospital, but he hadn't heard anything back, and that made him paranoid. What if the driver was never charged for their careless driving and it was only a matter of time before they were back on the road again, endangering someone else? Weirder things had happened.

Or worse, what if the accident hadn't been an accident after all? What if the driver had seen Russ and Liam holding hands and hit the gas instead of the brakes on purpose?

Russ checked all his medications three times. Sadly none of them listed paranoia as a side effect. His brain had come up with that all by itself.

Yay.

Then there was the uncertainty of his professional future. Erika assured him that there would still be plenty of interest in him over the summer, provided his recovery went according to plan. But even the doctors couldn't tell yet how completely Russ's collarbone would heal.

His whole life, Russ had planned and organized everything he could. That was how he'd made it to where he was today. Now, so many things were outside his control—if he played hockey again, and where; if he healed and how fast; what to have for dinner and whether he could sleep through the night.

And then there was Liam.

Russ loved that Liam was getting to show off for the world. He was fucking proud of the work Liam had put in, and he deserved all the recognition he was getting. It would've made Russ puff up with pride, metaphorically speaking at least, since the literal version would've been physically painful.

Except that it hurt too. He'd hoped to get to share these moments with Liam, and now he couldn't. And seeing Liam successfully take Russ's place on the team, knowing that his own career might be over, was bittersweet. But Liam didn't know Russ might never play again, and Russ sure as fuck wasn't going to tell him—he already looked at Russ like he might break, and Russ wouldn't put that guilt on him—so he had to suck it up and put on a happy face, because otherwise he just looked like an asshole.

Also—and this was *really not helping matters*— he was horny.

Russ hadn't thought much about how prone he and Liam were to getting each other off on every surface in the house—and on road trips—until Liam was suddenly afraid to touch him and Russ's dominant hand was in a sling. He wasn't going to be fucking Liam stupid in the weight room again anytime soon. So not only could he not physically take care of Liam at the moment, he couldn't take care of him sexually either. He'd started to become jealous of the time Liam spent in the shower in the morning.

All things considered, it probably wasn't the worst time for Liam to go on a road trip. Russ would be even more bored, but at least he'd have limited opportunities to take his attitude out on Liam.

Maybe by the time he was back, Russ would be able to hug him without hurting himself. Of course, at that point, Russ would be so desperate that a hug from Liam would have him coming in his pants.

"I don't like this." Liam huffed as he tossed his go bag in the back of his car.

"I told you, I'm a grown-up." *And you are going to smother me to death if you stay here another minute.* Russ could barely put down the TV remote before Liam jumped up and asked if he needed anything. "I can handle myself."

Liam's cheeks colored. "No, I know, I just meant…." He sighed again. "It feels weird that you're not coming along. I'll miss you."

Well now Russ felt like an asshole. "Me too."

And he would, even if he also enjoyed having the house to himself. But this time he'd make sure he watched the games and commented on them. He didn't want Liam to think Russ resented him or had lost interest.

Even though he wasn't on the road trip, Russ tried to be active in the team group chat, partly to keep himself accountable and partly to keep everyone else from worrying. Texting with his non-dominant hand sucked, so he didn't keep on top of it as well as he'd like, but he figured the chat was busy enough that he'd slip under the radar as long as he contributed once or twice a day. He forced himself to stay up for the games in Nashville and Dallas—he texted Liam about them separately and heckled Hughesy for eating shit right in front of Colorado's net.

But clearly he hadn't accounted for all of the variables, because the fourth day of the road trip, Russ's phone buzzed with *I'm coming over. Put on pants.*

Russ blinked. Pretty much everyone he knew who lived in Miami was on their way to Arizona. Shelly was eyebrows-deep in writing a thesis. *Who is this? And how do you know I'm not wearing pants?*

It's Gabe Martin. For a moment he just got the three dots of a message in progress. Then, *Who wears pants when they're home by themselves?*

Okay, fair point. Russ put pants on. Well, shorts. Should he put coffee on too? Or was beer more appropriate? Russ wasn't drinking—not with the various medications and the fact that even a slight stumble could cause a big setback to his recovery—but Gabe might.

In the end he decided on neither; Gabe was showing up basically unannounced and completely uninvited. He could get his own beer.

He probably should have anticipated that he would, in fact, bring his own, along with a pint of ice cream he stashed in Russ's freezer. But he didn't open either right away. Instead he grabbed a bottle of water for himself and Biosteel for Russ and not so casually bullied him onto the back patio.

"Reyna's at day care and I needed grown-up company." He inched the patio chair back until the morning sun could hit his face without the umbrella in the way. Then he tilted his head up into the sunlight, shades on. "Don't tell Dante I'm enjoying this weather. He'll gloat."

Russ cracked open his Biosteel. *We don't have earthquakes, we don't have hurricanes, we don't have alligators*, he thought to himself. Yeah. They also didn't have seventy-degree weather in January. "Dante who?"

"Exactly."

There wasn't an easy way to ask *so what are you doing here* without sounding like a dick, which Russ was actively trying to avoid. But after a few minutes of small talk, he forgot he wanted to know. Gabe asked about Russ's family, so Russ showed him the latest ultrasound and a picture of Gia, who was extremely round and shooting the finger at the camera.

"I take it she loves being pregnant," Gabe said dryly.

Russ snorted. "Can't blame her. I only have to deal with this"—he gestured to the sling—"for a few weeks and I'm already fed up with it. She's been a prisoner in her body for like nine months."

"I remember when I had my shoulder done the first time. Everything hurts and you suddenly realize how many things you need both hands for. And that was my non-dominant arm."

The first time—God, he'd gone through it a second time on purpose, hadn't he? If Russ remembered right. "Yesterday morning I got an itch on my back. Wrong side to get it with my good hand. I had to rub against a doorframe like a bear." Not to mention what his scalp looked like because he couldn't care for his hair properly, or any of the other thousand annoyances of suddenly finding oneself helpless.

"You should get one of those back scratchers," Gabe suggested.

Russ had always dismissed that sort of thing as being for old people who couldn't bend. Now he was thinking about placing an Amazon order. "Yeah, maybe."

Gabe finished the water bottle and screwed the cap back on. "Anyway, I've got a handful of errands to run today. Thought I'd see if you wanted to tag along. I've been stuck in the house before. It sucks."

There it was. But it didn't bother him, coming from Gabe, maybe because he'd sat where Russ was sitting. Besides, getting out for a change of scenery would be good for him. "Better than sitting around here all day for sure. Thanks."

Russ had worried that Gabe was humoring him, but it turned out he really did have a lot of things to do. "Honey-do list," he said wryly. "Reyna's got a birthday party to go to next week, so I need to find the kid a present, and go to the bank, and pick up a couple groceries because we're out of the yogurt Dante likes…." He flipped the car visor down to keep the sun out of his eyes. "You can still back out."

"I know what I signed up for." Besides, maybe he'd find a baby gift for his sister while Gabe perused the toddler section of Toys R Us.

The errands ended up taking most of the day, which suited Russ fine. His barber was a few blocks over from Gabe's bank, so after the toy store, while Gabe was talking about investments or money transfers or whatever retired people did, Russ went in to see if he could get his edges cleaned up and happened to catch them during a lull. Normally part of the barber shop experience was catching up with everyone else, but Russ didn't mind that it was empty if it meant Jarome could fit him in. When Jarome saw the state of his hair—frizzy from a week and a half of Russ's one hand and limited range of movement—he insisted on doing a conditioning treatment first.

"Don't you have someone to do this for you at home?" Jarome chided. "Handsome guy like you."

Russ thought about Liam touching his hair like this, and shivered. He wouldn't know what he was doing, but he took direction pretty well. And it would *definitely* end in orgasms, even if they just rubbed off against each other in the shower. "Never thought about it," he said. If he *had* to have Liam taking care of him, that was a much better use of his energy than putting the toothpaste on Russ's toothbrush.

"Hmm, dating a white boy," Jarome teased. Russ's eyes snapped open, because he would remember if he'd told Jarome something like that, but

Jarome just went on as though this was no particular revelation and he didn't care in the slightest, except that he wanted Russ's hair to look good. "He'll learn."

…. Yeah, okay, Russ was sold on this plan. He left Jarome an obscene tip for seeing him on short notice and for the suggestion about Liam, and walked down the street to meet Gabe in front of the bank.

"Looking more like yourself," Gabe commented. "You hungry? I hate grocery shopping on an empty stomach. There's a burrito place Dante raves about a couple blocks over. They do a really great blackened fish—"

"You had me at hungry." Plus he could eat a burrito one-handed if they wrapped it for him. "Lead the way."

The burrito place had a patio, which made everything taste better. Russ ordered a second one to go after taking a bite of the first.

"Ambitious," Gabe said.

Russ carefully put down the burrito and wiped a smear of sauce from his mouth with a napkin. "Practical," he countered. "I suck at eating right-handed."

Gabe quirked a smile over his Modelo. "Fair."

They lapsed into silence for a bit while they polished off their lunches. "You still eat like a hockey player," Russ commented when Gabe reached for his fries.

"I eat way more unhealthy stuff now," Gabe laughed. "Gotta keep up with the workouts, though. Can't let my husband think he's in better shape than me."

The subject was right there, the questions just waiting for Russ to ask them. But did he know Gabe well enough to do it?

Somehow he didn't think Gabe would be offended, so he sucked it up. "Was it difficult? Retiring when he's still playing, I mean."

"Yes and no." He wagged his hand from side to side. "I miss playing. I don't miss the travel, but I do miss him when he's gone. The truth is we were lucky to get to play together as long as we did, and if I kept playing, our luck was going to run out. One of us would've been traded or gone UFA eventually, and I didn't want to be separated. Plus we wouldn't have Reyna if I hadn't retired." He shrugged, not totally at ease but not upset either. "I would've liked another shot at the Cup, but there was only room for so much in my life. Not having hockey made room for other things that are more important."

Russ picked at his burrito wrapper, glad he'd finished eating before they got to this point in the conversation. "I'm not ready to retire. I don't know if I could do it. You know?" Who would he even be without the game he'd built his life around? He couldn't bring himself to say *I don't know if I could stay with Liam and watch him play while I can't.* Feeling it was bad enough. And it wasn't because he didn't—fuck—because he didn't love Liam enough. He did. But he loved hockey too, and to sit back and be a spectator in the life he used to live… he'd be so bitter. "I'd fuck it up."

"Do you think you'll have to?" Gabe asked mildly. "Retire, I mean. Not fuck it up."

He shook his head again. "I don't know. Depends how the break heals."

A crunch while Gabe chewed on another fry. "You want some advice about it?"

Did he? "Probably depends on the advice."

Gabe snorted. "All right. Here it is." He leaned back in his chair. "Don't borrow trouble." He paused. "That's trouble with a lowercase T. Not *Trouble* Trouble. You wouldn't have to borrow him, I think you're in the lease-to-own option."

"So just take it as it comes. That's your advice?" Easier said than done. "Any pointers how?"

"Beats me. I was never any good at it." His lips quirked up in a half smile. "It's probably some kind of karma that this is advice I have to give to other people now. It helps, though, if you can do it. Do your physio, follow the doctors' instructions, take your meds. Those are the things you can control." He coughed and suddenly took an interest in the underside of the patio umbrella. "As for the frustration, that's what sex is for."

Russ had been taking a sip of his water, but he almost inhaled it instead. He expected that kind of comment from Baller, not his husband.

Well, no. Baller would've said *just fuck it out* or something considerably more graphic. Still. Russ set his glass down and wiped his mouth with his hand. "Kind of tough to get up to much at the moment."

"Oh, God forbid you have to get creative. How will Liam ever cope." He rolled his eyes. "What are you going to do, not have sex for six weeks?"

Russ felt judged, but the man had a point.

He mulled over what Gabe had said while they meandered the grocery store—apparently there was no rush—and through most of the drive home, when the unexpected exertion of the day caught up with him.

"Healing's a bitch," Gabe said when Russ stifled a yawn against the back of his hand.

"It is miserable," Russ agreed. "Can't even run errands without needing a nap."

At this, Gabe made a noncommittal noise. "Rest is work. Can't heal without it." He flicked on his blinker and glanced over at Russ. "Doesn't mean it's not boring."

Reframing rest as work did help, Russ thought later as he climbed into bed for a snooze. He wasn't doing *nothing*. He was giving his body what it needed.

Most of what it needed, he amended when he woke up hard three hours later, chasing the remnants of an involved dream about Liam and various ways they could get creative. He fumbled for his phone to check the time—he didn't want to miss tonight's game—and found a message waiting.

It was a picture of Liam, or at least of Liam's side. He was holding his shirt up in the mirror to show off the mottled bruising, but as attention-grabbing as the colors were, Russ's eye kept tracking away from them, over to his nipples, down to his navel. The picture didn't show the edge of his waistband, so Russ's brain decided he wasn't wearing underwear. Too bad he couldn't scroll down.

I look like a Rorschach test, Liam had written.

He looked like someone who needed Russ's dick in his mouth, and Russ told him so.

The phone rang a second later. "Okay first of all," Liam said before Russ could get out a word, "very rude of you to say that when I don't have time to jerk off before warm-ups."

Russ's dick woke the rest of the way up from his nap. "Hello to you too." He licked his lips. "Sure you don't have time?"

"I literally have to walk out of the locker room to make this call. Baller was giving me the eye. He saw me take the photo."

Well, that was his first mistake. "I guess you should hurry home, then."

"You're killing me. Call you after the game?"

"I'll be up," Russ promised. Even if he had to guzzle coffee at ten o'clock. "Go crush some desert dwellers for me."

"You say the sweetest things."

Russ brought his phone down to the living room so he could message the chat while he watched, but the puck hadn't even dropped before he got another text message.

Pleased to introduce Caden Russell Brown, born this afternoon at 3:18, 6 pounds 7 ounces. Mom and baby doing well. Grandma cried.

There was a picture attached—a small wrinkly bundle in a yellow blanket lying on Gia's chest. She looked exhausted but over the moon.

Russ glanced back at his nephew's name. Caden Russell. He swallowed against a lump in his throat. *Congratulations. He's perfect.*

He opened a browser tab and ordered an obscenely large gift basket.

Thanks. Not sure who feels worse right now, you or me.

Russ snorted. *Probably you. Get some rest and I'll call you later?*

10-4.

If nothing else, the arrival of Caden Russell would keep his mother too busy to come fuss over him in person. She'd have to relegate herself to text messages.

Maybe if Russ got the okay to fly, he'd take a trip back to Winnipeg to meet his nephew. Not that he'd be able to hold the kid, but still....

No, better not. He could hardly do anything for himself. He wouldn't be able to help Gia and might end up being more of a burden on the rest of the family. No one needed another helpless person around. He'd stay here. He could visit once he recovered.

Russ told himself it would be ridiculous to get upset about missing out when he wouldn't have been able to visit if he were healthy. He'd have been too busy traveling with the team. He never thought he might be able to drop everything and go meet his nephew, so it didn't make sense to be disappointed.

He kept repeating that to himself as the puck dropped on the television and his team started their game without him.

By first intermission he only had a few notes, but that wasn't unusual really. The Caimans were playing well without him. Russ was glad—he needed them to make the playoffs if he wanted a chance to lace up before the season was over—but it was weird too. He liked to be needed.

When the feed cut to the talking heads, Russ hit Mute. He didn't need to spend twenty minutes listening to their analysis—he wasn't playing, and when he was, he had a coach for that.

The silence would've been strange, almost oppressive, except before Russ could appreciate it, his phone rang. The call ID showed it was his mother.

If Russ didn't pick up today of all days, she'd never forgive him. He put her on speaker. "Hi, Ma. Or should I say Grandma?"

His mother sighed happily. "I don't think that's ever going to get old. Unlike me."

Russ chuckled and turned away from the television. "How's Gia doing, really?"

"Sleeping, thank goodness. I think she wore herself out with all the swearing."

"Yeah, Ma, I bet it was the cuss words that did it."

She laughed, partly at him and partly at her own joke. "I raised three tough kids, but labor's called that for a reason. You should see Jason, though; he's walking around like he's on cloud nine. And Caden is just a dream."

Russ smiled. Of course she thought so. She was his grandmother. "I'm glad they're all okay."

She made a noise of agreement. "These premature births can be tricky. Lucky for all of us Caden turned Gia into the Very Hungry Caterpillar. He doesn't even need to be in the NICU."

For the next few minutes, Russ listened happily to his mother's account of everything Caden Russell had done since 3:18 that afternoon.

"Sounds like he had a full day," Russ commented when she finished.

"And the rest of us too." He heard a muffled flump like a pillow deflating—Russ's mom used speakerphone for the same reason he did—and imagined she'd finally collapsed on the couch or her bed. "But that's enough about us. How are you doing, honey?"

Damn. And here Russ had thought he was safe. He should've known. "I...."

He turned his head to look at the TV, which was showing a breakdown of a play that had led to the Caimans' first-period goal.

He missed his team. He missed Liam. He missed having control over his life and certainty about his future and being able to breathe deeply without his ribs complaining.

"I've been better," he said, surprised when his voice came out in a rasp.

"I know it," Ma said. "And I know I'm nosy and pushy and that makes it hard to talk to me sometimes. But you're my son, and I love you. I do want to understand, so if you want... I could listen."

Russ struggled with the sudden urge to tell her everything. "Ma...." He let out a long breath and glanced at the screen. The talking heads were still at it. He swallowed. "I might not play again."

"Oh, Russ. I'm sorry. I know how much you love it."

"Yeah. They're worried about soft tissue damage, so I just have to wait and see, and that...."

Ashlyn Kane and Morgan James

His mother suggested gently, "It's never been your strong suit."

He huffed at the understatement and ran a hand over the back of his neck. "And I've been doing it all year, with my contract, because I *can't* even talk to teams yet. But at least I had hockey to distract me." Not to mention Liam. Would Russ even have made a move if he hadn't needed something to take his mind off contract shit?

"That sounds hard."

"That's not even the worst part." The more he said, the more that wanted to come out. "Now I just have to watch, you know? With games on TV, it's like I'm looking at my future. And with Liam—"

With Liam, he had a whole host of complicating issues he'd decided never to talk to his mother about.

It was too late, though. "What about Liam, honey?" She paused. "I suppose it's another big change, him being gone on a road trip while you're home by yourself."

She had to know they were together, didn't she? And she was giving him an out?

Or maybe she didn't suspect at all and that was Russ's guilty conscience talking.

"That's part of it." He rolled onto his back on the couch to free up both hands. Sometimes being able to gesture helped him put things into words. "But it's also—he's my rookie. I've been showing him the ropes, helping him with his mental game…." He ticked things off on his fingers as though she could see him. "And he's so good, Ma. I knew I was training him to replace me. I just didn't think I'd still be here when it happened."

For a moment she stayed silent, as if she was digesting what he'd said, or maybe what he hadn't. Finally she said, "I thought you weren't sure about your recovery yet. That sounds like you've heard bad news."

"No bad news yet." His mouth had gone dry.

His mother's voice was uncharacteristically tentative when she said, "Well, forgive me, because I know I said I'd just listen, but sweetheart... maybe don't go borrowing trouble."

People kept telling him that, but everyone else who'd said it was making a joke about Liam on purpose. Russ's throat tightened. "I'm in the lease-to-own option." He raised his hand to cover his eyes. He was going to have to tell her.

"Russell? What does that mean?"

He swallowed. "I'm seeing someone, Ma."

Her sharp inhalation carried through the speaker. To her credit, she didn't immediately ask a hundred questions, even though Russ knew she wanted to. "Oh?"

"It's Liam. It's—he's my—" *Boyfriend.* Why couldn't he say that? "We're dating," he finished pathetically. Before she could say anything else, he pressed on, hoping to skip past the third degree. "And I thought, you know, we'd keep it kind of casual, since he's just starting out in the league and I was probably going to get traded. Or sign somewhere else. And then I'd be retiring, and he'd...."

"You thought he'd leave you behind."

The air rushed out of Russ's lungs so fast his chest hurt. He couldn't admit that to his mother—not if he wanted to live—so he skipped past it into "But he didn't want to break up when Erika said they were going to trade me to Colorado, and now I'm injured and he's still…." Making sure Russ could open his microwave dinners and sending shirtless selfies while Russ was trying to watch hockey.

"Well," his mother said finally, "I'm glad you picked somebody with sense this time."

The idea of Liam as *someone with sense* forced out a strangled laugh. "Ma—"

"Russell." Oh, she'd full-named him again. He pressed his lips together. "You worked hard to get where you are, and you deserve to be proud of that. But you seem to think the only thing you have to offer is being good at hockey."

While Russ's ears were still burning, she continued.

"And honey, I have to tell you, that's not on most people's list of what makes a good partner."

Russ opened his mouth to protest, but he couldn't think of anything to say to defend himself. Liam was good at hockey, sure, and sometimes that got Russ hot, but that wasn't what made Russ want him around. He liked Liam's attitude and his sense of humor and his open affection and the way he made Russ feel like it was okay not to be able to control everything.

Which begged the question: What did Liam see in him?

Before he could think about it, he asked, "Do you think I'd be a good partner?"

It must have taken all of her restraint to simply say, "I haven't been trying to set you up with every eligible bachelor in Manitoba because I think you'd be bad at it, sweetheart." He could practically see her expression, fond but no-nonsense and very wry. "You're a good man. You take care of your family. You're there for your sisters. Even if you never play hockey again, you have lots of insight to offer others. And you made that young man a home, didn't you?"

He hadn't thought of it that way at the time, but…. "Yeah."

"See? There's your answer." She paused while Russ tried to digest it all. "But I hope you're planning to bring him home this summer to introduce us properly."

LIAM HAD been afraid that a road trip without Russ would feel weird. Russ had always been there to facilitate his place on the team, even at the beginning, when Liam was only batting his ass at him and didn't actually expect him to follow through with fucking it. He spent most of his time with Russ, on and off the ice.

But it turned out he'd made better friends than he thought. Hughesy appreciated having someone to hang out with who wasn't such an old man ("Watch your mouth, kid, or I'll force-feed you my prune juice," Baller sniped back), and Sparky needed someone to listen to him recite Neruda for fifteen minutes before every game, because…. Liam didn't know why. Goalies were weird.

So the road trip was fine. They picked up eight of a possible ten points and Liam managed twenty-six minutes a night without wanting to die, at least until he got off the ice and into the ice *bath* that was supposed to help his muscles recover well enough to play a back-to-back.

Whoever invented hockey was probably a sadist.

The Caimans' game in LA was the last one before the All-Star Break, and Liam looked forward to going back to Russ's and doing nothing but each other for a week. He dozed off on the flight back east with vague thoughts of cashing some of the checks Russ's mouth had written on the phone the other night.

Russ must've been thinking about it too. Liam pushed open the door and didn't even have time to take his shoes off, because Russ was shirtless in the kitchen and Liam needed to be kissing him *right now*.

Russ had grown his beard out, and it rasped against Liam's lips and chin as he opened his mouth under Russ's. The heat of Russ's skin seared through his clothes and sent a shiver down his spine, even as his right hand sneaked under the hem of Liam's shirt and brushed over his side, gently, mindful of the bruising. Fuck, he'd missed Russ's mouth—the way he tasted, the way he kissed Liam like he could learn the world's secrets.

He could feel Russ's erection through the silky fabric of his basketball shorts. But feeling it against his own wasn't enough. He snaked his hand between them and cupped Russ's cock.

That made Russ inhale sharply and sink his teeth into Liam's lower lip. Heat flared through him.

"Your breathing's gotten better," Liam croaked when Russ released him. He hadn't even winced after the sharp breath. "And where's your sling?"

Russ ignored this and unbuttoned Liam's pants, and Liam's priorities reasserted themselves. Russ's arm wasn't going to fall off. Liam could scold him later. "I bought you a present."

Liam inhaled shakily as Russ mouthed over his Adam's apple. "Oh?"

Russ hummed into his skin. "Come upstairs."

Liam was definitely going to come upstairs, all right. Dazedly, he allowed Russ to herd him to the bedroom, all too aware of his unfastened pants and Russ's heat at his back. He stopped just inside the bedroom door and kicked off his shoes, too blinded by lust to take in anything except how much he needed to get naked with his boyfriend.

At least, until he saw the purple dildo suction cupped to the headboard. "So... I take it you have a plan."

"Problem?" Russ asked as he slid his hands under Liam's waistband and shoved down his shorts.

"Nope," Liam squeaked. He took a step out of his clothes and then yanked off his own shirt, not willing to risk Russ's range of motion. "You want to tell me what it is?"

Russ stepped up behind him and slid his hand down Liam's chest, his chin hooked over his shoulder so that his beard scraped the tender skin of Liam's neck and his lips brushed Liam's earlobe. "Well." He curled his hand into a gentle claw and carded his fingers down through the trail of hair below Liam's navel. He stopped just shy of Liam's cock, already hard and eager for Russ's touch. "We have the whole week off."

Yep. Yes, they did. Liam swallowed. "Uh-huh."

"Unfortunately, my ribs aren't healed enough for me to fuck you the way you like." He made a loose fist around Liam's dick and stroked him once, tantalizing, and stepped up closer so that his erection pressed between Liam's asscheeks. "So you're gonna have to do that yourself."

"'Kay," Liam said weakly, imagining it as Russ smeared fluid over the head of his dick. "What, ah, what about you?"

Russ pressed a kiss to the top of his shoulder. "Don't worry. You can take care of me too."

Yes, that. Liam wanted to do that. The sooner the better. Liam got one last, searing kiss before Russ shoved him one-handed toward the mattress. "On the bed, hands and knees."

Liam scrambled to obey. Sweat broke out on his skin even in the cool air of the bedroom. It prickled at the nape of his neck, the hollow of his throat, behind his knees. Russ slapped the back of his thigh and then dug under one of the pillows. The click of a cap opening sent another shiver through Liam.

He jerked when Russ scraped his beard over the top of his ass. "You've got freckles here too, you know." He traced a path with his tongue.

"Uhhhhh-huh," Liam agreed.

A slick finger pressed against his hole. The strength went out of Liam's arms when Russ pushed inside him. "Next time I fuck you, I'm going to come all over them."

Breath hitching, Liam rocked back into Russ's touch. His dick jerked between his legs as Russ angled his fingers just right. "Yes," he whispered.

Another finger joined the first two. "Today I'll settle for the ones on your face."

"Russ." Liam licked his lips. "Get on the bed. Please."

Russ didn't move, except to curl his fingers against Liam's prostate again. "What's the hurry?"

"Are you fucking—" Liam lost his words in a moan when Russ rubbed his beard over his ass. "You're the one who said I look like—"

Russ bit his upper thigh. "Like?"

God, he was going to make Liam say it. "Like someone who needs your dick in my mouth." He took another shaky breath. "You should do something about that."

"Hmm." Another scrape of rough facial hair on Liam's skin, this time on the hypersensitive insides of his thighs. Then Russ rumbled, "Since you asked so nicely. Turn toward the foot of the bed."

Somehow Liam obeyed, even though moving on the soft mattress when his legs wanted to shake with lust proved tricky. Russ smoothed his hand down his back, directing him into place. There was a loud sucking noise as he repositioned the dildo to the right height.

Then Russ guided him backward, until the slick tip of it nudged Liam's hole. "Good?"

In answer, Liam pushed down onto it, relishing the stretch. The toy was longer than Russ but not as thick, and Russ had angled it just right, so that the slightest tilt of Liam's hips had it rubbing over his prostate with each thrust. "Fuck," Liam groaned, pausing with the toy as deep as he could get it. He clenched down, and his cock dripped between his legs.

"I'll take that as a yes." Russ joined him on the bed, kneeling in front of Liam's face. Gently, he pressed his thumb into the hinge of Liam's jaw. "Open for me."

As if he had to ask. Liam opened, wetting his lips.

Russ cupped the back of Liam's neck and pulled him forward onto his cock and off of the toy, until only the tip remained inside.

Liam's stomach clenched at the taste of him, salt and sweat and sex. He sucked, pressing his tongue against the underside, breathing shallowly through his nose.

"I was right," Russ said. He brushed his fingers over the freckles on Liam's cheeks. "You do need it."

Liam shuddered at the pitch of his voice, low and intimate.

"Show me how much," Russ commanded. The words sent a wave of heat through Liam's body, pooling in his armpits, in his stomach, in his dick. "Fuck yourself on my cocks."

An involuntary whine escaped him, stifled by Russ thrusting gently into his mouth. Right—Russ wasn't supposed to do that. It was Liam's job to take care of him tonight. He leaned into Russ's hand on his face for a fraction of a second before swinging his body backward until his ass was flush with the head-board. It rattled against the wall and in Liam's head, his whole nervous system lighting up at the perfect pressure inside him. His erection leaked steadily between his legs, neglected, throbbing with want.

Liam ignored it and lurched forward onto Russ's dick. Russ made a satisfied sound, something that didn't filter into Liam's brain, and carded his fingers through his hair, and—

Everything faded into a blur of pleasure. Liam's mouth watered and spit slicked his chin as he thrust himself onto the toy in his ass and forward onto Russ's cock. It had been so long since they'd fucked, it felt like forever. He'd never come without someone touching his dick, but he wished he had, wished he could.

He could come once he'd taken care of Russ.

Russ was rock-hard in his mouth now, leaking salt-bitter fluid over Liam's tongue. It made his mouth water more. "Fuck, you're so good at this. You're going to make me come."

Yes. Liam sucked harder, frantically pushing his body back and forth. The dildo hit him perfectly, ratcheting his pleasure to almost unbearable levels. He curled his hands into the sheets as Russ curled a hand in his hair. He had the other wrapped around the base of his dick now, fingers bumping Liam's lips, until finally he pushed Liam back.

Liam closed his eyes as Russ's come hit his cheeks and lips. The head of Russ's pulsing cock bumped his mouth, smearing hot, bitter liquid over his skin. Liam shuddered, lapping at Russ's foreskin, his whole body taut with the need for his own release.

He was teetering on the edge when Russ drew back and brushed his fingers over his face again, collecting his come. Then he wrapped his slick hand around Liam's erection. "Come on," he rasped. "Finish it."

Trembling, Liam fucked forward into his fist and back onto the dildo. Russ tightened his grip perfectly as Liam thrust back hard. Stars erupted behind his eyes as his orgasm poured out of him, his balls contracting and pulsing.

Finally he collapsed onto his elbows, heaving. The toy slipped out of him and he winced, overstimulated.

A moment later Russ grabbed a damp cloth from a bowl on the bedside table. "Here, close your eyes."

Liam did, tilting his face up so Russ could clean the remnants of come off his face. Then he flopped over onto his side.

Russ sat heavily on the bed next to him and leaned against the headboard. Liam stretched a kink out of his neck and left his face pressed against Russ's knee. "I should go on road trips more often."

Russ laughed breathlessly, then groaned, and reality reasserted itself.

Liam sat up and turned toward him. "So… am I allowed to ask about your sling now?"

Russ nudged him with his knee. "Doctor said I don't have to wear it all the time anymore. The collarbone's healed well enough to go without for a while, as long as it doesn't hurt."

"Hmm. That's good." Except Liam could tell by the tightness in Russ's expression that right now it did hurt, at least a little. Or maybe he'd overdone it on his ribs. Spying the sling hooked over the end of the bedpost, he picked it up and tossed it gently in Russ's direction.

Russ gave him a flat, unimpressed look, but there was a hint of humor underneath. Probably. "I missed you too," he said dryly. He put the sling on, though.

"Don't be a baby." Liam stretched again, then frowned when the movement pulled the drying come on his thighs and stomach. "I need a shower. Wanna join me?" He walked his fingers up Russ's thigh. "I'll wash your back for you."

Russ captured Liam's hand in his right and prevented any further teasing. "Actually…."

Liam looked up at the sudden hesitation in his voice. It was unlike Russ. Liam waited.

With a little grimace, Russ said, "Can you help me with my hair? I need two hands and I don't have the range of motion yet."

Hearing the mighty Russ Lyons ask for help would've put Liam on his ass if he weren't already, but he knew better than to make a big deal out of it. Russ would get all prickly and uncomfortable and probably take back the request. Instead, he gave a slight, teasing leer and said, "Sounds hot. I'm in."

Russ rolled his eyes, but he also rolled out of bed and walked toward the bathroom, calling back over his shoulder, "You coming?"

So Liam figured he'd done all right.

RUSS USUALLY looked forward to the All-Star Break. By that point in the season, he was ready to sit on a beach, eat himself stupid, and sleep for twelve hours a day. He was still looking forward to it, but this time because it meant Liam would be home and he wouldn't have to lie around his house wallowing in his own boredom. Human company and sex on tap. Just what the doctor ordered.

And for the first two days of it, that was what he got. As a bonus, Liam turned out to be a quick study in scalp massage, and having him work Russ's moisturizer in while Russ sat on the stone bench in the shower and tried not to melt into a puddle didn't suck.

So obviously things went down the shitter on the third day, when Russ woke up to the news that the DA had decided not to press charges for the accident.

No one from the Miami PD had been in touch with him since he gave his statement, which made everything feel worse. To add insult to literal injury, he couldn't even work his frustrations off in the gym. Deep breathing exercises didn't exactly cut it, and watching Liam lift weights only made him jealous and horny.

This was dumb. "I'm going in the pool," Russ said abruptly and spent fifteen minutes power walking in the shallow end. It didn't help, but at least he didn't have to watch Liam do things he couldn't.

When he'd worked his body as much as he dared, he got out of the water and sat on the concrete patio for a few minutes, hoping the February sun would evaporate some of his mood. He wasn't sure it was working, but the warmth felt nice. He even did a little more deep breathing, mostly by accident.

The patio door slid open behind him and Liam stuck his head out. "You hungry? I made lunch."

Russ let out a slow breath. He was hungry, and there wasn't any reason to be angry Liam had made lunch. He picked up his towel and stood. "Yeah. Thanks."

Lunch was chicken sandwiches with a chopped salad of chickpeas, cucumbers, tomatoes, onions, feta, and olives. Russ had made the salad before, and he liked it, but he'd been planning to use the feta in a different salad, and Liam put mayo on his sandwich. Russ hated mayo.

He ate it anyway, because he needed food and it seemed petty not to, but he wished Liam had just asked if he wanted mayo. He must've bought it himself—Russ didn't even keep it in the house.

Liam didn't seem to notice his mood, which was probably for the best. He chattered away across the kitchen table as Russ methodically chewed his sandwich. "… Hughesy asked if I want to do an air-boat ride with him tomorrow, but then I saw the calendar on the fridge—you have a doctor's appointment?"

When *didn't* Russ have doctor's appointments, lately? "Yeah."

Liam nodded. "I'll see if he wants to go the day after instead."

Russ bristled. "You should go tomorrow. I can get an Uber. It's not a big deal." He would prefer to go by himself. If the doctors had bad news, he wanted time to process it before he had to face anyone who knew him.

A furrow appeared between Liam's brows. "I want to be there, though."

What about what I want? His career. His independence. A life where he could make decisions for himself and didn't have to fight the other people in it every step of the way.

"Go with Hughesy," he said again. "It'll be fun." And Russ would get a day in his house by himself without Liam hovering over him. He stood up to dump the rest of his half-eaten sandwich in the garbage.

"Okay," Liam said finally. Then, "Aren't you going to finish your lunch?"

Russ accidentally slammed the cupboard under the sink. "I'm not hungry."

There was another pause—one that made Russ grit his teeth—as he put his dishes in the dishwasher. His ribs twinged as he bent.

Then Liam said, "Why are you mad at me?"

All Russ's breath left him in a rush of broken ribs and bruised lungs, which hurt enough that he slapped his palm on top of the counter. "For fuck's sake, Liam. Not everything is about you."

Liam stared at him, pale under his freckles, his mouth slightly agape.

Russ felt like a complete monster when he snapped, "Can you just give me some fucking space for once?"

All at once Liam flushed scarlet—and not, Russ thought, with embarrassment. He stood abruptly from the table, leaving one of his sandwiches untouched. "Fine. If you're going to be an asshole, I'll see you later."

He snatched his keys from the peg by the door and stormed out of the house. A moment later Russ heard his car start and the roll of tires on pavement.

Deflating, Russ dropped back into his chair at the kitchen table. He thought he'd been doing so well. He'd even told his mom about Liam. He thought he'd figured himself out. So what was wrong with him? Since when could he not communicate his boundaries? He'd set them just fine with his busy-body parents, even if they occasionally needed re-minding. It wasn't like Liam was pissing him off on purpose. He thought he was helping. For any *normal* person, he would've been.

And if Russ hated to need help, that was a Russ problem, not a Liam problem. Without Liam, Russ would be far crankier. He'd have had a hard time even opening microwave dinners. Forget putting clean sheets on the bed.

He could've just told Liam to back off, so why didn't he?

Because Liam had specifically mentioned that he wanted to do things for Russ. To him, their rela-tionship had felt lopsided until now.

Russ might've been fine with Liam doing the laundry and making lunch and driving him to ap-pointments if he were still *capable* of doing every-thing he wanted to. But having Liam do all the things Russ used to do for them both felt now like salt rubbed in an open wound. And Russ might've ac-cepted that his hangups weren't all about hockey, but Liam still playing only compounded the problem.

None of which was Liam's fault, and none of which negated the fact that Russ needed help whether he liked it or not, and none of which excused him from being a dick about it.

He'd turned a bad situation into a total shitfest.

Needing something productive to do, he got up from the table, grabbed a Tupperware container, and put away Liam's sandwich and his lunch dishes. He found the lid for the salad bowl and tucked that into the fridge too. He contemplated taking out one of the beers—he was off the medications that made alcohol a problem—but decided against it. He wasn't going to wallow.

Which left him alone in his too-quiet house, asking himself what the fuck he was going to do now.

FOR THE first few minutes, Liam just drove—no music, no destination, just him and the car and the road. What was Russ's problem? He was the one who'd wanted a serious relationship in the first place. And as soon as things got *serious* serious—like, life-threatening-injury serious—he pitched a fit and pushed Liam away.

After five minutes, he realized he was heading to Baller's place. Two minutes after that he pulled into the driveway and parked the car.

But he didn't get out. Getting out would feel like giving up or running away or admitting he couldn't solve his own problems, and Liam wasn't ready to do that.

So, what *could* he do to fix this? Ideally he would text Russ to stop being a dick, and he would, and that would be it. But Liam wasn't *quite* naïve enough to think that'd work. He had to work out what Russ's problem was. Unfortunately Liam couldn't read minds, which meant they were going to have to talk about what was bothering them.

On second thought maybe he *should* just text Russ to stop being a dick. That sounded way easier.

He was drumming his fingers on the steering wheel and debating alternatives when a knock on the window made him jump so high he banged his knee on the dash.

When Liam's heart climbed back down from his throat and he could see again, he looked to his left and saw Baller smirking at him. He had Reyna in one arm and a hose in the other. He must've been watering the plants.

Liam rolled down the window. "Hi. Sorry."

"Nah, it's fine, we love an impromptu comedy show, don't we, Reyna?"

Reyna giggled and then faceplanted in her father's neck because she was shy.

Liam slumped in the seat. "I didn't come here on purpose." The last thing he wanted was to go groveling for advice. Hard pass. He told himself he'd come here because it was the last place he'd stayed that wasn't Russ's.

Ugh, he should've gotten his own apartment.

"Hmm. What do you think, kid, should we invite him in?" Baller made a silly face at his daughter. "Or maybe I should just spray him with the hose?"

"Spray widda hose!" Reyna yelled enthusiastically.

"We'll make that our backup plan," Baller agreed. He turned back to Liam. "Are you okay?"

Liam took a deep breath. He was pissed and hurt, but not devastated. He'd been in worse shape after the accident. And at least he'd had enough sleep the past few days. "I'm okay."

Baller nodded. "You know where you gotta be?"

Standing toe to toe with Russ and having it out over whatever crawled up his ass. "I know where I need to be."

"Great." Baller slapped the roof of the car. "Get lost."

Everyone on this team was so bad at pep talks. Liam started the car. "See you later."

The drive home gave him plenty of time to build up a head of steam, but for every one of Russ's transgressions, Liam developed a corresponding new thing to worry about. Russ was stubborn and noncommunicative and had basically kicked Liam out of the place he lived instead of having an adult conversation. Liam *couldn't* worry that Russ wanted to break up with him—Russ would've told him it was over to his face—so instead he worried about why Russ didn't want Liam to come to his doctor's appointment and whether that might be related to how clipped he got when talking about his recovery.

Oh God, what if he was dying?

No, that was dumb. Liam needed to focus. He wasn't going to talk himself out of being angry at Russ before he even got an apology.

Liam pulled back into the driveway twenty minutes after he left. He shoved the keys in his pocket and swept into the house, holding on to his righteous fury by a thread.

Russ was still in the kitchen, staring at Liam in a horrible parody of Liam's homecoming from the road trip. But he looked different. His face was drawn and tight, his posture full of misery instead of promise.

"You're such an *asshole*," Liam said at the same time as Russ said, "I'm sorry."

Liam had taken a deep breath, ready to launch into a detailed breakdown of why Russ sucked and why Liam wasn't going to put up with his shit, but then Russ's apology filtered into his brain and ruined everything. Against his will, he felt the indignation slowly leach out of him. "Are you kidding me?" he said helplessly. "You're apologizing before I even get to tell you why you're a dick?" What was he supposed to do with all these feelings now?

"I'm sorry," Russ said again, this time with a slight twitch of his lips. "Maybe I should tell you why I'm a dick instead."

That seemed to be his preferred method of apologizing. One day Liam was going to do all the telling. But today he wanted to know that Russ really did understand where he fucked up. He slouched into one of the kitchen chairs. "I'm listening."

Russ sat across from him and reached over the table for Liam's hands. Liam let him take them, annoyed at how much better he felt already.

But then Russ didn't speak right away.

"Still listening," Liam prompted.

Russ grimaced. "Sorry, it's hard to know where to start. I... you know I like taking care of you, doing things for you. Picking up the dry cleaning. Making dinner. That stuff."

"Yeah, I noticed." Plus Russ had said as much on their date.

"Right. And right now I can't do that, and you're doing all these things for me"—he winced. "I feel like I'm being smothered—"

"Smothered," Liam repeated. A flicker of resurging anger licked at his spine, and he yanked his hands away. "*I thought you fucking died* in that parking lot. And then I was in the hospital for hours before anyone tells me you're okay! So I'm *sorry* for caring about you!"

Russ's face had gone blank with shock during his outburst. "Hey, hey. I didn't know. Liam. I'm sorry." He caught his hands again. "I'm *sorry*," he repeated firmly. "I obviously didn't think about your side of things, and that was stupid. I'd probably be smothering you too."

If what Liam had been doing was Russ's definition of smothering, then Russ had an asphyxiation kink, because he'd been smothering Liam for months. Liam took a deep breath and then exhaled the anger again.

"Can I get on with the apology part now?" Russ asked gently, and when Liam nodded, he continued, "It's not that I don't appreciate it. If I didn't feel so helpless, it would be great. It's just hard for me to not be able to reciprocate, and I've been taking it out on you, and that sucks. So. I'm sorry."

There was no way that was everything that was bothering him, but it was a decent start. "Okay. I forgive you." But that didn't solve their problems. "But, like, you do need help with stuff, so what do you want me to do?"

"Can we compromise? I'll try to be less cranky and better about asking for help when I need it if you promise not to try to do everything for me before I even have a chance. It makes me feel like I…." His fingers clenched and released around Liam's, and a shiver ran down Liam's spine.

"Makes you feel like what?" he asked cautiously, a little hoarse.

Russ raised his eyes from the tabletop. His voice cracked when he said, "Like you don't think I'm going to play again."

Oh. Liam wet his lips and swallowed around the lump in his throat. He'd only thought Russ might have died for a few seconds. Constantly living with that fear couldn't be fun. "Is, um, is that a possibility?"

Russ let out a slow breath. "Maybe. It's… I have some scar tissue built up in my shoulder from the break. I'm having an MRI tomorrow to see how it's healing."

"But you don't want me to come," Liam said. Russ had told him to go on an air-boat ride with Hughesy instead and look at alligators. "Because I'm smothering you?"

"No." Russ looked up at the ceiling. Liam let him have that; this conversation was hard enough without prolonged eye contact. "Because if I get bad news, I don't want to take it out on you. I'll need time to process. It's hard sometimes because you're still playing, where I want to be. But it's not your job to manage my feelings about that."

Manage his feelings? "Have you been talking to a therapist?"

Russ's lips twitched into a parody of a smile. "Sort of. I got an earful from my mom while you were gone because I was kind of…. I got all tied up thinking about how this thing I really value about myself could go away, and that would make me a shitty boyfriend."

Liam's mouth dropped open. He'd done a terrible job of letting Russ know how much Liam appreciated him if he thought, even for a second, that he wasn't, like, the archetype of a good boyfriend.

Russ went on, a little sheepishly, "But Ma pointed out that actually no one has 'good hockey player' on their list of things they look for in a man."

Liam cleared his throat. "I'm glad she got you figured out." Then the full meaning of Russ's words hit him and he swayed a little in his chair. "Uh, you told your mom about me?"

"Um." Russ ran a hand over the back of his neck. "If it helps, I definitely didn't say *anything* about your dick."

Liam didn't have the slightest clue how to reply, so he didn't try. Instead he said, "I think we're off topic." He took heart from the fact that they'd come back together to talk things out, but they still had to actually do that talking. "You say you don't like feeling smothered. I get that. But can I still help with some things?" Like conditioning Russ's hair, which turned Russ into a gooey, horny puddle. But even aside from that…. "I know you like to take care of me, but I'm a grown-up too. We should take care of each other. That's what people who—"

People who love each other. That's who does that.

Liam's heart suddenly beat in his throat. Russ was still looking at him, still holding his hand, like he could see what was going on in Liam's head. He looked very soft about it, indulgent. Maybe a little bit smug.

Let him be smug. He was the one who'd fucked up here; he could say it first. "—people in relationships do," Liam finished. "It's not fair if it's all one-sided."

"Deal." Russ raised Liam's left hand to his lips and kissed the back of it. "And I promise I'll tell you about my shoulder eventually, just maybe not right away."

Liam figured *eventually* would happen soon if it was good news and God-knew-when if it wasn't, so he'd be able to prepare himself. "That's fair." He cleared his throat. "One more thing I want to get off my chest." He took a deep breath because it was kind of a big deal. "You asked for space today. Do you want me to find an apartment? I put it off because I thought you'd need me around, but—"

"No." Russ looked surprised at how fast the word came out. "I like you here. This is your home too. It was shitty of me to run you off. I can go for a walk if I need space so bad. Next time tell me to go fuck myself."

Liam's mouth twitched without his permission. "Absolutely not," he deadpanned. "That's my job."

Russ startled into a laugh, wheezed out a "fuck" when that apparently hurt, and then laughed harder, cursing the whole time. Liam kept his alarm under wraps. If Russ were hurting himself that badly, he'd have stopped laughing. Finally he stood up and beckoned Liam into his arms. "You're a lot of trouble, you know that?"

Liam shrugged innocently, but he went. He wasn't stupid. Postfight hugs were the best. He pressed his nose into Russ's shoulder and inhaled as Russ tucked his hands into Liam's ass pockets. "So they tell me."

Russ drew back until their noses brushed against each other. "Good thing I love trouble."

Yeah. It definitely was.

NOW THAT he could go without the sling for a few hours, Russ was cleared to drive short distances, and not a minute too soon. He took himself to his doctor's appointment, pretending his stomach wasn't trying to eat itself from anxiety.

"Mr. Lyons?" A scrubs-clad woman poked her head out of the door to the examination rooms. "We're ready for you."

At least they weren't making him wait for long.

Russ mechanically stripped down to his underwear and donned the stupid hospital gown. The tech hooked up an IV line for the contrast material.

And then he was in the big noisy machine, breathing as shallowly as he could to make sure they got a good image. Russ hadn't thought he was claustrophobic until his first MRI. Now he dreaded them. The sooner he got out of here, the better.

Finally the ordeal was over and Russ got to put real clothes back on. Considering the stakes, he would rather have had his hockey pads—some kind of armor against whatever was coming—but he had to settle for shorts and a T-shirt.

It was only a few minutes before the radiologist came in, followed by Dr. Chapel. "Mr. Lyons, I'm Dr. Ford." She shook his hand.

"Hi." Russ didn't have *nice to meet you* in him, but he pasted on a smile. "Let's not beat around the bush, okay? It's been a long couple weeks."

Dr. Chapel cleared his throat. "All right, well. I'll let Dr. Ford deliver the prognosis."

She gave him a professional smile. "I appreciate that this is a difficult situation, but this kind of medicine doesn't deal in absolutes. The good news is that from what I can see on your scans, I don't believe the bone will require surgery to reset. The less good news is that the broken bone did some damage to the surrounding tissue. You're likely going to experience a loss of range of movement and some loss of strength—"

Fuck. That was it, then. Russ was glad he was sitting down, because he thought his legs might've gone out from under him otherwise.

"—but I believe that with targeted therapies like TENS, ultrasound, and deep-tissue massage, as well as a specially tailored physio regimen, you should be able to regain enough function to play professionally, if not at the same level."

Now he was *really* glad he was sitting down. Russ let out a long breath and tried not to let his relief leak out the holes in his face.

"That said," Dr. Chapel said, taking over, "you can't start the massage course until the bone finishes healing. I'll set you up with a TENS machine you can use at home, though, and we'll have the therapists work out some exercises you can do to get the blood flowing to promote healing without causing yourself further injury."

Russ had never been so grateful to get homework. He thanked the doctors and walked out of the exam room in a daze.

He could keep playing. Maybe not for long, and maybe only in the minors, but maybe in the NHL.

When he got back to the truck he started the engine, but he didn't go anywhere yet. First he texted Liam. *Mostly good news. Starting limited physio asap.*

Liam texted back *!!!* and then a picture of someone holding a baby alligator by the tail, followed by a heart-eyes emoji.

It seemed like they were having a good time.

Russ went back home and carefully prepared dinner in the Instant Pot, feeling very much in charity with the world. While the meal cooked, he went outside and sat on the patio in the shade and closed his eyes, enjoying the breeze. For the first time in weeks, he felt like he could breathe. He might not be able to control everything in his life, but the things that really mattered—Liam, his health—were on track. He could worry about where he might sign next tomorrow.

As if on cue, his phone buzzed with a text from Erika, who'd probably just gotten an update from Dr. Chapel. Russ dismissed the notification without reading it. Scratch his earlier thought—*Erika* could worry about where he might sign next. Russ had just discovered he might still get to play this season, and he was focusing on that.

He must've dozed off, because the next thing he knew, Liam was touching his shoulder. He'd sunburned across his nose—Russ knew he should've made him wear sunscreen—but he was grinning and happy, even if he smelled like a swamp. "Hey."

Russ stretched, surprised when his collarbone didn't protest overmuch, and then pulled Liam down to sit on the lounger with him, between his legs. Liam didn't lean into him—bad idea with all the still-healing bones—but it was nice anyway. "Hey. Did you have a good adventure?"

"Yeah. Air-boat tour guides are crazy, holy shit."

Russ snorted. All those mosquitos, on top of the alligators? You'd have to be. No, thank you. "Not surprising."

"Right?" Liam half turned so they were facing each other. "I got a weird phone call on the way home, though. Like, it was the Miami PD looking for you. Not in a we-want-to-arrest-you way. Sorry, that was probably not the best way to phrase it."

"Probably not," Russ said dryly. "What did they want, if I'm not suspected of murder?"

"The lady said the officer who took your statement wrote your phone number down wrong. They've been trying to get in touch with you about the driver of the truck."

For fuck's sake. Of all the reasons for Russ to have been stressing out over the lack of communication. "What about them?"

Liam trailed his fingers through the hair on Russ's shin. "So I guess there was some problem with, like, HIPAA or something? I don't know. The doctors had to get permission to tell the police stuff, and then the police had to get permission to tell you, but I guess she wasn't drunk or anything. The driver, I mean. She had a seizure. That's why they're not charging her."

"Oh shit." Russ could've had so many more nights of peaceful sleep if someone had told him this weeks ago.

"Yeah. No history of epilepsy or anything. I guess we were lucky it wasn't worse." He stopped fidgeting with Russ's leg hair and laced their fingers together instead.

For the first time in a while, Russ *felt* lucky. It was a nice feeling. He'd missed it. "Guess so."

Then Liam leaned his head back and sniffed the air. "Oh man, did you make dinner? I'm starving."

He'd probably been too busy gawking at alligators all day to have lunch. "I did."

Liam closed his eyes in apparent ecstasy. "I love you."

Russ went warm all over. "It's just chili."

Liam climbed to his feet and offered Russ a hand up. Russ took it without thinking. "Oh, yeah, just homemade dinner ready when I'm hungry without me having to put any effort in. No big deal. Come on and feed me before I waste away."

Well, they couldn't have that.

LIAM WOULD have liked to say that, in the weeks leading up to the playoffs, he had his shit completely together. He got enough sleep, arrived at practice on time, played perfect games, and didn't bug his boyfriend about his physio regime.

But it would have been a filthy lie. At this point in the season, Liam didn't think such a thing as *enough sleep* existed. Russ had teased him about being borderline narcoleptic before, but these days, half the time he fell asleep in his dinner. And Liam really liked dinner.

Most of the time, he made it to practice without being late, and only one of his on-ice mistakes potentially cost the Caimans a game. But he managed not to bug Russ about physio, and somehow that was more important. Things at home were good—better than ever, or they would've been if Liam had been awake to appreciate them.

He regularly forgot to pick up his dry cleaning, but Russ had him covered. Liam would've felt bad for needing to be looked after, again, except the day before the All-Star Break ended, a storm blew in and knocked a giant palm tree across Russ's driveway. It would've prevented Russ from getting to an appointment, but if Liam had one non-hockey skill, it was clearing trees. He grabbed the chainsaw and a pair of safety glasses from Russ's garage and got the trunk rolled off to the side in plenty of time.

Of course, Russ was still late for his appointment, but that was because he couldn't keep his hands to himself when Liam was doing a lumberjack impression. The tree was happy to take the fall.

The point was, Liam wasn't dead weight for Russ to carry. They had different strengths. And that was good.

The end of the season flew by. Before Liam knew it, they were suiting up for their first playoffs practice. They had the second slot in the Atlantic Division, facing the third-place Toronto Shield. Liam felt good about the team and good about their chances, but the best part about this morning's practice was—

Mo whooped when Liam pushed open the locker room door. "Well, well. Looks like Trouble brought a friend."

"Fuck off," Russ said cheerfully. "Don't get excited, I'm only here to make you look stupid."

"You didn't have to come in for that," Sparky chirped, and then everyone piled on welcoming Russ back.

Liam got out of the way and let it happen. Russ was allowed to practice, but he'd be wearing the red no-contact jersey for a couple of weeks. That didn't matter to Liam—it meant he got to have Russ with him on the road, and it meant he was that much closer to recovery. If they were only going to have a few more weeks on the same team, Liam intended to make the most of them. He'd done okay with Yeti, but he wanted his regular partner back.

Even if, starting this afternoon, he was going to have to share him.

After practice, Liam drove home so Russ could rest his shoulder—just a precaution, but one they agreed on.

"It's not too late to run away," Russ said as Liam flicked on the turn signal to merge onto the highway.

"I'm not afraid of your mom."

Russ snorted. "That's because you didn't grow up with her."

Maybe, but Liam had enough overbearing siblings; how different could it be? "She gonna love me. I'm charming."

"She's gonna think I'm a cradle-robbing pervert."

Blithely, Liam flipped the bird to a sports car that had cut him off. "You are." Judging from the snippets of conversation Liam had overheard over the past few months, Russ's mom was so excited to finally be introduced to one of Russ's boyfriends that she'd be taking Liam's side in any potential disagreements from now until eternity. And if not, he could distract her by asking to see pictures of Caden. Grandmas loved that shit.

Besides, he still had an hour before her plane landed, and Baller had already told him that if everything went to hell, he could camp out in their guest house. It never hurt to have a Plan B.

At home they got out of the car and beelined to the kitchen, picking up the routine where they'd left off when Russ got injured. Liam got out plates, cutlery, and drinks while Russ rummaged in the fridge for the leftovers. When he closed the door, one of the magnets fell, and Russ's physio schedule fluttered to the floor, along with a handful of memos from their meal delivery service and something on a thicker piece of cardstock.

"Do you have secret hoarding tendencies?" Liam teased as he picked up the collection. He knew Russ didn't; Liam had never seen someone so dedicated to cleaning out the fridge every week.

"I forgot that stuff was back there." Russ shook his head as he went through the pile Liam had handed him. "Shit."

Liam cracked open his bottle of Gatorade and turned his attention to the microwave that would soon be providing his lunch. "Hmm?"

Out of the corner of his eye, he saw Russ lift the cardstock. "I totally forgot about this. I need to RSVP." He paused long enough that Liam turned around again. "What are you doing this July?"

"Aside from training? You."

Russ snorted. "Staking your claim?"

"Mmm." Liam made a show of craning his head around to ogle Russ's backside. Then he looked up again, coy. "Can't let anyone else think they might have a second shot."

Something about Russ's startled, sheepish expression made him stand up straight. "What?" he asked.

Russ gave a barely-there half shrug and shifted his gaze to somewhere over Liam's shoulder. "You're assuming anyone else ever got a first."

Liam's brain did a full record scratch. That night in his hotel room—their first night together—Liam had asked if his first time was special, and he'd said....

Yeah, actually.

Without admitting that it had been all of five minutes previously.

"I can see you getting weirdly turned-on by this," Russ said, voice laden with amusement.

"You are *such* a romantic," Liam accused. He reeled Russ in and planted a kiss on him. Unfortunately they didn't have time to get side-tracked, with company on the way.

In reply, Russ held up the card, which showed two cartoon men in tuxes and hockey skates holding hands. "Yeah. So, you wanna be my date to Max Lockhart's wedding?"

Liam plucked the invitation from Russ's fingers and scanned down to the date and location. Moncton, New Brunswick. "Sure. Since we'll be in the area… you want to take an off-season tour of a sugar shack?"

Lyons Signs PTO With Miami Caimans
By Rocky Sanderson

Veteran defenseman Russ Lyons has signed a professional tryout with the Miami Caimans.

Lyons, 33, made headlines earlier this year when he was struck by a vehicle and suffered multiple broken ribs, as well as a broken collarbone. The accident occurred just days before he was due to celebrate his 1000th NHL game, and a week before rumors say he was scheduled to be dealt to the Colorado Altitude to alleviate cap pressure for the Caimans.

Now it looks as though he may be sticking around after all.

"Miami's been home for the past six years," Lyons said in a video interview this morning. "Getting to stick around for another, maybe play my thousandth game here, it means something. Not everyone gets so lucky."

The Caimans had a strong season up until Lyons's injury and beyond, finally losing to last year's Eastern Conference Champions in the Conference Final. Lyons did not play during the series.

The Caimans play their first preseason game September 20 in Tampa.

POSTGAME

RUSS PLAYED his thousandth game in the middle of October.

He didn't play twenty-eight minutes a night anymore, and Liam had replaced him as the team's top defenseman, but Russ couldn't muster up much regret. The Caimans couldn't have afforded to re-sign him if he'd made a full recovery right away, and Russ was too proud to take a discount.

Besides, he was still improving. He'd only signed for one year. At the end of this season, he and Liam could test the free agent market together.

And if they couldn't find a team to take them both, well, Russ was thirty-three. He probably only had a few more years of hockey in him, and then he could freely follow Liam all over the continent and bully him about leg day.

They beat Toronto at home on Pride Night, wearing their rainbow-striped jerseys. Russ assisted two of Baller's goals and one of Hughesy's and, as a punishment, got dragged into an interview room afterward to talk about his milestones.

The interview had just wrapped up when Liam poked his head into the room. "Hey! Are you day-dreaming in here? Because it's your turn to tell your mom we're not moving to Winnipeg."

Russ's ma must've overheard, because her laughter followed Liam's pronouncement through the door. He'd finally told her that he didn't get along with Winnipeg's coach and would do whatever he could to avoid playing for the man. Now the whole thing had become a running joke.

"Wouldn't it be my turn to tell your mom we're not moving to Quebec?"

"You gonna do it in French?" Liam challenged with a grin. "Besides, what's wrong with Quebec? Good language, good hockey, good maple syrup—"

"—no earthquakes, no hurricanes, no alliga-tors," Russ finished for him. "We'll see, Trouble. Let's get through this season first."

"Well, I was trying, but you're in here talking about the meaning of life—"

Russ's interviewers watched their exchange with badly stifled laughter. Once he'd introduced Liam to his parents as his boyfriend, his glass closet had out-lived its usefulness. Russ shattered it just after the Caimans' playoffs exit, though he hadn't mentioned Liam in his coming-out statement.

Of course, their relationship didn't stay secret for long, between the fact that they lived together and the pictures from Max and Grady's wedding.

"Sorry," Russ told the interviewers. "This has been fun, but it looks like I'm needed elsewhere."

He let Liam pull him into the hallway, which was emptier than Russ expected. His parents must've joined the festivities wherever the team was gathering.

"They're gonna pie your face," Liam said apologetically just before they reached the door. "Pretend to be surprised. Oh, and Mo's already talking about his karaoke plans."

Of course he was. Russ sighed, long-suffering. "Never should've let him host the party."

Liam laced their fingers together. "Look on the bright side," he said. "Maybe we get locked in the pantry again."

Keep reading for an excerpt from
Textbook Defense
by Ashlyn Kane and Morgan James

Coming Soon

EMRIK TIGHTENED the knot on his tie, picked up his jacket, and checked himself in the mirror. He wasn't a vain man, but he didn't clean up too badly, especially in his tailored black tux. At times like this, he was glad one of the veterans years ago had convinced him it would be a worthwhile investment. A comfortable suit made all the difference during stuffy black-tie events.

Satisfied, he left his bedroom and headed for the kitchen to say good night to his baby.

As expected, Kaarina sat at the counter talking a mile a minute to Janice, who was cooking dinner at the stove.

"—and then Jake said I couldn't do it, but he was totally wrong, because I did!"

"Of course you did," Janice agreed with a nod that said she hadn't doubted Kaarina's abilities for a moment.

Kaarina beamed at Janice and continued her story. Not for the first time, and certainly not for the last, Emrik thanked all the gods and fates that had brought Janice into their lives. Her arrival hadn't been a miracle—Emrik had advertised for a nanny and she applied for the job—but she was a perfect fit in their household and was the only reason Emrik was able to be a "single" parent.

"Are you off, then?" Janice asked when she caught sight of him.

"Yes." He stepped forward to hug Kaarina and kiss her silky hair. "Love you, peanut. Have fun with Janice tonight, and I'll see you tomorrow."

"We're going to eat popcorn and watch movies," Kaarina chirped.

"Well, that does sound like fun."

"Doesn't it? Way more fun than a stuffy party that you have to dress up for."

Emrik chuckled. "Definitely." He gave Kaarina one last kiss, and she wrapped her arms tightly around his waist.

"Bye, Daddy. I love you. Try to have fun!"

"Thanks, peanut, I will."

Famous last words, he thought at the venue later as he adjusted his cuffs and looked at himself in the bathroom mirror. He looked significantly less pressed than he had at home.

He had arrived almost an hour ago, and he couldn't say he was enjoying himself. First the person on the door made a fuss about Emrik's missing plus one in a bubbling, overeager way. Then, in the main room, Emrik had hoped to find a glass of water to ease his parched throat, but every time he spotted a waiter or tried to move toward the bar, someone else popped up in his space, ready to chat about the Shield's latest and most disappointing season—which was how some people categorized any season that didn't end in a Cup win, no matter that a Cupless end was the fate of over thirty teams every year.

Emrik finally got his hands on some water, but the bartender turned out to be another armchair pundit who had the solution to all the Shield's problems.

By the time he spotted the sign for the restroom, he was desperate for a break.

Dinner wasn't for another hour. He had at least another three ahead of him before he could duck out gracefully.

Which was fine. Emrik was a big boy, and he could handle it. He took a deep breath and left the restroom… only to do an about-face when he recognized the woman walking into the ladies' room.

Fuck. Of course Alana was here.

Emrik didn't like to think himself a coward, but he had no intention of exchanging a single word with her. He took three long strides away from the restrooms to a small curtained-off alcove and stepped into it. He wasn't *hiding*. He was just taking a little time-out to get his bearings.

Except he didn't look *into* the alcove beforehand, and he'd stepped on someone's foot. "Ow," said a familiar voice. "What the fuck."

Emrik blinked as the man from the library—Rowan—scowled at him from a few inches away.

"Oh, it's you."

What was that supposed to mean? Flustered, Emrik opened his mouth and said, "What are you doing here?"

"Here as in the party?" Rowan gave a winsome smile, as if Emrik had not just accidentally caught him hiding in what amounted to a closet. "I was invited." Rowan paused, placed a finger to his lip, and amended, "Ordered at stiletto-point? Coerced? I'm here at the behest of Her Majesty Gemma Bancroft, ostensibly to entertain her every whim because the rest of the table is insufferable—"

That sure was a lot of five-dollar words.

"—just because I can't afford a thousand-dollar-a-plate dinner—"

"I meant here in this…." Emrik gestured around them. He didn't know the English word. "Hole."

"Hiding." Rowan deflated, then immediately puffed up again a glint in his eye. "Wait—what are *you* doing here? At this dinner, and also in this alcove."

Alcove. Yeah, Emrik wasn't going to remember that. "I was invited."

Rowan tilted his head. "Because…?"

Emrik hunched his shoulders. This was going to sound conceited. "The organizers asked people from the Shield to come to sell more tickets."

To his surprise, Rowan didn't roll his eyes. "Oh. Yeah, I can see how that would be a selling point if you're going to spend this kind of money on dinner." He peeked out from behind the curtain, swore, and plastered himself against the wall again. "So. Why are you hiding?"

You first, Emrik wanted to say. But something about Rowan's endless talking disarmed him. Maybe he shouldn't give the man too many excuses to talk about himself. "There's a woman…."

"Does she bite?" Rowan asked. "I mean." He waved a hand in Emrik's direction. "You look like you could take her."

As if Emrik was going to get into a physical altercation with anyone off the ice. He'd be thrown in jail immediately, and he'd deserve it. "She's…." This was so hard to explain without using the word *stalker*, which felt like overkill. *Puck bunny* was pretty misogynistic. Unfortunately the alternatives, again, made him sound self-important. "Obsessed with me."

But Rowan took it in stride, one corner of his mouth quirking up as he flicked his gaze up and down Emrik's body. "Ah. Well, at least she's got some taste. No restraining order?"

Emrik shook his head. "It's not… dangerous, or invasive, or anything. Her parents have money and she shows up to every event…." As well as some of the open practices and training camp scrimmages. It made him uncomfortable, but she hadn't crossed any lines. If she started showing up at Kaarina's school plays or something, he'd reconsider. "It's just awkward." And this conversation had become far too focused on him. "Your turn. Why are you hiding?"

Sagging against the wall, Rowan tilted his head as though to peer out from behind the curtain thing. "Same reason. Well, okay, not exactly. Do you know the fourth-richest man in Toronto? He keeps telling me his name and I keep forgetting it on purpose. Anyway, he's very talkative. *Very.* And that's coming from me, so that's saying something. He loves a captive audience."

He didn't remember the man's name but knew he was the fourth-richest man in Toronto? For a moment Emrik was perplexed, and then he remembered Rowan was here on orders from Gem. "And you're his favorite?"

If possible, Rowan slumped further. "I don't know if he's looking for a sugar baby or if I just remind him of his favorite grandchild, and I don't want to know. I am *actively avoiding* knowing."

That sounded like the best course of action to Emrik. Privately he was a little perturbed at Gem; knowing her, she'd brought Rowan along to be sacrificed to the man in the name of charity. Then again, she'd done the exact same thing to Emrik, and he didn't *really* mind. Except for Alana being present, of course. "What if it's both?"

Rowan yelped and then covered his mouth, as though afraid he might give away their spot. "That's horrible. Gods, *why*?"

To make you laugh. It had worked too; the mirth in Rowan's eyes danced in the dim light in their cubbyhole. Sanna would have called him *boyishly handsome*, with that slightly too-long hair that flopped over his forehead. Emrik would've bet he was older than he looked, but he couldn't say how much. "Sorry."

"Eh." Rowan waved this off. "Nothing I haven't thought before, even if I somehow had the restraint not to say so out loud." But now he was looking at Emrik speculatively. "You know, we might be able to help each other out here."

Emrik could guess where this was going. "I technically have two tickets." Because he was a softie and knowing there were kids in the city with so much less than Kaarina and so few people in their corner made him hate the world a little bit. "So there's an extra seat at my table. No Gem, though."

Rowan grinned. "Under the circumstances, I think she'll forgive me if I abandon her to play pretend boyfriend with you all night." He paused. "Actually she'll probably send me a bottle of champagne; she's made her opinions on my previous actual boyfriends *very* clear."

"Subtlety isn't really her strong suit."

"Yes, that's why we get along." Rowan linked his arm through Emrik's. "So, all right, are we stepping out of this alcove with our outfits disheveled like we can't keep our hands off each other, or am I going to have to pretend subtlety as well?"

"If it won't kill you," Emrik said. "I prefer not to make a scene."

With a put-upon sigh, Rowan twitched the curtain to one side and peered out. "If you insist. Looks like the coast is clear."

"Then let's go have dinner."

Rowan led him by the hand out of the alcove. "Let's have *drinks*," he corrected. "Then dinner. And we'll make sure everyone sees we're so besotted with each other that we couldn't possibly notice them."

Bemused, Emrik allowed himself to be pulled along for the ride. "Have you done this before?"

Rowan tossed a look back at him over his shoulder. "Why, do I seem like some kind of fake-date slut?"

His eyes were dancing again. "My parents threw a lot of intolerable parties when I was growing up."

They bellied up to the bar. "Intolerable?"

"Over-the-top. Very boring. Self-important." This time Rowan's grin was a little strained. "One learns to make the best of the situation. Sometimes that means having a little fun at Mummy and Daddy's expense—literally and figuratively. What's your drink of choice? Since you're being a public figure, I'm assuming no hard liquor."

He just skipped from one subject to another like a fruit fly. "Safe bet," Emrik murmured.

"So, wine? Beer? Coke? The blood of your enemies?"

A smile tugged at the corner of Emrik's mouth. Something told him Rowan was far more likely to be the blood-of-his-enemies type than Emrik. "Beer."

"Great. Light, medium, dark? Any allergies?"

"Medium, and no," Emrik answered. Why was Rowan asking so many questions? Surely he knew Emrik could order his own drink?

"Lovely." Rowan fluttered his lashes at the bartender—thankfully a different one from before. She didn't seem very impressed, but she did smile.

"What can I get you?"

"A couple of beers, please," Rowan said with an easy smile. He unlinked their hands and placed a finger on one of the fancy menu cards in front of him. "Amber for this one, and the light IPA for me." He leaned forward conspiratorially. "I prefer blonds."

Oh, so that was the game. Emrik smiled ruefully in spite of himself, and shook his head.

The bartender laughed. "I see that. Coming right up."

"You are enjoying this," he observed.

"Oh, *immensely.*" The bartender slid their beers across the bartop, and Rowan thanked her and passed Emrik his with a little bow. "Here you are, darling."

Emrik wasn't used to being doted upon. It was weird, but Rowan's enthusiasm made it easy to go along with. "Thanks." He shoved some money in the tip jar as they swept away from the bar.

"Aw, babe," Rowan crooned, leaning into his space. "Handsome *and* generous."

The kicker of it was, the ruse was clearly working. Emrik could see people noticing him, even looking in his direction and turning to whisper to their companions, but everyone kept their distance. Rowan and his feigned affection provided a perfect buffer.

"Well, with you occupied, she might be the target of the fourth-richest man in Toronto. She's earned it."

Rowan laughed and found a table for their drinks. "And he's clever and thoughtful too. I'm a lucky man."

Shaking his head, Emrik set his drink down. "Are you always like this?"

Rowan blinked at him, the picture of innocence. "Like what?"

Loud. Friendly. Flirty. Outrageous. Emrik gestured, hoping he didn't come across as critical. "You're very… on. All the time. Doesn't it get tiring?"

"Does a fish tire of swimming?" The words came out teasing, but the expression on Rowan's face, the slight tension at the corners of his eyes, the crease in his forehead, told Emrik he was taking the question seriously. "I'm not, actually. Always like this, I mean. But I would never let on about that to a fake boyfriend. He must think I'm an utter, unfettered delight all of the time."

Unfettered was another unfamiliar word, but Emrik thought he got the gist of it, in context. Over Rowan's shoulder, he spotted Alana heading in their direction. He'd have to take a page from Rowan's book and try something a little less subtle. "Are you an unfettered delight who dances?"

Rowan followed his line of sight and inclined his head in understanding. "My dear, I do whatever is required of me." He offered his hand. "Shall we?"

ASHLYN KANE likes to think she can do it all, but her follow-through often proves her undoing. Her house is as full of half-finished projects as her writing folder. With the help of her ADHD meds, she gets by.

An early reader and talker, Ashlyn has always had a flair for language and storytelling. As an eight-year-old, she attended her first writers' workshop. As a teenager, she won an amateur poetry competition. As an adult, she received a starred review in *Publishers Weekly* for her novel *Fake Dating the Prince*. There were quite a few years in the middle there, but who's counting?

Her hobbies include DIY home decor, container gardening (no pulling weeds), music, and spending time with her enormous chocolate lapdog. She is the fortunate wife of a wonderful man, the daughter of two sets of great parents, and the proud older sister/sister-in-law of the world's biggest nerds.

Sign up for her newsletter at www.ashlynkane.ca/newsletter/

Website: www.ashlynkane.ca

MORGAN JAMES is a clueless (older) millennial who's still trying to figure out what they'll be when they grow up and enjoying the journey to get there. Now, with a couple of degrees, a few stints in Europe, and more than one false start to a career, they eagerly wait to see what's next. James started writing fiction before they could spell and wrote their first (unpublished) novel in middle school. They haven't stopped since. Geek, artist, archer, and fanatic, Morgan passes their free hours in imaginary worlds, with people on pages and screens—it's an addiction, as is their love of coffee and tea. They live in Canada with their massive collection of unread books and where they are the personal servant of too many four-legged creatures.

Twitter: @MorganJames71
Facebook:www.facebook.com/morganjames007

HOCKEY EVER AFTER BOOK ONE

WINGING IT

Falling for his
teammate wasn't in
the game plan....

ASHLYN KANE
MORGAN JAMES

Hockey Ever After: Book One

Hockey is Gabe Martin's life. Dante Baltierra just wants to have some fun on his way to the Hockey Hall of Fame. Falling for a teammate isn't in either game plan.

But plans change.

When Gabe gets outed, it turns his careful life upside-down. The chaos messes with his game and sends his team headlong into a losing streak. The last person he expects to pull him through it is Dante.

This season isn't going the way Dante thought it would. Gabe's sexuality doesn't faze him, but his own does. Dante's always been a "what you see is what you get" kind of guy, and having to hide his attraction to Gabe sucks. But so does losing, and his teammate needs him, so he puts in the effort to snap Gabe out of his funk.

He doesn't mean to fall in love with the guy.

Getting involved with a teammate is a bad idea, but Dante is shameless, funny, and brilliant at hockey. Gabe can't resist. Unfortunately, he struggles to share part of himself that he's hidden for years, and Dante chafes at hiding their relationship. Can they find their feet before the ice slips out from under them?

www.dreamspinnerpress.com

THE WINGING IT HOLIDAY SPECIAL

ASHLYN KANE
MORGAN JAMES

Hockey Ever After: Book 1.5

Hockey's started, holidays are looming, and NHL player Dante Baltierra's husband is keeping secrets.

Of course, secrets aren't unusual this time of year, but Dante is pretty sure Gabe isn't being squirrelly about a new flat-screen or tickets for a second honeymoon. Whatever is eating Gabe is more serious than a surprise under the tree. But as much as Dante wants to help, asking about it would be fruitless. Besides, he has a theory about the problem—and the solution.

He's just not sure Santa has the power to deliver what Gabe really wants this Christmas.

www.dreamspinnerpress.com

HOCKEY EVER AFTER BOOK TWO

SCORING POSITION

You miss
100 percent of
the shots you
don't take.

ASHLYN KANE
MORGAN JAMES

Hockey Ever After: Book Two

Ryan Wright's new hockey team is a dumpster fire. He expects to lose games—not his heart.

Ryan's laid-back attitude should be an advantage in Indianapolis. Even if he doesn't accomplish much on the ice, he can help his burned-out teammates off it. And no one needs a friend—or a hug—more than Nico Kirschbaum, the team's struggling would-be superstar.

Nico doesn't appreciate that management traded for another openly gay player and told them to make friends. Maybe he doesn't know what his problem is, but he'll solve it with hard work, not by bonding with the class clown.

It's obvious to Ryan that Nico's lonely, gifted, and cracking under pressure. No amount of physical practice will fix his mental game. But convincing Nico to let Ryan help means getting closer than is wise for Ryan's heart—especially once he unearths Nico's sense of humor.

Will Nico and Ryan risk making a pass, or will they keep missing 100 percent of the shots they don't take?

www.dreamspinnerpress.com

UNRIVALED

Love
doesn't
pull its
punches.

ASHLYN KANE
MORGAN JAMES

Hockey Ever After: Book Three

People say there's a fine line between love and hate. If you ask Grady Armstrong, the line's as obvious as the one across the middle of a hockey rink.

So he can't explain why he doesn't walk away when his Grindr hookup—a guy who accused him of impersonating himself—turns out to be Max Lockhart, a rival player Grady once punched in the face. Apparently Max can goad him just as well off the ice as he can on it.

Max Lockhart showed up thinking he was going to expose a fake. Instead he hooks up with a guy who claims to hate him. And has a good time. A really good time. But that doesn't mean players from different teams can be together.

Max has always wished Grady would relax a little. When the season starts and Grady accepts Max's offer of help with finding someone to date for real, Max gets his wish. But he should've been careful what he wished for, because now that he knows Grady is a big softie under that prickly shell, he'd rather keep Grady for himself.

Grady only goes on a handful of dates before he realizes he has a lot more fun with Max. But he can't be falling for a rival player… can he?

www.dreamspinnerpress.com